IN CONCERT

IN CONCERT

A Symphony of Danger, Ransom, and Redemption

RAE RICHEN

In Concert
A Symphony of Danger, Ransom, and Redemption
by Rae Richen
Copyright@ 2017, re-issued 2024
All rights reserved.
Published in the United States of America by

Back Beat Publications
an imprint of Lloyd Court Press
3034 N.E. 32nd Avenue
Portland, Oregon, 97212
www.lloydcourtpress.org

Cover art by Owyn Richen, Cover design by Diana Kolsky
Book Design by Amit Dey

ISBN: 978-1-94360-94-2 Paper
ISBN: 978-1-94360-96-6 E-book

Publisher's Cataloging-In-Publication Data
(Prepared by The Donohue Group, Inc.)

Names: Richen, Rae.
Title: In Concert: A Symphony of Danger, Ransom, and Redemption/
                  by Rae Richen.
Description: Portland, Oregon: Back Beat Publications, an imprint of Lloyd
                  Court Press, [2017] re-issued 2024
Identifiers: ISBN 978-1-943640-96-6
                  ISBN 978-1-943640-94-2 (ebook)
Subjects: LCSH: Women violinists--Fiction. |
                  College teachers--Oregon--Fiction. |
                  Kidnapping--Oregon--Fiction. |
                  Organized crime--Europe, Central--Fiction. |
                  Bach, Johann Sebastian, 1685-1750--Manuscripts--Fiction. |
                  Oregon--Fiction. | LCGFT: Thrillers (Fiction) |
                  Romance fiction.
Classification: LCC PS3618.I34 I5 2017 (print) |
                  LCC PS3618.I34 (ebook) |
                  DDC 813/.6--dc23

For Margaret Arwain Price

Musician, teacher, humanitarian

And you will know why…

"If the missing Bach manuscripts were ever discovered,
I would beg God for a second lifetime and a better violin."

Overheard in the library of a musicians' retirement home.

PROLOGUE

1979

Sixty-five-year-old Raphael Atemvoll listened as his twelve-year-old viola student, Otto Rákóczi, played a Beethoven sonata. At the same time, he heard the timid knock of the new student, the young child he expected next. He waited, listening for more boldness, both from the violist and from the new student.

Within moments, both the sonata player and the knock became more certain. He smiled. Boldness, sureness, Otto grows. *The new student will grow, as well,* he thought.

At the end of the sonata movement, Otto put down his instrument and asked, "Would you like me to open the door, sir?"

"That would be very kind of you, young man."

The boy, a promising conservatory scholar, walked up the stairs from the studio to the front door. Raphael heard him turn the doorknob and pull it open. Its hinges squeaked. The boy said, "Uh. Uhm. Uh."

That surprised Raphael. Otto hardly ever seemed tongue-tied. Raphael stood, thinking something must be wrong. Then he heard a child's voice. "Aren't you going to let me in? I think I have the correct address. Dr. Atemvoll?"

"Um, yes," the boy said. "Uh, his studio is downstairs."

"Where are the stairs?"

Ah, thought Raphael, the new one is sure of herself, articulate – all good. But what has happened to the boy's tongue?

He heard the clip of patent leather shoes, but not the usual smack of violin case on narrow stairwell walls. He waited. And then he saw as she came down.

She was short but seemed tall for eight years old – tall because of attitude. Her posture proud but easy, not stiff; violin case held vertically in front of her as if she had solved narrow staircase problems many times in her short life. Her reddish-brown hair fluffed all around her small face, her green eyes gazed calmly, taking in the expanse of the room until her attention finally arrived at the seated professor.

"Professor Atemvoll," she said in an unhurried manner. "I'm pleased to meet you at last. We're you not finished with the viola lesson?"

It was at that moment that he realized the telephone call he had assumed came from a soft-voiced mother, actually had been from this child. His mind raced over the remembered content: list of pieces played; scales and arpeggios practiced daily; use of certain finger exercise books; study of Sevčik bowing exercises as needed by repertoire – yes, she had used the word *repertoire*.

She waited for his answer. So did the boy.

"You are correct. We are not finished, Miss Zolesku. I would like to introduce you to Otto Rákóczi. You may choose a book and read until we are done." Raphael gestured at the bookcase and plush chairs at the other end of his studio room.

"Thank you, sir," she said, and headed toward the library table with the cloth upon it. She set her violin case on that cloth. Raphael gestured to the boy to resume their lesson.

Otto glanced at her, and Raphael didn't blame him for hesitating. Darya Zolesku was an enigma – a small child comfortable with adults, with herself, with hoisting her heavy violin case. She hardly seemed eight years old. Raphael wondered if her parents even knew she was here.

As they resumed the sonata, Darya gave an admiring smile toward the full tone the boy produced, and then she chose a book. Raphael felt his skin tighten as she pulled it out – a small book, bound in leather and sewn together by hand. A book only he ever read.

She took the book to the dark rose chair and she lay it on the side table. She scooted herself completely into the chair before picking it up again. Raphael breathed relief at her care for it. Her short legs hung above the floor, her patent-leather shoes flashed in the light of the nearby lamp. Her short, thick hair hid her face as she read.

Raphael smiled up at the boy as he finished the middle movement of the sonata. "Very nice, Otto," he said. "I like the changes you have given it – much more interesting dynamics. The pianissimo is very well controlled. There is one . . ."

"Yes, sir," the boy said, "the shift to B."

"Exactly. Remember to take your thumb up the finger board – it is your luggage on the flight, and you don't want to be without your luggage."

The boy tried the long shift to the upper fingerboard and missed twice, each time glancing at the little girl, who seemed mentally buried in the book.

Raphael said, "Take that first finger up to the G and then plunk down the third finger on the B. Practice that a few times now."

During this discussion, Darya never took her eyes off the book, but when the boy hit the G and then the B, she nodded to herself, and kept reading. Her left foot shifted toward the right each time the boy's finger slid up the fingerboard toward the high G. Her right foot plunked down as he hit the B. Raphael was certain this motion was completely unconscious. It stopped when the boy played the whole passage for a last time.

When Otto's lesson was over, and while he packed up, Darya lay the book again on the side table before scooting from the chair. She carried the book to the shelf, held the nearby books away from its space to reinsert it.

Where did she learn such reverence for books? Where, for that matter, did she learn to talk to prospective teachers as if she were an adult?

She took out her half-sized violin, plucked the strings softly, tuned the flatted E string and then took out her bow. Raphael saw that this instrument was beat up. Marks on the case indicated it belonged to an institution – her school perhaps. He guessed it probably was a frustration for her – bad tone, wouldn't hold its tuning, strings not responsive enough to facilitate fast play. And the bow . . . even worse.

Otto climbed the stairs, taking a last puzzled look at the girl, before he disappeared upstairs and out the studio door.

She came to stand where the boy had stood. Her hair shone in the light of his lamp, and her green eyes seemed to probe his emotions. "May I ask you a question, Professor Atemvoll?"

"Yes?"

"Was that little book about Sospiro made for you?"

His heart thudded. Whatever question he had expected was far from this one. "What has made you think so, Miss Zolesku?"

"Atemvoll – filled with atoms, air – breath. And Sospiro, that means something about breathing, too, doesn't it?"

He gazed at her, a child, and not a child. His heart began to open. He felt it unfurl like the slow blossoming of a rose, petal upon petal sighing its fragrance out to the summer air.

"Darya, please give me your violin and then bring the book to me."

She handed the violin and bow to him. He set them on the table next to his and waited. When she returned, he took the book and gestured for her to sit in the wide chair next to him. Opening the book, he said, "See here, the signature of the artist?"

She nodded, "Annensky."

"He was my friend when I was small. He made this book for me as we traveled through – through very dark places."

"So, that is why all around the little boy it is dark and the bears' eyes gleam in the blackness?"

"Yes, but do you see this light near the ground?"

"The sun?" she asked.

"Yes. It rises."

"And the boy blows out," she said, "and the air whooshes across the land to blow away the bears and the wolves," she pointed at the next page.

He said, "The air is the Sospiro – the sigh, the warm west wind. It is hope."

"Do you still blow the Sospiro?"

"Our music, yours and mine, that is the Sospiro for everyone who hears us. We play to blow the warm air for the earth, for other people."

"And your friend painted the warm air to help you not be afraid – I mean when you were little?"

"Yes. And it works even today."

She smiled up at him. "I like that book. I like that Annensky."

"Yes, his paintings bring happiness and understanding to all who see them."

"Is Atemvoll your real name? or Sospiro?"

He hesitated, thought about the truth of his past, and about her very young age. He said, "When I was three, I told everyone I was Sospiro, the west wind. Here, in Hungary, my name is Atemvoll.

Now, let us begin your lesson by finding out if your mother knows you are here?"

For the first time, she wouldn't meet his eye. "No," she whispered.

"Where does she think you are?"

"She gave me the money for my lesson, but she believes I'm studying Hebrew with the rabbi's wife."

"And how far away from your home are we?"

She looked up at him, earnestly, "Only one bus ride . . ."

"One bus ride from . . .?"

"Well, it is the other end of Andrassy Ut."

"My dear, I think our first job is for us to take that bus back to your home and explain the truth to your mother."

"Us?"

"Yes, Us. You are my last student today."

Her eyes filled, but tears didn't spill. "Couldn't we play a little first?"

He looked her in the eye. "We will not play one note until we have your mother's permission."

Her gaze took in his hair, his face, his hands and then her gaze moved around the room, as if seeing a beloved space for the first and last time.

He felt another rose petal open. "Come," he said. "Let's pack our violins for the bus ride."

BOOK ONE

CHAPTER ONE

**FIFTEEN YEARS LATER
EARLY SPRING, BUDAPEST, 1994
SOON AFTER THE BREAKUP OF THE SOVIET UNION**

Raphael Atemvoll slipped into the back of the large lecture hall at the Franz Lizt Akadémia. He sat immediately left of the door where the lecturer wouldn't notice him. Darya wasn't lecturing at the moment. Instead, she answered questions from one of the one hundred fifty students who had signed up for her course on the History of Music and Western Culture.

"Yes, Mr. Nagy?"

"What is rococo music?"

"That term, rococo, usually refers to decorative arts and architecture in France around the time of Louis the Fourteenth – seventeen twenty to about fifty. . . a reaction against the straight lines and supposed stiffness of the previous generation of the arts."

She glanced at the same student who had his hand raised again. "Mr. Nagy, Zoltan?"

"Why react to straight lines?"

She smiled and turned to the whole class. "Each generation longs to remake the world and believe it has created the first true art and music. Our parents reacted against the world of their parents, too. Mom and Dad are not the fuddy-duddies we like to pretend."

The class erupted in laughter.

"Our grandparents, now they really were old pudding – in fact, very much like us."

Raphael saw startled recognition on many student faces.

Darya answered Zoltan Nagy by pointing out the relationship between playful and asymmetrical architecture and the rococo movement in music. To demonstrate, Darya lifted her violin from its table and played a heavily ornamented and humorous phrase from a French court dance.

"Some courts in Europe retained the love of rococo far past its popularity in France," she said. And then she played the opening of a Russian court dance. "That is Anton Batislav, Russia, early 1900," she said.

Raphael smiled. She is so free, open and inventive with her examples. That little joke about Anton Batislav is aimed at me, so she knows I'm here.

He loved her as if she were his own granddaughter and had loved her from the moment she walked down the stairs to his studio. He had also seen to it that her younger brother received lessons on the piano – a selfish wish for her to have a loved one to share music. Piotr had become an intelligent and quick-witted accompanist and soloist.

But today, Raphael wanted to hear for himself why Darya gathered such a big following for her lectures. Ever since he had recommended her as his replacement on the faculty, he had heard that her lectures grew with each term and were now held in the biggest classroom.

In the student news, one reporter had written, "Miss Zolesku explains people by playing for us the music that people created to explain themselves."

Raphael thought of Darya as the eight-year-old who innocently brought out all his memories and sadness.

Today, as he watched Darya in this classroom at the Akadémia, another situation weighed heavily on Raphael. The leader of a gang of hoodlums searched for something of great value that only Raphael knew about.

He knew it was time to pass it to someone. He would have given it to the Akadémia except for the inability of the school to protect it.

After a lifetime as a professor, he certainly had no money to guarantee its security. He had thought of the state museums. He had thought of many places where the manuscripts could be held for all scholars to study and for all people to see, but security in the changing times of this new government was no guarantee that the music would be safe.

And then there were the recent messages in the newspapers. "Raphael Czigler, lawyers for the estate of Feodor Czigler seek you to give you an inheritance."

A bald lie. A trap.

Whoever they were, they would figure it out soon. They had to know about Grandfather Anton Batislav. They had to have followed the trail and figured out who had adopted the heir of Count Czigler. Knowing that, they would soon know who protected the manuscripts.

So, he believed the recent extremely polite phone calls meant they knew Raphael Atemvoll had been born a Czigler.

They must never suspect his relationship to the student he had recommended as his successor in the department. He should never have sent her music for her birthday.

Her reputation already grew, here at the Akadémia and at the concert halls of eastern Europe. Darya would be in their awareness, perhaps already in danger. He couldn't burden her with the hidden manuscripts.

But he had to do something with them.

As he listened to her discuss the short-lived era of rococo music and art, he remembered a letter she had shared with him when she was about thirteen years old. Her uncle – the one who escaped Hungary during Soviet times.

Tobias Kossuth had written to her describing his new home in New York City "This old building is a rococo throw back, with nymphs and dandies painted on every wall and ceiling, and flush toilets that still work by pulling a chain." Uncle Tobias had said.

This was her uncle who had paid for her music lessons and the lessons of her brother, Piotr. As a result, Raphael had Tobias' address in his files.

A trusted uncle in New York. Museums with money and security. Raphael knew he had to get the manuscripts away from his office and home and keep them away from Darya until these people gave up. He must find a way to send the music under cover to Tobias Kossuth.

Someday, Darya would be asked to play solos in New York. When she does, she will visit this uncle. She will figure out what it is he has. And she will know what to do with it.

Now, I have to figure out how to get it to her uncle without attracting attention to it.

At that moment, her class came to an end. Raphael noticed that the student, Zoltan Nagy came forward and spoke deeply with Darya.

Raphael remembered her mentioning this student, a cello player, very talented and very involved in movements to reform their new democracy.

"He makes dangerous and impetuous decisions," she had said. "I hope this doesn't get him into great trouble."

Raphael watched the young man lean toward her, gesturing in the way of the vehement young who believe they have found truth.

* *

THAT AFTERNOON, 1994, BUDAPEST, HUNGARY

In his modest home near the broad, tree-lined Budapest boulevard of Andrassy Ut, eighty-year-old Raphael Atemvoll heard the final click at the other end of the phone line, and then the dial tone.

Raphael breathed heavily. He asked himself, how did Steiermark discover that I must be the one?

And as he moved toward his library, he thought:

Why did I not foresee that he so soon would give up pretending polite interest?

During two previous phone conversations, Garig Steiermark had attempted to convince Raphael that he was a benefactor, and a gentleman who devoted himself to finding lost music manuscripts. Steiermark claimed he wished to make certain they were in a wonderful museum, available to all scholars of music. He wondered if Professor Atemvoll had ever run across the missing violin concerti by Johann Sebastien Bach.

During the first disturbingly friendly phone call, Raphael had heard the arrogance in the man. The valuable, the irreplaceable, the beautiful should become exclusively his.

Also, during each call, Raphael had pretended amazement that anyone would think he could have such a valuable manuscript.

After the first call, Raphael had visited young Judge Otto Rákóczi, once his viola student. From Otto, he learned what he already suspected. Steiermark was a thug, well-spoken, perhaps, but a vicious bandit in a family of bandits who had come to Hungary from Russia at the end of the Communist Revolution. He was a bandit who owned vast properties in the northern mountains of Hungary. Steiermark controlled that whole region as if it were not part of the newly liberated

Hungary. It was his own kingdom. Steiermark devoted himself to theft, ownership of rare things, and to expansion of his bandit empire.

After these revelations, Raphael had then begun sending all of his music manuscripts into storage in the building belonging to a friend he trusted, but who was nowhere involved in music and wouldn't be a target of Steiermark.

Raphael regretted the two gifts of music that he previously had made to his student, Darya Zolesku. If Steiermark knew, he would go after her next. The rest of the music was now in the storage unit.

The rest except the three.

After today's call, Raphael knew what he had to do. It was very risky, but he should have done it much sooner. Steiermark would come here, and could arrive at any moment. It was not far from Hungary's mountains to Budapest, and the man might be even closer than that.

Raphael turned to his bookshelves and quickly removed a handful of books. From behind the books, he ratcheted the combination lock, opened a safe, and pulled out the three folios, notebooks of music. He opened the first of the notebooks and allowed himself a second to caress the back and front covers. Inside the cover, hidden by the glued cover paper, lay the oldest piece in each notebook – each a composition worth millions of dollars at auction.

Raphael's own teacher, Anton Batislav, had hidden these manuscripts in the linings of these notebooks long ago. Anton had taught Raphael to read the politics of any country and to be very careful about where these manuscripts came to the light at last. When Russia was Hungary's over-lord, neither Anton nor Raphael had trusted the government.

And when the new Hungary emerged from the Soviet Union, Raphael had waited to see the direction it would take, and the power it might have to control and protect its libraries and museums.

His house wasn't safe any longer. He didn't know if he had minutes or hours to get them out of here. He closed the safe and put back the camouflage of books, pulled out his desk drawer and retrieved three large manila envelopes. He stuffed each folio in a separate envelope and grabbed the nearest pen.

In a nervous hurry, he wrote: "Medical Service of New York, attn. Tobias Kossuth," Darya's beloved uncle.

After adding the street address, Raphael wrote in a slash across each package, "Returned. Incorrect copies. Missing pages."

"That should keep sticky-fingered postmen from stealing the contents," he whispered.

The return address was a post box he rented near the *Zeneakadémia*, the Franz Liszt Academy of Music. He used the name Feodor Sospiro for that post box. If clerks looked for anything from Raphael Atemvoll, they would not look at these manuscripts.

Raphael hoped these messages and addresses would misdirect the avaricious postal clerks, even any who might owe allegiance to Steiermark.

He shuffled to his front windows where he looked out onto the ash and sycamore trees of Andrassy Ut, searching for anything unusual. No unfamiliar cars. Maybe he had time. If he hurried to the bus stop, he could take them to the national post office. He stepped outside, locked his door, and hitched his arthritic legs down the steps. As he worked his way past the nearest Metro stop, he glanced around him and then headed for the stop three avenues away. No one followed him that he could see. Once he arrived at the stop, he stepped into the alcove for a small coffee shop and book store, a doorway out of the wind and out of view.

Given time to stand still, Raphael realized that he had put Darya Zolesku in grave danger. His home and his collected manuscripts were listed in his will as an inheritance for Darya. And there was the fact that he had sent her a few of his own compositions for her twenty-fourth birthday last month.

He knew she didn't presently have room to store his music collection, but he also knew she had loved looking through his library when she was his student. He still remembered how, as a small child, she had sat for hours, humming and turning pages. What a delightful prodigy she had been, a wonderful granddaughter for a lonely old man.

Last year, when she turned twenty-three, she had been hired to take over his teaching position at the Zeneakadémia. As a celebration gift, he had sent to her home several manuscripts from his library. If Steiermark knew about those birthday and celebratory gifts and the gifts of this year, her whole family was in danger.

He stepped inside the bookstore and asked to use the telephone. In the back room, he called a member of his Friday evening string quartet, explained the danger to Darya and convinced the man that she and her family had to be moved immediately to a safe place.

The friend knew Darya, of course. He could pick her out in a crowd – the short young woman with the regal posture, dark auburn hair and a mischievous smile that lit a stage. The friend also knew her brother, Piotr, so the family would trust that Raphael had sent them.

His friend planned to take them to a niece's farm near the border with Austria, a drive of a few hours, and far to the west of Steiermark's lair.

By the time the next bus arrived at the bookstore, Raphael had decided to mail each manuscript from a different branch of the Hungarian postal system. He couldn't trust their safety to one place or one postal clerk.

An hour and a half later, he had mailed all three. He decided not to return home. Steiermark might be waiting for him there. Instead, he stepped off the bus and walked to his office building near the Oktogon, the intersection of Terez korút and Andrassy út, near Liszt

Ferenc Terrace, the musical center of the city, where his friend, the quartet member had said he would meet him when the trip to the farm was over.

In his teaching sanctuary, he could outwait Steiermark.

Inside, Raphael rested against the wall on the first floor, exhausted by his trip and his fear for the manuscripts and for Darya. Outside the front door window, he noticed parked cars, a yellow Skoda, a beat-up Peugeot, a long black sedan with an odd license plate – 656-ABS. Maybe from Ukraine. He stared closely at the cars. No one sat in any of them. They were benign.

After a few moments, he climbed to the second floor. Raphael reached his key toward his studio, but the door swung open.

There stood Garig Steiermark, a young man of hard features and a suit of fine wool. He yanked Raphael into the office and closed the door. Behind Steiermark, another man pulled music manuscripts from his old wooden file cabinet and tossed them on the floor.

Steiermark's man had a scar down the side of his face. An ugly sneer showed his character. He stared at Raphael with narrowed eyes.

Nevertheless, Raphael let himself find hope in their presence. It meant they had not followed him to the post offices, and they were not at Darya's home.

"Maestro Atemvoll, where are the concerti?" Steiermark asked. The mocking respect was familiar from the morning's phone call, smooth, even gentle, but edged with impatience and entitlement.

"Concerti? Mr. Steiermark, as I told you, my teacher, Anton Batislav, was a minor musician at the Russian court. Why would anybody give him such valuable manuscripts?"

"You can make this easy," Steiermark said, "by just handing them to me."

"I have no such manuscripts, Herr Steiermark." Raphael said. He felt for the edge of his piano, a warm contact with wood that bolstered his courage.

"I traced their path from Count Czigler to Batislav to you, so either I make a mess here or you just get the Bach concertos out and hand them to me."

"Young man, Count Czigler wouldn't have even noticed a simple violinist, certainly not given him anything as valuable as what you ask for."

Steiermark grabbed Raphael's left arm, twisted and broke it. Raphael fell against the piano. Great pain swept from his arm to his fingers and up to his chest. It brought sweat to his body, and a red darkness to his vision.

"There is more of this for you, if you don't tell me where they are."

Raphael started to turn toward Steiermark when a blow knocked his legs from under him. He fell hard, knocking his head against the piano leg. He gritted his jaw, but a cry escaped. Through the fog of his old eyes, he saw the pleasure his pain gave to Steiermark.

"Now. Tell me." Steiermark said.

Raphael gestured toward the files, hoping to prolong their search. The scarred man kicked him in the stomach. He coughed up blood, and thought, *He knows I have gotten rid of them. He will kill me.* And then, he blacked out.

* *

In the late afternoon of that same day, twenty-four-year-old Darya Zolesku whistled as she tugged on her blue wool coat. Her last private violin student had left an hour ago. She had practiced for her upcoming concert at Sopron and had waved at the last of her colleagues as they left for home and dinner.

Feeling great, Darya buttoned a scarf around her neck. This year, spring made a late entrance in Budapest. After a day of teaching and practicing, she was ready to go to her parents' warm home and play duets with her brother, Piotr. Later, she and Piotr would meet friends at the Baltazar Theater.

Before leaving her studio, she lay her teaching violin in its case on the side table and then stood in thought. She raised her arms, humming. While pretending to air-violin, she tried out the playfulness of a catchy phrase from a little Kodaly piece.

Last week, her teacher, Raphael Atemvoll, had sent her a birthday gift of manuscripts from his own library. Last year on her birthday, he had also sent manuscripts, celebrating his retirement and her new job taking over his classes at the Akadémia. Among the pieces he sent was this Kodaly gem.

She loved Raphael Atemvoll, that brilliant gnome of a man, her musical and life grandfather.

Still humming the Kodaly, Darya locked her studio, took the stairs down to the lobby, walked past the elegant green and gold lobby columns and out of the Liszt Academy of Music, the *Zeneakadémia*, into her beloved city. She turned to wave at the carved cherub orchestra on the façade. The little imps always laughed with her at the fun of making their music.

Budapest glowed with afternoon sunlight. The ash and plane trees poised to unfurl their leaves. The air smelled less of the mountains and snow than yesterday. The fragrance of grasses and loam floated in from the plains – a promise of good things for the New Year.

Free and happy, Darya marched to Kodaly's beat and onto Liszt Ferenc Terrace, the pedestrian-friendly gardens in between shops and restaurants. She passed the statue of the pianist Liszt – his long fingers and self-importance exaggerated by the sculptor. She smiled at the humor – the poking fun at the revered pianist.

Life in Budapest grew more open. The world encouraged humor and optimism since the Soviets had pulled out, starting in 1989. The groceries now stocked bread, fruit and eggs. The violent gangs operated mainly in the north, near the borders with Poland and Ukraine. And, mostly, anti-Semitism was a whisper only under certain conversations with the older generation.

Her mother's brother, Uncle Tobias, was even flying in from America for her concert. He had promised never to return until Jews could move freely and could live openly in his home country once again. Uncle Tobias had paid for her lessons and for Piotr's. She longed to meet him and be able to thank him for all he had done. Letters went only so far in hugging such a generous soul.

As she left the terrace, turned and swung down the wide Andrassy Avenue, a long and immaculate black sedan slowed. She squinted at it. This same car had sat outside her parents' apartment this morning. Also, yesterday morning. While she practiced in the living room, she had noticed the license: 656-ABS.

As it approached, her neck cooled with fear. She hurried her steps.

The car passed her and drove on. She relaxed. It meant nothing, a coincidence. It must belong to someone who lived new to the area. There was no reason to fear when so many strolled nearby – many students were leaving the *Zeneakadémia. A*fternoon shoppers poked into the small stores, the coffee and book shop or the grocers. Fear belonged to the old Soviet times.

Two well-dressed couples walked toward her, probably heading to the nearby Opera or a restaurant. She raised her gaze to the ash trees, searching for a bird whose evening voice she loved.

At that moment, one of the men on the sidewalk stepped back from the woman with whom he walked. The woman didn't even seem to notice, but continued to tell a humorous story to the couple in front of her. The three passed Darya.

Behind them, the man stopped as if to check his belt. Darya began to walk past him.

Suddenly, his belt whipped out of its loops and over her head. He wrapped her arms. Screaming with anger, she fought the power of the belt. In the man's face, she saw only hard-jawed hate, gray eyes, and a scar from his brow to the corner of his mouth.

Behind her, a second person threw a dark cloth over her eyes. Rough hands jerked her head against a man's chest. An arm wrapped her waist and lifted her.

She yelled for help from passersby, but the man pushed her head down and tossed her into the back seat of a car. She kept screaming as she fell onto the lap of yet another person. That third man tied the scarf tightly over her eyes. Then, his hand slammed across her mouth.

"Shut up, Jew slut."

The door thudded closed. The car sped away from the scene. She twisted her nose from his fingers and gasped for air. The first man grabbed her left hand and twisted hard. "Hold still, bitch, or you'll never again play the violin."

She held very still. *He knows who I am.*

She couldn't see the car, but the smell of leather and lemon cleaner told her it must be the immaculate black vehicle – 656-ABS. She should have paid more attention, not been so secure. Her stomach and her bowels tightened.

Taken from the streets. She had heard of this . . . the gangs kidnapped the famous, the rich.

Why me?

"And now, Miss Zolesku, you will be quiet for the next few hours."

She felt a needle stab her left arm. Heat surged through her veins. Her mind whirled away to fear and the certain knowledge that this was a mistake, yet she would die.

CHAPTER TWO

Darya had no idea where she was. She knew they must have driven a long time, and much farther north, but that was a guess based on how cold it was in this region. Her dank cell had walls of hard rock. It seemed to have been carved long ago. Moss covered the walls. Moss on top of old moss two inches thick in the few places where light entered from a slit close to the ceiling.

So far, each time the head man beat and questioned her, a different guard came first. Each guard wore a uniform of dull gray green that she could barely make out in the darkness. The guard would tie her hands and then cover her face with a blindfold.

And then the other man arrived, the evil, smooth voice. She heard him click open his lighter and then smelled his cigarette.

Starvation, thirst, and beatings left her disoriented. The cold nights of a delayed spring left her freezing in a cell beneath what she guessed was a large prison. The only thing she knew for certain was that on that first day, they had taken her blue coat, checked that her blindfold held, and then beat her. Since that night, she had been blindfolded, drugged, and beaten many times, while the smooth voiced man asked her the same questions over and over.

One man directed all the others. Though she could not see him through the tight scarf, she knew well the fine weave of his suit pants, the feel of his beard on her face and throat, the smooth insinuation of his voice. She would not soon forget the smell of his after-shave or of his cigarette. She knew the fiery burn on her shoulder would not soon heal.

"You can go home, you know. You can play the concert at Sopron, but only if you give me the Bach Concerti."

"Why?" she had cried that first time. "You can buy them from Editio Musica, in Budapest."

He smacked her jaw and knocked her to the floor. The cigarette and lighter came out again. She heard the flick, smelled the tobacco and knew he would soon touch her with the burning end.

The third time he came, he didn't even speak, merely threw her down and fell on top of her. She scratched and clawed until he grabbed both of her hands and pulled them above her head. Someone else tied her hands while the man in the suit pulled down her underpants.

"Does this seem like a joke to you?" He hissed.

He forced apart her thighs and thrust himself into her. Shocked pain tore her insides. What he said next was barely audible over her agony. "I know you have them."

During his repeated assaults, he kept asking "Where is the Bach? The lost concerti?"

"I have only . . ." she screamed as he ground himself into her.

"The missing Bach. I know you are the one Atemvoll sent them to."

"You hurt Raphael?"

"He admits he sent them to you. And my people saw you receive the packages from him."

Darya didn't believe him. No pain would make Raphael Atemvoll put a student of his in danger. Raphael had given her gifts of music, but no handwritten manuscripts, other than his own compositions.

The packages were at her mother and father's, but she didn't want this man anywhere near her family, her brother.

"He sent me his own writing. And Kodaly. No Bach."

As she said this, his long fingers had tightened on her thigh, digging into her flesh. "Jew Bitch," he sneered. He rolled over her once more, whispering, "They are not at your home. So now, you will tell me."

She had only a moment to realize that he had done something to her family.

And then he used her again. In agony, she turned her mind away and dreamed of strangling him with her silk scarf.

After two days, coming every two hours, he rose from her, opened the cell door and gave her to the head guard. The last thing he said was, "Do whatever pleases you, Viegelund, but do not destroy her mind, or her hands and arms. I will be in Budapest. Call when she agrees to talk."

So, her reasoning mind said to her bleeding and trembling body, so, the man in the suit wants to ransom me. But who does he think will pay? Papa works for the railroad.

After he left, the guard, Viegelund laughed. "Missing Bach? He saw you and wanted you. The manuscripts are his excuse."

He kicked away her broken shoes. "I need no excuse, Jewess," She heard him whip out his belt, just as he had on the street. He was the man with the scarred face.

And then he hit her in the face with the buckle and yanked open her dress.

*   *

Hours later, alone in the low light of her cell, Darya held one hand to the cut on her cheek as she tried not to touch the shoulder that Wool suit had repeatedly burned. With great persistence, she lifted a broken piece of concrete and scratched a third line in the moss on the wall. The third day after the kidnapping. She huddled on the thin mattress and tried to figure out why the man in the fine wool suit kept talking about Bach. What was it he really wanted? Money? Wealth? To lie with her?

But he had left after the first painful days, leaving her with the sadist, Viegelund. Wool suit had said he was going to Budapest. To stalk or beat her family? Where was Raphael Atemvoll? She prayed he was still alive, but he, too might be imprisoned.

The fine wool suit man had not returned. She would remember his perfume, his fine suit and his hateful, cajoling voice.

He could not think she had anything of value, certainly not manuscripts by Bach. She would have known immediately when she saw them, and she had played every piece that Raphael had given her.

She knew what the guard, Viegelund wanted. He hated Jews. Wanted to destroy her. She vowed to kill him if she ever got her hands on anything sharp.

Then she would search out the man in the fine suit. License 656-ABS.

She closed her bruised eyes and rocked. Her revenge would never happen. She had only this crumbling piece of concrete. They didn't even allow her a spoon to eat the thin gruel they brought her yesterday.

No one would ransom her. She had nothing of value but her concert violin and her music. And the concert violin had been made by Raphael because she could not afford the Guarneri he believed she deserved. His creation had lovely, deep tone, but that did not make it valuable to any but her.

It was in her apartment. If he had stalked her family, Wool Suit probably also knew the location of her apartment. Probably Wool Suit already had the violin.

Darya watched a sliver of light move across the farthest wall. Light revealed the seep of water from outside dirt to inside the rock foundation. Funguses and moss grew thick. Roaches drank and copulated in the lichen.

And that was when she noticed the package crumpled near the wall. She picked it up. Cigarettes. Fingerprints, she thought. She knew the blue, black and white brand. French. *Gitanes brunes. Dark-fired tobacco called Gypsy woman.*

She stuffed the package into what was left of her pocket.

Her cell door creaked open. She tensed.

Not again, so soon.

She clutched her torn dress and closed her eyes, awaiting the blow.

"Miss Zolesku?"

At the soft pretense of respect, her body cringed.

"Miss Zolesku. I am Nagy, Zoltan Nagy."

She opened her slits of battered eyes and stared into the darkness. The man knelt so that the light revealed his face.

"You won't remember me. I took your music history class in the mornings. I play the cello in the *Zeneakadémia* orchestra."

But she did remember: bright, a fine cellist, ardently political.

He took off his coat and held it out to her. Underneath he wore a uniform with the insignia she had seen on Viegelund's shirt the day she was kidnapped, the gray green uniform of the prison gang. Nagy, Zoltan Nagy – a part of this terror?

When she didn't move, he took her hand and put her arms to the sleeve holes. Its warmth on her arms and back made her aware of how cold her feet were.

"I have food." He reached behind him and brought out a partial loaf and a small block of cheese. He took her right hand and closed her fist around the bread. "Eat quickly. I can't stay."

"Why are you . . .?"

"I came to these mountains because I thought Karl Viegelund an idealist. He made a speech at Hösök Tere, at Heroes' Square, all about freedom and the courage to change the old ways.

"And then, many times I met him at the taverns with friends. He asked me many questions about your teaching, did I ever hear you playing music that I couldn't identify, that sort of thing. I thought he admired you.

"After class four days ago, he put me on a bus up to this fortress. I was stupid. He is nothing. Greedy. He does dirty jobs for rich men – men like the one who left you here. That man is a rich gangster, supposedly owns a castle in these hills near this prison. That man owns Viegelund. Karl Viegelund owns other men . . . and women, and me. I can't escape."

Darya shuddered at the memory of that man who owned all. "Who was he? The man in the suit?"

He shook his head. "No one speaks his name. I know only that he hired Viegelund to bring you here."

"His car license, 656-ABS, not a Hungarian style plate."

"I've seen it. I could look it up if I were not a prisoner here myself."

"But . . ."

"Eat."

She bit into the bread and then the cheese. "Zoltan," she said. "You are better than..."

He shook his head. "I wish that were true."

"It can be," she whispered.

He said, "I must tell you something. You have to remember me and this moment. Not all men are like this place. Remember me. Be my freedom."

His voice seemed prophetic and far away. *My freedom?*

"Your freedom," she said, "You must leave this Viegelund."

He stood and backed toward the door. "I will return as soon as I can and let you out of here. I have to figure a way."

At that moment, they both heard the sound of many boots. Her cell door banged open. There stood Karl Viegelund, backed by five others.

"You!" Karl shouted. "Jew lover!"

Darya stood, "He did nothing."

"Brought you food," Viegelund pointed out. He turned toward his men. "Not the first time he's defied orders to help a prisoner. Take him to the south yard."

The men grabbed Zoltan. Karl Viegelund grabbed Darya. "We'll see him to hell," he hissed, "and you we'll bury under a glacier."

She heard Zoltan's boots dragging along the hall as he cried out. Karl yanked her by the waist to his chest. Through Zoltan's thin coat, Viegelund's hands covered her breasts and roamed down her body. "You have a date to keep," he whispered, "or I would enjoy you one more time."

She shuddered. Who but the fine suit could keep Viegelund from her?

Then Viegelund pulled her out of the cell, pushed her around the corner to the spiral stairs and forced her, stumbling and running, up to the light of a muddy yard. Off to the south, toward the setting sun and out of sight, she heard the others jeering at Zoltan.

"Tear off his shirt," one yelled. "He won't be able to wear it anyway."

She heard a lash whistling through the air – someone warming a strong arm.

Viegelund pushed Darya north, toward a small building. Her body tightened, waiting. She closed her bleeding eyelids and willed her mind to separate from her body against whatever he would do next.

He laughed. "Oh yes, I would take you again. And if you don't make it, I will have that pleasure. But your ransom has been paid."

She opened her eyes. "Who?" Beyond his back, she saw they stood near the entry gate to this building – a castle wall, ancient stone.

Viegelund sneered. "I said it has been paid, but it only bought you a chance to live. See if you can stay free long enough to meet him."

"Who? What does he want of me?"

Viegelund's smile ended. "What would any man want?"

"Where is he?" she asked.

"He said he would be in the cherry orchard at the bottom of this road. But he forgot to ask me nicely to bring you there. Besides, I can't be gone that long or take a jeep without others noticing."

How can I escape them both?

He pushed her chest. "If you can't get there, what is that to me?"

"You lie. There is no one."

"I had a very good price for you. More than the Bach would ever bring to me."

"Who?"

"I didn't get his name. He didn't offer it. I'm not sure you'll like him any better than me. Big fellow. Rich."

Escape. Escape and avoid the one who paid. They're all filth.

Into her mind came the words of Zoltan Nagy. *Men are not all like these men.*

Reacting to a sound from the inner prison courtyard, Viegelund moved quickly, grabbed her by the hair and shoved her toward the open prison door. "Better to freeze than live," he taunted. "Go and find your benefactor, if you can." His tone insinuated more.

His next push sent her beyond the prison walls. She sprawled on her hands and knees in the snow of an open field. She expected to be dragged back inside. Instead, there was only silence. She dared to breathe. Viegelund, Karl did not come.

There is no hiding from him.

Through battered eyelids, she saw a hulking castle prison behind her. It slumped atop one of Hungary's northern hills. Karl stood for a moment in the open doorway. He had thrown her out into a larger prison, to play with her mind, make her dream of freedom.

He brought me alone to the north tower, so no one would see him let me go.

Gusts of late afternoon wind picked up ice crystals and sent them in a dance of mockery about her bloody arms.

Mockery. That explained why he threw her out. Tonight, as Viegelund, Karl left for town, he would hunt her down. No one could hide – not on this exposed hilltop, nor in the surrounding fields of harvest stubble. Behind her, Viegelund's contempt and laughter rolled over her. Then he slammed shut the outer door.

She had become two people, the battered woman and the other who could no longer feel or hear. Darya smelled her own coppery blood and, on her clothes, the pervasive odor of moldy walls from the castle dungeon. From her hair, a stick of bedstraw fell to the mud. The evil smells mixed themselves with fresh pine pungence blowing across the plain. Beyond the castle, she saw the famous broad-shouldered silhouette of Mount Kékes.

Now she knew she was in the Mátras, the central mountains, far from Budapest, far from any real help.

Shivering, she pulled Zoltan's thin jacket closer about her neck. She pushed to stand, but pain slowed her movements. She must move from the gate before the next guards arrived.

A human cry rang out behind her. She stiffened. Above her, in reaction to the cry, a raven cawed. The bird jumped up and down on his spruce branch. A second human cry reverberated around the castle walls. And then another and another in a crescendo of anguish.

The thugs whipped Zoltan Nagy. He had begged her, "Escape. Become my freedom." She swayed in pain and grief. Now was the moment when even Viegelund might be watching Zoltan instead of her.

She moved forward, and forced herself to find reasons to live. Mama, Papa, Raphael Atemvoll, even Piotr, they also might be prisoners. She must remain free, learn more. Darya dragged her feet through the snow toward the raven's tree. The raven paid no attention to her.

Inside the castle walls, Zoltan's cries stopped. The raven stopped its excited call. The guard would look out again soon, if he weren't already watching her.

She slid behind the low hanging branches of the spruce, a small and useless hiding place. Beyond the tree, and to the south, she saw that volcanic boulders and ragged lava created a steep precipice falling away to the valley below the castle.

From the silence, she guessed that the guards inside had retreated to the warmth of their beer hall. She imagined Zoltan's body lying in the snow. For him, for her family, she must get away and find help.

Reaching up into the tree, Darya broke off a low branch. She backed toward the southern cliff, brushing out her tracks. As she peered into the steep drop, snow devils enveloped her.

CHAPTER THREE

At the edge of the steep incline, she turned her back to the void and climbed downhill from the obscuring tree. By the time her bare hands and feet could no longer grip the cutting lava, she had achieved almost fifty feet of distance below the level of the tree. She chose a large volcanic crag and crept around it to the side away from the road. Darya decided to stay as close to this level as possible while she moved. Here she could hide from the road and from the valley until dusk. In this coat, she would appear to be part of the lava if the light were gray.

She assumed all traffic with the castle arrived by the road. She planned not to be visible when the night guards arrived, and the day guards left. By the darkening gray of the sky, she could only guess that it was nearly five in the afternoon. Already, the oak forest below her was deep in shadow. This night would be long.

Her feet – she couldn't pay attention to her feet, had to focus on pretending to be warmed by the cotton jacket. Through the oaks, the valley below her hiding place showed no sign of a friendly farmhouse, only of the village where she had learned that the guards lived and spent many Forints of brazenly stolen money. No one in that village would have the courage to help her, or Zoltan.

This was their Hungary, ruled by this gang, this Viegelund, Karl, as her Hungarian countrymen would call him. This Viegelund knew there would be no help for her.

Darya had no idea who the thugs in this castle-prison might be, only that they lived outside the laws of the new Hungarian government – the lawless result of sudden freedom from Soviet rule. Some of the gangsters spoke German, some Hungarian, some Russian. A polyglot group. Viegelund hated Jews, this she knew, but Jew-bashing wasn't his primary purpose. He thought someone would pay.

And now someone had, but she couldn't trust that person any more than the others. Did that man also believe she had these imagined manuscripts? Did he think she was someone else? Someone worth a lot of money? She had to find a way to avoid Viegelund, and the man in the fine wool suit and the man who had paid for her. And she had no idea what two of those men looked like.

As darkness grew, she edged around the lava outcrop and worked her way toward the valley, keeping well below the road. In the darkest part of evening, across whisper-soft snow, Darya heard the arrival of the night guard. Above her, they rode up the hill in an ancient and noisy automobile. She held her breath and forced herself to stand still. She worked to stop jittering with cold. Fifteen minutes later, a jeep filled with the hated day-time guard squirreled its way down the steep road, the men laughing and jeering at each other.

She waited to see if Viegelund and Karl came to the cliff's edge. He might have watched her begin to descend and have an idea how to find her. Many minutes later, as silence settled over the plain, she decided he had gone with his comrades. She dared to continue her work downward. Her feet had become so cold she couldn't feel them, couldn't tell her toes to grip the rock. Her work across the cliff face had cost her many detours toward easier handholds. After another hour and a half, she came to a place where the cliff intersected the road far below the castle. She stopped and tore the lower half of her dress. One half of the fabric she tied around each foot.

In the ambient light of cloudy sky above bright snow, she followed the hardened tire tracks of the jeep, hoping the rags of her dress on her feet helped disguise her footsteps.

For two hours she hobbled down the turns of the road. She listened, alert for any need to disappear into the rocks. At last, near the base of the hill, she turned aside into a scrubby walnut orchard. The snow seemed softer under the orchard trees, so she broke off old branches of a fern plant and used it to disguise her exit from the road. Then, hidden by the gnarled trunks, she rested against a leafless, black-barked walnut tree. She stared out at the road, wondering how much further she could go on her bleeding feet.

She had to move forward and think of nothing but each step.

However, she found she couldn't push herself away from the walnut tree. Her mind raked over the last minutes before he put her out.

It was all too easy. What was the Viegelund's game? Was he watching her? Coming after her?

Behind her, a twig cracked. She whirled, ready to fight. A big man in a dark overcoat appeared next to a nearby pine. Darya shrank against the walnut.

He was supposed to meet her in a cherry orchard. But he must be the one. Dear God, how easy for him.

In the near darkness, he spoke softly in Hungarian. "Darya, I am your Uncle Tobias."

"You lie." How could her uncle have found her here? And so big compared to her mother.

The man lifted his Astrakhan hat and stopped walking toward her. The lambs' wool hat reminded her of the Russian bigwigs who once strutted down the streets of Budapest. One of his hands rested in his pocket – probably on a gun.

The man shifted from one foot to the other. "Truly, my little niece," he said, "Karl Viegelund, up in the castle, believes he now owns a whole building in the United States. And both of us have cold feet by now. He promised to drive you to a cherry orchard, but I didn't trust him, so I waited here, a mile closer to the castle."

She held up her bleeding hands. "Not likely," she said.

"He and his men did crash around in the cherry orchard last night, but I was here, and hidden until I heard you coming down the road."

"Bribery might explain Karl," she said, stiffly, "but you may be working with the other one. Anyone might know I have an uncle in the States."

"Yes, they might. You are right to be careful."

"Why did you not bring a limousine to the castle door?" she taunted.

His laugh seemed gentle, designed perhaps, to put her off balance. "I usually take the Bronx subway, not a limousine."

Uncle Tobias' letters had mentioned the Bronx and the subway, but this was not enough proof. She could think of one way to know for certain if this man were her mother's brother, the uncle she had never met except in his letters to family.

"Your patients must miss you terribly," she said.

"My patients are all dead," he answered.

"Tobias!" she whispered.

He nodded.

"How did you find me?" she asked, still reluctant to believe.

"I came hoping to hear you play at Sopron two Fridays from now, but they'd already kidnapped you. Somehow, your parents had already been taken as well. They had ransacked their home and thrown everything to the floor.

"Then two days ago, a ransom note arrived at your parents' home. The gang leader, Viegelund wanted to make a deal on his own, and behind the back of the one who paid him to take you."

Darya whispered, "The other man, the rich one, thought I owned the missing Bach concertos."

The big man shook his head. "Why would he believe such a thing?" Tobias asked. "Even the Viegelund thought it farfetched. He believes ransom is a faster way to wealth. I met him last night at the edge of the village."

Darya imagined the danger, and Tobias' courage.

He smiled, as if he knew her thought. "I had back up," he said, and pulled a gun from within his coat. She stepped back, ready to run. He dropped his hand to his side.

"The arms are for Viegelund, Karl, not you."

She breathed again. Then she asked, "Mama? Papa?" And then, she added a ruse, just in case. "How is Anna?"

"I do not know Anna. But from your apartment, I have your violin and your music. Remember? You sent me a celebratory key when you first rented that space?"

"It is you!" The key was their joke and her encouragement for him to return to Hungary.

It came to her that he had said this last in Yiddish. "Sweet Poppy," he whispered.

At her mother's nickname for her, she gasped, "Tobias! Oh, Mama."

He stepped forward, pulling her into his generous embrace. "The Festival at Sopron needs to hear your wonderful music one more time before you also disappear, and then, we must search for our family."

"Raphael?"

He shook his head. "I cannot find him. His office and home also have been torn apart."

She saw a pain flit over his face. "What? What are you not telling me?"

He looked at her and said, "You are freezing, I will tell you everything, but after we get you to safety."

She looked up toward the prison. "Uncle, I must find help for Raphael, for my family, and for someone else still inside the prison. They will die."

He frowned down at her, then glanced up through the darkness toward the looming hill. "I have friends in Budapest and Sopron," he said. "They will know what may be done. Follow me."

"He has hurt Raphael, I'm certain. And Mama . . ."

He shook his head. "They destroyed everything, but I cannot find anyone, your parents nor your brother, and not Raphael."

Darya's heart seemed to freeze. "For this music?"

"No one knows," he said. "Only to you and to Viegelund did he give the fantastic excuse of the music."

"Where are they all?"

"I have friends trying to find out."

"Where will I go?"

"To a safe house with me to recover. To Sopron to play once more for your people. And then to New York as a new person with a different name."

"But Mother, Piotr, Papa."

"Friends are searching." He stepped back into the orchard, offering her his coat as he moved. She felt the safety promised by her uncle's big arms. She wanted that safety, but more, she wanted to get Zoltan, Raphael, and her family to safety with her.

"Damn," he said, "Bach's concerti are not worth the pain and danger they have caused."

CHAPTER FOUR

THE YEAR 1748

In the music parlor, Johann Sebastian Bach played the piano-forte softly as he spoke to his wife, Anna Magdalena.

"And," he said, "the orchestra will move on down to resolve into the D minor chord, with the foundation in the bass and the cellos." He let his left hand run down the harpsichord keys, taking the lower voices to the finale.

Anna Magdalena wrote quickly as he had taught her to do. She noted the small bird trills of the violin and then the last entry of the theme. An octave below the cellos, she heard and notated the progress of his bass viol. The bass rose to meet the cello, giving resolution to the final moments of her husband's newest violin concerto.

Anna Magdalena leaned over the harpsichord to hear what he did with the third of the chord. She wrote as fast and neatly as she could.

"And the violin leads them to heavenly rest," Johann laughed, "but not much rest." He let his orchestra accompaniment run on to a suitably exuberant cadence where he truly ended.

His fingers lifted from the keyboard to touch her face.

"And heaven it is," she said, leaning her cheek against his caressing finger. "But let me get that on the page first."

He chuckled, "First before you make breakfast for the masses?"

Anna smiled at his joking way of referring to their children, and his grown children by his deceased first wife, Maria Barbara.

*   *

Johann watched her calm smile. It always amazed him how patient Anna could be, and how motherly, even for the boys who were not much younger than she. Carl Phillipe Emmanuel, his most responsible son, still enjoyed being clucked over and fed. Wilhelm Friedemann, on the other hand, appreciated no one who had high expectations for manners and responsible actions. Yet, his Anna took care that even that snotty boy-man received food and a good bed.

Anna said, "Breakfast is ready, save for cooking the fresh eggs from my hens. And the children will wait while their father's concerto is completed. Besides," she glanced at Johann, "Carl has not found Wilhelm Friedemann yet."

Johann sighed with worry, then watched as she quietly worked on, copying his last measures on her page.

"Sweetheart," she said, "This is fun and beautiful. Wonderful. Let's take the manuscript to the window where you can see that it is all there." She rose, swished her skirts away from the side chair and led him to the window bench.

He took the manuscript, held it to the light and very close to the side of his face where his failing eyes could still see the notes. Conducting with his right hand, Johann hummed the parts completely through.

"Well done, Popkin," he said at last. "What a gift you are to this old, blinded fool."

"I love this old fool," she said, and leaned toward him, kissing his cheek.

He responded warmly, as she had hoped. Then he drew back. "People say I should never have brought you to this house of chaos, all these children, all this copying for a man whose music is going out of style."

"People know nothing. And you are not out of style. The next generation only wishes that were so."

"Well, our boys need their musical day in the light."

"And our girls."

"Well, yes." He nodded, aware that his focus on the boys' education had long been a tiff between them.

She smiled, lifted the manuscript, and set it on the small table before them. Then she took his old hands in hers and lifted them to her lips. "Many years from now, when people will read any of your violin concerti, I hope they see my love for you in the handwriting. I know they will hear your genius in the beauty, the complexity and the exuberance."

"Dear Anna, you were a gift the day you walked into my life. No ordinary bride, you were, and now, a wonder of a woman."

She leaned toward him, but outside the study, a heavy door slammed. Booted feet stumbled into the entry way. "Out of the way, you bugger sister," a slurred voice said.

"Best step aside, Regina Susanna," said another young man, more quietly. "He needs to sleep off his night."

Anna whispered to Johann, "Carl Phillipe has found Friedemann at last."

She started to rise, but Johann held her next to him. "Let Carl take the burden of his brother alone. There is nothing you can do that Friedemann will appreciate."

She sat back, evidently resigned to that truth, and laid her hand on the concerto's first page to test that the ink had completely dried. After a moment, she said, "Johann, what will we do with Friedemann?"

"Wilhelm Friedemann is old enough to care for himself, and should move to his own apartments again. He will have to look at himself in the mirror and try to shave the dissipation from his face."

"Move out? Do you think he can live by himself, safely?"

"He is not learning to do that by living here, my Anna."

Both of them feared for Wilhelm Friedemann, a consummate musician of dissolute habits and argumentative nature. Friedemann never said no to his hangers on, and was always willing to play the dice, drink the next drink and talk about the jobs he should have had, and would have someday, when he practiced more and kept appointments.

Anna stood and lifted the manuscript. Johann saw sadness slide into her being, sadness for her lost babies, and sadness for the boy who would not be a man. She placed the violin concerto on the side table where later she could copy the orchestral parts. The concerto had been promised for a concert this spring, the violin part to be played by a friend of Carl Phillipe Emmanuel.

She returned to the window seat to help Johann rise, but he wrapped an arm about her waist, pulled her to him, and whispered, "I do love you."

"I know that Johann. I hear it in everything we do together. In each lovely melody and especially in the adagio movement of this violin concerto"

She leaned down and kissed him long and warmly.

CHAPTER FIVE

THE CONCERT, SOPRON, HUNGARY, 1994

At the outdoor theater of Sopron, the night shone with stars of early spring. Darya shivered, remembering cold mountains and ugliness. Her body still recoiled from the touch of others, but five days in her uncle's care had brought back her hands and her music. Five more days had healed her cut face enough for makeup to cover the last yellowing damage.

Her greatest relief came from knowing that Raphael Atemvoll had had time to call and get her family to safety in some unknown place. They were still hidden away somewhere known only to a friend. The friend didn't tell her, and she didn't want to know, in case tonight didn't work and she was captured again.

But even the friend did not know what had happened to Raphael. When he came to get him at his teaching studio, the place was torn apart and there was only Raphael's blood on the floor and on the piano leg.

So, for all their sakes, tonight had to work as Uncle Tobias planned.

As she looked out toward the open lawn from behind the proscenium arch, she saw no hint of the Viegelund, or any guards she recognized, but she knew that other man must be around. His fine suit might be hidden in a wool overcoat, but she knew he would have a ticket for this night, and he wouldn't give up easily.

What she did see were hundreds of faces, happy people, bundled in winter coats, sitting on chairs or on blankets, waiting for the orchestra to settle and for her to arrive on the stage. Tonight, she would play the Bach Violin Concerto in A minor, her favorite of the Bach concerti that still existed.

Why does the man believe I have the others? We know so little about them, not even if they really existed. But he was so certain ...

But Raphael Atemvoll had in no way sent her such manuscripts.

There in the first row of the outdoor theater, a seat stood empty. Tobias had saved it for her teacher, Raphael Atemvoll. She feared what Viegelund's gang might have done.

Gazing at that empty chair, she worked to keep her tears inside.

Her uncle, Tobias Kossuth, had spread the rumor that Darya Zolesku never had been kidnapped, but had been merely practicing at a remote location on the outskirts of Budapest, unaware that there had been a search for her. He added a small hint in all the rumoring. The whispers spread. The whispers told of a Darya Zolesku who might seem a bit odd in recent days, more tense than expected, more easily on edge.

Thus, Uncle Tobias' rumors had at once calmed the fears of the recording studio which hoped to work with her next week on her next disc. He had calmed the radio announcers, newspaper reporters, her students, and the whole police-search apparatus. And at the same time, he had set in motion the speculation that would follow.

At this moment, she had to do the hardest thing. She had to fail.

"What about the cigarette package?" she whispered to Tobias.

"The police identified the fingerprints. His name is Garig Steiermark. He is untouchable, at least within Hungary."

"And if he ever left Hungary?" she whispered.

"Well then. More is possible."

"That man and his gang will be out there," she said.

"We must convince him, my Darya. You must do this," Tobias said, "For your teacher, for your family. Yes, even for our friend Bach."

Ready to perform, Darya took her gaze from the front row, gave her attention to the gathered audience, pushed back her hair, tucked her violin under her arm and stepped upon the stage of her country's most famous festival. The audience welcomed her warmly. Many in attendance had been her colleagues, her musical friends, her students. But her family remained in hiding, still in a barn somewhere unknown even to her.

And Darya Zolesku was damaged, angry and fearful, no longer the naïve girl these people thought they loved.

She pushed down memory of the days in the castle prison and took her place before the orchestra. This concerto was beloved. She had played it since she was thirteen years old, musically growing with it each year.

Unlike concertos from other time periods, Bach's three existing concertos waited for no long introductions, they whirled right into the business of laying out the opening theme with the violin in the lead, the orchestra supporting. Darya had always believed his three lost concerti would have been as exciting and as beautiful.

She lifted her violin to her shoulder, felt the burn of the cigarette, but placed her bow on the E string and nodded to the conductor. He smiled, raised his arms, flicked the point of his baton to give the orchestra the speed, and then brought his baton down.

As she played the opening bars, Darya forgot all else. She played the allegro with the orchestra as if all of them had stepped together into a tale of heroic adventure. Every syncopation and lick of strong rhythm led them all in a dash toward triumph. At the end of that movement, the orchestra moved directly into the second movement.

In the opening four bars, the orchestra imitated guitar-like strumming, setting eight insistent, slow beats. The harmonic changes brought the audience to a yearning anticipation of the violin. When Darya entered, her notes came as the softest voice in the far-off hills, a lament sung by a mother for her child. Darya played, imagining Bach and his wife, and the children Anna had lost. Father and mother, crying for the touch of their soft hands, for the young arms around an old neck. Increasing key changes brought out the sorrow, as if the parents searched for the missing ones, or at least an explanation for death ...

And then the movement ended with as silent an audience as Darya had ever known. She held them in her palm and didn't want to do what she had to do next.

She began the last movement, a dance of life. It rang with joy, a follow-me-to-fun-and-love nine beat jig that could not stop, could not slow down – a dervish of motion and sunshine.

She saw smiles on the face of her friends and others in the front row.

And then, when the rhythm changed, she began to speed up the basic beat. The orchestra followed her, or at least most of it. Many scurrying measures later, where Bach brought the violin's dance to a full stop, Darya ignored the two beats of rest and sped into the next section well ahead of the celli, who were supposed to reintroduce the main theme.

She sped, faster and faster. Behind her, the orchestra fell into disarray. Darya slid over the sixteenth note runs by herself and then headed into what should have been the violin's accompaniment of the orchestra, a whirl of string crossings and chords that blurred more and more as she moved faster and faster. The concert master worked to catch up, to figure out where Darya had gone. And his leadership brought most of the orchestra back by the time she reached the Tutti where all should have been playing together.

But there, she quit, stared at the audience, stared at the empty chair for her teacher. Her eyes brimmed with tears. She glanced with regret toward the concert master and the conductor, then ran off the stage. Tobias pulled her swiftly away from the stage and into his rented car.

*   *

Hours later, in the hills above Sopron, Uncle Tobias turned their car onto a remote road and drove uphill several miles. No one passed them the whole time they were on that road, though they passed a farm with a gaggle of geese penned near the lane. Later, Darya saw two cows and four horses grazing in a field. At last, well after sunrise, Tobias brought the car to a halt near a limestone cliff. He opened his door.

"Move into the drivers' seat and put your hands on the steering wheel," he said, removing his gloves.

She came around the car and did as he asked. Then he handed her the car rental papers.

"Wad these up and put them on the ground, well away from the turn-out, and weight the wad using this," he said.

He handed her a rock.

She took the rock and the papers. She saw her name on the rental agreement. As she stepped from the car, wadded and placed the papers under the rock, he walked into the woods. In a moment, he returned carrying the body of a woman with dark hair, a dead woman dressed in one of Darya's dresses. "Open the car door again," he said.

She did. He slid the woman into the driver's seat.

"Who is . . .?"

"She was already dead, unclaimed, headed for the teaching hospital. I cannot tell you more."

Darya stepped back, sick in her stomach. "But she . . ."

Tobias stood apart from her and next to the woman. "God," he said, "take this woman's soul into your care. She saves my family from harm. We thank her and will remember her all of our lives for this moment."

Then, he strode to the trunk and removed everything except Darya's suitcase and her violin case.

"My violin . . . Atemvoll . . ."

"It must be here when they find the car. The metal maker's-mark on your bow, your violin, these will identify her."

"But her finger prints, her teeth."

He looked at his shoes. "Darya, stop asking questions. Stop . . ."

He did not look well. She could only guess what he had done.

Uncle Tobias took a flask from his pocket. Lifted it and said, "Lighter fluid in disguise."

He poured the contents on the front seat and on the woman. He pocketed the flask. Then he lit a match, tossed it inside and slammed the door.

"Quickly, before it explodes. Push."

She ran to the back of the flaming car and pushed with him. Within moments, it began to roll toward the cliff. The car did not explode until it hit the bottom, three hundred feet down.

Three days of hiking followed. On the third night, they stood on the reedy shore of the Neusiedler See, called in their native Hungarian, the Fertö Tö – the lake that borders Austria and Hungary. Forty miles from the site of Darya Zolesku's suicide, Darya and Tobias stepped into the lake and began swimming away from Hungary, from the border patrols, from possible identification of Darya, and, they hoped, away from the lawlessness of greedy men.

Darya knew from childhood swims that the lake was not deep, but the bottom could be a tangle of reeds and deep mud. She dared not put her feet down.

The power of water, and a wind from the north sapped energy. The nausea she had been feeling since before the concert swept over her several times. But she could not give up. Giving up would take Uncle Tobias down with her, so she swam, one arm, kick, kick, other arm, breathe and kick, one arm . . .

When she thought she could swim no further, a row boat appeared in the darkness. She dodged it, afraid. The man in the suit had found her out.

"Tobias," the rower said, "Tell her to climb in."

She swam away, watching with wary fatigue. The rower's shadow bent toward her.

Tobias' voice came from the other side of the boat. "Darya, this is my friend, Gabriel Kolya. Help him pull you in."

She reached her arm to the boat. Within minutes, both she and Tobias were in the small boat, wrapped in blankets, shivering, and watching the northern shoreline approach.

"I've made arrangements for both of you to live with me."

Tobias said, "I have a reservation for both of us at a pension."

"I find that unsafe. Too many will see her. I took the liberty of canceling that reservation."

Tobias tightened his grip on Darya's shoulders. His voice grew icy. "That was too much liberty, Gabriel. Don't make decisions for me or for our guest."

"I'll be sure to ask in future. I think it is dangerous for her to be in public."

Tobias went silent, but his hands continued to warm Darya's shoulders. Then he whispered to her. "He means well, but ...."

Though she shivered almost beyond control, she nodded.

"We're beyond any border guards," the dark-haired man at the oars said, "Here we are well into Austria."

A half-hour later, they pulled into a small dock at Podersdorf am See. When Darya stepped out of the rowboat, the rower tried to take her hand. She yanked her hand back.

"I will walk for myself," she said. She knew her harsh response came out of the days of beatings. She knew this man was a friend of Tobias's, but she didn't ever again want to be controlled by others.

*   *

Days later, hidden in Gabriel's apartment in Vienna, they planned how to get Darya to the United States. Tobias visited the U.S. embassy in Austria, asking what would be involved if a friend claimed need for asylum.

The answer, of course, was that the need for asylum had to be investigated, and the country of origin had to be shown to be incapable of controlling the gang who might have threatened the friend.

So, they knew that route was closed to her. Any suggestion that the death of Darya Zolesku might not be final would bring with it the specter of police investigations and news interviews.

Darya Zolesku was too well-known in Europe. A Darya who might have survived and who requested asylum, clearly would bring the attention of the hoodlums from the mountains of Hungary. So, she had to try to enter the U.S. as a different, totally new person.

And by that time, Darya was certain the nausea she felt each day was caused by a new life. She spent each day arguing with herself about her situation, the ugly reason for the existence of a baby, the baby's place in the world, and her rights and responsibilities. She had clear reasons not to want the child, but she was loathe to do what made sense. She had a deep feeling that the child would be a light and not a reminder of darkness.

Gabriel Kolya, the tall rower, was, it turned out, a famous Austrian-born pianist who had become an American citizen. Gabriel offered to solve their immigration problems.

"We can get a false Austrian birth certificate and passport. Darya can become my wife and enter the United States with ease."

The idea stiffened her back with renewed terror. "No," Darya said.

Both Gabriel and Uncle Tobias looked at her in surprise.

"I will not marry anyone." She kept her gaze on Tobias to emphasize to him her resolve. Uncle Tobias would think she refused because of the days in prison, but there was more.

Darya feared what she believed was Gabriel's will to control.

"But . . .," Gabriel began, until Tobias put up his hand to stop discussion.

"Gabriel, we need to find another way. It is too soon."

*   *

A few mornings later, she entered the bathroom, trying desperately to be quiet about throwing up. When she was down to dry heaves, she stood, tried to breathe deeply and make it all stop.

After her stomach stopped roiling, she brushed her teeth and threw cold water on her face. In the mirror, she looked a ghost.

As she left the bathroom, Gabriel met her in the hallway.

"I know a place," he said.

"A place for what?"

"To help you not have this child."

She felt slapped. Backing from him, she said, "I won't."

He stepped toward her. "But it is a mistake child. The child of evil."

She faced him. Pointed her fist at him and said, "No."

Just then, Tobias came into the hall. "Darya will decide what happens to her and for her. I recommend you allow her the time and space to think for herself."

"But …" Gabriel began.

"Leave her alone," Tobias said.

*   *

One early morning soon after this confrontation, Darya slipped out of Gabriel's stifling apartment and sought the libraries of Vienna to begin her own investigations of the Bach violin concerti.

She walked down the út, remembering to think of it as a street, or in the German of Vienna, a strasse, and a square or platz. She found Heldenplatz, and then Josefsplatz and stared in admiration at the palace where one wing had become the National Library of Austria. Minutes later, she entered the front door.

"Hello, Fraŭlein," the greeting librarian said. "How may we help you?"

"I wish to see your collection on music history, especially the history of Johann Sebastian Bach."

"Please sign into the visitors' book." The young man moved a large book on a turntable toward her. "Your accent . . . Hungarian, nein?"

Darya stared at him, realizing that she had to put on a bluff and not draw his interest.

"Hungarian, yes," she said as she hesitated over the page. He might ask for identification.

Boldness, she thought.

Then, remembering one of her teacher's childhood fantasies, she took the offered pen and wrote, "Rebecca Sospiro."

"Danke, Fraulein Sospiro. Our music hall is on the second floor of the Hofburg section of the old Imperial Library. You may take the stairs to the left."

As Darya clung to the iron banister and climbed the worn stairs, she said a prayer for her teacher, her mentor, her beloved Raphael "Sospiro" Atemvoll.

Where are you, my teacher-grandfather?

The room she entered rose to a height that forced her to grab for the wall. Its leaning shelves filled with volumes, its enormous statues and painted ceiling made her stop. Her mind tried to understand where Gods, heroes, draperies and painted perspective left off and true marble corbels existed to support the central dome. The contrast with her recent days in an underground cell, and then suddenly in a small apartment took away her breath.

"May I help you, Fraulein?"

She turned toward an elderly man who hovered.

"I am looking for the catalog of books concerning music history."

"This way, Fraulein. You read German as well as Hungarian?"

"Yes."

"You may begin here, then."

After negotiating the card catalog and its not quite complete electronic replacement, she found several listings for the works of Bach. Among the actual manuscripts, she found that some contained quotations from known or reconstructed examples of the missing works.

As she had been taught by Raphael, two of the missing violin concerti were supposed to have been re-written for other instruments. Bach often borrowed from himself and rewrote music for other occasions and other instrument combinations.

As her brother, Piotr, had often said, "When the violinist is away, the oboe will play.

Others, including "Bach's sons and music colleagues, had done the same borrowing and rewriting from Johann's works.

Thus, it was believed that two of the original violin concerti had been re-used for the harpsichord. As harpsichord music, they contained obvious solo right-hand parts – the parts believed to have originally been for solo violin, or perhaps the oboe.

All of this, she understood, was intelligent guessing by trained scholars. However, the original manuscripts would answer many questions, and because of the great esteem for Bach, any page from any one of them that was a proven original would now be worth a fortune to a museum or to a collector.

She knew the man in the fine wool suit wanted them only for himself. If ever he did find them, no one else would see them as long as he lived.

*   *

After two fruitful hours in the library, Darya had learned that the manuscripts had probably been sold by Bach's son, Wilhelm Friedemann. But these speculations had been put about long after the deaths of anyone involved. She discovered that some even believed Friedemann had sold them to a Russian count.

If that were true, there would be no way that her beloved Raphael Atemvoll would have had them. He told her that he had lived his childhood years among the Slovaks, and then most of his adult life in Hungary.

She returned past Saint Stephen's cathedral and wound her way through the market streets to Gabriel's apartment at number 5 Domgasse. The door flung open and Gabriel pulled her inside roughly.

She pushed away from him.

"Where have you been?"

"Don't touch me like that."

"You can't just disappear. I'm responsible for you."

"You are responsible only for you."

At that moment, Tobias came into the living room. "Gabriel sit down."

Gabriel glared at Tobias, but sat.

"Darya," Tobias said, "please leave me a note if you decide to go for a walk. I . . . we thought you had been kidnapped again."

Darya suddenly realized what fear she had caused. "Uncle, I am so sorry. I felt . . . this town is so beautiful, I just wanted to get into it. I wasn't thinking."

Gabriel said, "I can take you on a tour, but please, don't leave us in this kind of situation again … We can't even call the police to look for you."

"I won't do that again without telling you. But I do need to go out, to find out more about the concerti. About why they think I have them."

"Where did you go?" Gabriel asked.

"To the National Library. It is quite close."

"But you have to sign in to visit there."

"Yes," she said, turning to Tobias. "I have a new name."

Tobias raised his eyebrows.

"I am Rebecca Sospiro."

"Sospiro?" Gabriel said. "What kind of wacky name is that?"

Darya/Rebecca saw Tobias smile. He remembered the story of Raphael/Sospiro from her childish letters about her lessons.

"I'm going to my room," she said to Gabriel.

*   *

On their second approach to the immigration problem, Gabriel Kolya visited the embassy and told a different story in order to gather information. He came back to inform Darya that her pregnancy, lack of a supportive father, and her lack of verifiable history would get her turned away at all entry points.

Yet, Darya again refused Gabriel Kolya's generous offer of marriage. She could not fulfill the duties of a wife, not after what had happened to her in the prison. In fact, when Gabriel was near her, her mind recoiled and disappeared into a dark cave.

Moreover, she knew that Gabriel, as husband, would not be able to accept the child within her. He had already badgered her several times about having an abortion. Not just asked, but insisted it was the only way. He believed the child was the product of a devil.

But her mind returned to Zoltan's words, "Be my freedom," he had said.

How can I do that for you, Zoltan?

She could not compound the evil that had happened to her by condemning the child. That way may have been smarter, even okay in the eyes of God, but for her, she knew that she needed to turn the evil into good, to accept the child and create love where there had been hate and rage.

"Be my freedom," Zoltan had said. She could not be his freedom if she tied herself to Gabriel Kolya, a man who refused to understand her need to let the child be a child, create joy where there had been so much fear.

*   *

At last, an Austrian medical examiner, a friend and colleague of Tobias, provided her with identification papers making Darya Zolesku into Rebecca Sospiro Gregory, the widow of a recently deceased American who had been living abroad and who had no other family.

Thus, Rebecca and Tobias were the only attendants at a very small funeral for the man, Lemuel Gregory.

Rebecca approached his open coffin. Through the mask of embalming makeup, she could see that he had been a sad and possibly even a gentle man.

"Thank you, Lemuel," she whispered. "You give me new life. I will not hurt your name and reputation."

And then she whispered a petition to God for Lemuel and for the woman in the explosive car.

A name and other necessary information made it possible for Tobias to bring Rebecca to New York in time for her son to be born a U.S. citizen.

CHAPTER SIX

THREE YEARS OUT OF HUNGARY, 1997, NEW YORK CITY

Rebecca Sospiro Gregory set her music bag on the piano in her studio in New York City. Ever since crossing the Atlantic and moving to Uncle Tobias's apartment building, she'd established herself as Rebecca, not Darya. She'd come from Vienna, not Budapest. Her accent was recognized as Hungarian only by other Hungarians and Germans, who believed she had spent her youth in Podersdorf am See, a town so close to the Hungarian border that she was bound to have picked up the cadences and pronunciations of the neighboring country.

To all, she was the widow of Lemuel Gregory, an American who had died of heart complications while living abroad.

"An entirely new identity," her uncle had said. "You live and teach in your own apartment in my building. Who knows that you are my niece? No one."

Rebecca also had established herself as a fine violin teacher, who played in the New York Philharmonic, never played recitals, but often played music with friends.

Her normal excuse for not playing in public was that she wanted to devote her attention to her two-year-old son. Her colleagues would only accept that excuse because they also enjoyed her son, and because they sensed a grief in her beyond the ordinary.

The truth was that possible discovery petrified her. She felt certain that a public music career, even as Rebecca Gregory, would lead to her being found out. Garig Steiermark, the man in the fine wool suit, was not one to give up easily. He would figure out that the bastard Viegelund had taken a bribe and allowed her to escape. He might have realized that she had an uncle in New York. He probably searched for her, still believing the Bach manuscripts existed. He would not believe the truth, and he would not stop.

"At least you get to play music," Tobias often said.

"I love it," she told him. "And the philharmonic is wonderful – friends who care and who also love music."

"Well, some love music. Others . . . well, others love gossip, so be careful."

So, she played music, but not as the world-class musician Raphael Atemvoll had believed she would become.

At her studio table, Rebecca/Darya pulled some manuscripts of music from her bag and caressed the old pages.

Raphael Atemvoll. She would have recognized his compositions even without his name on the front page. Her violin teacher's distinctive calligraphy and his musical humor shone from the pages.

And part of his humor seemed to have been to send his entire collection of music away from any possibility of capture by Steiermark's hoodlums of the Hungarian mountains. Darya/Rebecca feared that his mailing ruse had cost him his life. She had not heard from him since her kidnapping. It was probable that only his manuscripts remained.

Soon after Darya's suicide, and their trip to New York, a friend of Tobias' in Budapest wrote.

"Tobias,

I am devastated to learn of the death of your niece, Darya Zolesku, and also the possible death of her teacher, Raphael Atemvoll. As you know, I own a building of storage spaces. During the year before these sad events, Mr. Atemvoll had brought boxes of sheet music to my storage building. I enclose a note written to me by Mr. Atemvoll and ask you what I should do with these boxes. There are several of them."

The note from Raphael was included in the letter. It said:

'These manuscripts belong to Darya Zolesku, professor at the Zeneakadémia, and are a gift from me to her for purposes of assisting in her teaching and in her concert career. If something happens to me, please make certain she knows they are stored here.

"Thank you for your attention to this important library of music.

"Sincerely,

Raphael Atemvoll."

Tobias asked his friend to mail the first of the boxes to one of the buildings he owned in New York. The building manager promised to call when they arrived.

"I sensed they had something to do with your kidnapping, and with Raphael's disappearance," Tobias told her. "I wanted to get them out of the country as soon as possible, but I don't want anyone to follow their route to you."

When the boxes came, Tobias and Rebecca discovered ten banker's size boxes of manuscripts, quite a tower of them in Tobias' apartment.

"If they know he had these," Tobias said, "They will try to trace them. So, my manager thinks they are for a friend in Chicago. I propose we store them in yet another building."

"There is another building?"

"I own five buildings in Manhattan. That's probably the sum total of the low-income housing in this city – one hundred forty apartments for folks who need to live in this city, but can't afford most of it."

"You once said that Viegelund believes he owns a building in New York City."

"That address is in the Hudson River, and he does not know my name."

"He might have found my letters from you . . ."

Tobias smiled. "Pink treasure chest painted with Disney princesses?"

"You know where I kept them?"

"I have them."

*   *

There were, of course, no Bach manuscripts in Raphael's boxes. Along with the boxes, they found three envelopes at Tobias' medical examiners' office. He had hardly looked at them because a message on the outside had indicated they were something unimportant. Then, his secretary had opened them and found more music.

But still, no Bach. Not Bach at all. The handwriting on the envelopes was very scrawling, not Atemvoll's controlled calligraphic style, perhaps hurried for some reason. However, they seemed also to be a collection of his own writing.

The reasons for all this transfer of music were a puzzle and news of his supposed death, a sadness. After a time, Rebecca overcame grief to look at the three notebooks. Inside the notebooks were copies of Raphael Atemvoll's writings and many compositions of his old teacher, Anton Batislav.

Yet, nothing they had received was even close to a Bach manuscript.

Rebecca believed the mailings and the storage meant that after Raphael had sent the celebratory and birthday gifts to her, he had realized she was in danger from his music collection. But how had he known? And why begin transferring the boxes to storage almost six months before his death?

Had he become aware much earlier of the man in the fine wool suit?

Now, in her studio, and in remembrance, Rebecca played again through the three notebooks of those mailed manuscripts. Such beautiful music. Great encores and solo pieces. She remembered his self-deprecation about composing. "Mere bagatelles," he had called them.

She put her head down on the piano and remembered Raphael's impish grin, his optimistic beliefs about human kind and his grandfatherly care for a little girl.

Uncle Tobias appeared in the doorway of her studio. She glanced up and noticed the worry in his face.

"Rebecca, are you still searching for the Bach?"

"No, Uncle. I'm just enjoying memories of Raphael. We have searched enough."

Tobias nodded. "I've been through every box a third time. You've been through them four or five times and found nothing – no hint of Johann Sebastian Bach."

She nodded. "True, but we did find that Corelli manuscript."

Uncle Tobias said, "I've asked Abe Friedenberg to take over negotiating for that. He believes the school of music at Stanford will be the best place to take care of Corelli."

"He would really know best," she said. Tobias's friend, Abe, lived and taught in Portland, Oregon, but he seemed to know everyone in the musical world of the United States.

Last year, for summer term, he had hired Rebecca to teach music at Reed College where he and his wife, Miriam, both taught. Lovely people, beautiful, calm yet vibrant city. Except for missing Tobias, it had been very hard to return to New York City for the first philharmonic rehearsal.

Tobias said, "What we have found by Raphael Atemvoll is lovely and well worth introducing to the world."

Rebecca ran her fingers over the manuscript now on her music stand. "You heard his first concerto? The one I practiced again last week?"

He smiled. "Wonderful! But if you introduce it, people will ask how you got it. They will want to know your connection to Atemvoll."

Rebecca studied the pages, and then her uncle. "Abraham Friedenberg could bring his music to the attention of other violinists."

"I suppose that's a little safer."

"And the little dances by his teacher, Batislav – very fun," she said. "I think we should play them for friends at holiday parties."

"Gabriel won't play them with you." Tobias said.

She laughed. "Gabriel Kolya is a – how you say?"

"He's a snoot."

She nodded. "Snoot, then. And he isn't the only accompanist in New York, as much as he'd like to think he is."

Uncle Tobias frowned. "Gabriel believes he owns you because of that little row-boat trip into Austria. He will sabotage any other pianist you work with."

Rebecca took in a deep breath, feeling the oppression she always experienced when she thought of Gabriel. "Uncle, I don't understand why he continues to push. I won't play in public, and I've told him this many times."

"Yet, he believes he can break your resolve and create a famous duo. He wants Rebecca Gregory to be as famous as Darya Zolesku once was, but he wants to be in charge."

"The man is … that word you used … obtuse!"

"Yes. Obtuse. And he's dangerous for you. But does he care?" Then Tobias smiled. "Speaking of obtuse, your very sharp son has just awakened from his nap."

Rebecca laughed and followed Tobias upstairs.

On the piano music desk and inside Rebecca Gregory's music bag, hidden behind the glued-down end papers of three music notebooks, yellowing manuscripts lay hidden and safe, but unheard.

*   *

In Budapest, Raphael Atemvoll rolled his wheelchair into the office of the young judge, Otto Rákóczi.

The judge rose. "Mr. Sospiro," he said. He came to Raphael's side, took over pushing the wheelchair and brought him smoothly toward the sofa and chair at the fireplace end of his office. Raphael noted the viola that sat on the side table and the wooden music stand that stood in a corner.

"Nice digs, Otto," Raphael said.

Otto chuckled and sat in the chair next to him. Both of them sat for a moment, each knowing the other's sadness.

Then Raphael sighed and put his courage and his trust in his young friend. "I have something to tell you, but it must remain a secret. You must not pursue justice in this case. I could not bear to lose you as well."

Otto sat up straighter, his face tight with worry.

Raphael pushed on. "A young man is accused of raping Darya and causing her suicide. It is not true."

"But how can you be sure?"

"Otto, you must promise this goes nowhere."

"How can we let him go to jail for something he did not do? If you know something …"

Raphael raised his hand to stop his friend's questions. "What I know you must use to do what you can, but the information cannot be whispered outside of our friendship."

Otto put his hand on Raphael's arm. "I trust your judgement. I will keep this in confidence."

Raphael nodded. He took a deep breath and finally told Otto the truth. "Darya is not dead." He felt the jerk in Otto, but continued. "The body was from the morgue, on its way to the teaching hospital."

"But the violin, the bow …"

"They were hers."

"The rental car, the papers …"

"Yes. Let me tell you how it came about, and how I know."

Otto leaned forward. "Let me tell my clerk to hold all calls."

An hour later, Raphael drank a small glass of Zwack.

"Better?" Otto whispered, as he wiped his own eyes.

"Yes."

Otto wrote the name, Nagy, Zoltan, on his note pad. He wrote no other notes. "I will steer this case to me. That is tricky, but my relationship to you and to Darya is not well-known."

Raphael nodded. "Thank you, Otto."

"And now that her uncle has corresponded with you through this storage unit, can you write to her?"

"Not at all. After those months in the hospital, Steiermark believes I have died. Safer to be Andras Sospiro, safer for me. Safer for her. Any contact from me will put her in danger again."

"Your pension …"

"It's amazing how corrupt a music school secretary can be. My pension was inherited by my Sospiro doppelgänger."

Otto shook his head, smiling. "So long as you lay low, and don't take on another violin genius."

Raphael nodded, "Many great ones," he said, "including you. But you had more interest in justice even than music, so the world lost a very fine violist." He nodded toward the music stand. "So, you keep at it."

"It helps me enjoy life and plow through tough times. After her death, all of the cello suites and the violin sonatas couldn't ..." At Raphael's smile, Otto added, "Do you remember that day, her first lesson?"

"Oh, yes."

"I knew something certain in that moment when she asked to be let in. 'This bright star', I thought. I always wanted my lesson to be before hers, so I could watch what happened."

Raphael laughed, "So, that was the maneuvering. I thought it was love."

Otto looked startled. "She was so little. So, always ... well ... not quite little sister, but something very like."

"And her death took you down, too."

Otto nodded. "It did. But it helped me to save you, to give you your new identity – a mend in the fabric of the world."

CHAPTER SEVEN

The New York Philharmonic's opening concert of the 2000 season had arrived at a desperate moment. Months ago, the conductor had scheduled a premier performance of the Violin Concerto in E Major by Raphael Atemvoll.

Programs had been published and a world-famous soloist hired. The soloist had practiced the concerto all during the previous summer, proclaimed it one of the most beautiful concerti of all time, and then had come to town with much fanfare. A story about the concerto and its missing composer had filled the first page of the *About The Town* section of the *Times*. The violinist already had rehearsed three times with the philharmonic.

But, on the night of the concert, the soloist could not even leave his hotel room on his own feet. A norovirus gripped fifteen percent of the inhabitants of his hotel, and he was among the first to be taken to the hospital.

This soloist's crisis was unknown to Rebecca Gregory, who for four years had played in the back of the first violin section of the New York Philharmonic. All her friends in the orchestra believed her to be Rebecca Gregory, Austro-Hungarian widow, and mother of a charming three-year-old tow-headed boy, and occasional duet partner at home concerts with the flashy Austrian-born pianist, Gabriel Kolya.

They also believed her to be extremely shy in spite of the fact that any musician who had played duets or quartets with her knew she had extraordinary skill and a beautifully thoughtful singing style in her playing.

Rebecca Gregory believed she had hidden the depth of her musicianship from these kind friends.

But today, in the back halls of the rehearsal space, her accompanist, Gabriel Kolya, told the conductor, "Rebecca Gregory is the only person I know who has ever played this concerto by Atemvoll. I have heard her practicing it at her studio. She is marvelous. We have to put her on in the maestro's place."

"Gregory?" the conductor was totally taken aback. "She can't even look a camera in the eye. She is so shy she could never stand on that stage in front of the cream of New York music lovers."

"Just get her to stand in for the maestro during this first concert. You will see."

The conductor believed in Gabriel Kolya's good sense, but to be certain, he accosted the concert mistress before he made a decision.

"Rebecca?" the concert mistress said, "Yes. Gabriel is right. Give her barely a moment to think about it and then call her up. If he says she knows it that well. Do it."

Gabriel nodded, "After the musical introduction, she will be in the music totally. Nothing outside of the music will phase her."

"I suppose if it doesn't work for this Saturday concert, I could send out desperation calls for a replacement violinist. How does she know this piece?"

Gabriel hesitated.

The concert mistress answered. "Isn't it possible that Austrian musicians know more about this contemporary Hungarian composer than others? Neighboring countries and all that."

Gabriel added, "Yes. Kindred spirits. Believe me, she knows it in her heart."

*   *

Backstage, Darya-Rebecca warmed her fingers with scales and arpeggios, facing the fact that tonight, Raphael's concerto would be well-played by someone else. She rejoiced that some part of Raphael Atemvoll would soon be known to the world. She had read the article in the *Times* and felt only deep sadness when the story confirmed what she already knew. Her teacher had not been seen since the day his famous student had gone missing.

Even two weeks later, when that student had reappeared to play her infamous concert at Sopron, he was not in the audience. After her apparent suicide that same night, a more desperate search had been made for Atemvoll. Many feared he was somehow mixed up in her disappearance, reappearance, disastrous concert and suicide.

No one had ever found him. The authorities concluded that he, too, must be dead.

That conclusion crushed her heart, making it difficult to do anything other than play her violin.

After reading the article, all Rebecca Gregory could hope for was that Raphael's music would gain acceptance and that her beloved teacher's memory could be appreciated for all his talents.

It was this acceptance of reality that Rebecca dealt with. She warmed her heart and fingers with the exercises which he first taught to her when she was eight years old.

Then her friend, Maria Shining, the concert mistress of the philharmonic, sat down in the chair beside her and said, "Becca, I have a big favor to ask of you, and I am asking for the whole philharmonic."

As she heard Maria out, Rebecca first had been stunned, then very afraid that by playing the concerto she would be recognized as Darya come to life. But then, within minutes, she knew she must do it. She had undergone so many changes since the kidnapping, and now she had to trust her new identity. She had to do it for Raphael Atemvoll.

An hour later, wearing a black dress loaned by Maria, Rebecca Gregory stood in the wings of Philharmonic Hall. Her uncle, Tobias Kossuth, stood next to her.

* *

Looking down at her, Tobias realized that she had a real chance to make her life as Rebecca. This night could succeed.

He too had been very afraid when she told him of the philharmonic's request and of her decision to play the solo. He also felt certain that Gabriel was behind this maneuver. Who else knew that Rebecca could do this? The man would stop at nothing to bring her to public attention. He wanted to record with her, play concerts with her, and at some level, he still held out hope of making her his wife. He wanted control.

Yet, this concert might be a good thing for her. She needed freedom from fear. Tobias hoped the time was right.

Four years ago, his friend, a plastic surgeon, had changed her overbite, but not the Magyar slant of her eyes. He had changed the curve of cartilage in her ears – something he said was often used to identify the missing. He had taken away the dimple in her chin, but not the dimples in her cheeks. She really was different. Why shouldn't she have a life free of fear? She was no longer Darya. Tonight, she could become the real Rebecca Gregory.

Tobias, however hopeful he tried to make himself, was sweating. He'd been foolish to have mentioned this concerto to the conductor of the philharmonic during a party for symphony supporters. Soon after, at the conductor's request, he had his friend Abraham Friedenberg mail a copy of the violin part with piano accompaniment. The conductor's interest in it had been sparked. He had asked Abraham to send the orchestral parts.

So, Tobias knew he was responsible for Rebecca's present predicament, or opportunity – he hoped it was the latter.

Until tonight, her illegal entry into the United States had been – if not easy to keep under wraps – at least manageable.

Next to him, Rebecca waited, apparently serene, listening to the Wagnerian overture that opened the concert. It seemed to Tobias that the loaned concert gown flowed like dark water with her movements. Her face was composed and concentrated. Her eyes seemed alight with enjoyment of the music that her friends made on stage.

The overture ended. Rebecca touched Tobias' arm. "It is time," she said.

He glanced down at her, hoping she looked enough different from the frightened girl he had met in the woods, hoping no one would recognize her almond eyes and red-brown hair, hoping she was fully Rebecca Gregory for the rest of a long and happy life.

"Give Raphael's concerto a great evening," he whispered.

She smiled, a small hint of fear in her trembling lip. "I will," she said, and turned to carry her violin onto the stage.

Then, as her friend had predicted, the music took over. From his place backstage, Tobias watched her, and watched the audience reaction. The lively opening tune reached out and plucked the audience to alertness. The Hungarian dance rhythms created tension and fun that kept them on the edge of their seats. The lovely, spun confection of the middle movement brought smiles to the faces of young and old. In the final movement, the composer's surprise laughter of a melody, and the brash risk-taking in the technique kept raising the suspense and answering "Yes!" to the question "can you wring any more from a violin than this?"

At the last orchestral chord, Tobias saw that Raphael's concerto had won new devotees. To his pleasure, he realized that Rebecca now also had a devoted following. This would not be the last of the attention paid to the newly discovered violinist from the back of the philharmonic.

*   *

By two years later, Tobias had allowed himself to become complacent. Yes, Rebecca was well-known in music circles of the United States. Yes, she had recorded three compilations, all including the works of Raphael Atemvoll along with other modern and classical composers from middle Europe. Yes, she had a strong following. However, perhaps because they didn't understand the power of classical music in people's hearts, the paparazzi had not taken up the kind of adulation and annoyance that they inflicted on famous film stars.

And the best part, Rebecca became accepted as Rebecca, without deep delving into her origins.

Their story held up to inspection. But Tobias had grown afraid to test it. Their one visit to an emergency ward, for a tricycle injury to her child, had resulted in police questioning. The nurse had suspected that someone, perhaps Rebecca, Tobias or some love interest of Rebecca's had caused the boy's foot to tangle in the spokes. The questioning included a request to see her passport and then her marriage certificate.

"We keep such things in the bank," Rebecca had answered. "My husband's death certificate is also there. Would you like for me to get them on Monday morning?"

"Not necessary," Officer Richards answered at last.

The matter had been dropped. But the experience had kept them from hospitals and other institutions ever since.

To Tobias, the whole question of "some love interest" for Rebecca worried. Gabriel Kolya wished desperately to be that love interest, but he had no chance, and, it seemed, neither did anyone else. Rebecca had many friends, both male and female, but her capacity for physical love seemed gone.

She had admitted to Tobias that when a suitor attempted any kind of closeness, even just holding hands, her mind left her and hid in a dark place.

"A heavy black door slams shut, and I am gone for minutes."

She had worked hard to stop this reaction, had forced herself to try, but time and again, her mind took control. She had given up, and concentrated on music, her students and her women friends.

Her familial love focused on her son, Benjamin, and on her uncle.

* *

On a Friday afternoon, Tobias picked up five-year-old Benjamin from preschool. They drove to the studios of Columbia Records and waited in the lobby for Rebecca and Gabriel Kolya to finish today's recording of the Kabalevsky violin concerto – a charming and fast-paced addition to their upcoming album.

When they arrived, Tobias grew disgruntled to discover that Gabriel's agent, a round piece of poison, already took up three chairs in the lobby seating area. One chair had been devoted to the man's brief case, one to his butt and one to his size eleven dress-shoed feet.

Tobias nodded to the man, pulled a free chair close to the carpet and another chair for Benji. Benji plopped to the floor, took his two match-box cars from his backpack, and began making putt-putt noises to assist the forward motion of a jeep and a BMW.

The agent frowned and rattled papers in his fat fist. Tobias ignored him.

Tobias sat staring at the poster of Rebecca and Gabriel that would be on the back cover of the new album. It pleased him that the color was beautiful, the overall look impressionistic and the faces, softly fuzzy. Rebecca's curls were more in focus than her features, and her face turned toward her violin more than toward the camera. The look said, "Art" and not portraiture.

Those Hungarian buzzards will never see Darya in that photo, Tobias thought.

Benjamin glanced up from playing with his cars. "Uncle, are they done yet?"

"Any minute, Benji," Tobias said, glancing into the hall toward the recording studios. "This is Kabalevsky day."

Benji stood, holding his two cars. He made them drive toward each other, near-miss each other and then drive away, all while humming Kabalevsky's hoppy tune at a very fast clip.

Gabriel's agent kept flipping through contract papers.

"Kid," the agent said, "Don't you ever keep quiet?"

Tobias was about to give the man an ear boxing, but Benji said, "I'm sorry. Are you trying to learn your letters?"

The man stared.

"At school, also, my friends need quiet when they learn their letters," Benji said.

Benji left the cars, sat in his chair, reached into his backpack, and pulled out his copy of *Frog and Toad*.

Tobias raised an eyebrow at the huffing agent. The man shut up.

A few minutes later, Gabriel and Rebecca came out of the studio with the happy producer. The agent tried to have a word with Rebecca, but she only gave him a polite smile, handed her violin case and her bag of music to Tobias, and swung Benji up in her arms.

Ever since the famous premier concert, the agent had wanted to sign her up as a client. She never gave him more than her "no thank you".

Gabriel tried to capture her attention as well. She said, "Thank you for a great time with music, Gabe."

He pointed to his agent, but Rebecca said, "No." She whipped out the door and into Tobias' parked Volvo. Tobias had grown used to hurrying off, helping her avoid these agent and contract discussions.

As she buckled her son into his car seat, Benji said, "Did you have fun playing Kabalevsky?"

"I did."

"Did Gabriel have fun, too?"

"I believe he did," she said.

"He doesn't ever have as much fun as you, though," Benji said.

"Well, someday he will figure out that the music *is* the fun."

Benji said, "Kabalevsky, Kabalevsky, Kabalevsky. The words *is* the fun, too." Then he stuck his thumb in his mouth and hummed for five minutes until he fell asleep.

As they arrived in their parking structure, another blue car exited. Tobias frowned. The blue Chevrolet was not familiar. Neither was the man in the brimmed hat who drove it.

Tobias said, "We have no new neighbors in this building."

"Uncle, they may be visiting the Charltons," Rebecca said. "Stop worrying about every change. We are fine."

But as soon as Tobias unlocked and opened the door to their apartment, they knew. Every cupboard had been emptied. The mattresses had been ripped, the music cabinet overturned and ransacked.

And in her daylight-basement studio, the same chaos appeared.

The Charltons had had no visitors. Mrs. Charlton took a still-sleeping Benji in to sleep on their sofa while Tobias, Mr. Charlton and Rebecca turned the mattresses to disguise what had happened, and cleaned the messes. Especially, they cleaned Benji's room. Rebecca didn't want Benji to guess at the fearsome thing that had happened in their home.

When Benji slept again in his own bed and Mr. Charlton had returned to his apartment, Rebecca sat down on the coffee table.

"This is what you found at my parents' house, isn't it?"

Tobias nodded slowly. "But it has been six years since that night. Others may use the same method to search for valuables."

"But nothing has been stolen. They are looking for something that doesn't exist, and they have discovered again the person they believe owns it."

Tobias said, "We must get help."

"Can you report this to the police and keep my passport, my status out of it?"

"I can try."

At last, Rebecca burst into tears and into Hungarian. "Damn these gangsters. I want a life for Benjamin."

Tobias felt his heart rip.

CHAPTER EIGHT

NEW YORK CITY
A MONTH LATER, THE YEAR 2000

On tiptoe, five-year-old Benjamin Gregory grabbed the sleeve of his great uncle's black coat. His high voice echoed off the dark red, blue and green tiles of the Third Avenue-149th Street subway station. Tobias scanned the crowd as he took Benji's hand and leaned closer to answer. A train entered the tunnel, drowning out Uncle Tobias' reply.

Near them, sat Rebecca. She stopped watching her family to glance warily at the waiting passengers and the arriving train. It was not their Number Two train to the old Mott Avenue Station. People exited the train and moved swiftly up to the street level. No one looked toward Tobias and Benjamin. Rebecca let her attention return again to her tow-headed son and her silver-haired uncle. The two of them huddled in conference under the brilliant colors of José Ortega's mosaics. *Una Raza, Un Mundo, Un Universo.*

She smiled at her son, at her uncle, at the whole *Universo* which surrounded them.

We were right to come out, she thought. Benjamin loves the zoo. Uncle Tobias and I, we should not be so afraid. The damage to our apartment a month ago – that was a random break in. The bad ones have forgotten me. I am dead.

She hoped to wipe the destruction of last month and of six years ago out of her mind. Since last month's chaos, the building superintendent had changed all the locks. He'd hired a guard for the entry door. There would be no more vandalism in their apartment or in her teaching studio on the lower floor.

Rebecca relaxed her muscles, shifting her net bag farther onto her shoulder. She checked the bag's contents once more: a notebook of Professor Atemvoll's sheet music to read and catalogue on the ride home, student compositions to grade, coin purse, blue furry bear.

Today, Benji had whirled through the Bronx Zoo asking everyone questions: the custodian, the little boy or girl standing next to him, other moms, even dads. Rebecca enjoyed watching his easy affection and exuberance with people. She had lost optimism and trust six years ago, but she worked hard not to teach fear to her beloved son. She wanted to rid herself of fear, as well.

A second train whooshed out of the Third Avenue Station. Its departure sucked a gust of air down the subway steps, bringing with it the stench of old urine and the heat of the New York City streets.

From her vantage point near one wall of the station, she worked to blend in. Rebecca had perfected the art of disguising wild auburn hair under a summer hat. The slant of her brown eyes was easily hidden behind sunglasses. On the streets of the city, she wanted anonymity. Today no one noticed her. The outing had been a success for Benjamin, and for her.

At that moment, she caught sight of a uniformed policeman – a man of middle weight and broad shoulders. He approached them tentatively. She tensed. His black eyes squinted at her. Then she knew there was a mistake. Beneath his regulation NYPD pants, the man wore baby blue Nike athletic shoes and white socks.

"Uncle!" She reached for Tobias and Benjamin.

Tobias glanced up. In that moment, the policeman swooped on Benjamin, grabbing him by the waist. Tobias' grip tightened on Benjamin's hand; Rebecca heard a sickening give in her child's shoulder. A screech escaped her even as she lunged at the attacker's back.

"Mama!" Benjamin screamed.

The man kicked out, sending Tobias to the ground.

From behind the man, she hooked her arm around his neck, yanking his greasy hair with her other hand. Startled, the man dropped Benjamin. The child lay in a whimpering heap, between the attacker and Tobias. Tobias crawled toward Benji, gathering him close to his chest.

Still wrapped around his neck, Rebecca hit at the man's ears, his nose, his back – any part of him she could hurt. "Help my son," she screamed at the waiting crowd.

But people backed away.

The man shook her and clawed at her. Rebecca's arms bled from the dagger-sharpness of his dirty fingernails. The man lunged at Tobias, carrying Rebecca on his back. He booted Tobias' kneeling body and knocked him to one side. Tobias' head whacked against the tiles. The attacker grabbed again at Benjamin's limp arm. Benjamin screamed with pain.

The crowd on the platform surged toward him. The policeman drew his pistol, aiming it at Tobias. The crowd backed up. But Rebecca jammed her knee into the man's kidney. He shrieked, dropped his gun and crumpled to the pavement. Benjamin crawled free of him.

Rebecca scrambled over the man, reaching for his gun on the floor, but he kicked at it. It skittered across the tiles and onto the tracks. The man came to his feet again, yelling, "Grab them. Drug sellers and child stealers."

The crowd surged toward Tobias and Rebecca.

"Liar," Rebecca shouted. "No policeman wears shoes like that."

One man in the crowd yelled, "Get 'em all. Let the police figure it out."

The police . . . only God knew what would happen to them then.

"Get up", Rebecca yelled to Tobias, praying he could move at all.

A few in the crowd seemed ready to grab at them, but she glared at them. "The man is no policeman."

Her uncle pulled Benji into his arms. "Come, Becca," Tobias grunted. He wove groggily toward the stairs.

"Mama," Benji cried. "Boo Bear!"

Rebecca grabbed her bag with his Blue Bear and her music. She swung the bag at the one person who reached to stop them. He backed off. She dashed to the steps. Behind her, a woman with a cell phone yelled, "Get me the police." The rest of the crowd turned as if to help the policeman.

Tobias was right to run.

But their attacker pushed through the crowd and stumbled after them, yelling "Stop them." His face contorted in rage. Rebecca leapt the rest of the stairs two at a time.

On the street, idle loungers watched the flight of the old man, the child and the woman as if an unbelievable movie unfolded before them. What would have been a five-minute ride on the subway was now a two-mile race among other people's streets and apartments. Rebecca glanced over her shoulder at their pursuer. The fake policeman still followed.

She pushed her bursting lungs harder as she ran after Tobias. He had amazing speed for a man of sixty. In Tobias' embrace, Benjamin hung limp, holding his cries inside.

Behind them, the kidnapper yelled, "I know where you live, girlie," he yelled. "You'll see me too late."

A snarl of anger escaped her as Rebecca ran. Tobias breathed hard. His forehead bled. Still, he ran, seeming as strong as in his youth when he ran great distances, or as strong as the day, six years ago, when he helped her escape the outlaw border gangs in Hungary. Rebecca feared that now his strength was pure adrenaline. She blamed herself for this situation. She'd let down her guard because she wished, for this one sunny day, to be free of fear.

"Uncle, let me carry Benji."

"Becca," he panted, "a cab. Get home fast to care for Benjamin."

"Hospital," she began.

"A hospital makes police reports," he stated.

Rebecca's throat tightened on her desperation. "Yes," she whispered.

She glanced behind them. The man had stopped running after them.

Tobias slowed, watching her. For her uncle's sake, for Benji's sake, she had to continue. She took Benji from her uncle, murmuring, "My turn."

They began to move again. "Few cabs come to this part of town, Uncle," she said.

"Then we keep running."

CHAPTER NINE

In their apartment, an hour later, Tobias slumped against the bathroom sink. Sick sweat dripped from his chin. His stomach threatened to turn. As a medical man, he knew you sometimes hurt people in order to help them. As an uncle, he hated it. It didn't matter how good his pain killing technique, the child's fear was enough to make Tobias ill.

He'd sewn cuts on his Benji twice, and now he'd had to wrench Benji's dislocated shoulder back into its socket.

Wrench. That's what it was, no matter what obscuring medical terms you used.

No surprise to him he'd become a medical coroner. You can't hurt the dead.

He closed his eyes on the image of a woman on fire in a falling car.

Hearing song from the room beyond the bathroom wall, his mind returned to today. Rebecca singing Benjamin's lullaby. Her untrained voice was pure. Her low tones relaxed the fearful child. Singing was one activity Rebecca didn't do publicly, yet Tobias loved her songs.

He rinsed the sweat from his face, slapped cold water on his neck, then peeked into the bedroom. As he stood in the doorway and leaned against the doorjamb, Rebecca adjusted the bedcovers. Benji sniffed and grabbed her hand.

"Mama, do Asian elephants fight African elephants?"

Benji's curiosity did not suffer.

"I have not studied this," Rebecca answered, "but perhaps you can ask the zookeeper next time we're there."

"How about the ants? Will the red ones fight with the black ones?"

"I'm not sure, Sweetheart. Why does this worry you?"

"Gabriel said we shouldn't trust . . ."

Tobias winced, but Rebecca gently stated Benji's fear. "I know. Gabriel believes we should distrust those who are not like us, neh?"

"The man at the train station, he is maybe not like us."

"The one who hurt you is just like us, except he has not learnt to care about people. It is nothing to do with whether the man goes to synagogue."

"You are sure, Mama?"

She nodded. "Benjamin, a good person can keep the Sabbath at a cathedral or Shabbat in a synagogue. Another might pretend to keep Shabbat but does not keep it in his heart."

Benjamin sighed. He let go of his mother's hand, wiped at his nose with his fist and smiled at Rebecca. His small, square hand fingered the blanket ribbon. Tobias relaxed as Benjamin closed his eyes. He gazed at Benjamin, awed anew. His nephew was a small copy of Rebecca. Benjamin's redgold curls promised to become the same rich auburn as hers. Two asymmetrical dimples accented the soft curves of his face. They replicated the features that captivated Rebecca's admirers.

But where her eyes were dark, and her emotions veiled, Benjamin's were often illumined by eagerness. Until this incident, Benjamin felt free – like Rebecca before her kidnapping and imprisonment.

Tobias noticed Rebecca watching himself. Her appraising glance made him stand up straighter. Running scared wore at both of them.

He wished she'd allowed him to call off dinner with Gabriel Kolya tonight. Rebecca insisted they not tell Gabriel about the attack because he would use it to push his own agenda.

To avoid Gabriel's interest, Tobias had to discuss the subway incident now. From habit, he slipped into Yiddish.

"Becca, until today I thought someone merely tried to scare us for sport. Today went beyond sport."

Rebecca gestured him to follow her away from the sleeping child. In the sunny yellow kitchen, she reached with shaking hands to check on the Szekely goulash. The crock-pot lid rattled noisily as she tried to replace it. Light from the broad kitchen window reflected on the pot's glass top and on the tears of fear that stood in Rebecca's eyes.

Finally, she blurted out, "Why take Benjamin? Why? I hoped Hungary had thrown off the yoke of vicious men. I thought danger from the old country was past."

"But our letters to your father return unanswered," Tobias reminded her. "Raphael's quartet friend has no word from them, nor from Raphael. Who knows what kind of gangsters are still in power among the low life there?"

She whispered, "My family, Raphael, . . . and Zoltan . . ."

Tobias wished he didn't have to open up that old wound in her soul. His friends in Hungary had tried every avenue to find out what happened to Zoltan Nagy, her young student. And her family had gone into hiding as Tobias had urged, but now he could not contact them. No one she loved was safe as far as he knew – including her revered violin teacher.

"Perhaps," Tobias began tentatively, "We blame Hungary too easily for what happens to us. Look at the discord in our new country . . .Look at those who sell hate."

"But their hate is no longer for Jews," she said. "They sell hate of Mexico and the Middle East."

"Who then?"

"And why?" she asked.

He shook his head.

"We are not rich," she said. "I have nothing of great value, but they would not believe me. It must be revenge. It must be those men – those gangsters at the castle prison."

"Whoever it is," Tobias said, "they will try again."

Tobias was not ready to reveal the note he'd found as they cleaned the rubble of her invaded apartment last month. However, he now knew that because of that note, he must convince Rebecca to get out of New York. He began to tick off his evidence.

"Becca, the apartment super said a man asked about the vacancy next to us. He wouldn't accept the one in the next building – said he liked the view better from here."

Rebecca started tearing lettuce for salad. Tiny pieces fluttered into the salad bowl.

"Rebecca!" he said, taking the shredded lettuce from her. "Look at me. Listen to me."

She inhaled and squared her shoulders before she would look at him.

"We have to face the truth," he said quietly. "We have made mistakes. You were safe in the back of the orchestra, never trying to move forward.

"You played the concert," Tobias continued. "What has happened since comes from that moment. Somebody from the old country must have recognized you."

"How could they?" She attempted humor, raising one dark slash of eyebrow. "You said I grow fat and sassy here."

Affectionately he circled her wrist with his big fingers. "In Hungary, my little niece, you were a leaf, a matzoth, a skinny waif with long, long hair."

He lifted her arm and smiled at her. "The difference is great. Still, you have such a distinctive face, even after the surgery."

She shook her head.

Tobias became insistent, "Those may have been random breakins at your studio, and at our apartment," he said, "but you can't deny the look on that guy's face today. He'd spotted his prey. Next time, they will send someone more clever, more strong."

"How can we protect Benjamin?" She put a trembling hand to the countertop. "Not with the police?"

"No. You know what questions police will ask."

She leaned her forehead onto the golden oak of the cupboard doors. When immigration looked deeply into her situation, they would send her . . . where could they send her, she didn't exist. "There is no safety for us."

"Becca-ley," he said gently, "last summer, after your master classes in Oregon, Abraham Friedenberg offered you that position in Portland, at Reed College."

Rebecca raised her head from the cabinet door. She stared out at the building across the street. Memory seemed to invade her gaze. "In Oregon it rained, but the rainbows were wonderful."

Tobias smiled. "Take Abe's offer. Secretly take Benjamin to Oregon, until these people give up."

"I felt . . ." as she straightened her back, Rebecca seemed to light up. "I was healthy the whole term that I taught at Reed College."

Tobias understood. He knew of the episodes of mental darkness when men got too close to her. She had only suffered that problem twice in her time at Reed College, and those had been with a friend who meant no harm.

"You could be completely well if you were away from . . . from us." He didn't say 'away from Gabriel Kolya', but he thought it.

"Yes," she said, smiling and stretching her arms out to hug Tobias' old shoulders. "Yes," she laughed. "Yes! But if Abe still invites me, you must to come with us."

He shook his head. "We can only throw these *mosheniki* off the track if I stay – make them think you're still here."

"But I can't leave you . . .," Rebecca whispered.

"They're not after me, Becca. I can go to the police, but only if you're not here."

He saw Rebecca blink. He realized as soon as he said it that, indeed, he would be safer if she were gone. If he didn't have to answer questions about her background, her immigration status, he'd be free to report trouble to the police. He could hire a detective, a lawyer, get any help he needed to sort out the threat to them all.

"But our recital."

She always referred to it as 'our recital', saying, "Gabriel puts more fingers into any recital than I do." Their recital was sold out. Indeed, that triumph was now a source of fear for Tobias. But after all their work . . . well . . . he supposed, there would be even more news coverage if she cancelled than if she played.

"Rebecca," Tobias said in a low, firm voice. "Directly after your recital, I need you to leave."

She looked stunned, a moment of gray-faced disbelief. For Tobias, this was harder than sewing on Benji. He had to do it. He watched her swallow hurt. She glanced away.

"Yes," she said, gathering her rough voice by coughing once. "I will call Abraham. Miriam will love having Benji again." Rebecca laughed. Her laugh was tight with pain, but she talked on. Tobias' skin grew cold watching her convince him of her courage.

"It is best, Uncle. Leaving New York will keep my picture out of the newspaper until things settle down in the homeland. I will not play concerts or create any more disks. They will forget me."

Yes, that's it. Teach, but don't play concerts."

"Maybe soon we will know how the new Hungary will deal with its thugs."

Tobias nodded, encouraging.

She said, "Some New York newspapers are available in Budapest. But newspapers from the western coast of America – never." She waved the West Coast, Oregon and Reed College out of Hungarian attention. Rebecca's dramatic gestures were tight – a robotic, programmed effort to act carefree about stepping off a cliff. Tobias's throat tightened with the pain of watching her.

"In Budapest," she said, her voice rising, "Oregon doesn't exist. If I leave New York secretly, Benjamin will be safe." She added, "Mother, Daddy, Raphael, Piotr, Zoltan, they are all still alive in Hungary. I know it. They will be safer too. They will be . . ."

Tobias could stand it no longer. He reached to pull her into his bear hug, to give her safety once more. But the doorbell rang. She turned stiffly toward the entry hall. Tobias sighed.

Gabriel Kolya was always early for dinner and rehearsals.

CHAPTER TEN

Three nights later, Tobias regained his seat as intermission ended. Lights lowered to announce the second half of Rebecca Gregory and Gabriel Kolya's recital. Tobias loved Rebecca as his own child and his pride in her tonight grew boundless. When she played, every element of humor or tenderness in her music wove itself into the soul of the audience.

Rebecca moved calmly onto the stage of Alice Tully Hall. The toes of her maroon shoes barely showed beneath in her rose and cream gown. Gabriel Kolya followed her onto the stage, exuding his usual aura of protective closeness.

In the many faces turned toward the stage Tobias saw rapt attention. Several women watched only Gabriel as he bowed. But Gabriel's gaze turned toward Rebecca.

To Tobias, her gracefulness made her seem taller than five feet four inches. When she stepped forward with her violin, all eyes followed. She commanded space.

Gabriel seated himself at the piano. Tobias again glanced around the rows of eager listeners in Alice Tully Hall.

A new gentleman appeared off to one side and three rows in front of him. The new man's European suave and slender body-type smoothed the way he moved toward his seat. A high-boned stoniness carved his elegant face. Tobias grew certain the man had not been in that seat during the first half.

Rebecca began with the *Sonata in A major* by Cesar Franck. For several measures, Tobias saw only his niece. Then as the first theme ended and Gabriel introduced the second theme, Tobias noticed a movement in the newcomer. He glanced toward him and discovered the impassive face had changed to one of intent study. From that moment, Tobias could hardly take his eyes off the new customer.

Rebecca began the wonderful *Carmen Fantasy* – Sarasate's tour de force tribute to Bizet's famous Gitane, a gypsy woman. As she played, Tobias noticed that the new man's attention seemed a sinister dissection of Rebecca's motions – an interest that held nothing of the usual audience awe of her musical passion and the lyric voice of her instrument.

Later, as Rebecca and Gabriel played the last movement in the Brahms' *G Major Sonata*, Tobias turned from the man to watch the rest of the audience. He needed to check his perception of normal audience behavior. God knew his brain could be searching for ominous portents everywhere.

What he saw, however, confirmed his suspicion that this one man watched her with predatory intent. The man's hand reached inside his suit coat. For a moment, Tobias feared he reached for a gun and he almost stood to stop him. Then, suddenly it dawned on him what the man was doing. The fellow touched his chest and gave himself pleasure as he watched Rebecca's body and violin dance through the encore, a *Sarabande* by Bach. Tobias stomach roiled.

Forcing his mind back to the stage, Tobias watched Rebecca's fingers and tried to forget fear for a moment. But he could not dismiss the disgusting image.

Tobias knew he had to keep that man away from Rebecca. Tobias wanted this evening to end. He wanted her journey to begin.

Her last note echoed through the auditorium. She tucked the instrument under her arm and smiled. Tobias knew what happened now. The old woman in the private box and the fresh-faced student in the last row of the balcony, each felt warmed by her radiant pleasure in being able to play for them.

The new man, however, rose during the last note. He gestured to another fellow stationed at the nearest exit. As the two of them left the auditorium, the man pulled a familiar cigarette package from his coat.

Can't even wait to smoke, Tobias thought.

While the audience still cheered, Tobias knew he must get backstage before Rebecca and Gabriel walked blindly into a trap. He rose and began to move toward the aisle as Rebecca played a second encore – a *Bagatelle* by her teacher, Raphael Atemvoll – a charming and harmonically very Hungarian piece.

The new man didn't even turn at the door to see what she played. Everyone else cheered and called for more. "Encore Maestra Gregory," the woman at the end of his aisle shouted.

In that moment, Tobias realized that what he had seen was the blue, black and white – the distinctive package of Gitanes, the cigarette smoked by Steiermark as he held Rebecca prisoner. The cigarette which he had used to burn her left shoulder.

Tobias pushed past the people in his row, and thanked God Rebecca obliged the general encore request with the fun of Kreisler's *Praeludium and Allegro*. Out in the hall, he couldn't see Steiermark. He ran down the nearest stairs, expecting at any moment to run into him.

The man had disappeared. But the smell of the cigarette lingered like a threatening cloud.

Getting backstage before Rebecca came off stage would give Tobias a chance to steer her away from the man he now believed to be Steiermark.

Rebecca held the audience in her thrall. No one in the room knew this was Rebecca's farewell to New York City, no one except himself and Gabriel.

Minutes after her last wave to the audience, with Gabriel's help, their trio avoided the man by moving from the stage out to the main street entrance along with the crowd. To Tobias' surprise, there was no sign of the repulsive man anywhere between the theater and their car. He probably had thought he would catch her at the stage door.

Once in the back seat, Tobias told Rebecca what he had seen. Gabriel glanced at them in the rear-view mirror. "Many Europeans smoke Gitanes," he said. "Gitanes brunes are supposed to be the best."

"Do they smell strongly?" Tobias asked.

"I've heard that they have a smell like well oiled saddle leather."

"That's it," Rebecca whispered. "That's exactly the smell. And cologne.

Within half an hour they were at home and safe, certain no one had followed them.

Benjamin wandered in from his bedroom when they arrived. He was ushered by Mrs. Charlton, their careful neighbor and baby sitter, his arm sling askew, pajama shirt buttons not quite straight. His pajama footies scuffed happy, sleepy steps as he ran to his mother.

Benji even braved the usual cool reception from Gabriel to hear about his mother's recital.

Ten hours before their flight. Tobias already missed his little family.

After their neighbor left, Gabriel wanted to stay and celebrate their triumph. Rebecca poured three champagne goblets and a goblet of juice for Benjamin. They congratulated each other. Gabriel pleaded that Rebecca not leave him for such a backwater place as Oregon and Reed College, but she held firm. Tobias let go a sigh of relief at that moment.

"You must plan to come play a recital with me in Portland next spring," she said. This idea gave Tobias the chills.

"Ha! Portland," Gabriel harrumphed, "so provincial."

Rebecca laughed. "Provincial is believing your town is the center of the world."

Gabriel glowered.

"Gabriel, you cannot tell anyone where I am going, or why. You understand that, of course."

Gabriel glanced at Tobias, who held his gaze, waiting to hear his answer. Gabriel shifted his stare toward a painting on the wall. "Do you think me an idiot, Liebchen?"

"I think you drink when you feel sad," she said to Gabriel, and took his arm to walk him to the door. She ducked one maudlin attempt to kiss her and ushered him into the outer hallway.

When she closed the door, Tobias saw that Rebecca leaned on the jamb just long enough to bring her mind back from that dark cave she had described to him.

He now was very glad that they had planned for her to disappear to Portland. The strong memory of the smell of Steiermark must have thrown her. Gitanes and cologne – a cologne she had no name for, but had once described as overpowering sweetness.

Tobias knew that at the very least, she must get away from Gabriel. The man refused to keep his hands off her, or to believe, or even care about the destructive effect of his attempts at affection.

Tobias wished he had not told Gabriel where she would be going, though he was certain Gabe would have guessed. He'd made an almighty fuss last summer just because Rebecca was gone for three months to teach in Portland.

Tobias also didn't believe that tonight Gabriel would go straight to his home. He would take wounded pride to an after-concert party where he'd have to make excuses for his lovely violinist.

After Rebecca closed the door, she smiled at Tobias and took Benjamin to his room. Soon, Tobias heard their lullaby. Since that day when his niece told him she was pregnant by an unknown – probably one of the prison guards, Tobias had been amazed at how protective he felt of the child.

There were times like this, when Tobias wished he hadn't arranged that watery meeting with Gabriel. But he did worry that Rebecca seemed to want no man in her life. In six years, she'd never dated anyone more than twice.

Tobias laid a fire. His own fear left him cold. He also had a second need for fire. From his pants pocket, he drew a wrinkled note, crumpled from being concealed since the break-in at their apartment. Its message was still starkly clear.

"Darya, we know what you and your uncle have done. He will suffer unless you contact us by September 27, Post Box 946, East 42nd Street, New York. You know you have the means to obtain our silence."

The name 'Darya' jolted him. Darya was dead. She must remain dead. If Rebecca saw this note, she would never leave him for Oregon. With her away, and protected by Abraham and Miriam, Tobias had a very good idea how to find out more about these pissant scoundrels who broke into their home, and how to find the man who tried to kidnap Benjamin. He now was certain they were related to the too-handsome man at the concert tonight. He had asked an investigator friend to keep a watch on that post box. So far, no one had attempted to open it.

Tobias reached for yesterday's newspaper on the table. There on the front of the entertainment section stood Gabriel with his arm around Rebecca. Thank goodness Rebecca had seen the camera coming and turned her face away.

She was beautiful and talented. Newsmen felt compelled to spin speculative fantasies about her. Most imagined her practically living in the piano with Gabriel Kolya. And Gabriel did nothing to dispel those ideas.

Was it a newspaper story like this that had brought the man to the concert tonight? Was it Steiermark, or just another predatory man who happened to smoke Gitanes?

Tobias wrapped the threatening note in the photo page and quietly rolled a paper log. He tossed it into the fireplace and then sat in his chair. The fire nibbled at the edge of the news, then caught and burst into short-lived flame. In Tobias' mind, the note and the flame became fiery death – a deep ravine, an automobile, a woman.

He shuddered.

CHAPTER ELEVEN

THE YEAR 1756

Carl Phillipe Emmanuel Bach stepped into the darkened taverna. He could see nothing, yet he knew his brother was there. No one played the clavier with such clear enunciation and no one else so clearly brought out every melody that arose from within the harmony. And beyond wonderful pianistic style, Carl recognized that the clavier player created sarcastic spoofs on their father's contrapuntal music. Only the anger of Wilhelm Friedemann would bother with a spoof of a forgotten musician six years in the grave.

Carl sidled toward the sound, avoiding the dull shadow of a raised arm – a man lifting a tankard, he assumed. The tavern wench came to a halt in front of him, her tight curls barely visible in the light of the failing fire.

"Ow! Near made me spill 'em all," she complained.

"I'm so sorry," Carl said. "I'm headed toward the clavier."

"We already got a player. Pays him in beer and bed. Don't need you."

"Wilhelm is my brother."

Her head leaned to one side. Her voice became harsh. "Didn't know Willie had family. You ain't been before."

Carl wasn't sure why her tone made him feel guilty, but it did. "Been traveling," he said as he scooted around her large skirts. "Back now, though," he added to let her know he might be around to keep track of his brother's women, and she'd better not be stealing from Wilhelm.

Carl thought, Wilhelm Friedemann should be the one who feels the guilt. We've brothers and sisters – fourteen Bachian mouths to feed and he does nothing for any of them. He allows the women in his life to believe he's got no one.

In the dark, Carl began to see the tables, the men whose heads lay on the boards, and his brother's once white shirt that should have gleamed in the low light, but now showed only gray dimness. He worked his way toward that grayness. Friedemann didn't stop playing the keyboard, just sniffed, and began singing.

"Something flowery this way comes, and the stink gives me the runs."

A weak guffaw arose from a table behind them, making Carl retort with his own loud verse.

"That's the beer within your vein. Makes digestion runs and pain." Carl dragged a chair to the upper end of the keyboard. He plopped onto the chair, scooted Friedemann out of the way, and began playing something grandiose he had learned from his trip to Italy – no contrapuntal sarcasm for him. His brother sat up straighter and listened.

"What dramatic hash is that?" Friedemann asked.

"Something about the great Dido. A beautiful tune and even greater variations – for the violin originally, by Giuseppe Tartini."

"Dido, Aeneid's wench?"

"Queen of Carthage. A real woman." Carl glanced at the wench of the tavern. She didn't even seem to hear their argument.

Friedemann slapped the keyboard. "Why are you here, Carl? It can't be to borrow money."

"No, brother, it is to offer you money."

"For my playing?"

"You might think about accompanying my friends when they ask. But that's not what I offer money for."

"Your friends ask at inconvenient times. That last one . . ." Friedemann waved his hand toward the past.

"The last one?" Carl asked. "the great home concert where our mother had to fill in for you at the last minute, and then Anna Magdalena had to apologize to everyone for being so forward as to walk on stage like any man . . .?"

"Mother! Anna is nothing but our stepmother. And there was no need for her to do that."

"The violinist needed an accompanist. The hostess, a duchess, no less, could not wait, and Anna Magdalena knew the piece."

"Our stepmother always was a pushy woman."

"Pushing you to be a man? Well, there is no more need to worry about her attempts to help you stay sober. She has died."

"And where, Carl, where? In the poor house. Our father . . ."

Carl stopped playing the keyboard and put his nose in Friedemann's face. "Don't you bring our father into this when you spend your afternoons making fun of his music."

Friedemann stood and glared down at him. "You offer money. For what?"

"For your portion of father's music."

"Why?"

"Because," Carl also stood, to be on a level with his brother. "Because you have so little regard for any of it. And also, because the great violinist, Tartini, has asked for the three other violin concerti. He heard the G minor when Papa played it . . ."

"Hah! Too late brother. I have sold them. The whole lot."

Carl sat hard on the chair. "Sold?"

"Gone. A Russian count. And I hope he takes them all to Siberia and buries them."

IN CONCERT:
BOOK TWO

BOOK TWO: CHAPTER ONE

THE YEAR 2000, NORTHERN IRELAND

Thirty-five-year-old Lewis James strode down the empty main road in Ballybly, Northern Ireland. He carried a sign nailed to a stick. On each side he'd printed the words, "Where are they? Jesus searched for lost sheep."

On one side of the street, the curb stones at each corner were painted red, white and blue stripes. The other side green white and orange – the demarcation between Protestant and Catholic neighborhoods.

This ugly divide between two communities had created the abyss that swallowed Dicken and Molly, his brother and brother's wife – a divide of centuries that mostly fed the armament makers and the explosives dealers, while leaving everyone else in Northern Ireland to live in poverty and fear.

Molly and Dicken had been missing for two months.

Behind Lewis, incessant, angry honking broke out. Willem, the one driver on that road in mid-Sunday morning, yelled obscenities, some of which Lewis hadn't heard since he left Ireland ten years ago to teach in America.

Lewis turned around, and shouted, "Willem McIntyre, I'd forgotten the blue of your diction. Let's share a pint, so I can stretch me mind."

"Move your arse, you Taig. I've places to go."

"You used to be more creative with your insults, boyo," Lewis said. "I'll be movin' as soon as you help me find Molly and Dicken."

"Look in your father's garden. Dig in the loose soil."

"Come along," Lewis said." I'll get two shovels. We'll dig at your place as well. Prove everybody wrong."

"The hell you will, Bastard. We all know what happened."

Lewis shouted. "Half the town says you buried them in your meadow, and the other half that my mother fed them arsenic pie and stuffed them in her rose garden."

"You come in me meadow, I'll shoot you."

"Threats. Accusations. Shootings in the dark of night. Not one of you helped search for them."

"No need."

"Don't you want your sister back?" Lewis asked.

"Why would I? She was ruined. And Dicken's guilty."

"They were married."

"Father Morrissey says not."

"Then Father Morrissey can't read, or refuses to."

"Bans and a license from some London priest can be faked."

"Come to Belfast and London, Willem. Help me look for them."

"They're dead, and you know it. Now bugger off, Orange Man."

Lewis turned and marched slowly up the middle of the street. Willem continued honking and revving his engines. Lewis silently thanked Willem. He drew a crowd.

Out of the Catholic parish hall poured men and women in Sunday best. Out came the priest.

From the Anglican sanctuary, the skinny young pastor and his elderly flock. From the pubs crowded the young men and women, friends of Willem, and once, also friends of Molly and Dicken. Some even had been friends of Lewis.

The young men laughed. The priest and the pastor tried to shoo their followers back into each fold.

But this spectacle was now. Jesus could wait.

"Help find them," Lewis shouted. "Stop fighting each other long enough to search."

Lewis saw his younger brothers and sisters, his mother hovering over his little sister, Brenna. They merely gaped at him as if he were crazy.

Except Brenna, who reached out for him. Their mother grabbed her arms.

"Hello, Brenna. Thank you for caring," Lewis shouted to her.

His mother turned Brenna's back to him, but Brenna looked at him over her shoulder, and tried to shrug off his mother's hands.

In the back of the other crowd he saw Molly McIntyre's mother.

"Mother and, Sarah McIntyre, these are your children. Come together. Work together. You love Molly and Dicken. You know each other."

Molly's mother turned her back to him. His own mother tried to hide Brenna behind the pastor.

The priest shook his fist at Lewis. "They chose to defy their mothers. They reap what they sow."

"Molly and Dicken sowed love," Lewis said. "But none of you wanted that harvest. Now, you reap hatred and fear, the only weeds you cast about in the hard ground of this God-forsaken town."

"How dare you," shouted the young pastor.

Behind him, he heard Willem slam the door of his truck. Several of the men from the pub pushed forward to see what Willem would do.

Lewis whirled, but too late. Willem's rake handle whacked him in the jaw. As he collapsed, he heard Molly's mother shouting, "Get him on that plane. Send him back where he came from."

But his little sister, Brenna, screamed, "You, Willem. Leave him alone."

Someone cried, "Lewis! Lewis!"

He hoped that was the voice of his mother.

Then he saw the rake come at him again.

CHAPTER TWO

A MONTH LATER, THE YEAR 2000
LONDON, ENGLAND

Lewis sat in the pew of Saint Ignatius Catholic Church on Stamford Hill in London. His head still ached, but at least he could see straight. What he had seen in Ballybly was the fear that people teach each other. Back in Ballybly hospital, Brenna had been able to visit him only one time, and for that, she was punished with flunking school for the term.

Here in London, he had more help. On one side of him sat Sister Kathleen Moran, fingering her beads and pleating the front of her habit over and over again.

On his other side, back lit by a window depicting Jesus talking to the elders in the temple, sat Father Gillooly.

The father leaned toward him. "Yes, I performed their wedding. They had witnesses from college. I had noticed Molly . . . Mary Margaret McIntyre visiting many times, and Sister Kathleen knew Molly as a student in the college."

"Yes," Sister Kathleen said, "she was in my Medieval Literature class and, later, in the small discussion group on themes in post-modern theater. Very bright and thoughtful student."

Father Gillooly said, "Your brother was a gentleman about the requirements of the church. He came to all the classes and took communion. He loved Molly very deeply."

Sister Kathleen said, "I suspect they believe everyone in the hometown wants them to disappear. They probably don't have any idea you are searching."

Lewis shook his head. "I've taken out ads in the major London and Belfast news. A half page ad in each and several days of smaller ads. Nothing."

"They went home once," Sister said, "to test the waters. They came back very discouraged. And Dicken was beaten, like you."

Lewis leaned his head in his hands and imagined his little brother's pain. More than the pain of the rake handle.

"What might Dicken be doing for work?" Father asked.

"Since he graduated in Maths, he could be teaching," Lewis said, "or working for a company that needs mathematicians."

"Molly was offered a scholarship at Royal Holloway, but she's not registered," Sister said. "Maybe she couldn't afford the difference – the books and room."

Father said, "Lewis, considering the beating you got from her brother, I guess, we have to face the possibility …"

Lewis raised his bandaged hands. "God, don't let it be so."

"Amen."

After several silent moments, Father asked. "When do you have to return to America?"

"Three days. I'm back to Belfast, tomorrow and then catch the flights home."

Father nodded, "We both have your information – where you are in Reed College and your address in Portland, Oregon. If we hear anything …"

Sister added, "I may be able to find out something from students who are friends. People here liked them both very much."

"Anything. Any clue." Lewis said.

"Son, a word o' warning. Ditch any bandage you can before you take flight. Airlines are suspicious of Irishmen with signs of police workin' on 'em."

"I'll do that. Though it feels like the bandages hold me head together."

"Don't I know."

"Even you, Father?"

"These days, the cassock brings the English police like flies to dead meat."

CHAPTER THREE

SEPTEMBER, THE YEAR 2000

In the crowded Denver airport, Lewis James pretended to read the newspaper – a ruse he often used to avoid talking with the people who surrounded him in places like this. Last he looked in the airport mirror, his face looked fairly normal, but his head ached fierce. And his hands still puffed under his too long shirt sleeves.

He needed to be alone, to think and to relax.

These days, all air traffic in the U.S. seemed to be routed through Dallas, Chicago, or here in Denver. He had chosen a waiting area near but not at his plane to Portland, Oregon, close enough to hear boarding announcements, but far enough away that he was unlikely to meet his colleagues or students.

September. Thousands of professors and their postpubescent hatchlings migrated to the fall feeding grounds. Lewis noticed plenty of long hair and Birkenstocks wandering around. Sooner or later he'd meet a "Reedie", as his students mockingly called themselves. He wasn't in the mood to answer questions about his sabbatical year.

He needed to get the taste of his native Ballybly out of his mouth before he talked to anyone from Reed College.

So, with his back to the sunny windows and his front to the mirrored wall, Lewis buried himself in the fascinating financial facts of the *Wall Street Journal,* keeping one eye on the mirror, just in case something interesting came along.

Everywhere he went, he found himself watching for Dicken and Molly.

Thirty minutes into his hermit life, however, Lewis saw a new and arresting reflection. Behind him, an auburn-haired Aphrodite and her golden child entered the lounge and showed up in his mirror. She wore a green suit of fine design and easy swing, not the Levis and loose shirt he was used to seeing on traveling mothers.

Professor Lewis James might occasionally be a-social, but never would he ignore such an elegant goddess. Thank Zeus the mirror made it possible to sneak a watch on the woman.

Lewis smiled to himself, as much as his pained jaw allowed. He could imagine how his colleagues in the philosophy department would justify observing her as "an opportunity to reflect on the deeper meanings of myth and beauty in man's psyche."

As a professor of physics, he recognized the attraction for what it really was – magnetism.

Too bad she would be taking the plane to Los Angeles that this waiting area served. This pleasure would prove far too ephemeral.

There was something about her toss of red-brown hair that pricked familiar – something. But the boy's constant motion interrupted Lewis's search for the image.

Her child had one arm bound in a protective sling. Lewis imagined a playground accident. In spite of the sling, the little boy proudly carried his own small backpack. His mother carried a larger pack slung over her right shoulder. In her left hand, she carried an oblong violin case. She set her pack down in the row of chairs behind Lewis, one of the few empty spaces in the room.

The woman's short auburn hair was curly and thick, so thick that the sun couldn't shine through, but warmed the Titian highlights of the outer layer. The sun also warmed her large, hazel eyes. An elusive dimple flickered in each cheek. At the corners of her mouth, a hint of sadness betrayed her.

She walked away from her pack, still carrying her violin. She knelt twenty feet behind Lewis and next to her child. The boy stared out the window. As she answered the boy's questions, her English revealed the dark hues of central Europe. The boy's English was crisp and careful. He seemed about five years old. Loose curls of blond, turning red caught the sunlight from the window, a bright frame for his serious face.

The boy's mobile eyebrows were up and down, knitted and wide apart with every new thought. He was a boy of many new thoughts – his eyebrows were never quiet. Standing next to her at the window wall, facing the runways, the child questioned everything he saw: how the trucks knew when to get out of the way of the big airplane; how soon the sun would set; how airplanes take off after dark. The boy's questions were about the machines he saw, and the machinery of the earth and stars. Her answers to him were clear, concise and memorable.

Lewis wanted the child to keep asking, plumbing the woman's understanding of the very things that Lewis loved.

When she stood to stretch, Lewis sat tall so that in the mirror he could let his gaze travel the length of her legs, enjoying the sensation the view gave him. In truth, the sensation made him move uncomfortably in his chair. She walked toward his back. Lewis turned his gaze hastily to the *Wall Street* headlines.

Placing her violin in the chair behind him, she fished in her pocket, handed the child a coin and knelt down again. Lewis sat up very straight. In the mirror, he saw the top of her smooth curve of forehead.

"Mama!" the child said. "I'm going to stand up and see if the penny will land on its tail."

In the mirror, Lewis' glance met the child's. Lewis winked. The boy's eyebrows shot up. He gave Lewis a wide grin and made an effort at winking back.

His mother's dimples, Lewis realized. Charming on the boy. On her, heart stopping.

The boy flipped the coin, waved at Lewis and ducked down to see the results of his flip. After a few trials and several clandestine exchanges of winks with the man in the mirror, the child said, "Mama, standing and sitting doesn't make a difference. It falls how it falls. Heads and tails, my statistics don't change much."

At the word 'statistics' Lewis made an abrupt reassessment. Yes, it still appeared the child was a child. Not a short adult.

The boy wandered back to the window.

His mother stood from her crouching position. This presented a pleasant view of her softly flared skirt. She moved the violin to the floor, smoothed her skirt in a most delicious way and sat down behind him with her hair not six inches from his. Lewis nearly leaned back, then sat bolt upright. He needed to get a better rein on his mind.

The perfume of Jasmine. He recognized it from evenings in his own garden. Her scent nearly compelled a bold move of introduction.

However, at that moment, the son raced at his mother. In the mirror, Lewis saw him coming, but saw too late. The boy hit her lap in a flying leap and knocked her head into Lewis' head with a resounding crack. Lewis was on his feet in an instant. Holding his pained head, he bounded across the seatbacks to her side. Her son backed away. Lewis leaned over her, checking her pupils.

"How's your head? Something cracked inside one of us." He felt the attention of the other passengers on him and wished them all to disappear.

Her eyes grew very wide. Lewis leaned a little closer. Her right hand rubbed the back of her head, but as he neared, her left hand came up to ward off his advances.

He smiled and straightened away from her. "Involuntary reactions, quick as ever. Pupils dilating normally, I see. No sign of concussion. How about the mouth? Isn't that where he hit you?"

The lady touched her fingertips to her mouth, which, under his inspection, must have felt vulnerable.

"My mouth is just fine. Thank you."

His gaze rested on her mouth for a moment. "Yes, just fine," he whispered. She tried to sit up, to regain her command of the situation without being any closer to him.

He asked, "And your memory? Your name?"

The child said, "Rebecca . . ." but he was stopped by his mother's raised hand. She reached out for her son, clearly seeking protection from the boy's closeness, as much as offering it to him.

She gave the child a reassuring smile and then turned to Lewis, saying, "Memory in working order as well, thank you." Her dimples deepened slightly, but her mouth maintained its melancholy.

"Well, Rebecca Whoever, are you the victim of such attacks from young men very often?"

Lewis thought she jerked as if hit. Then her jaw tightened.

"Only from Benjamin." Her voice seemed to caress the name, accenting its first syllable – Ben'-yah-meen.

"Ben'-yah-meen." Lewis pronounced the name as she did. "Ben'-yah-meen, mothers are very precious and should be taken care of. You have a particularly fine one, my boy. I hope, in future, you'll be gentler."

Lewis, playing the innocent, concentrated on the child. The boy's curly head nodded gravely before he climbed into her waiting arms, put his finger on her swollen lip and whispered, "Sorry, Mama."

"Well done, lad." Lewis smiled at her puzzled indignation. "Now, ma'am, if you'll excuse me, I believe they're calling my plane."

His own head hurt, plenty. Moreover, he felt he'd played his hand beyond the hilt and ought to be gone. He hadn't been able to stop himself. Her mouth was too sad and soft not to tempt him into this pleasant diversion.

Now, he was forced to go to the next lounge and board a plane for Oregon, a country, heretofore fully satisfying to his senses – but, bereft of her, a desert.

CHAPTER FOUR

THE YEAR 2000
PORTLAND, OREGON

Even as Rebecca and Benjamin waited for their flight, a certain Harald Steinmetz exited from his limousine in downtown Portland, Oregon. His real name was Garig Steiermark, but when he wanted to leave his lair in northern Hungary and pretend to be a gentleman, he employed this second identity.

Steinmetz/Steiermark settled his dress hat on his straightened well-cut hair, rose from the back of the limousine, straightened the crease on his fine wool suit slacks, and strode through Portland's brilliant sunshine toward the door of the Heathman Hotel. Kenneth Russmann, his second in command, followed him up the stairs.

At the front door, Steinmetz glanced down the street. Next door to the hotel sat the ornate Arlene Schnitzer Concert Hall. One block south of the concert hall, Portland's theater district flashed neon signs over Broadway Street. Location and ambiance made the Heathman Hotel a home for international artists visiting the Pacific Northwest.

Thus, the hotel staff neither hovered nor gushed because of the extraordinary wealth of a German named Harald Steinmetz.

This was expected whenever Garig Steiermark left his lair to play the wealthy philanthropist.

The freshly re-decorated penthouse had been set aside for his indefinite stay.

Steinmetz arrived to negotiate with the Portland Art Museum for a showing of his famous collection. Garig-Harald held his great-grandfather Steiermark in disdain, but, during his Parisian years, the old man had the foresight to pay the food and wine bills of several destitute painters, including Sisley, Bonnard, Manet, and Pissarro. Paintings were his thanks from the artists. Garig never exercised the same profligate generosity as his great-grandfather, but he appreciated the old man's eye for investment.

In the new century's business climate, Garig searched for less generous ways to increase the family holdings. Some of his ways included kidnapping for ransom, and outright stealing of valuable art and historic manuscripts. Even as Harald, he never attempted to justify his methods. Others would have used them if they could have gotten away with them. Business was business. And he was very good at business.

He lived up to the expectations of his wealth-acquiring great grandfather and grandfather. His own father had been a nonentity, ousted from the family by the time he was five years old.

His mother and his aunts had not known how to get their hands directly on the family fortune. Early, his grandfather had made it clear that no woman would inherit anything more than a trust fund. Garig was the only male heir. Thus, the miserable women spent his youth trying to make little Garig distrust his intelligence, hate himself and trust them – but to trust only one of them.

Always the scheming and subtle jibes at each other. His childhood had been a time to learn manipulation of women.

As soon as Garig Steiermark had attained his majority, he had dismissed the lawyer who hoped to control all. He had set up his mother and aunts together in one house in Budapest, forced to live on dwindling funds. From his hideout in the mountains of Hungary, he had received the well-paid butler's reports of their fights and hatreds. Elegant payback for their years of selfish planning. He never visited them but knew more about their schemes than they themselves.

As he smiled to himself about the latest reports from the butler, Garig-Harald stopped at the hotel entryway, nodded briefly to the green and gold uniform of a Heathman doorman.

A very nice touch for a small town like Portland, Oregon. Old world elegance.

He climbed the inner marble steps to the lobby and entered an elevator waiting to take him to his floor.

Steiermark-Steinmetz recognized everything that his man, Russmann, had done to smooth his way into Portland, right down to holding the elevator, so they would not spend time in the lobby. Of course, he would never tell Russmann he noticed the preparations.

After the elevator door closed, Steinmetz held himself silent for a few moments, but finally had to have news. He stared at the elevator buttons and asked, "She is here, yes?"

"Her flight lands in half an hour," Russmann said in his quiet voice.

"The child is with her?"

"He is."

"Very good. Soon, we shall see if the child shows Steiermark qualities. Possibly . . ."

"She met a man in the Denver airport," Russmann said. "Very brief. Viegelund's team on her air flight suspect he may be a bodyguard hired by the uncle."

"Viegelund? That Hungarian hoodlum couldn't keep her when he had her locked up. Why did you hire any of his men?"

"He has something to prove, so will be more careful. He says that the one who allowed her to escape is in jail, and accused of her rape as the cause of her suicide. And after six years, I've made certain Viegelund's men are much better trained."

"Huh! We'll see."

"They have my orders not to touch her."

"You say there was a bodyguard in Denver? Describe."

Russmann shrugged. "'Big, but fast', they said. Jumped the chairs in the airport to talk to her."

A show-off, then, Steiermark thought. Easy to get rid of that type.

Steinmetz realized his sharp jealousy was absurd. His money and his looks – he always put other men at the disadvantage. Moreover, it wasn't as if he'd want her for long. Women grew whiny after a few months.

By that time, he'd have what he really wanted, and possibly the child as well – an heir to train as Grandfather had trained him.

When his sources told him that they had discovered his musical prey alive and in New York, he'd decided to take a new look at her. He'd flown in from his castle in the hills of northern Hungary to attend her fall recital at Alice Tully Hall. During the recital, even as she played the Carmen Fantasy as if solely for him, he'd decided on an exciting way to get what she owned, and he desired. He had set the plan in motion that night, even before she began the *Praeludium and Allegro.*

He'd ordered Russmann to have his men follow anyone who seemed to know her well. They had the great luck to call Steinmetz to a tavern where her accompanist grew drunk and loquacious.

After that maudlin conversation, Steinmetz ordered his men to allow the woman and her child to enter Portland undisturbed. The men were only to find out the location of her new apartments. He decided to make her feel safe, but to keep a watch on her while he negotiated with the museum for the art event – thus becoming a city benefactor and opening doors for social connections to her.

He would also put on his musical historian hat, developing a story which would allow him to be near her during a university term or, if she proved exciting, two terms – whatever it took to get what he wanted. He had already made himself known to the research librarians and music professors at the universities in the region. He had established his credentials as Harald Steinmetz, a German music historian and researcher. They might as well have been real credentials – he loved finding valuable manuscripts. He loved owning them, as well.

Within the next two weeks, he expected to know her schedule, her routine. The local historians, art lovers and musicians would know and vouch for him. Then, he would introduce himself to her, and be able to watch her son for Steiermark/Steinmetz intelligence. The maudlin New York pianist had not given the child positive marks, but that could be jealousy speaking.

Steinmetz's elevator door slid open, revealing a hallway with thick carpets and soft lighting. Russmann indicated a right turn and handed Steinmetz the key to his penthouse suite. The two men walked silently to the door. Once inside the room, Steinmetz tossed his hat to the dining table. In the mirror, he noticed, and approved of the suit he wore.

He gestured his desire for a drink. Russmann retrieved the hat and headed for the bar where he pulled out two glasses. Steinmetz pulled cigarettes from his pocket, but before he lit one, he noticed a bowl of fruit on the table near the window. While he searched the fruit, he tossed Russmann the lime.

"I've been over that bowl and everything else in this room," said Russmann.

"Tell me about this man she met in Denver." Steinmetz continued his inspection of the fruit.

Russmann squeezed the lime into the gin as he explained. "This big fellow talked to her, then he got onto the flight from Denver before she did. Our guy says the fellow sat in the row in front of her on the plane, hid behind the newspaper as if he didn't know she'd arrived, and hasn't talked to her during the whole flight."

Steinmetz lit his cigarette, lay the blue and white package on the table near the fruit, and then gazed out the window at the languid pedestrians on Broadway. Their lack of push reminded him of the slow social mixing on the street in his home village in southern Austria. He'd forgotten that people could stroll, greet each other and stroll on. He took a deep breath and let it out.

Since the concert where he had created his new plan, he had been in too much hurry. He wanted her manuscripts, at least, but he could take time to work great pleasure into his game.

He faced Russmann and said. "We must isolate her, encourage her, later, to turn to me for protection."

Russmann cocked his head and frowned. "I thought we were after manuscripts, Garig, not playing cat-and-vole with this woman."

"What I do with this woman is my business."

The startled tension in Russmann's face pleased Steinmetz. His lieutenants always had to learn to follow orders, not give advice. Some had not learned quickly enough. Harald Steinmetz wanted complete control over the next few months. Russmann better deliver on that. That was what his money bought, and his power demanded.

Russmann's cell phone rang. Steinmetz ground out the used cigarette. He stared at the buildings across the street from his hotel. There was something oddly bright about this town – far more light than he liked. He finally decided that the airiness resulted from buildings too short to be making money, leaving too much visible sky, and streets far wider than necessary. The trees . . . why so many trees?

Russmann spoke into the phone, "He's right here," and handed Harald the phone, mouthing the caller's name.

"Yes, Sidonie?"

"The moving van driver is kaput. No muss. No fuss."

"What have you done? I told you not to go near her things."

"They will be careful. She will never know."

Steinmetz's eyes narrowed.

This one is out of control.

He could hear the familiar drone of his Lear jet. "Sidonie, you are already in the air."

"Toronto to Helsinki to Vienna."

"Good for you. I will see you in a few weeks in Vienna, darling."

"I want to come to Oregon, Garig."

Steinmetz merely laughed.

Sidonie's voice came back, petulant, "By the way, Garig, the van driver, he died very quick and very happy."

He turned off the receiver. Steinmetz whispered to himself, "Someday, Siddie, you will die the same way."

"Did you order her to search the van?" Steinmetz turned on Russmann. "Damn you. They alerted Miss Gregory to danger."

Russmann seemed totally unconcerned. "I warned them not to change anything. Viegelund's men know what they are doing."

"Do you believe her stupid? She has the manuscripts hidden in a bank vault, either here in Portland, or in New York. I want her to feel safe when she meets me."

"And then what?"

"We destroy her illusions of safety. And I become her savior."

Russmann nodded, his smile tight and forced.

"Meanwhile, you leave her alone. Do you have that?"

"Yes, sir." Russmann stood at attention – a posture he rarely used. Steinmetz liked the feel of it.

Fear and respect. Sidonie needs to learn these things before she dies.

Steinmetz added, his hands raised in the ancient gesture of wait-and-see, "Meanwhile, I am here to meet with the museum curator. Then, I introduce myself to the head of her music department."

"Yes, sir."

"And you watch her, report her habits, but do nothing."

"Right."

Steinmetz turned back toward the window, thinking, Soon, I will see just how beautiful and warm Miss Rebecca Gregory can be.

He had noticed the tension in Russmann's neck. He recognized the symptoms. Too bad this man had begun developing his own agenda, Steinmetz thought. His personal assistants might remain with him longer if they could follow orders and not care about why.

The phone rang again. Steinmetz gestured for Russmann to get it, then gazed out at rose-colored buildings and leisurely human beings. A new tempo entered his blood, slower, more sensual.

I am finished with heated lust.

Steinmetz basked in the languid warmth of new perspective. Six years ago, Darya Zolesku had been almost a child. He took her to create fear. Now, as Rebecca Gregory, she'd become a remarkable woman, and far more interesting to him. Pursuit could bring him more, much more than valuable baubles.

His memory had begun to inform the way he would define success this time – his memory of Rebecca Gregory in concert, of her grace-filled presence and her passionate music., the Carmen Fantasy, as if she knew he was present, and wanted him.

And there was that possibility of an heir . . .

He reached into the bowl of fruit, lifted out a sweet mandarin and began to peel back the skin.

CHAPTER FIVE

On the airplane, Benjamin's thumb slipped into his mouth as he stared out his window. Rebecca didn't notice his drift toward sleep. Her mind ran deep in study of one of her violin teacher's sonatas. When she was a child, he had taught her many of his shorter pieces. Raphael had never taught her his larger musical pieces like this sonata.

His five violin concertos she had learned on her own, because they were beautiful, and because she loved him.

Seven years ago, after her first year of teaching at the university, the orchestrations for his concerti were in the first box he sent her.

Overall, he'd sent away twenty-three boxes of sheet music. Ten of these had been in the first shipment from his friend's. Then, when those had been acknowledged by Uncle Tobias, thirteen more had arrived. She had catalogued about half of them, but she had been through all of them many times trying to figure out if there was any reason he might have had original Bach manuscripts.

Three little notebooks of Raphael's music were the ones she kept close to her always, because they reminded her of his humor and his care. All three were presently in her carry-on bag. She couldn't bear to have them sent on the moving van or mailed. They were among the best she had of him.

Rebecca glanced out the window of the airplane and noticed they were now flying over the Rocky Mountains. Broad shouldered and rugged peaks poked through late afternoon cloud cover. Rebecca started to show Benji the changing landscape, but found he had his thumb in his mouth and his head on his pillow. She covered him with her coat and let him sleep.

After the mountains were behind them, Rebecca's mind drifted once more to her teacher. Since playing his concerto, she had played shorter pieces as encores at recitals. Delighted audiences called for more.

Rebecca glanced outside again and saw the silhouettes of the Cascade Range – Mount Hood, Mount Jefferson, and The Three Sisters. She remembered all this beauty from trips with Abraham, Miriam and her students of the previous summer.

Benjamin slept. She watched scudding clouds begin to obscure the mountains and decided not to wake him.

The music Raphael had sent her also included some by the man who had raised him, Anton Batislav. Raphael had told her,

"The Russian Court of Tsar Nicholas II wanted imitations of French and German dances, so that is what Anton gave them. Of course, he wrote other music for himself and his family."

Remembering these moments, tears pooled in Rebecca's eyes. An ache tightened her throat.

Above her, the seat belt lights blinked "On", for descent into Portland. Rebecca swallowed her sorrow with a soft sigh. She replaced the notebook of music in her pack with care and then reached over Benjamin to check his belt.

She leaned back to struggle with the problem of carrying their packs, a valuable violin and a precious son from the airport to the air-porter limousine and at last, to the apartment.

As the airplane nosed down through scudding clouds, the drops of water on Benjamin's window announced the added problem of the notorious Portland rain. Rebecca searched through her carryon for his jacket and hat.

She decided to let everyone else get off the plane before she tried to hoist Benji. At forty pounds, he was no easy load, yet she knew she could lift him; she'd done it many times before.

Other passengers scurried to empty their overhead compartments and then shuffled in line toward the front of the plane. She noticed a nearby balding man who had arrived at the New York flight at the same time as she. His arrival now, at her secret destination made her suspicious. She wanted no connection between herself and New York.

The man put on his fedora, a hat she thought marked him as old world and out of the mainstream. The man shuffled off the plane from a row not far in front of her row. Rebecca let out a sigh. He didn't wait for her. Good.

When almost all the passengers were gone, Rebecca turned to Benjamin and lifted his inert body.

* *

At the beginning of the flight, Lewis saw Rebecca Gregory and her son enter his plane to Portland. Though grateful to the god of luck, he had slid his tall self far down in the seat. He feared his presence on her flight would frighten her. At the end of the flight, he waited and waited so she could get off first and not see him. He guessed she would believe he'd somehow followed her to Portland.

But after slouching during the entire flight, his back cramped, and his legs tied in knots. He could wait no longer. He stood up, in-so-far as the ceiling of the cabin allowed, and saw her problem at once. Benjamin's eyebrows were immobile for the first time since Lewis had met him. His long, blond lashes lay against his cheeks.

Lewis stepped to the aisle, opened the overhead compartment and took down her violin. He whispered, "If you'll carry the violin, I will carry Benjamin until we find your greeting party."

She cried out. "You! Where?"

He had feared his presence would startle her. Yet, the vehemence of her cry surprised him. "Look," he said in a gentling voice, "My name is Lewis James. I'm a teacher here in Portland. I teased you inexcusably in the Denver airport. But, in truth, I'm a pretty honorable fellow. Won't you let me help you?"

"I need no help from strangers," she said. "Please give me my violin."

He handed her the instrument case and said, "I'm on my way home from a trip to visit my family in Ireland. I had no idea you would be on this same flight."

The flight attendant hovered near, anxious to clear the plane. Rebecca put one hand to her forehead. She seemed tired and defeated.

Lewis waved off the attendant with a gesture that allowed no protest. He sat down in the opposite aisle seat. Something about Rebecca's frightened eyes told him that one touch from him would drive her away forever.

"I don't know what's happening to you," he said, "but I'm not part of it. In the Denver airport, your son provided me with an easy opening for introducing myself. I teased you a little and then left. I never expected to see you again, and I felt sorry about that. I was already on this plane when the two of you rushed on board, a little late, if you'll remember."

She looked up at him. "I'm not crazy. I know it must seem thus. But, I must be careful, now. You are so . . ."

At that moment, he realized there was something very real behind her fear. And he would not know what it was until she trusted him.

He spoke with friendly persuasion. "I'm not part of the problem," he said. "But if you'll let me, I could be part of the solution."

* *

Rebecca watched his mouth, his eyes and his smile lines. His frank declaration dazed her. She'd grown tired of being afraid – wanted very much to believe him. His face became hopeful and quizzical. His thick eyebrows went up in a question just the way Benjamin's eyebrows would behave. That gesture turned the tide of indecision for her.

"If you could help me take our back-packs to the airporter limousine, I would appreciate it." She heard the fatigue in her voice.

"How about if you stand in the aisle, then I can hoist the bags."

She hesitated. She knew he must have seen distrust re-enter her thoughts, but he smiled. "You can hit me with the violin if I get out of line. In truth, you can."

She bit her lip, whether from attempting to hold in laughter or tears, even she wasn't sure. At last, she handed him the backpacks and said, "I will carry my son and my violin."

He shrugged his shoulders into the pack straps, picked up the boy's backpack and cradled it close to his chest as if it were a child. He gave her a smile that said he accepted her limits. She glanced at the violin, at her child and again at him before she nodded her agreement.

* *

Lewis followed her out of the airplane and down the long concourse toward the escalators. In the emptying hallway, only one straggling passenger followed them. Lewis stepped onto the escalator first. As she hesitated, Rebecca noticed that he glanced up at her. She put on a brave smile and stepped on the moving stairs. But her smile lasted a mere moment.

Looking down, over the shoulder of her sleeping son, Rebecca saw a dark-haired man push into the revolving doorway between the baggage claim area and the street. In that brief moment, Rebecca recognized the greasy hair and piercing, dark eyes of the man from the subway station, the man who had tried to steal Benji.

*   *

Lewis watched the merest glimmer of a smile disappear with frightening speed from Rebecca's face. He whipped around – sure she'd seen something beyond him, something that shocked her. Several people milled through the revolving door that led to the street. A couple seemed to have been caught in one section. Someone pushed the door faster than they could manage together. As their door section opened onto the street, the couple fell over each other onto the sidewalk. Beyond them, a dark-haired fellow scrambled to his feet and darted in between shuttle buses.

Lewis glanced back at Rebecca and her son. Behind her, the man wearing a fedora crowded onto the escalator. Lewis recognized the man as one who had boarded the plane in Denver soon after she did. But he also remembered that this man left the airplane long before Rebecca. He should have been down at the baggage claim area by now. The man seemed more intent on watching Lewis than on keeping track of Rebecca.

Rebecca's violin and the long-legged child's body hampered her mobility. If she had a reason to be afraid, this man might be the cause.

That boy weighs too much for her, Lewis thought as he stepped off the escalator and moved to the side of it to protect her. The man in the fedora stepped off and proceeded toward the baggage carousels. No threat there, after all.

Rebecca caught up with Lewis. He could see her apprehension, either about him, the mass of people, or whatever she'd seen beyond him. He glanced at the crowd in the baggage claim area and made a quick decision.

"Rebecca, you sit on this bench with Benjamin and your violin. Give me your claim checks and describe your bags to me."

"I have no baggage," she said. Then she sent him a piercing gaze. "You're in this together, aren't you?"

"I don't know what . . ." Lewis hesitated, afraid he would say the wrong thing.

At that moment, an older man bumped into Lewis and turned to apologize. "Excuse me . . . oh! Lewis James, isn't it?"

"Yes. Ah! Dick Street's father?"

"Right on. Arthur Street. Here to pick up Dick's brother." The man reached to shake Lewis' right, the hand that hugged the child's pack. "Dick enjoys your class. Hope you're back from Ireland to stay." The man beamed. "That your wife's backpack?"

Lewis glanced down and laughed. "No. No, this belongs to my friend, Rebecca." Arthur Street eyed her and her child a bit speculatively. Lewis saw that Rebecca's eyes had lost their accusing hardness. She watched Arthur Street closely. Taking advantage of her new indecision, Lewis hastened to add, "Mr. Street, please tell Dick I'm looking forward to seeing him in class again this year."

"Sure will. He says you're the best."

Lewis felt his face redden. "Thank you," he replied. In ordinary times, he might have taken such a compliment in stride, but at this moment, he very much needed her to hear it.

He saw obvious relief on Rebecca's face as she followed this interchange. Arthur Street had accomplished something Lewis could never have prayed for. At least, it must seem to her that this stranger who offered help was what he claimed – Lewis James, the Oregonian, a teacher just back from Ireland. His students liked him. Their families appreciated him.

After Dick's father nodded a goodbye, Lewis smiled at Rebecca. He set the backpacks next to her and said with an air of casual friendliness, "My teaching colleagues left my van in the parking lot. May I give you a ride?"

She blinked and shrank under the burden of her child and her violin. She became mute and wouldn't even look him in the eye. Then she glanced over his shoulder. Horror tightened the muscles around her eyes. "That man," she whispered. "That man. Please get us away from him."

Lewis glanced behind him just in time to spot the same dark-haired man returning through a different revolving door on the far end of the baggage claim area, three carousels away. His squinty eyes made a quick survey of the crowd. Then he moved toward Rebecca.

Lewis grabbed the packs. He took Rebecca's elbow with his free hand and ran with her toward the conveyor belt that fed the nearest United Airlines carousel.

"Hang on," he said. Lewis lifted Rebecca, her child, and her violin across the in-coming baggage conveyor belt. He jumped over the belt, lifted her onto the exiting belt, pulled her head down and ducked with her through the short doorway that led to the baggage loading room. They were within yards of today's landing runway. A baggage truck headed their way.

In a moment this area would be swarming with people tossing suitcases. Behind them, between the swinging rubber door covers, he saw the shadow of two men running toward the carousel bed.

Lewis put his arm about Rebecca's shoulder, lifted her off the carousel and pushed her toward a metal doorway signed *Employees Only*. At their abrupt entrance into the office, a startled cigarette-chewing secretary jumped. Next to her stood a tired woman in a disheveled United Airline baggage-handler's uniform. Lewis closed the door and leaned against it. Behind his back, he turned the lock and tested the handle.

On the other side of the door, he could hear the running footsteps of at least two men.

"What are you doing in here?" the secretary blared at them.

Lewis decided to go for soft-voiced Blarney. "It pains me to admit that me van's been left at Employee Parking. 'Twas my neighbor, Forgetful George. Used it to get his own-self here this morning for work."

Behind him he heard a noise that could have been suitcase tossing. He wasn't sure if it was real baggage handlers or Rebecca's pursuers searching for her. He went on with his story about his car.

"George, the poor auld fellow, sure an' he forgot me and the misses would be needing our van at the end of the day."

The baggage handler gazed at him, narrow-eyed. But the secretary nodded as if she knew George, and could believe he was forgetful.

Thank goodness the door she pointed at led away from the baggage area where Lewis now heard two angry voices.

An angry wrench tried the door, but Lewis held the knob still and leaned hard. The man gave up.

The secretary pointed toward a door on the far side of the room. "He tell you what aisle?"

"No, ma'am," Lewis said, pulling Rebecca toward the opposite door, "Me friend George, he didn't let on where he put it, but I'd be willing to lay a thick wager it'd be the only orange VW bus out there."

The woman laughed. So did her companion. "Out this way," she said. "You'll find it."

His bluff and his Gaelic lilt seemed to charm them. "Ta," he waved and gave a quick twist to the exit-door handle. Glancing around outside, he checked for any followers, found none and escorted Rebecca onto the cool concrete smell of wet parking lot.

CHAPTER SIX

He could tell she'd grown numb with fatigue and fear. He whispered, "Best I could manage to get us away from the black-haired fellow. That was who you were afraid of, wasn't it? The man with the beady eyes? The one who crowded out the near door and returned by the far door?"

She nodded.

"We have a hike to my car. Now that you've followed me this far, may I carry Benjamin?"

A moment's hesitation, then she nodded again.

He lifted the boy from her arms. His hand brushed against her waist. They both recoiled from the touch. He looked at her questioning eyes and soft mouth and realized something in him would not leave her alone, no matter what haunted her.

This fear for her came on him because he had listened to her talk to her son. A free, open and intelligent woman, she was, and then this – to be stalked. That should happen to no one.

He knew, too, that she found something in him to trust. He intended to nurture that seed to a ripe harvest. Pulling himself together, he led the way to the employees' elevator, which they took to the roof parking and out into the cool night air of the public lot.

In the dark, Lewis kept his attention on the shadows. Possibly, her pursuer knew the airport well enough and had guessed Lewis' intentions. To his relief, within four very shadowy aisles, Lewis found his metallic brown Explorer. He glanced around one more time, saw no hint of trouble, so, opened the side door to buckle Benjamin into the back seat.

"I'm sorry I don't have a booster seat for him," he said to her.

"Taxis in New . . . in my city don't use them. I need to buy one now that I'm here."

The overhead light awakened Benjamin before Lewis could flick it off. The boy turned his face and felt Lewis' chin and jaws with his small fingers. Something the child noticed woke him. He looked Lewis in the eye and said, "You're not Uncle Tobias. You're the man with the sand hair and crinkles."

Lewis whispered to him, "I'm a friend. I'm Lewis James."

"Lewis," Benjamin memorized the name. His drowsy voice said, "When we ran, Uncle Tobias' beard sweated." The boy dropped his head back onto the seat and slept as soon as his thumb found his mouth.

When were they running with Uncle Tobias? And what were they running from?

He closed Benjamin's door and then Rebecca's. As he climbed into the driver's seat, Lewis smelled the warm Jasmine scent of her. He tried to speak calmly. "This man we are escaping – what did he do?"

She glanced over her shoulder at the child in the back seat. Lewis looked at him, too. A more sound sleep he hadn't seen in a long time.

"It can't be the same man," she whispered. "Looks like him. Just looks like him."

"You were sure of him when we were in the airport."

"I've been very careful to keep this trip a secret. No one knows I'm here."

Lewis decided to accept her assessment for now – a pretty transparent hope to be free of something that gave this woman the terrors. He wanted to give hope.

"If you see anyone else who looks like him, will you tell me? I want to know who frightens you."

"I . . . I will Mr. James."

"Now about your baggage . . ." he asked.

"We sent the rest of my belongings in a moving van. But, you didn't pick up your suitcase."

"I'll call later and have the airlines stow it for me." Lewis backed the Explorer out of its space and grabbed the parking receipt off the dashboard. "First, let's get you some safe place."

Rebecca had difficulty with her unfamiliar seat belt, but Lewis knew he'd better not try to help her. Close contact would fuel her fears. Close contact would drive him crazy. He slowed down until he heard her buckle click. Letting out a sigh of relief, he headed toward the exit. He paid the three days' parking costs necessitated by his and his friends' inconvenient vacation schedules and gunned his Explorer onto Airport Way toward Eighty Second Avenue.

Rebecca seemed to study the dashboard. After a moment she said, "It is not orange. Nor is it a Volkswagen."

Lewis grinned, "If that fellow talked to the ladies in that office, I wanted him looking for something we don't own."

"A very quick lie, Mr. James." Her solemn voice made him give her a swift look.

"I'm not in the habit of prevaricating," he said, "but there are times when a bit o' bunkum puts the hounds off the scent."

"I don't understand," she raised her eyebrows and twisted toward him in her seat.

Before Lewis had a chance to explain, a red sports car distracted him. It hung off his left side in the next lane. A red Ford Probe, powerful little car, annoying and close. After a few moments, the sports car dropped into the lane behind him, allowing Lewis' mind to refocus on Rebecca.

"I speak English too fast," he apologized. "I'll slow down."

"Bit-o-bun-come?"

"A little humbug. A lie to send your dark man on the wrong trail."

"Ah. A good humbug."

The stoplight at Eighty Second Avenue gave Lewis a chance to catch a glimpse of the other driver in his rear-view mirror. Approaching headlights lit the red Probe's interior and gave Lewis the impression that the driver had big shoulders and wide hands. The lowered visor obscured the man's face, but showed a light-colored coat they had not seen in the airport – not her dark-haired pursuer – the man Lewis now thought of as "The Bird Dog".

Lewis glanced at Rebecca. She seemed not to notice his preoccupation with the follower but appeared to be studying the wind in the tall cypresses along Airport Way. In the shadowed lighting of occasional streetlamps, Lewis studied her exotic beauty. She had an Eastern European face. An image from some old picture book of the AustroHungarian Empire flashed through his mind. Of the many peoples once ruled by Austria, 'Magyar' was the term that came to mind. Her eyes were wide-set ovals of darkness, her nose small, straight and slightly turned up. Dark curls framed the wide gentle curve of her cheekbones. Raindrops from their moments in the night air still glistened on the outer surfaces of her hair.

The red car behind him honked its frustration at waiting during a green light. Aware that the Probe could have gone around him, Lewis began watching it again, with more care. As he drove, he hoped to keep her from worrying about the car, so, he tried to remember what they'd been talking about, but it was Rebecca who supplied the opening.

"You put words together . . . very impetuous."

Lewis laughed, glancing in the rearview mirror. "It's called brashness." The red sports car plodded in his wake.

"And where did you learn to speak this Brashness?" she asked.

Lewis chuckled, realizing she too could tease. "I grew up in Northern Ireland, speaking English at school, Gaelic at Grandfather's, a hybrid at home and Latin in church. Rebecca, was Benjamin born here or in . . .?"

"Born here," she said, turning her gaze out the rainy window to her side.

Lewis took the hint and stopped questioning about her past.

"So, he grew up with English, and you?"

"Austrian-German and … and other languages of the region."

He recognized the hesitation, the hiding of some detail she wasn't ready to share with the stranger that danger had thrown her way.

He decided to take some side roads to lose this persistent hanger-on. He turned on Cornfoot Road and passed the Air National Guard base. As he crossed Columbia Boulevard, he took the curve up Forty-Seventh Avenue, then Forty-Second Avenue and into the residential district of northeast Portland. The little car stuck with him.

Rebecca glanced at Benjamin, still asleep in the back seat. Lewis didn't want her frightened by the persistent vehicle.

"By the way," Lewis said with as much brass as he could muster. "I don't know your last name." He hoped to distract her, so she'd stop looking back.

"I am called Rebecca Gregory."

"Ah." The wonder of his good taste and timing amazed Lewis. "I recently bought your Kabalesvky concerto, with the little pieces by Kodaly, Elgar and the dances by Atemvoll. What a refreshing combination."

"Thank you." She glanced down at her hands in her lap. In the dark it was difficult to see if she looked as embarrassed as she sounded. In fact, the dark reminded him of why he had not recognized her right off.

"Your photo on the cover – very fuzzy and shadowed."

"Yes. Impressionistic, they tell me." She glanced back again toward her son.

"So, Rebecca and Benjamin Gregory, I expect I'd better find out where we're going, eh?"

Rebecca pulled down the visor and studied its mirror. "Let us lose the little red car first, no?"

Lewis grunted. "Sorry. I didn't want you worrying."

"I noticed him as soon as we came out of the toll booth for parking."

"All right, Rebecca," Lewis pulled over and parked the car on the side of the busy road. "Lock your door."

The sports car pulled around them and scurried down Forty-Second Avenue, turning right at the next corner.

"Tighten your seat belt," said Lewis as he gunned the Explorer into a U-turn. Rebecca threw a protective arm over the seat back. Lewis, glancing out of his side mirror, assured her, "Benji is buckled in tight."

He took the corner back onto Columbia Boulevard on two and a half wheels and headed east to Cully Boulevard. "Thank Father Abraham for giving us a full tank of gas," he muttered.

She laughed at that. "Better to thank your friends."

"Uh-oh!"

Rebecca glanced in the visor mirror to see the red vehicle he'd spotted coming after them. "It is red," she said, "but bigger."

"Hold on Honey, we're turning right."

She flung her left arm over the seat back toward her sleeping son again. Her right hand braced against the dash. In the middle of the turn onto Sixtieth, Lewis realized what he'd just said. The turn occupied his mind at that moment, so he said no more. Besides he didn't think any explanation of 'Honey' would make the situation better. He just hoped the silence from Rebecca represented distraction and not indignation.

As they righted themselves, he saw a red Chevy pass their intersection and drive on down Cully. "Right. It wasn't him. Did you recognize that guy in the sports car?"

"I could not see enough of him, only the shoulders and hands. He had one very large ring on his right hand, though. Gold with many pieces of glass."

Lewis drove past the cool green of Rose City Cemetery. "That probably wasn't just glass," he said and then realized she was smiling at him – a true smile, eyes and mouth and every part of her.

"God, you were joking," he laughed. "That's beautiful."

She ducked her head, but not soon enough. In the light of the streetlamp, he caught sight of the rose tint of embarrassment rising in her cheeks. She was wonderful. His throat hurt with new knowledge.

Lewis drove around a block and headed south until he could turn right onto Sandy Boulevard. He tried to speak but couldn't. It hit him all at once. The sole reason she sat in his Explorer was that she feared the dark-haired man more than the unknown.

And he, Lewis James, was the big unknown. He had no right to protect her, to insist she explain, to find her a place to stay that he knew was safe. He was their temporary refuge and scared for them. Scared of something he knew nothing about.

"Rebecca," he said, feeling his way into her confidence. "Can you tell me what is going on?"

She let out a long sigh. "I don't know. In New York City, someone broke into my studio. They take nothing. They throw things around inside our locked apartment. Then that man, two weeks ago he tried to steal Benjamin when we were in the subway station. I knew I had to leave New York."

Lewis didn't like this at all. "If that was the same man in the airport . . ."

"It cannot be. I make bad mistake." Her English suffered when she was afraid.

"I think you played it safe." Lewis drove down wide Sandy Boulevard, past a brightly painted rococo theater front. On this central pathway into the city, he saw no sign of the small sports car. Lewis wandered without aim, hoping she would soon feel safe enough to tell him where to take her.

"My Uncle Tobias and my accompanist, Gabriel, only they knew I moved here," she said, as if trying to make herself believe.

"Is anyone meeting you at your new home, anyone safe?"

"Ach, I didn't tell. I am to live in an apartment, near a hotel by the Willamette River."

"Near the River Place Hotel?"

"Yes. River Place."

"I know the area." Lewis geared down. His jeep grumbled up a small hill toward a terra-cotta tower topped by an incongruous 7-Up advertisement. In spite of his concern, Lewis smiled to himself. He enjoyed listening to Rebecca's near perfect English. It was the imperfections, the misplaced accents, the not-quite-correct verbs, these teased his ear.

He pulled his car into Interstate Eighty-Four heading toward the Willamette River. She spoke again, telling him more. That surprised him. She had previously seemed reluctant to give him many details.

"I have a teaching studio in my apartment," she said, "I can be at home with Benjamin."

"Great set-up," he said, figuring she must be warning him that Benji would be protected by adults all the time.

She asked, "Do you know the schools in Portland?"

"Only the one where I teach. It's for older youngsters."

"I thought perhaps you were teacher for small ones."

"No, but I have little brothers and sisters."

"Are you able to see them now?" She asked as if his answer was of great import, pivotal.

His whole frustrating summer hit Lewis all at once; he'd spent three months in futile search for his open-hearted youngest brother, Dicken, and for Dicken's Catholic wife. Lewis didn't want to talk about it – didn't want to add to Rebecca's troubles, so he just said, "I saw most of my family this summer in Ballybly – that's near Belfast. We call each other often. And of course, there's the email and Skype."

Rebecca smiled at him, the smile he already recognized as wistful. She glanced down at her hands and said, "It must give you great happiness to be able to talk to them."

He noted her intensity. "Rebecca, who is it that you can't contact?" A silent moment, a tightening of her fist in her lap made him afraid he should not have asked about her lost loved ones.

In a rough voice, Rebecca whispered her most private sorrow. "My mother, my father, my brother Piotr, my . . ." her voice broke and the litany stopped.

Lewis, his eyes on the road, reached out for her hand, held it, said nothing and let her be silent in her grief.

CHAPTER SEVEN

ewis James carried Benjamin up to Rebecca's apartment and laid him in her arms. "I'll just hand you his backpack and pop off home."

When he'd deposited Benji's pack inside her door, Lewis showed her how the lock worked, made sure it would lock after him and left. She smiled at the thought that an Oregonian felt it necessary to show a New Yorker how to use a lock, but she appreciated his concern. She'd been foolish and easy to frighten. However, Lewis James proved sensitive enough to leave them alone as soon as possible. For that, Rebecca was grateful.

She felt small in a very big and dark apartment. She checked the lock on the front door once more and decided to have at least two others installed tomorrow. To chase away her fears, she went back to Benjamin's room. He slept, sucking his thumb and fingering the ribbon on his blanket. She left the lights on in the hall as she returned to the dark living room.

A large expanse of colorless drapery hung cross the main windows. Rebecca yanked the cord to open them. She wished to savor the dark river and the wooded quarter east, across the Willamette River. The city of Portland reminded her of Budapest, a composite city bisected by a river – precipitous hills on the west side of the river, a rolling plain on the east, with scattered small and long-dormant volcanoes. On that plain across the Willamette, nestled in the woodlands, stood Reed College. Abraham and Miriam Friedenberg's home sat near the college. Next week they would return from Colorado where Abraham conducted a summer music festival.

To her right, near her apartment, in one of the ravines and wooded stretches of the West Hills stood the synagogue she'd attended last spring. Nearby stood the home of Rabbi Stamps who had smoothed over her newness in the congregation. Portland was a city, but the kind of small city where everyone knew someone you knew. It was like being part of an extended family of cousins and remote relatives – a real *mishpocheh*.

At last, she felt easy about this move. It could succeed. There were people here she loved, and a welcoming community. She'd been over-tired. That's what had her imagining that the dark-haired man followed her. During her last three days in New York, Gabriel again had created fears in her mind – fear of being far from his protection.

But the little man ran in the same manner as the false policeman – and his greasy hair, the same.

As Rebecca stood at the window, her eye caught sight of a brown Explorer – Lewis still parked below her window. *What is he waiting for?*

Her dream of being safe faded. She should never have let a stranger bring her to the apartment. Now, he knew too much. How stupid of her! It was true he had evaded the red car which seemed to be tailing them, but now she wondered if that was a show to make her afraid, to keep her seeking Lewis' protection.

She'd been exhausted. He'd been very kind, and she'd wanted to trust him. Backing away from the window, she drew the drapes.

*   *

In the Ford Explorer, Lewis had been about to turn the key in the ignition when something stopped him. In his rear-view mirror he watched the corner phone booth. A man shoved into the phone booth. Something about the man nagged at his instincts.

While watching, Lewis realized he'd seen this man twice before on this day – the last person after Rebecca to get on their flight from Denver, and after their arrival in Portland, this man had disembarked long before Rebecca. Yet, at the escalator the fellow had been right behind her.

The shadows of his wide-brimmed hat hid most of his features. The hat had been off his head once, during the time that he had followed Rebecca onto the plane. Lewis could remember that he'd been balding, blond and of medium height, taller than Rebecca, but shorter than Lewis, and stockier.

Lewis distrusted this coincidence. These apartments were out of the common way. When the man took off his hat to scratch his head, Lewis saw the shine of the bald spot in the streetlights. The hand with the hat gestured upwards toward the building. Lewis looked up to see Rebecca's drapes closing.

The man hung up and walked past Lewis' car to a blue Chevrolet Impala. He drove the car up the street and turned right onto Front Street. Lewis followed as soon as the Impala reached the corner. The Impala turned left through a stoplight and headed toward the hotel district. Lewis started to pursue through the stoplight, but a city bus barreled down the street in the oncoming lane. When Lewis finally could turn left, he couldn't find any sign of the blue Impala. After half an hour of driving around the hotel area, Lewis realized the car wasn't parked on the streets. It could be in any number of garages.

The clock on Lewis's dash glowed midnight. He hadn't been in Portland for several months and grew aware of how much he wanted to see his home again.

Tomorrow, he'd pick up his dog from Abraham and Miriam Friedenberg. His little beagle had probably been spoiled beyond spoiled during the year he'd been on sabbatical.

Lewis headed east onto the Hawthorne Bridge, across the Willamette River and into the wooded, rolling plain near Reed College.

Still, the questions raised by the existence of the man in the fedora nagged at him. What were these men doing?

CHAPTER EIGHT

Music rang out in the blue and gold salon, home of Count Czigler. The final chord of Bach's violin concerto echoed off the painted angels and cherubs that graced the ceiling. The last high tones of the violin reverberated from the carved golden festoons and brocade walls. Count Feodor Czigler glanced up from the keyboard. He smiled at his music teacher.

Anton Batislav tucked his violin under his arm.

"So," Anton said, gesturing toward the handwritten manuscripts on the music stand "how long have you known that you owned these three concerti?"

Feodor placed the violin manuscript inside the piano part while he tried to find the best way to answer. "Papa showed them to me as soon as I finished studying Bach's "Well-Tempered Clavier" with you."

"But that was, what? Ten years ago, before your marriage, before the ... before the birth of your Raphael."

Feodor noted that Anton still could not mention the death of Maria Anna Etnova – the death that attended the birth. Feodor himself had trouble talking about her – Anton's other favorite student, the laughing, calming and lovely girl, his beloved wife, no longer of this earth.

"Yes, long ago, Papa gave these to me and he told me about the night my grandfather died."

Anton's face tightened with remembered fear. "About the siege at the dacha?"

"Yes. Papa told me how you shot the invaders, and that you recognized one of them."

Anton closed his eyes in remembered sorrow. "The shot that hit your grandfather came first. We were playing duets, just as . . . I wanted to save your grandfather, but it took me a full minute to realize the truth of what was happening."

"Papa told me he saw it all from the barn where he was working."

"And where he had no gun," Anton said.

"Papa trusted you, but he learned that night to trust no one else. As soon as you recognized the pianist among the dead, he began making inquiries. They were part of a lawless gang that lives on the border between Hungary and the Ukraine."

Anton touched Bach's manuscripts. "Your father believed they were after these concerti?"

"Yes. They had negotiated with someone in our household trying to be certain my father did own these."

"You mean my wife, the Batislava," Anton could be blunt when it was needed. Under questioning, Anton's saucy and vicious wife had admitted to an affair with the pianist. She had been sent to prison because she also had stolen and sold to the gang many pieces of the household's stored art, the life collection of Feodor's father and grandfather. At the trial, music had not been mentioned. Feodor's father had wanted the fact of its existence, and even the suspicion that it existed to remain a secret.

Feodor said, "When Batislava confessed, she told Papa that they were after this music more than anything else she gave them. She had begun to fear them, and told them she'd never seen such music, that we never played it. But they were certain. They had traced it from Wilhelm Friedemann Bach to my great-grandfather. And they knew."

"And," Anton said, "they had to have it . . . she . . . once she started in with them, with him, she couldn't stop the greed of such men." Anton raised his glistening eyes to the ceiling.

To avoid Anton's look of hurt, Feodor also looked up. He suspected they both gazed at the same slight angel on the ceiling of this room – the golden-haired one that was Maria Etnova at twelve, the year the painter, Annensky noticed how beautiful she would become, and the year that Feodor himself realized how important she already was in his turbulent life.

Feodor felt unsure about how to tell Anton what must be said. "You know how much Papa admired you, so, it was not that he didn't trust you, it was that the gang was the beginning of our end – the lawlessness of our aristocrats, the tottering indecision of our Czar Nicholas, the border gangs, the rising workers mobs – Papa felt the approach of disaster – the disaster of our own making – this disaster that is now upon us."

Silence followed his statement, as if both of them listened for the inevitable hammering at the door. Tsar Nicholas in nearby St. Petersburg, had just abdicated his throne. His brother, the grand duke, had refused the crown unless elected. The new Provisional Government and the Petrograd Socialists, who vied with each other for power over the country, were poised to descend on the rich homes of the suburb of Tsarskoe Selo.

Count Feodor Czigler knew time ran out for his family. His friend, the painter Annensky, reported a large troop contingency had boarded the train in Petersburg Station, bound for Tsarskoe, fifteen miles to the south of the city.

For their safety, last week, Feodor already had sent all his servants on the last train to his country estate to live among his father's freed serfs. This hour interlude of music, the need to reveal the three missing Bach Concerti to Anton, this was Feodor's last act before the mob arrived. Anton was dressed for travel, his satchel and his pack leaned against the white painted salon door.

Anton put his hand on the manuscripts. "These are beyond price – lost these one hundred and sixty years – why keep them from the world until now?"

"Papa knew their value, but he also knew that the gang still exists. The new generation still is aware, and with our people in turmoil, there is no safe place for these in most of Europe in this year, and maybe into the next."

"They cannot stay hidden forever."

Feodor said. "You are right. But if the Border Gang doesn't get them, The Nazis will claim them. I beg you to take these and one other precious jewel with you as you escape the coming storm. What happened two nights ago at the palace in Saint Petersburg will come here within hours."

"I am ready. But I won't leave you and Raphael."

"Annensky says Tsar Nicholas is on the train as a prisoner. I've no doubt we will all be prisoners soon, if we stay here."

"You and the child must come. Wear your threshing clothes, your work boots, become the farmer you truly are and . . ."

Feodor raised his hand to stop the torrent. "I am known. I am easy to recognize. If they stop me, they also arrest you. I need you to take your violin, take these pieces hidden among your own manuscripts, and most of all, I need you to take Raphael."

"Your son! How can you send away your son?"

"Because I must. My mother cannot travel. I must find a way to hide her here."

"But . . ." Anton sat hard on the piano bench next to Feodor.

Feodor put his arm around the thin shoulders of his teacher. "Raphael loves and trusts you, my old friend. I must do my duty here. And I must pray that you get across the Baltic and the North Sea to England, if they will have you, or to the neutrality of Switzerland. I pray you and Annensky will find a way through the weakest part of this storm of war and revolution."

"What am I to tell Raphael?"

"You are on a big adventure. Tell him he is now the real Raphael Sospiro – remember that name he made up for himself when he was two years old?"

Anton's smile came with sadness. "Yes. 'I am Sospiro, the breath of the west wind'."

They sat, leaning against each other, remembering how the child created stories to go along with the music he played on his small violin and on the piano.

Feodor straightened. "My friend, I burden you because I have no choice. I trust you more than anyone in this world. When you are safe, do what you need to do, sell the music to the highest bidder, to a university or a library, if there are any libraries left in this chaos. Do whatever you need to do to take care of Annensky, yourself and Raphael."

In the distance, they heard the arrival of the train from Saint Petersburg.

Feodor stood. "The mob will come. It can't be long. I will bring Raphael to you. Annensky has already brought the horse and cart. His paints are buried under the hay. He will drive you as far as roads can carry."

Anton nodded and put his violin in its battered case – made to look like the abused case of a country fiddler. He put the manuscripts inside his own and enclosed them in his traveling satchel.

"My beloved Feodor, I will care for your Raphael with my last breath."

"This, I know full well."

CHAPTER NINE

FALL, 2000

Benjamin loved lunch with Mama in these funny restaurants. They had been in Portland for two Fridays, so they'd had lunch in this restaurant twice already. Mama always found a place with beat up tables, and sandwiches you couldn't fit in your mouth. Places like this always had yummy desserts.

Benjamin decided not to wait while Mama paid for lunch. He would go find a good table. He could sit there until Mama brought the lunch. Today, he hoped for a booth because the booths in this place had tall wooden backs. The backs had words carved in them and he could use the carved words for his new game. His Mama said some of the words didn't mean anything, but he could sound out lots of them.

He strode toward the farthest booth – one he'd never gotten to sit in. As he looked round the back of the bench, he found a surprise – a great surprise.

"Hi!" He put up one hand in greeting. Lewis didn't hear him, maybe because he read. Benjamin tried again, going for the sleeve this time. "Hi!"

* *

The tug on his sleeve woke Lewis from his book. "Oh!" he exclaimed. "Benjamin! How did you get here?"

"I came here for lunch. You're in my favorite booth. How did you get here?"

"I walked from work. Will you join me in your favorite booth? Where's your mother?" Lewis looked around the restaurant.

"She's bringing our lunch." Benjamin started the climb into the bench opposite Lewis. He lurched into the table causing Lewis to lift his soup bowl to save the contents. When Benjamin settled, he turned with a grin. "What's your lunch, Lewis?"

He noticed that Benjamin remembered his name after two weeks. "This is Minestrone soup. If you bump the table again, it will be StrewninManyPlaces soup."

The giggle from Benjamin pleased Lewis. He glanced out of the booth again to see if Rebecca searched for her son. Benjamin had handed him a great excuse to break his selfimposed exile from her company. He'd known she needed time before she could accept even the mildest attention from him. He'd driven past her apartment every night checking for the menacing red Probe or the blue Impala. There'd been no sign of either car.

* *

Rebecca discovered that Benji had left her side while she paid for their lunch. Frightened, she rushed toward his favorite booths. Moving down the aisle, she grew concerned. Benji wasn't in the usual ones. Toward the back, she nearly ran into a tall tweed jacket. She looked up and met the puckish smile of Lewis James. His smile had appeared in her mind during violin practice for the last two weeks.

"Your son has joined me in the last booth." He moved on down the aisle ahead of her. "Here she is Benjamin. She found us at last."

Benjamin stood up in the booth. "Hi, Mama. See who I discovered?"

"Yes, Benji," Rebecca looked up at Lewis, "Mr. James, I don't want to interrupt your lunch, we can …"

Benjamin interrupted, "Not James, Mama. His name is Lewis."

"Your Mother is right, too. I'm Mr. Lewis James. Please, Mrs. Gregory, do sit with us." He stood aside in the aisle for her.

Rebecca couldn't ignore her sudden feeling of brightness at this surprise encounter. After all, she'd vowed to be more careful with him if she ever saw him again. She was aware that her head was level with his shoulder. Even when he stepped aside, there wasn't room in the aisle for her, so as she moved, she brushed against the sleeve of his jacket, setting free the heather and fresh air smell of tweed. She felt surrounded by him.

As she settled in, he studied her tray. "Hot tea for Mom, I assume, and a juice for Benjamin, no doubt."

"Thank you, Mr. James." The warmth of his indulgent smile bolstered her courage.

He continued guessing the tray's contents as she removed them to the table. "Let's see … and split an enormous sandwich with a reward of half a piece of chocolate cake to follow, right?"

Benjamin's curiosity rose. "That's right, Lewis. Did you and your mama split sandwiches too?"

"No, there were too many of us to split a sandwich. We often split a pot of soup." He set the tray on an empty table nearby and folded himself into the opposite side of the booth. Careful as he seemed, his knees had no place to go and brushed hers on the way by. "Excuse me, Rebecca. These booths were built for the little people."

She struggled to think of anything intelligent to say. The closeness of the booth tied her mind up. The feared darkness began closing in on her. Her breathing became quick and shallow.

Ever since the days in prison, this darkness came every time someone got close to her. She could not black out in front of Benjamin. It would frighten him. She had to stop this . . . grab at reality and hold it.

She looked at Benjamin. He showed such glowing pleasure in being with Lewis that she made herself sit there. For his sake, she would breathe and stay. She pushed away the darkness by concentrating on cutting their sandwich. One minute . . . each minute might be easier.

*   *

Lewis caught the look on her face and the sudden stiffening of her body when he bumped her. He thought for a moment that she might bolt from the place. Then she cast a look at her son and stayed for his sake. The key to this mysterious woman was the boy.

Give her time and as much space as you can, Lewis, he thought. Talk to the boy who wants to know everything.

"Lewis? What are you reading?" Benjamin climbed up on his knees and hung over the table toward Lewis, endangering his juice.

"This is a book about stars and planets. It has a lot of pictures which we can look at when you've eaten your lunch." Lewis moved the juice to the wall end of the table. "Now that your mother has cut the sandwich, how about if you start on it?"

Benji took his sandwich apart and dragged out all the sprouts. He squished down on the remaining contents and lifted it to his mouth. He saw Lewis watching the process, so he explained. "These are bigger even than Mama's mouth. We have to excavate and condense them."

Lewis laughed as he glanced at Rebecca, the source of the big words. "Your son does a good imitation of you."

She smiled, relaxed a little and turned to excavating and condensing her own sandwich, looking up once to see the twinkle in Lewis watchful eyes. He winked and answered Benjamin's queries about the stars and planets.

"Are you an astronaut, Lewis?"

"No. That'd be fun though, wouldn't it?"

"Yeah! I'd be the pilot . . . vrooom!" Benjamin airplaned his hand across the table, missing his mother's tea pot because Lewis' hand reached out and deflected the plane to a safer course, and then continued their conversation.

"You could be the man who goes outside the spaceship to set up experiments," Lewis said.

"Boy, that'd be great! I've seen those guys in a movie at OMSI, the science museum. Are you going to do that, Lewis?"

"No."

"Then why are you reading about the stars?"

"I teach kids about the stars so that they can try to be astronauts if they want to when they grow up."

"Could you teach me about the stars? I want to learn about how they get out to the stars."

"Sure. At my cabin on Mount Hood I have a telescope for looking at the stars. Would you like to see it sometime?"

Lewis sensed the return of Rebecca's tension even as he invited Benjamin. "Of course, we'd have to do it sometime when it's convenient for your mother."

"Can we go, Mama? Can we?" Benjamin's eyes were shining with excitement.

Her eyes clouded as she looked at her son's expectant face.

Lewis interrupted Benjamin's badgering, "Benjamin, there's lots of time. We'll find a time, don't you worry." He whispered to Rebecca, "I'm sorry. That was thoughtless of me."

Rebecca looked at Lewis, her eyes darker than usual. "No, you're very thoughtful. I'm sorry not to be able to accept as quickly as you offer, Mr. James."

"I can wait, Rebecca." He sat back in his corner opposite Benjamin. "I see that you need time to get things sorted out." He turned back to Benjamin, encouraging him to eat his sandwich.

*   *

Watching Lewis James, Rebecca could almost imagine him teaching a room full of high school students. They no doubt adored him, his energy and quick wit. He listened with care to Benjamin and helped him find the right words to express big ideas. He treated Benjamin's curiosity with respect.

After drawing a map of the solar system on a napkin, Lewis had turned the conversation to maps in general. They went through several napkins, with Benjamin drawing a map of his bedroom. Then Lewis drew a map of the city, including Benjamin's home and his own. The restaurant and Lewis' school were placed in relation to the Willamette River. It appeared to Rebecca that Lewis' school might be quite close to the college. She'd not known there was a high school so near.

During the conversation with her son, Lewis included Rebecca with an occasional flash of smile or raised eyebrows when Benjamin said something humorous. She warmed to his interest in her son and could have listened to the two of them for a long time. Something about their relationship seemed so right that she lapsed into a comfortable silence, watching the expressive face of her son's friend.

She decided that Lewis James' attractiveness could not be captured in a portrait, yet he was attractive. His aquiline nose seemed too aristocratic for the rest of his features, which were rarely still. Soft folds surrounded his bright green eyes. His face became a map of laugh lines whenever he enjoyed himself. His strong jaw had a hint of dimple in the center, just enough to turn what might have been a stern face into a mockery of severity. His hair lacked discipline. His long fingers often attacked his sandy waves, raking through as he searched for a word or a thought.

She became aware that his eyes had turned toward her. She could tell by the selfmocking rise of one brow, that he was aware of her scrutiny. His open and vulnerable face asked if she liked what she saw.

At that moment, Benjamin remembered the reason he'd come to this booth in the first place. "I can read the words on the booth." He turned to show off. "RICK , that's RRRick. CK says "Kuh" doesn't it, Mama?"

"Yes, it does."

He went on deciphering, "LOVES, that's loves. And SUSAN is SOO SSANN. Is soossann a food?"

"Suzan. It's a girl's name."

"Oh!" The light dawned. "Rick loves Susan." He began looking for something else.

Lewis's eyebrows lifted, "What are you looking for, Benjamin?"

The child's small square hands traced the carvings of memorized physics formulae and other, more political, graffiti. "Where does it say that Susan loves Rick?" he asked. "I can't find it."

"Maybe," Lewis said, "Susan doesn't know yet that she loves Rick."

Rebecca replied. "Maybe Susan has already enough people to love."

Lewis answered, "I suspect, that Susan is missing out on a great guy."

Rebecca had to laugh at his temerity. She looked down at her empty plate and at Benjamin's. "Benji, it's time for us to go. Can you gather your napkin maps and say goodbye to Mr. James?"

"Maybe Lewis could go with us. I can show him all the places to hide in our new building."

Lewis chuckled. "I'm glad you enjoy my company, but I need to trek back to my school and get to work. My students pour in next week."

Benjamin took one of the napkins and a pencil and began writing with the cramped grip of child hands.

"What're you writing, little buddy?" Lewis asked.

"Here's our telephone number, so you can call me."

Lewis raised his eyebrows at Rebecca. "Is this all right with you, Becca?"

She considered a moment before she looked up at him. "Yes."

He was pleased at the firm tone of her voice. "Thank you. I won't use it to bother, but I do enjoy both of you. I will call."

After they left the restaurant, Benjamin skipped ahead of them down the block. Lewis took advantage of his absence. Holding out a napkin with some letters penciled on it, he asked Rebecca, "How do you pronounce this word?"

She looked at it, whispering the letters she saw, and then glanced at him. "I don't – it's LEH' vee. I can't say the `double u' as you do. I don't know. . ."

"LEH'vee, Levy. That's what I like. It's better than any other way I've heard my name pronounced. And here is my phone number, for emergencies. Would you use it?"

She expelled her pent-up tension in laughter at how he got around the barriers she put up. "Yes, Levy. You don't mind that I can't say it as Benjamin does?"

"I want you to say it your way and often. One other question Rebecca?"

"What's that, Mr. . . .Levy?"

"You are skitterish as a squirrel among dogs. I know you thought once that I might have been sent to hound you. But the other night at the airport I thought you'd made up your mind to trust me."

"I know of no reason to distrust you, Levy. I am a cautious person. Please do not be offended if I want to get acquainted slowly. It is how I must be."

The smile that radiated from his eyes to his ears was infectious.

"Thank you," he said. "Getting acquainted `slowly' is a big improvement over `never'. I cannot be offended."

After they parted, Rebecca tried very hard not to look after his tall, cocky figure. When she could stand it no longer, she glanced over her shoulder to see him still at the corner, a block away, looking after her. He waved and strode off down the street to his right.

*   *

Harald Steinmetz stood at the doorway to the restaurant and watched Rebecca walking with the man she had met for lunch.

So, she passed my table twice without any notice. She doesn't recognize my face. The child doesn't even recognize me. Russmann was right to introduce me to the hair dresser.

The very compliant and dead hairdresser.

It will be safe to introduce myself, but I cannot get too close at first. She won't know the smell of my aftershave. American brands are hard on the nose and not subtle, but it will throw off her senses. And clothes, different western wear.

I'll have to force myself not to caress her – that will be the hardest part – not to take her by force as in the old days. I can take time. Enjoy the process.

And then take that bright child. He is mine.

CHAPTER TEN

arly September had come at last, to Abraham's and Miriam's delight. Now that they'd returned from the Aspen Music Festival it was party time at the Friedenberg home near Reed College. Abraham had his 'to-do' list in hand while he listened to Miriam bustling about in the kitchen.

Abraham stopped his work for a moment to glare at his wife's small blue and green bird with disgust. The one thing he'd never understood about his wife was her affection for little dodo heads such as this.

During their year of dog sitting for Lewis James, Abe had been surprised at the dog-bird communication. The beagle howled. Blue Boy whistled and set off another round of howling. Cute, but noisy.

Abe plopped the "bird cozy" over the cage to shut out the sounds and sights of tonight's party. According to Miriam, the noise of a faculty party might frighten or corrupt her precious Blue Boy. Abe was sure no idea, naughty or otherwise, had flitted through that bird head in all its six years.

His mission accomplished and myriad 'to-does' crossed off, Abraham climbed the stairs to change his attire.

Years ago, he and Miriam had become the selfappointed parents of the faculty.

Reed College may not have known it, but it benefited as much from the warmth of the Friedenberg's as it did from the vast bequests of its famous alums. Brilliant young professors came here, attracted by the latest in lab equipment, academic freedom, and competitive salaries in a great city. They stayed because somehow, they couldn't bring themselves to say goodbye to the latenight discussions in the Friedenberg salon.

Miriam had been the sole female member of the Reed faculty when Abraham first met her. A biochemist and a fine essayist, her explanations of scientific ideas were so clearly written that her science column was carried by most major newspapers in the United States. Abraham was persistent and creative in his studies of music. His fascination with all the performing arts had been the impetus for several books, and his knowledge was sought by colleagues from around the world.

Tonight, on the eve of another school year, they had invited the faculty members to enjoy each other's company – an event anticipated by all.

Abe heard his wife climbing the back stairs. He glanced into the upstairs library, where Miriam began to set out Legos. "When is our little man arriving?" he asked.

"Rebecca's coming about five o'clock to get him settled in. She says she has some new manuscripts to play for you . . . some more things of Atemvoll's she's been looking at."

"Good. Benji and I can build Pirate Island or something while she plays the pieces. When is Lewis coming to help move the piano?"

"About 5:30."

"Good. Oh, and Miriam, did I tell you about the visiting musicologist? – a Harald Steinmetz. He's here to do a study of Oregon composers and their colleagues, zeroing in on Bloch, Avshalomov and Svoboda . . . some book he's preparing."

"Rebecca doesn't need match making, Abe. She needs to be left alone."

"They don't have to become romantically involved."

"No, they don't. But you keep thinking she should . . ."

He turned his florid, innocent face toward Miriam. "You needed me. I needed you. I don't want her to miss out on life . . ."

Miriam kissed him fondly and shook a finger at him, "After the hell she has been through she's not going to approach life the same way you would."

"I will merely introduce her to Steinmetz."

"That was a mistake last year for both Joseph and Rebecca. He was hurt, and it didn't need to have happened."

"I promise, Mama." Abraham kissed his wife and helped her get out the toys they kept for their favorite young guest. Soon they heard the slam of the backdoor screen. Smiling, they listened for pounding little tennisshoed feet.

"Boppa? Grandma? I'm here!"

Abraham grinned at Miriam, "Rex Magnus has arrived. Let the festivities begin!"

She laughed. "Benji, come on up. Boppa has all the Legos out and now the building can get under way."

Benjamin burst into the room and hugged the legs of his 'Grandfather'. He reached up to hug and kiss his 'Grandmother'. They loved it.

His mother's more serene arrival was no less important to them. Miriam welcomed Rebecca with a hug, but had to excuse herself to answer a ringing front doorbell.

Rebecca hugged her violin case and a folder of music. Abe took them from her and kissed her cheek. "Hi, Little Mother. Glad to see you. We have time for a long session with this stuff you've brought."

"There are wonderful pieces here, Abe. I think Raphael wrote most of them himself, but he was careless about signing his shorter pieces."

Abraham reached for her notebook and began flicking through the yellowed sheets. "Ah! Composing theater interludes didn't seem important to him, I expect – something to keep the audience in order."

Abraham had known Raphael Atemvoll in their youth. Throughout Europe, Raphael's reputation as a teacher was legendary. His reputation as a composer of lyrical pieces for the violin was no less.

While Rebecca and Abraham talked, Benjamin built. "Boppa, I builded a theater. You can play the music in here."

Abraham got down on the floor and checked the strength and colorfulness of an overwhelming tall front wall while Rebecca tuned. Benjamin added "one hundred and fifty thousand seats" to his theater.

* *

Downstairs, Miriam greeted Lewis James. He came laughing out of her Pouter Pigeon hug and accepted the lemonade she offered. They retired to her big kitchen where Lewis perched on a tall stool and submitted to the motherly questioning he expected from Miriam. She mixed the juice.

"Lewis, I can't tell you how dull it was last year without you."

"It's nice to be missed, Miriam, but you can't have a dull year. You couldn't know how."

"Well," she shrugged off his disbelief, then confirmed its accuracy. "There were one or two lovely young people added to our lives last spring. But we did miss you, my boy, and looked forward to all your letters. Tell me about your last three months. Did you find that wayward brother of yours in Ireland?"

His eyes clouded with distress. "No, I didn't. Dicken was so full of love – until they disappeared, they were the only ones who seemed untouched by the `religious' warfare."

She reached out and touched his arm. "I hope they turn up soon."

Lewis covered Miriam's hand with his, thankful for her friendship. "I keep imagining them trying to figure out what to do about the hatred in Ballybly. I hope they just left, but why not write to me?"

"Could they think you agree with all that negative thought?"

"Hard to imagine why, unless someone lied to them about me."

She let that comment hang in the air just long enough for him to realize that each faction in Ballybly had been lying about the other for generations.

"Yes," he said. "Lying serves their purposes."

Miriam looked him over, and moved away from that hurt. "Tell me about the time you spent in Germany with the physicists."

He sat up straighter on the stool, trying to remember back to the good part of his year. "They were cordial. We shared our research – came away with a passel of new ideas for each other. I've spent this last three weeks in my office trying to write an article based on our conversations about more efficient fuel for rockets."

"Did you do anything beyond physics while you were there? See any castles? Any fencing matches? Lots of plays?" She handed him a frosty glass of lemonade.

"Thanks. I did do some fencing, even acquired a new and dashing scar on my arm. Kept me in good shape. As for the rest," he wiggled his eyebrows at Miriam, "Yes, I had a social life. There are many nice young ladies in Germany. But it was on my way home that I met the woman I'm going to marry." He looked at her from under his thick brows, a light that wasn't mischief shone in his eyes.

"What?" Miriam had become used to his brief flirtations. Women went after Lewis James, but so far, none could hold his attention away from his beloved science.

"The very one. She is breathtaking."

"I hope she doesn't live in Cincinnati or some other distant clime."

"Amazingly, she lives in Portland. Miriam, she is worth the years of waiting."

"Who is she?"

Lewis felt a superstitious wish not to say her name, lest the evil ones should take her from him. He answered according to his instincts rather than his intellect. "I will tell you her name just as soon as she is mine. She is yet to be won." He brightened at the prospect.

Miriam was amused. "Hard to come by? You're attracted by the game itself."

"No. The attraction is the woman – intelligent, skilled, thoughtful."

"And beautiful."

"Very. But she's barricaded herself behind a succession of well-built walls. I no sooner scale one wall than I find another. But she cannot build as fast as I climb. I know that the last wall will have a door. She's going to open the door and let me in."

"It's the *game*! You don't even know her."

"Oh, I know her, Miriam. There is a mirror near her, a very clear, small mirror, reflecting her true self. It reveals more than she knows. I understand very well what it is I am pursuing."

"Oy! I've never seen you so intense."

Embarrassed, he set down his empty glass. "Well, I came to move the piano before this party gets going. So, I'll just carry on. Lemonade hit the spot."

Miriam gazed at the swinging door, still moving after he departed. She'd gotten used to the idea that the most eligible bachelor on the faculty was not eligible. He'd been claimed by the muse of science. That this could change in his thirty-fifth year was nothing short of amazing.

Walking from the kitchen to the music room, Lewis strode past the stairwell. From upstairs, he heard a recording of some enchanting lyric violin. He stopped to listen to the tune and stayed to memorize it.

He thought he recognized the style, both of the composer and of the violinist. Of course, Abraham would know the recordings of Rebecca Gregory and those of Raphael Atemvoll. Abraham was a noted collector of such works. Lewis smiled at the thought that Abraham might be a way for Lewis to establish himself with Rebecca.

When the recording upstairs stopped, Lewis stepped into the main-floor music room and picked out the tune on the grand piano, tried out some of the harmonic progressions he thought ought to accompany it and then moved the piano to the middle of the room. He felt a moment of grateful thanks for years of study with his mother, a woman frightened of Catholics, a bigot, surely, but the best classical piano teacher in Northern Ireland He was also glad for his twelve years' acquaintance with American jazz and theater music.

He shook off the last memory of his mother turning her back on him, and opened the piano to half-mast. From the keyboard, he could see the famous Friedenberg gardens, the buffet spread and the people who came in the front door. He could keep track of a party while never leaving the piano bench.

His conversation with Miriam had left him a little frazzled. Tonight, he hadn't wanted to think about Dicken and Molly. He *did* want to think about Benjamin and Rebecca Gregory.

Off in the entry, the doorbell rang. From the music den, Lewis saw the first guests arrive. Abraham had not yet come downstairs. From his studio upstairs, Lewis heard the strains of another song for violin. He edged closer to the stairs wanting more. He knew by the tone and the fluid singing style that this also was a recording of Rebecca Gregory, but it had to be a new one. Before he met her, he'd already owned the two she'd made in New York.

Miriam interrupted. "Lewis, I'd like you to meet Harald Steinmetz. He's a visiting musicologist – here using the Reed library for his work this fall."

Lewis tried to drag his mind from the recording to pay attention to the dark-haired and handsome fellow. Steinmetz, a man as tall as Lewis, dressed in a suit of denim that sat oddly on him, as if it were a fabric he couldn't get used to. His finely sewn linen shirt seemed more like the man – Flemish or Irish linen.

The man pushed his straight hair off his forehead in an awkward gesture, and then offered to shake hands with Lewis.

Lewis could tell that Harald Steinmetz hailed fresh from Europe, a man used to elite parties where wool and linen would be considered Bohemian attire. The slightly longer hair as well as the denim pants and jacket must be what he thought defined Oregon casual.

Lewis extended his hand, "Glad to meet you, Mr. Steinmetz. What research brings you to this corner of the world?" Steinmetz's hand was cool and smooth.

"It's Harald," Steinmetz said, his smile genial. "And you are …?"

"Lewis James, physics. What is your particular interest here?"

"Northwest composers, Svoboda, Avshalomov, Barton, Adams …" Steinmetz seemed to watch him for any recognition of these names.

"Thomas Svoboda – good," Lewis said, "Jacob Avshalomov – wonderful start." Lewis said, "and how about Susan Alexander? Obo Addy?"

Steinmetz frowned, "An oboe player?"

"Drums, Ghana. Driving."

Steinmetz's eyebrow rose, "Fun, I believe. However, my research is in Northwest composers."

"Ah, well then," Lewis said. He reminded himself to introduce Rebecca and Benjamin to Obo Addy's Ghanaian rhythms. Addy had moved to Oregon thirty or more years ago. The composer lived, in fact, two miles north of Abe and Miriam.

Steinmetz turned to greet Abraham who had just arrived from upstairs.

Abraham said, "Ah, Steinmetz, I am so glad you two have met." He turned to Lewis and said, "Mr. Steinmetz comes with the best of credentials, publications in *The Strad, Piano Quarterly* and *International Pianist.*"

Steinmetz glanced at Lewis. "We were just becoming acquainted, Abraham. And I hope you will feel free to call me Harald, even though we have such brief knowledge of each other."

The three of them discussed news of changes in the Tschaikovsky Competition voting system and then moved to Steinmetz's interest in Svoboda's *Overture of the Season.*

Lewis was impressed with Steinmetz's knowledge and articulate manner of discussing compositions. He knew the man felt uncomfortable in the denim, because he pulled at the lapels and cuffs frequently.

Others joined their conversation, and after a time, Lewis left to find old friends. He caught up with Ben Jones, the Reed choir conductor and voice teacher. Thus began a round of news sharing and laughter.

By a half hour into the party, Lewis grew uncomfortable. He'd heard the name 'Dr. Gregory' spoken in tones of awe, tones of reverence, and even in tones slightly suggestive. It didn't take long to realize that Dr. Gregory was Rebecca, and that Rebecca was the most sought-after woman on the Reed campus. The syllables of her name seemed to float at him from six or seven groups at once. When he heard Harald Steinmetz ask about her expected arrival, Lewis grew annoyed.

He retired to the music room and began taking his frustrations out on the piano. Politeness ignored, he played the most bombastic Schumann he could think of. Lush chords and arpeggios occupied his mind enough to cool it off. By the time he'd toned down to play some lighter pieces, his friends gathered nearby. Requests for Broadway musicals, Gay Nineties fare and Sondheim operas occupied him for at least forty-five minutes.

Wearying of group singing, Lewis asked Ben Jones to sing the "Simple Song" which Leonard Bernstein and Stephen Schwartz had written for Bernstein's Mass. Lewis loved this poem and unpretentious tune. It soothed him as no other song he knew.

*   *

Upstairs, Rebecca finished reading to Benjamin and left her son building another Lego kingdom. She heard someone downstairs begin an angry rendition of *Les Papillons – The Butterflies* of Schumann. These were not butterflies the pianist portrayed. These were bald eagles at war. She laughed, wondering what caused such violent emotions. The pianist was skilled. Les *Papillons* was hard to play this well, with or without anger.

The pianist's dark mood was soon followed by friendly accompaniment to humorous songs. As Rebecca arrived at the top of the stairs, a tenor began a song with the pianist's accompaniment.

"Sing God a simple song". She'd heard this piece only once before. But this tenor's voice rang softly, sure and accurate. The accompaniment was reminiscent of a lyre. She halted on the first step, captivated by the psalmlike poem. As the applause downstairs died, a sense of fulfillment came over her. She wanted to learn this song.

So many people filled the music room that, at first, she couldn't see the piano. From Miriam's buffet, she chose a smoked salmon pâté on toast to carry with her, and moved from group to group.

Abraham introduced her to a visiting musicologist. "Harald Steinmetz, I want you to meet Rebecca Gregory." She looked up to see a handsome man in a stiff denim suit smiling down at her. He bowed and took her hand.

"Ah, yes, I have heard you in recital, Miss Gregory."

His touch – she froze. This is crazy, she told herself as she pulled her hand back. Why am I having this reaction?

She recovered enough to speak. "I have only played one recital this year in New York . . ."

"At Alice Tully Hall. Mere weeks ago. Wonderful concert."

"I . . . I thank you, Mr. Steinmetz. . .?" So, he had been there. Hundreds had been there . . . it meant nothing that he knew of her. But she had to get away from him before her reaction became evident. "Please excuse me, Mr. Steinmetz. I must greet an old friend."

She turned to avoid the man who brought memories of New York to her new home. At last, she faced the piano and could find out who had played the fighting butterflies. To her amazement, Lewis James long arms and fingers dwarfed the keyboard. His wild sandy hair fell over his temple.

* *

Lewis took a deep breath and, aware of her, flicked a glance over her dress, then back to the keys.

"Jasmine," he whispered, watching her.

"What?"

His smile was mischievous as usual. "You always smell like jasmine."

Her quick retort was unguarded. "You always smell like heather and fresh air."

"Do you like it?" he asked glancing at her dark green dress and its sleeves.

"Do I like this song?"

"No, the heather and fresh air."

"It's a good smell." She gestured indifference.

He watched her dark sleeve, floating like a veil around her slender arm.

Behind her, Lewis saw the new musicologist watching them. Abraham hovered nearby, engaging the man, Steinmetz, in conversation, but Steinmetz kept glancing at Rebecca.

The man couldn't be faulted for noticing her, but Lewis wanted to keep her attention for as long as possible. He neared the cadence.

"Jasmine is tantalizing," he whispered, "a nectar designed to attract bees. Your actions and your fragrance give off opposing messages. Which am I supposed to believe?"

She started to give a sharp answer to his comment about the jasmine, but his piano improvisation distracted her. He finished the repetitive song he'd been playing and took off into an ending cadence that seemed familiar. She relaxed into laughter and sank to the bench beside him. "Mozart's style."

"Glad you recognized it. And this?" He scooted to make more room for her while he played. He noticed a disappointment on Abraham's face as Lewis claimed her attention. That reaction from Abraham puzzled Lewis.

Steinmetz had moved on to meet another group from the faculty. Lewis began a new style variation on his theme.

"Scott Joplin," she said.

He was impressed. "Where did you hear his music?"

"On Tour in Yugoslavia."

He tried other American composers in rapid succession.

"Oh!" She smiled with pleasure, "George Gershwin . . . Aaron Copland . . . Jerome Kern! America has such good music!"

"Sure does! But this old German guy is still the best . . ." His fingers began to bounce with the joy of a well-known piece.

"Bach. The third prelude," she said.

"Yep. This is a jolly piece. Very dancy." He played the insistent little hopping thirds with precision and humor. Toward the end, he gazed at her, holding the last chord until she looked up.

"Any requests?" he asked. Though the crowd was noisy, there might as well have been no one else in the room. His eyes held hers, probing, asking questions.

Miriam came in with a tray of desserts. He saw that Miriam noticed the exposed fragility on Rebecca's face. Lewis glanced at Miriam and nodded. She took his hint and began distracting her guests with chocolate mousse.

He recognized her effort. He whispered, trying to keep Rebecca's attention on him. "Do you have any requests?"

She was reminded of her reason for coming to the piano. "I want to learn the psalm you played with Ben."

His eyebrows shot up in surprise. "The Simple Song". How long have you been in the house?"

To him, everything before this moment seemed ages ago. "We came at five, to play songs for Abraham."

"Ah … that was not a recording of you, but the real you." Realizing that the "Simple Song" had pulled her to him, he began playing its accompaniment. Her face took on hopefulness – the sadness and fear he often sensed, washed away with the chords.

"I'll teach it to you," he said.

Understanding her need for strong belief, he began the song.

"Sing God a simple song: Lauda, Laude …

Make it up as you go along: Lauda, Laude …

Sing like you like to sing. …"

As he taught her the rest, Lewis glanced at her. She watched his fingers on the keyboard. He knew she smiled inwardly. Her face had grown radiant. He played on, the melody following the patterns dictated by the words. The directness, like the old psalms and the Latin *Laude* – praise, bridged the gap between their two religions, a healing salve for both of them.

She sang it back to him, searching for one unusual interval. Then again, she sang, sure and clear. Her voice had none of the strength of a trained singer, but was flutelike, the voice of a shepherd in the echoing hills. When she finished, a hush filled the house and garden. She seemed aware only of the song and of his presence. Their friends remained silent, waiting.

Lewis's instincts grew alert. He brought her out of her trance by playing other pieces as he talked to her. Behind him, Miriam began party-frivolous conversation guaranteed to distract the others from Rebecca and Lewis. The expectant hush was broken.

Lewis felt, as much as saw that Harald Steinmetz stood near the music room window, watching Rebecca and caressing the stem of his wine glass.

*   *

From the kitchen door, Miriam saw the fragile white clay that had been Rebecca being fired. For her safety, the source of the heat had to remain constant. If Lewis persisted with care, Rebecca could become a fine white china. Given the flaws in her history, an inconstant heat would leave shards of kaolin clay.

*   *

For Rebecca, the pleasure of discovering the song hung like a mist around her, separating her from reality. When she looked at Lewis, the mist began to evaporate in the light of his gentle smile. She felt comfortable near him today, even though she recognized the extra glint in his eye that heralded a teasing.

His lips pursed in a brief, unsuccessful effort to keep the tease inside him. "According to the gossip in this party, you, Goddess of Music, have dumped a soaring career in Parnassus to slum with mortals here."

"Parnassus is not all it's advertised to be," she quipped. "So many muses in one place . . . a cacophony, very distracting. One can't even play in tune for the pipes and poetry all over the town."

"Are Oregon's mortals less frightening, now that you've been here a while?"

She stared at him, reminded of how tonguetied she'd been when they were together in the restaurant. The thought that blurted from her was too revealing. "You bring intensity to life that is . . ."

"Do I frighten you?"

Rebecca sat in momentary silence. How could she be honest with this man whose kindness and warmth she wanted to share? — honest and yet not repel him. Try his own technique . . . She looked at him with an imitation of his own mischief, raised one eyebrow and whispered, "You don't scare me. Not in large crowds like this."

Lewis chuckled. "So, I must resign myself to meeting you in airports, crowded restaurants and large parties. I can stand it, if you can."

With feigned nonchalance, she shrugged. "I'm used to it."

"You did well the other day," he said, "a very small booth with a very large man, and yet you were able to make yourself stay for almost half an hour."

"My son enjoys your company very much."

Lewis realized she hoped to deflect this conversation away from herself, but he kept playing Della Joyo and steered their talk back where he wanted it.

"And I enjoy Benjamin. He's a lively and curious boy. I think he gets that from you, but you keep the freer side of yourself for him alone."

Rebecca seemed exasperated with her own tension. "I am alive!" The intensity of her whispered declaration stopped his fingers in midpiece. "You just don't recognize symptoms. I sneeze when flowers bloom. I blink when the sun is in my eyes. Look for subtle signs!"

This was the whimsical, humorous woman he'd heard on the airplane talking to her son, not the careful and guarded woman of their encounter in the restaurant.

"In Oregon," she declared, "I begin to be alive. I want to throw rocks in rivers, run in the college quadrangle, make echoes among tall buildings."

"Soon." he whispered. "Soon you'll be able to do all that, and more that you think you'll never be able to do. Stay with us . . . with me. Don't return to Parnassus."

She studied his face. "Back there," she said, "I was kept in a bell jar and only let out for eight o'clock concerts. Here, I may learn to breathe real air all day. I might learn to eat junk food and sit on grass."

He laughed with her at her choice of freedoms. He ached to know her, to help her get free of whatever kept her locked inside those thick walls. The cooling night air blew through the garden window and reminded him of a way to get Rebecca out of this crowd.

"Goddess, let me show you a vice that mortals indulge in. Miriam asked me to make the coffee for this crew when the evening begins to cool."

Without awaiting her answer, he took her by the hand and led her toward the kitchen.

*   *

Their progress through the crowded room was followed with a few raised eyebrows. Rebecca had never before been led by the hand anywhere, by anyone, as far as her colleagues could remember.

"That won't last long," predicted Williams of the music department. "Five to fifteen minutes tops, then she gives him the heaveho," (himself having suffered the heave-hoes last spring).

Jeffreys, a physics colleague, stuck up for Lewis. "I think you under-estimate the Jamesian charm. And, they have a common interest in music."

Williams snorted. "A parlor musician? They'll soon founder in the desert of his musical knowledge."

Crandall, professor of English and cynicism, had grown tired of Williams' figures of speech. "When you foundered, Williams, it must have been in poetic justice."

Abraham, fearful lest this party split along departmental lines, stepped into the conversation, putting an arm around Williams while asking Crandall to expound on his latest medieval poetry find. Jeffreys, amused at Abe's obvious hosting, drifted toward the punch bowl, away from Crandall's 'Lay of the Persian Rose'. The title reminded him of his interest in the whereabouts of a certain dance teacher.

Instead, he bumped into a fellow in a denim suit.

" 'Scuse," he said.

The man stepped aside, still staring at the kitchen door.

CHAPTER ELEVEN

In the kitchen, Lewis watched Rebecca hoist the large coffee urn into the sink to fill it. He hunted in the freezer for the coffee beans. "Let me know," he mumbled over his shoulder, "I'll take that out of there when it gets full."

Rebecca laughed. "I happen to have sufficient muscle for the job, sir."

He rummaged in the freezer, unsuccessfully. "At over sixty-two pounds the cubic foot of water, that coffee urn will weigh about eighty pounds topped off."

"Musicians develop very strong muscles," she said. "This is very easy lift for violinist." She turned off the water and reached for the handles at the top.

He gave up on the contents of the freezer and watched her strain against the weight. Crossing the room, he reached one arm around each side of her to get a grip closer to the urn's center of gravity. "We'll take it up and to the right counter. Ready? One, two, three!"

They lifted it steadily and moved to the right together, setting it safely on the counter. He left his hands on the urn a split second longer than necessary. He backed off and began bantering with her again.

She continued to face the sink, closing her eyes and breathing quickly. He realized he'd made a mistake. He turned back to the freezer to give her room.

"Rebecca," he chuckled, "violinists develop muscles it's true, but your massive muscles are not the muscles needed for lifting coffee urns which are nearly as tall as yourself."

Her back straightened. She faced him with renewed liveliness and announced, "So, tall pianists poke fun at short violinists."

"No, no." he dismissed the idea. "The average tall pianist will take care of the little violinist when she's about to ruin years of skill development in a moment's female bravado."

She lifted her head. "And pianists could not possibly hurt themselves?"

He smiled down at her. "Not possible. But this pianist could use a little help finding the coffee beans."

She closed the freezer door and reached into the refrigerator section to pull out a sack of decaf and another of regular.

"Good thinking, my dear Gregory," he said.

As he ground the beans, Rebecca leaned back against the counter, folding her arms across her. She seemed relaxed, enjoying the interlude between their bouts of teasing.

"You know, Levy," she said, "I was under the distinct impression that you taught children … `youngsters' was how you put it, I believe. I did not expect to find you at a college faculty party."

He chuckled. "To me, college students are youngsters. After all, I'm thirty-five and growing older."

Gazing down at her fresh face, his mood changed. He reached out, brushing a glance over her cheek. "You, Rebecca, are much closer to them in age. I'll wager there are many young men in your class who suffer from love of the unattainable Dr. Gregory."

As soon as he said it, he sensed a sudden rigidity in her. To his horror, she withdrew into the fortress and closed the gate. Her eyes looked directly through him. She barely breathed. He was afraid to move.

In the darkness, Rebecca felt oppressive air. A young man, once her student, huddled in silent anguish. Zoltan.

Lewis saw Miriam enter the kitchen. He waved her off. He had to find the way through to Rebecca or what he had done would remain a barrier between them.

"Rebecca, you are safe with me."

Slowly she relaxed. After minutes, her eyes opened. She tried to draw away. "I'm sorry, Levy. I was . . .."

"I am sorry, too. Whatever I said, I didn't mean . . . I didn't know."

"It is not what you said. Just a flash of sad memory."

But to him, it seemed that she had lost great energy in that sadness. Lewis glanced at Miriam for confirmation of his next statement. "Miriam can take you upstairs, so you can rest."

Miriam nodded.

Lewis went on. "You've many friends here. Later, come back down and be with them. They care very much about you."

Miriam turned her toward the stairwell door.

Rebecca stopped suddenly. "No. No, I'll join the others." Rebecca started a wavering course toward the door.

Lewis feared to interfere.

Miriam stopped her progress. "Rebecca, I don't think your body is with us yet. Wait a moment, breathe a little before you face them. That's it. Much better. Now, can you manage to look less glassyeyed? Don't want them to think you found Abraham's brandy."

Rebecca whispered, "Tell him it was my fault."

"I will." Miriam opened the door for her to rejoin the party.

After Rebecca left, Lewis slumped against the counter, raking his fingers through his hair. "I don't know what I did to her, Miriam."

Miriam bit her lip, trying to decide just how much she had been given permission to tell him. Most of the story should come from Rebecca when she could tell it. For now, only a little of it would have to be told.

"Lewis, in her homeland, she was . . . she was mistreated. It doesn't take much to put her back there, though the power of that memory weakened last year while she was here. Now after a time in New York, it has regained its strength. Something – no many things in New York are harmful to her."

She studied his reaction. For Rebecca's sake, she didn't want to discourage this young man. For his sake, she did not want to mislead him. What he asked her next made her heart shrink.

His voice had the soft strength of passion under taut rein. "Is it because I touched her?" He watched Miriam carefully.

She considered her answer for a long moment. "If I didn't know you well, Lewis, I might have thought that was the reason. But, you would approach her with great care . . . you told me so yourself this afternoon. I've sent her mind into that dark place with no more than a casual remark. Abraham has found her there when they've just been sitting quietly, sharing a recording."

Lewis passed his hands over his tired eyes then looked directly at her. "Miriam, on the night we met, she believed someone had been sent to hound her. Is someone still threatening her or is she imagining it?"

"Something has begun to happen during this last year. Her Uncle Tobias told Abraham that their apartment and her studio were ransacked. And someone has tried to steal her son."

Fear gripped him. "Benjamin? Where is he now?"

"He's upstairs, building with Legos." Miriam smiled. If Lewis felt so strongly about Benjamin, he was hooked for the right reasons. "You could go up and see him if you want."

Lewis surprised himself with how possessive of Benjamin he felt.

"I. . . yes, I'll find Benjamin." He tried to shake off his foreboding about Rebecca and clear his mind for the little boy. "I haven't played with Legos for a long time," he said, forcing a smile as he climbed the back stairs.

CHAPTER TWELVE

s soon as Rebecca re-entered the music room, Abraham got her into a conversation with Harald Steinmetz. Lewis James was a nice fellow, but unlikely to commit to anyone. The business with Joseph Selig last year had been a mistake, really. Nothing in common with Rebecca other than the synagogue. With Steinmetz, he believed he had the right combination.

But, as Steinmetz talked to her, Abe looked closely at Rebecca and thought that if she didn't get out in the sun more, she was going to fade away. She seemed to struggle to be polite.

"I do hope all your things arrived from New York in one piece," Steinmetz said.

"Everything I brought with me on the plane was fine. From the moving van, some of my sheet music boxes had spilled out and been stuffed back in. I've usually had better luck with UPS than that."

Abraham noticed that at the mention of trouble with UPS, Steinmetz's face tightened.

"I hope nothing was missing." Steinmetz said. "Making claims on things like that can be discouraging."

"No, nothing missing. I brought my most fragile music with me, which was lucky."

Abe noticed Steinmetz appreciating her looks. He did it in a more subtle way than most, but Abe was gratified.

"You have fragile manuscripts?" Steinmetz's gaze drifted to her fingers. "I expect you have some very old music from your childhood teacher."

She looked sharply at the man. After a moment she said, "Why would you think that. My teacher, Dr. Ronen, is still in Austria."

Abe noticed that she had put up an immediate defense.

Then Steinmetz said something that Abe knew would put her off.

"I would like to hear some of those encore's you often play, Raphael Atemvoll famous songs, Dr. Gregory."

She frowned. "I'll be playing some of them in a small concert in the Reed Commons later this fall."

Steinmetz shifted gears. "I have tickets to hear the Symphonic Choir sing a new Tomas Svoboda piece set to some Mayan poems. The concert is this Saturday. Would you come with me?"

"Thank you, but – string quartet to coach that night . . ."

Abe had heard this put-off too many times before, and knew it to be only occasionally true, but Steinmetz seemed to shrug off his second disappointment. "Perhaps we can find another time."

Rebecca stepped back to invite other music faculty into their conversation. Disappointed, Abe knew she was setting things up so she could leave this conversation smoothly.

She didn't like invitations. Abe let it go. But he feared that if she continued this way, she'd never get over her past.

*   *

Out in the garden, Rebecca shook off the crazy tightness that meeting the new man gave her. She couldn't figure why this one gave her that dark feeling.

She decided to check in on Benjamin again. He often played in a special part of the garden that Abraham left open for his trucks and cars, but he wasn't there. He could play for hours with a set of blocks, but she was surprised he hadn't come downstairs to greet old friends.

Inside, someone, she assumed it was Lewis, began playing the piano. As Rebecca searched for Benji, she half listened to the piece. It seemed familiar, and melancholic. The piano's haunting melody followed her upstairs.

In the upstairs hall on the bookcase sat the stack of music she'd brought with her. Glancing at the first of Atemvoll's songs, she understood why the piano piece seemed so familiar. It was the same song with a different accompaniment. How could Lewis know that song? She had only ever played it for Abraham.

She opened the door to the Lego room. In the middle of the carpet was the most elaborate structure she'd ever seen. A battery-operated crane still bobbed up and down.

Benjamin was gone.

She looked out the window into the garden, thinking she'd missed him, but he wasn't there. She went to the bathroom. The door was closed. Rebecca fidgeted for a moment, then knocked.

"Benjamin? Is that you?"

"Rebecca? This is Yvonne. Benjamin isn't in here. I haven't seen him."

"Thanks, Yvonne." Rebecca bolted for the downstairs. In each room she entered, she saw no sign of her son. There were so many people. They were too tall. She couldn't see him through them.

Feet! That's it! Get down and look for small shoes and legs.

She dropped down close to the floor – high heels, black wing tips, Reeboks . . . no child's Keds. She felt a hand on her shoulder.

"You all right, Sweetheart?" Abraham asked.

"Abe, I can't find Benji. I was looking for his shoes."

"I think he's got his shoes on. He's on the piano bench with Lewis James, getting on famously."

"Oh!" Relief swept through her. "I didn't think about his feet not touching the floor."

"He's not ready to use the pedals yet."

Rebecca gave Abraham a kiss on the cheek and didn't explain herself. The conversation was far too muddled. She wound her way into the music room. The top of Lewis' rumpled hair could be seen as he bent over his companion. They played Three Blind Mice with an oompah accompaniment by Lewis. She stood in the doorway enjoying their fun. At the end, Benjamin hopped up on the bench and hugged Lewis, nearly knocking him off.

As he straightened up, Lewis's gaze locked with hers. One eyebrow shot up questioning her state of mind. She smiled. His wink told her that the mugging he was getting was fine with him.

Rebecca was happy for Benji, but afraid that when the dark memory seized her in the kitchen, Lewis had lost interest. Many before him had become discouraged. Last spring, Joseph Selig had said when he touched her, he only burned his hands on her frozen surface. She'd tried for him, sensing the same needs in him as in herself. But it hadn't been enough.

*   *

Lewis watched Rebecca hesitate in the doorway. For the first time he noticed that on this warm evening she was the only woman whose arms and throat were covered. Beautiful as the dress was, he wondered at the significance of her choice. Distracted by her, he encouraged Benjamin to play a song for him while he kept an eye on Benji's mother who was deep in thought.

Benjamin played quite well. The little folk song, *Adieu,* demanded some technical skill. Benji ended his song with a little clap of triumph, so pleased with himself that he hugged Lewis.

People near the piano clapped. The response embarrassed Benjamin. He hid his face in Lewis' shirt front. Lewis motioned for Rebecca to come rescue her son. Benjamin had his thumb in his mouth and was pulling on the smooth front of Lewis' shirt with his other hand.

Lewis made room for Rebecca next to them. "I think your son is looking for a ribbon blanket."

She looked startled, "How did you know?"

"Many little brothers and sisters."

Benjamin took the thumb out of his mouth. "Lewis, you be my bed. I'll sleep on you." His eyes closed firmly, squinched tight. He had deep laugh dimples which he tried to keep smooth.

Lewis cozied Benjamin into a tight little ball and began rocking back and forth with big uneven motions. "This is the way the rocking chair rocks, the rocking chair rocks. . ."

"Let me out!" Benji giggled and squirmed.

"Is my rocking chair too broken for you, little buddy?"

"You are a galumphing chair!"

"Good name. Where would your mother like to have you deposited?"

Rebecca laughed. "How about depositing him on the back seat of Abraham's Volvo. That's our chariot until I can afford to buy one of my own."

"Yes, my lady," Lewis said, then he whispered, "I'm glad to see you back to good health, Rebecca. What can I do to prevent that from happening again?" He knew he was taking a risk, but he could not leave unspoken discomfort between them.

"As soon as I know, I will tell you," she said.

"Thank you." He lifted Benjamin in his arms and gestured for her to lead the way to the car.

*　*

As the piano player and Rebecca took the child outside, Harald Steinmetz studied the three. He had grown certain of several things. Rebecca Gregory truly was Darya Zolesku. She did not know who he was. And the child most probably was his, a clear Steinmetz/ Steiermark child – smart, charming and musical – definitely his.

CHAPTER THIRTEEN

Days later, Rebecca answered the knock on the door. In front of her stood Harald Steinmetz. He lifted a brief case and held it open.

"Rebecca, I've brought some duets. Could we play them?"

"I just put Benjamin to bed."

He looked startled. "Doesn't Benjamin like music for bedtime?"

"Mr. Steinmetz . . ."

"I know. I should have called. But you would have said "maybe next week. Maybe the month after next . . . and I enjoy your company, so I thought I'd take the direct approach."

Rebecca glanced out at the sunshine streaking the apartment hall from the windows at either end. She glanced at her watch. And then she looked back into Harald Steinmetz's hopeful gaze. Something about this man seemed too forward. Here, away from the party and where Lewis's piano playing didn't provide background music, Harald's voice seemed too smooth.

He smiled and pointed at his briefcase. "Debussy and Beethoven."

She thought about the piano parts, and realized that if he suggested these duets, he must play piano very well, indeed. And she needed to stop being afraid of others all the time. Rebecca steeled herself to step into unfamiliar friendliness.

"One hour of duets. Then I must work."

He grinned. "Oh, thank you, Rebecca. You won't regret it, I promise. Dvorak, Brahms, Franc – and any music you have that might be fun."

She opened the door and let him in. And she left the door wide open while she pocketed her cell phone, with the phone number of Abraham all ready to dial.

She realized right away that Harald played well, leaving out some notes that were reachable only by very practiced pianists. But he kept the rhythm and played through his mistakes. After forty-five minutes, he asked if she had some music of her own. "Aren't you in the process of cataloguing your teacher's music?

"No," she said. "I'm cataloguing the music of Austrian and Hungarian composers who are not well known."

To avoid his gaze, she opened one box.

"What's this?" Harald asked, pulling out an empty envelope. "Looks like someone in Budapest mailed this to you."

"They mailed it to Uncle Tobias, probably something from the hospital's medical staff." And then she found herself lying even more. "Tobias must have gotten rid of it. 'Incorrect copies' you see."

"Ah yes," he said, putting the envelope on the side piano desk. "What else do you have?"

"Songs from famous operas," she said, lifting out a notebook filled with transcriptions of operatic arias. As she handed it to Harald, she lifted two more envelopes out of the box with the 'Incorrect copies' inscription. She held them two next to her skirt, so he wouldn't notice.

Harald studied the opera notebook, frowning as he paged through. While he was engaged in silently reading music, she set the envelopes low on the nearby book shelf., bending over as if searching in the box. She didn't want to talk to him about Budapest, Uncle Tobias or Raphael Atemvoll. Rebecca Gregory's violin teacher supposedly was a man in Austria, but Harald Steinmetz had guessed she catalogued Atemvoll as her teacher. She decided to protect herself.

Harald glanced up, "I've heard some of Atemvoll's encores that you've played. Beautiful." He flipped another page. "Could we play those?"

She hesitated and then decided the best thing was to put a brassy face to his thinking. She pointed at a notebook with Raphael's pieces.

"I found these in a shop in Vienna."

"Are these all Atemvoll? Or are there other pieces in here?" he asked.

"His and someone else named Batislav – court dances from early in the century – waltzes and minuets, even a couple of fox-trots."

He smiled, turning pages to find them. "Let's play those."

So, for fifteen more minutes, they rushed through several Batislav pieces. She enjoyed hearing them again, but Harald could hardly get through them fast enough, turning pages back and forth between pieces to see if there was anything more interesting in the volume.

When he did this for the fourth time, she said, "That's it for me, tonight. Time to go home."

He stood, setting the manuscript on the piano side desk. "You meant an hour on the dot, didn't you?"

"Got to get ready for my lecture tomorrow," she said, putting her violin on top of the piano. She handed him his coat. "You play very well, Harald. Do you enjoy it?"

"With you, very much," he said, gazing at her, and then back at the box and the piano. "Let's do this again soon."

"Maybe next month," she said. "I'll have to check my calendar."

He put out his hand to shake hers. "Thank you for taking me on at such short notice, Rebecca. I appreciate it."

She looked at his hand, felt a tightening in her stomach that she couldn't explain. Instead of shaking hands, she led him to the door that she had left open.

After he left, she stood on the inside of the door, leaning against its cool wood.

"Why?" she asked the uncaring air. "Why?"

Pushing herself to move, she returned to straighten the piano desk. Then she remembered and opened the envelopes with the two "incorrect copies'. Inside the sturdy covers were more dances and interludes by Batislav and newer interludes and songs by Raphael – music compiled in the same manner as the notebook that Harald had not enjoyed. She had looked at all three notebooks many times and each time rediscovered that they were what they appeared to be, Raphael and Anton's compositions.

Thumbing through Raphael's beloved songs, she smiled, hummed the opening of the first one and then remembered the day he had taught her this song. Her heart seemed to seize. Grief poured out as she leaned on the curve of the piano.

Where is Raphael? Did that Hungarian hoodlum murder him?

Minutes later, she straightened her back and wiped her tears. She set the two manuscript notebooks on the bookshelf, took the third notebook off the stack of "already played music" at the side of the piano and put it in the bookshelf as well.

It was as she reached into the lamp stand to turn out the light that she saw the return address must be from a post office near the Zeneakadémia. Would the academy have mailed Tobias pieces by Atemvoll and Batislav? It had to have been Raphael himself who asked them to do it. But why mark the package as 'incorrect copies'?

Then she remembered the tariffs that had once been onerous. Many people mailed things marked 'Uso' or 'Used' or 'Incorrect Copies' as if the contents were nothing important. This practice avoided the postal costs of mailing valuable things.

The practice also discouraged pilfering by mailmen who might be looking for valuables they would love to intercept and never deliver.

Rebecca chuckled. She'd never have suspected the secretaries at the Zeneakadémia of being so clever and sly.

*   *

Lewis met Rebecca twice in the next week, once at the Art and Music room of the Multnomah County Central Library, a room whose arched windows let light shine on her hair and illumine her face. On that day, he discovered, Benjamin was staying with Miriam, so Lewis invited Rebecca to lunch. They walked together down all ninety-two steps of the gracious winding stairway, she smiling, and chattering over her discovery of the clarinet concerto by Mozart.

"The whole score," she said. "We could follow along with the recording."

"I have an old recording of Benny Goodman playing it."

"Do you mean dance-band Benny Goodman?" she asked.

Lewis laughed, "One and the same guy. You've got quite a background in American music."

"Well." She shrugged. "What we could get ahold of in Hun . . . in Austria."

Lewis noted the slip. Was Hungary somewhere hidden in her past?

"Do you miss Austria?" he asked.

She stopped near the last landing of the marble stairway and stared up at him. "Miss Austria?" for a moment she seemed flustered, then she said, "I am so busy learning to enjoy America that I rarely think about Austria."

He accepted that, for the moment. "Let's try the Mexican restaurant in the next block."

During lunch, they poured over her Mozart find, and his library copies of old blues artists' recordings, Robert Johnson and Muddy Waters.

The second time they met on purpose in her office and practice studio, to play through the score of the Mozart, and then to have some fun with sight reading recent compositions for violin and orchestra. Lewis's mother had taught him how to reduce a whole orchestra score to piano as he read it. As they played along, Lewis thought with sadness about his mother's actions of last summer, but said a prayer of thanks for her early insistence on this skill. It brought him this hour and a half of closeness and enjoyment with Rebecca.

*　*

Harald Steinmetz persisted. A week after the first visit to her apartment, he invited her to the opera and Abe talked her into accepting.

"So, you are in public, in a crowd – what could happen?"

Abe worried about her so much, that she decided to practice a wider social life.

Abe even had offered to take care of Benjamin at their home, so she could go.

She planned with Harald to meet him at the opera house. Instead, Harald came to her door, coat in hand.

Startled, she twisted the handle on her door, but it was already locked, so she said, "We'll take the bus. Much easier than parking."

He whipped the hat off his longish brown hair as his eyes widened with appreciation.

"Here, Rebecca, flowers from my hotel's courtyard garden. Could we put them in water? I want you to remember a pleasant evening when you see them tomorrow."

Being ready and out in the hall, she intended to keep her distance from him, or any other gentleman.

"No," she said. "I will wear them on my coat."

Pansies? Most men brought or sent her roses, in numbers varying according to what they'd read about the symbolism of such things. Pansies seemed to bring more of the giver with them. Maybe she had underestimated him.

"Let's go." She said. "Curtain time is in twenty minutes."

At the opera, Harald kept his distance and was a charming companion. Once during a tender moment in the story, he stole a glance at her. Otherwise, there was no hint of unwanted affection from him.

The dessert they shared afterward was okay. He sat on the far side of the table and told stories about the lives of contemporary composers. They seemed every bit as colorful and unpredictable as their predecessors.

When the bus pulled up near her apartment, he got off with her to walk to his car. "Rebecca, I don't want you walking into your apartment building by yourself. I'll walk you to your door and then leave. You won't have to push me out or anything. Promise."

She frowned. "I've returned at night many times without mishap. Honestly."

"I'm sure you have, but if something happened to you tonight, I would never forgive myself."

As Rebecca unlocked her apartment door, Harald shrugged his shoulders, "Thanks for indulging me. Good night, Rebecca."

Relieved that he really did mean to leave, she smiled, "Good night, Harald. Thank you for the evening, and for worrying."

He bowed with grave ceremony and turned to walk down the hall. She opened the door, flicked on the lights and gasped.

Everything in her apartment had been overturned, pulled apart, thrown down.

She heard Harald running back to her doorway, but could pay no more attention to him. She ran quickly to her violin case. Nothing missing or broken, just opened and dumped. Her old records and disks were here, the players shoved around but not unplugged. She stood, leaning on the piano to breathe a moment and then started back to Benjamin's room. Thank God he was staying the night with

Abe and Miriam. Maybe she could get all this cleaned up before morning, so he wouldn't need to know.

She didn't want to let any other thought intrude – thoughts of who and how, and why?

*   *

Harald Steinmetz stood silently. He watched her progress around the room, noting what she checked. She was very shaken. He followed her into Benjamin's bedroom.

His men had destroyed this room. The sheets and blankets had been torn from the bed. As she approached it, Harald saw that the mattress had a long gash down the middle.

The sight of that slash broke her already shredded selfcontrol. She cried out and hit at the wall of the bedroom. "Damn it. This will stop." She yelled.

"Is that your son's bed? What are they trying to tell you? What is it they've taken, Rebecca?" He watched her eyes, holding out his arms, waiting for her to cry on his shoulder.

Instead, she hissed at the mess. "I can't tell what's missing. But who could know for days?" She pushed past him. "I must clean all this up before Benjamin comes home. I don't want him frightened." She began picking up blocks and papers from the child's floor.

Harald got down beside her. "Rebecca, let's do this systematically. Start with the most valuable things, check where they are and then clean that area. Let me help you."

"No Harald. I need to do this myself. Thank you, but I must be alone now."

"Rebecca, this is overwhelming. Don't tackle this all alone."

"Harald, please! Being with people now is overwhelming. Leave me alone. I need to be by myself."

"It's not safe. Let me . . ."

Rebecca's body shook as she faced him. "They have whatever they came for. Go. I insist!"

He watched her trembling anger, then let out a sigh. "All right. I go. Lock the door and call me if you get too . . . if you need anything. Get me at night if you need me."

He knew she wouldn't call the police, and he certainly didn't suggest it. She would be afraid to answer all their questions. He left her to pick up the pieces of her shattered life.

*   *

Sitting in his car while her apartment lights stayed on, Steinmetz took deep breaths. She didn't look for anything, but checked the child's room and the violin. The concerti are not in her apartment. What did she say about 'most fragile music'? She admitted to fragile music without any thought to hide that she had it. I'm certain she meant the music of Raphael Atemvoll, even though she denies her relationship to him.

A startling thought occurred to him. She doesn't know she has them. They are there. They have to be there. Count Czigler's mother screamed at him while my father tortured him. "Tell him and save yourself." My father wrote her exact words. "You gave them to somebody. Tell him."

And after the count and his mother died. My father followed the trail . . . Batislav and Annensky and the child Raphael. The war hid them. The invasions of the Soviets hid them.

Not in Switzerland, as Madam Czigler guessed with her dying efforts to save her son. Not in Switzerland at all.

I finally found them in Hungary. And I know that Raphael Atemvoll doesn't have them anymore. He sent her music for her birthday twice, so they are there, but she does not know it. I am close to them. I can feel it. So close . . .

It was at that moment Harald remembered the empty envelope addressed to Tobias Kossuth. The treasure had once been in that envelope. But the envelope is opened, so where?

Count Czigler, Batislav, Atemvoll, Zolesku. It was the only possible trail of ownership.

CHAPTER FOURTEEN

As soon as Harald left, Rebecca lifted the phone and called Abe and Miriam. While Miriam put Benji to bed at her home, Abe came right over with a locksmith to change the lock on her door. That accomplished, she paid the locksmith, let him go back to his home.

And then Abe stared at Rebecca. "Steinmetz never suggested calling the police?" Abe asked.

"No."

"As if he knew that was out of bounds?" Abe said.

"How could he know that?"

"Perhaps," Abe said, "it's just that where he lives, police are not to be trusted."

"I thought he lived in Vienna," she said.

"But there is no way he could know you can't go to the police, is there?"

"I've read music with him once and attended a concert with him," she said. "He knows nothing."

"Let us see what they took," Abe said, "And then I want to hire the people who help clean our home for parties.

They began picking up the mess. As she straightened the music on the piano, Rebecca thought of the Bach someone believed she had.

How could anyone imagine such valuable music came to Raphael Atemvoll? People have searched for the Bach concerti for two hundred years.

But, please God, where is Raphael?

* *

Later, Abe called in the Bridge City Home Cleaning crew to help restore the apartment. He wanted Rebecca to come live with them, but she refused.

"I can't continue to live with fear, Abe. Living with Uncle Tobias didn't keep me safe, and it made Tobias a target as well."

"But Benji . . ."

"Yes," she said, "can we work out a way to keep Benji with someone all the time?"

"I want to be sure that happens, starting yesterday," Abe said. "While you get out your calendar to plan for Benji, I'm going to install this alarm system."

"Where did that come from?" she asked.

Abe studied the box, as if it held the answer, "Um . . . it came from Home Depot." He hauled out his screw driver and drill and set to work.

* *

Rebecca had to admit that after the nightmare of her weekend, she anticipated a healing contact this Monday morning at ten o'clock. At that fresh hour, she crossed the campus from teaching a class in one of the annex houses toward her next student in the music building. On the way, every morning of the term, she met a longlegged physics professor whose bright green eyes were undeniably laughing. His sandy brown hair danced about his face as he strode toward her. His thick eyebrows rose in greeting as he neared. His lips pursed in an effort to contain his mirth. At the last moment he would tip a nonexistent cap at her and say "Mornin' Becca." His smile would flash forth at last, his uncontrollable warm gaze would sweep over her, his legs would carry him past and she would be left grinning foolishly, walking slightly above the grass, happy to have seen the interest and fun in his eyes again.

* *

Lewis thanked the registrar's office for having the sense to put him in contact with Dick Street. Not only was Dick a challenge to keep up with, mentally, but, because his wheel chair couldn't negotiate the stairs in the physics building, he had to be tutored in the cafeteria. This exciting responsibility took Lewis across campus every morning at nine o'clock.

And brought Lewis back across campus at ten o'clock, in time to cross paths with the most distracting woman. Lewis loved to watch her walk toward him, her graceful sleeves and skirts flowing about her in the wind, clutching at her body in ways that would have embarrassed her, had she known. Her modesty was legendary on campus. The wind in the quadrangle knew nothing about modesty.

On most mornings, as he walked toward her, he sent the wind out before him, asking it to play with her hair, caress her throat, throw itself against her slender legs. And when the wind had given him about fifty yards worth of pleasure, he would draw near, see the bright amber of the morning light in her dark eyes and hear the near perfect English of her "Good morning to you, Levy".

* *

This Monday morning, he appeared around the corner of the Commons as usual, but she noticed immediately that the swing of his legs was not so free, his eyes not so bright. When he neared, the raise of his eyebrows was less a greeting, more a question. His pursed lips held back not mirth but concern. He tipped his hat and said "Mornin' Becca?"

"Good morning to you, Levy?" He passed on. She walked stolidly on the grass, not relieved of the weekend's fear and bad memories.

"Becca?"

She turned and saw him running back toward her. He crossed the quadrangle in a few smooth strides. He was always more graceful than she thought a tall man could be.

"Rebecca," he took her arm and walked toward her original destination. "Rebecca, I can be late to class this morning since it's a lab and the students know what to do. May I ask about a plan I'd like to work on with you?"

"Yes. What plan, Levy?" His hand on her arm was warm.

"I'd like to plan a series of lectures for the physics and music students on the physics of sound production, harmony as it relates to the physical properties of vibration, acoustics . . . that sort of thing. Would you work on it with me? make it a joint lecture?"

"When would we do these lectures?"

"In February we could do the first one between your recital series in January and the symphony concert in March. Others we could space out over the next term."

Her brows lifted in quick surprise. Then she smiled up at him. "Interesting. Of course, we'd need to work up an outline . . ."

"Great idea. How about in your office after classes?"

"Let's see," she frowned slightly. "I attend a concert tonight. How about Tuesday or Wednesday?"

"Fine. Either . . . or both if we need both . . ."

"Tuesday then, at five, for an hour. I must get Benjamin from Miriam's by six-thirty. By the way, how did you know my concert schedule?"

"Abraham. He also told me about your breakin last weekend. I'm sorry, Becca."

She tried to keep her voice light and unconcerned. "It is all cleaned up now and nothing seems to be missing. Thank you, Levy. Abraham put in an alarm system Sunday night. I think I am well guarded."

She didn't want to be the gloomy victim type for this man. She'd shown him too much of that dark side of her life already.

*   *

Lewis noted the contrast between her devil-may-care words and the tremor in her arm. Ignoring her fear, he pretended to accept her lack of worry. He didn't tell her that he'd bought the alarm system and given it to Abraham with express orders not to mention his name.

She also didn't need to know that he still made a trip past her apartment each night, on the lookout for the balding man or the Impala. She wouldn't recognize Lewis' small sports car, only the van he'd had at the airport.

It embarrassed him to have been nearby when Steinmetz had steered her inside after their date last Saturday night. He wasn't spying on her social life, just checking on her safety. He had also seen Steinmetz come out and sit in his car for a few minutes. Later, Lewis had heard from Abe that Steinmetz tried to help her with cleanup, but she had rebuffed his help.

This morning, he was reluctant to close their talk on such a sinister topic, so he added, "I look forward to hashing out the lecture series with you, tomorrow."

"Hashing?"

"Discussing."

"Ah," she laughed. "I'm glad you suggested it, Levy."

He grinned and shrugged, then glanced up at the gothic portico they were approaching. "You're just about on time for the next class. See you tomorrow." Reluctantly, Lewis let go of her arm.

*   *

Bemused, Rebecca entered the music building and started up the stairs to her classroom. She turned back one last time to watch him run to his class. Through the glass doors, she was treated to the delightful sight of a grown man leaping in air and clicking his heels together as he ran. She laughed with pleasure at his expression of how they both suddenly felt. Lewis's lecture idea was a good one, but his ulterior motive was even better.

CHAPTER FIFTEEN

Over the next days, Lewis searched for more ways to protect her and Benjamin, more ways to be with them much of the time. He got his next bright idea while not working on his research project. He was tiltback, nearly tip-over-top in his swivel chair, hands behind his head, eyes closed, dreaming about her. This past week they'd worked two times on their proposed lecture series.

She had been brilliant with suggestions about how to help students understand the over-tone series.

Plus, it was nice close quarters in her office – close enough to leave him wanting, wondering. He knew from his friend Abe that they were all being more careful that Benjamin was never alone. Perhaps he could offer to help with his childcare.

But she didn't yet know him well enough for that. So, discard. Next idea!

Ahha!

His chair came upright as his feet hit the floor. He searched for a phone number. Finding the telephone itself was not so easy. He closed several physics manuscripts until he unearthed the battered instrument. A quick call and within minutes, he had the information he sought.

He rose swiftly, donned his worn wool jacket, and dashed out the door, leaving his swivel chair bobbing.

At the desk of the River Place Athletic Club, he bought a family membership for Rebecca and Benjamin Gregory, and then he bought a membership for himself. When the membership cards had been duly encased in plastic, he returned to his office in the physics building. There, he ripped the beginnings of what ought to have been a journal article on fuel efficiency out of his typewriter and began a letter on his `Reed College' letterhead.

Dear Rebecca,

I'm hoping you will accept this membership for you and Benjamin in the River Place Athletic Club, the swimming facility across the street from your apartment. I hope you will find the swimming at River Place relaxing after a day of work.

I look forward to hearing that young Benjamin has learned to swim, so that he can be safe near the rivers and oceans of Oregon.

Please let me know if there is any other way, I can be of help to you in your adjustment to Portland and to Reed College.

Sincerely,

Lewis James

Lewis noticed the clock – nearly time for his next class. Taking his letter out into the hall, he read it over to himself as he walked toward the office department. Oblivious of all but his own satisfaction, he nearly stumbled over Dick Street's wheelchair.

"Professor," said Dick. "I didn't know you liked to help people with their adjustment to Portland."

Startled, Lewis looked at his letter to see if the words showed through the back side.

Dick laughed and leaned as far forward as his brace would let him. "Careful what you say," he whispered. "Dick Street reads lips." He wiggled his cherubic blond eyebrows and continued, "But, Dick Street also keeps secrets."

Lewis leaned down and whispered back. "Thus does Dick Street get straight A's."

Dick's hearty laugh rang out. "I wish. See you in class."

Lewis wended his way a little more carefully toward the office where in pen, he added his office location and his home and cell phone numbers to the letter. He enclosed the letter along with Rebecca's and Benjamin's membership cards in a licked and stamped envelope, plopped the missal in the outgoing mailbox of the physics department and went to his next lecture feeling very happy with his gift.

His students knew something distracted him as soon as he launched into a lecture about the stars in a class on wave theory.

*   *

On the second Monday morning after he'd mailed the membership, Rebecca called Lewis at his home before he left for school.

"Benjamin and I want to thank you for the swimming membership."

"My pleasure," he said, fiddling nervously with his car keys.

"Could you join us for a swim this afternoon at 5:15 after Benji's class? There is free swim time until 6:30 p.m."

His key hand stopped moving in mid-air. "I . . . I'd be delighted Maybe, after, maybe we could go somewhere for dinner." He sounded like such a dolt.

"That would be great fun. We'll see you at the pool."

Lewis whistled as he gathered his trunks from the `not used often drawer' of his dresser. He'd neglected swimming since he left Belfast for graduate studies, and he'd nearly forgotten how exhilarating it'd been to dive in the River Lagan near his home. At the last minute, he hauled his camping refrigerator out of the basement and put it in the car trunk.

After giving several extremely lively lectures and one pop quiz, (when he was entirely out of patience with the slow clock), Lewis met with his tutorial students for an hour and then hightailed it out to the car. A quick stop at the grocery store cost him fifteen minutes. He put the perishables and a bag of ice in his camp refrigerator.

He swung into the club parking lot near Rebecca's apartment at five o'clock on the nose. Cautiously he approached the front desk. Seeing no Rebecca or Benjamin, he handed the clerk his own membership card.

It didn't take him long to change and arrive poolside with a blue towel slung nonchalantly over his shoulders. He entered a large pool area enclosed in an arched dome of glass. There were three pools – a hot tub big enough for eight or ten people, a shallow children's pool about twenty feet square and a lap pool with eight lanes. Besides himself and the lifeguard, there were five lap swimmers and a small class of mothers and babies just leaving the shallow pool.

He stopped at the shallow end of the lap pool, watching Rebecca give her son a ride down the length. Benjamin held onto her shoulders and kicked his sturdy legs to help propel them to the other end. When they turned around to swim back toward the shallow end, Benjamin saw Lewis standing at the head of their lane.

"Mama! It's Lewis! Hi Lewis! See me swimming? Mama, can Lewis swim with us? He could give me a ride sometimes, too."

*   *

Rebecca looked up and felt the warmth of friendship in her heart as she focused on Lewis' smiling face. For the first time, she was aware that the broad shoulders inside his tweed jacket were his own and not the tailor's, and she realized he must do more than sit in a physics lab all the time.

As they neared the shallow end, Rebecca stood up. Smiling and disentangling herself from Benjamin's tense grip on her shoulders, she pulled him around one hip.

"Hello, Levy. I'm glad you were able to come." she said.

Benjamin let go of her arms to wade to the edge close to Lewis before climbing out of the pool and wrapping his arms around Lewis's leg.

*   *

Now that he stood so close to her, Lewis felt intensely like a voyeur. In the pit of his stomach was a knot of guilt. Rebecca in a swimming suit was more beautiful than his imagination. Her Lycra suit was a dark rust color, fitting her smoothly from firm hips to slender waist and on up over full breasts to a turtleneck halter collar. The parabolic curve of the back didn't even swoop so far down as her waist.

She rose out of the water on the ladder. He tried, but could not take his gaze off of her as she approached him. Yes, her slender arms and back did have the same rosy hue as her cheeks. And her legs were long, and strong – the legs of a soccer player. The nearer she came, the more out of place he felt.

"Levy," she said, "You're the only other Reed faculty member that I recognize here. If there are those I should know, would you be sure to tell me their names? "

"Of course, Rebecca." Lewis picked up Benjamin to distract himself from the sight of her. "I haven't seen any other faculty here. Not many live close to this pool."

"Is your home nearby?" She shook the water out of her thick dark hair.

"My house is just at the other end of the Hawthorne Bridge. Very convenient."

Lewis thanked his cleverness in finding a place where the other young faculty members could not see the charming sight of this woman dripping wet, with auburn tendrils forming a damp frame for her face. He knew that he'd better get in the pool very soon or everyone in the room would know just how deeply that sight affected him.

Benjamin had become his shield and his excuse. "Well, young swimmer, you're shivering. Would you like to do a few turns in the shallow pool with me so that your mother can swim some laps?"

"Sure, Lewis! Can I jump to you?"

"If that's all right with your mother."

*   *

They both turned questioning eyes to her and for the second time since they had met, she was struck with a feeling that the eyebrows of Lewis James were operated by the same clever puppeteer as the eyebrows of her son.

She laughed at them both and said, "You may jump Benjamin, if Levy wants to catch."

Benjamin grinned and race-walked Lewis to the children's pool. Rebecca watched Benjamin jump and knew, from the abandon with which he leapt, that her son trusted this man.

*   *

Lewis could see the admiring eyes of everyone at the pool follow her fluid motions. Only her son took her grace for granted.

But, Lewis admitted, Benjamin got the best part of her. He got her clear answers to important questions. He got her unconditional love and he got her whole-heart laughter when he said something funny.

Benjamin left Lewis little opportunity to watch Rebecca swim as he claimed the attention of his favorite man in the world.

"Lewis, see me jump up and down in the water?"

"I sure do young man. Let's play a game. It's called ring around the rosy."

"I know that one! Grandma Miriam plays it, too."

"Well, bless her heart. And does she fall down at the end with you?"

"Oh, no! She says that she'll do that when I'm big enough to pick her up. I think her legs are not exercised enough."

"Well, that may be the reason, all right. I can pick myself up again, however. So, we can both fall down. We hold hands and pick each other up by pushing our feet on the bottom of the pool. Ready?"

"Ready."

The first time Lewis came up, he saw dry curls on Benjamin's head and knew that the boy was afraid to get his face in the water.

"That was a good practice session, Benji. Now, when we play the game, the fellow who has all of his hair dripping wet, even on top . . ." he put Benjamin's hand up to feel his dry hair," that fellow wins the game."

Benjamin evidently had a streak of competitiveness. The next time they came up, his hair was very wet. He put his hands up to check the top and grinned at Lewis.

"I win! I'm all wet!"

"You sure are, Benji! Good job!"

"But Lewis! You're all wet too!"

"Yes? Well then, I guess we both win."

"Two can win a game?"

"Sure. There are lots of games where everybody wins. Does your mother ever play music with other people?"

"Oh, yeah. She plays lots of duets with Gabriel."

"Are they both having a good time?"

"Sure! They play a lot. When they are playing, Gabriel looks happy. Lots of other times, when they just talk, he looks sort of angry or sad . . . yeah, sad."

Lewis ached to ask more about this Gabriel, but he didn't want to take unfair advantage of a child. So, he moved back on topics. "Well, playing music is a game where everybody wins, isn't it?"

Benjamin's eyebrows knit together, then shot up. "Oh! It's a game where you win if you're having fun. Can we play `ring around the rosy' again?"

They played, falling down into the water many times before Benjamin got tired of the game. "Lewis, I need to go to the bathroom. I'll go get Mama."

"I can go with you, if you want."

"Can I go in the men's room? I've never been in the men's room."

Lewis smiled, anticipating the interesting conversation that Benjamin's curiosity would generate in this new experience. "Sure, Benji. We'll do that."

Lewis gave Benjamin a piggyback ride to the ladder. He turned to call to Rebecca.

"We're just going to the restroom, Becca. Back in two minutes."

She smiled at them and nodded. They both climbed up and began walking out of the pool area.

*   *

Rebecca kept an eye on their fun whenever she swam toward them. She was unsure about her relationship with Lewis, if that was what one called it. He amused her . . . no . . . it was more than that. She felt relaxed and happy with him. She liked the attention he paid to Benjamin.

She glanced back and smiled at them, heard Lewis voice, but didn't understand what he was saying. She turned the corner for what, she'd decided would be her last lap, and saw the two of them rise out of the pool and go hand in hand toward the dressing rooms.

A cold knife of fear cut through her heart. She swam to the side of the pool and tried to pull herself out. Panic turned her arms to soft lead. She tried again, floundered on the side and rose, running blindly, calling Benjamin's name.

CHAPTER SIXTEEN

Lewis and Benjamin were near the door to the men's room when they heard her. Benjamin turned toward her with a puzzled look. Lewis held Benjamin's hand and put his other hand out to slow her as she came toward him. She evaded his grasp and reached for her son, saying his name over and over.

"Mama, what hurt you?" The boy cried and wrapped his arms around her neck as she knelt next to him.

"Becca, what is it?" Lewis asked.

She saw no monster in Lewis's face, only concern. Her free hand covered her face as she tried to gather her flying thoughts.

At last, she was able to gasp out one word. "Where?"

"Rebecca, I thought you heard me tell you."

"I need to pee," Benjamin cried. "Lewis said it to you."

"One of us better take him soon."

"Oh Levy!" She looked at him over Benjamin's shoulder. "I'm – forgive me."

"Mama, can I go in the men's?"

Lewis whispered, "I'm sorry we didn't make sure you knew where we were going, Becca."

Benjamin stood there crying. "I gotta go," he whimpered.

Rebecca offered Benjamin's hand to Lewis.

Lewis said, "We'll be back in a minute. When we come back, I want to talk to you while Benjamin plays."

"Yes, Levy."

* *

He watched her get in the hot tub as he and Benji hurried to the bathroom.

On the way down the hall, Lewis spoke to the pensive little boy. "We'll wash the pee from your suit while we're in the bathroom. Won't take a minute."

"What's the matter with Mommy?" Benji sniffled.

"Mommy's all right now. She was afraid we might get lost. But, we'll be back to her in no time."

Benjamin giggled. "She didn't think you would get lost, Lewis. You're a grown up. She thought I was going to the ladies' room and wouldn't find you again."

"Maybe that's it all right, son."

Lewis hurried Benjamin into the toilet, then into the shower to rinse his trunks. On the way back, he explained about the funny toilets. At the pool side, he noticed that the other lap swimmers were toweling off and leaving. He was grateful to have a few minutes with Rebecca alone before any new group might arrive.

He waved to Rebecca and got down a swim bubble for Benjamin, showing him how the inflated bubble would help him float and play in the water. Benjamin enjoyed his new freedom in the children's shallow pool, as Lewis stepped to the hot tub, a few feet away.

"May I join you, young lady?" he asked Rebecca in an old man's voice. His attempt at humor seemed to overcome her embarrassment. She laughed as he came down the steps to join her.

"Rebecca, I should have guessed taking Benjamin out of your sight would frighten you. Miriam told me about the kidnap attempts."

She looked away from his probing gaze and whispered. "I'm sorry Levy."

He shook his head. "'Sorry', I accept, but please trust me all the way. What do they want?"

*   *

She began to relax. The swirling water encouraged her. She knew she could trust him as Benjamin did, yet her story was difficult to tell.

"Someone believes I have valuable music, very valuable."

"You mean something original? Old?"

"Bach. Lost violin concerti." She glanced up to see his eyes widen and his brows pinch.

"Wow!"

She nodded. "Wow, yes. But impossible."

"But those – there were three missing, right?"

"Yes. That's what some people believe. Though at least one piano concerto might have originally been for violin and piano."

"They think you have original manuscripts?"

"Yes."

"They've been gone for two hundred . . . you don't have them. You've been looking."

"I've catalogued everything Raphael sent me. None of it is even in Bach's handwriting. It is all Raphael and his teacher, Anton Batislav, and other pieces he used for teaching."

"Raphael Atemvoll?"

"Yes. These gangsters believe he gave them to me."

"Why?

"It makes no sense. Raphael came to Hun . . . to my country from Russia, not Germany, so why on earth would anyone think he might have them?"

"Rebecca," Lewis said, "That's the second time you have almost told me you are from Hungary and not Austria. Why hide the truth?"

She closed her eyes, floating back to another time, a murkier water. She and Uncle Tobias were swimming in the night. The Neusiedler See in spring was a swampy wetland, warm and debilitating.

But the Hungarian patrols made the swim the only way to escape without alerting the gangsters that she was still alive. She prayed as she changed strokes, "Please, let the boat be there. This sickness comes so often. God, let me have strength for this. I can't drown. Tobias will go down with me."

*   *

She opened her eyes. Aware of Lewis' worried gaze, she tried to explain. "I couldn't even write to them. They would be in danger if anyone knew the truth."

"Rebecca, tell me all of it."

They watched Benjamin bobbing with a floating toy, throwing it and swimming after it. Lewis touched her hand. "Now, Rebecca. Tell me now, please."

She began, groping for where to start. "Someone has been breaking into my apartments and studio. In New York, they broke into my uncle's home and the home of my accompanist, Gabriel. The other night, while I was at a concert with Professor Steinmetz, someone got into my new apartment and knocked all my books and music off the shelves. They never steal anything, just throw things around. But what scares me the most is their threat to kidnap Benjamin They slashed his mattress."

Lewis closed his eyes. "Damn."

"Abraham bought a new one for him, but …"

"But the message is clear…" he finished her thought. "Miriam said there were two attempts to take him in New York."

She pulled back. "Miriam told you?"

"Miriam and Abe have known me for many years. They know I would do nothing to hurt you."

"I trust them," she said slowly.

"Good," he said. "Now, please tell me about Benji."

At last she said, "The first attempt was early last August. We were together in the subway station, coming home from the zoo when a man tried to grab Benjamin from my Uncle Tobias. They almost ripped him in two, but I was able to jump on the kidnapper as they struggled. Tobias picked Benjamin up and we ran two miles to the apartment, carrying him."

Lewis said, "I think Benjamin remembers that time. In fact, at the airport, he woke up and realized that I wasn't Uncle Tobias because I didn't have a beard that was sweaty from running."

She shivered. "I wish he could forget the pain and fear. He still wakes with the dreams."

Lewis nodded. "When was the second attempt?"

"The next week, just two days before our flight here. A stranger entered our apartment play yard. He offered to show Benjamin an electric train. Benji refused to go with him, but the man insisted. One of the other children came to get me. I ran out. The man dropped Benji's hand and ran."

"What did that man look like?"

"I was never close enough to see him, but the children said that he had curly hair and was taller than I am. He wasn't the same man who had tried to take him in the subway."

"Would Benji recognize him?"

She glanced at Benjamin again. "Yes. He has described him to me many times. Tall, curled hair, brown suit, blue shirt." She stopped.

"Hard to convict. Tall to children. How about to you?"

She glanced at him, and he saw the irony.

"Okay tall to children and small violinists. But the curly hair would help."

"Yes, it would."

Rebecca silently watched her son at play. Her throat felt tight.

*   *

Lewis wanted to put his arms around her, to protect her, but he dared not touch her. He settled for lifting the warm water in his hands and pouring it over her shoulders. She turned to him with a grateful look.

"You're more patient than any man should have to be. Please, forgive . . ."

He touched her lips with a finger to stop her. "No forgiving because there is no guilt. Yes, I want to know you better, but you have built a fence around yourself for a reason. When you decide to put a gate in the fence, I hope you'll invite me in. I am a patient man." A gleam of humor entered his eyes, "Frustrated, but oh, so patient."

She could nearly feel the touch of his hands in the sensual embrace of his gaze. For the first time since that night long ago, she found she did not shrink from the thought of a man's desire for her. It was this man, this tousled, laughing, strong and patient man who could make her want again.

*   *

Her almost imperceptible movement toward him brought his already taut senses to a high pitch. His hands caught her waist, finding smooth warmth in her supple body. Her eyes grew wide with what he thought was fear. He forced himself to draw away.

*   *

For the first time in almost six years, Rebecca grew aware of wanting more from a man than he had given her. When his hands left her waist, she felt isolated and imprisoned.

His voice was rough when he spoke again. "Let's go get our little one – your son." He looked apprehensively at Rebecca. "Would you let me take the two of you to dinner at my home after we're dressed?"

Rebecca felt gratitude for his offer to stay with them a little longer. Her apartment was going to feel very modern and cold tonight. "Is your home appropriate for a wiggly five-year-old?"

"Oh, yes." His teasing twinkle was back. "There's lots of space for him to play when he finishes his meal before we do."

"You certainly do know little ones," she said. "How old were you when your youngest brother or sister was Benjamin's age?"

"Let's see," he began figuring as he lifted himself up to sit on the side of the pool. "I guess I was fifteen when Dicken was born, so I was twenty when he was Benji's age. By that time, I was finishing up my undergraduate degree in Cambridge, but I hitched my way home, every saint's day it seemed like, to celebrate one sibling or another."

He reached down absently, intending to help her up. Clearly, his thoughts were still on his family. "Baby Dicken was a dark little fellow, always questioning the statusquo – asking why we couldn't visit his friends down the road who were not Protestant. Why did we have to be wary of neighbors who followed the Church of Rome? Why couldn't we just talk to each other?"

Lewis' hands held Rebecca's upper arms, lifting her as if she were weightless. He looked at her as he brought her up toward him. Suddenly, thoughts of Dicken vanished. He could see only her glistening skin, her accepting eyes, her soft, full mouth.

All his pent-up desire became a flame that burned in his kiss. His arms held her suspended half out of the water before him as his mouth tasted the yielding sweetness of her tentative acceptance.

He was suddenly brought back from passion by a small square hand on his shoulder.

"Mama's going to fall back in, Lewis." His voice tensed with worry.

Lewis pulled away, looking at Rebecca for a sign that she might be pulling back inside her gate. Her face flushed with that beautiful peach color he'd first seen when they bumped heads in the airport. He finished lifting her out of the water, seating her next to him, carefully not leaving his arm around her.

He turned to Benjamin, "No, son. Mommy is just coming out. She'll be safe. You'll see. Now, let's all get dressed and go to dinner. What do you say, my swimming friend?"

"Can we, Mama? Can we?" Benjamin clamped his arms around his mother's shoulders, his wet little legs danced in delight and pushed his mother toward the water.

Lewis' hand on his back stopped the dance. "Watch it, little man. It's you who will drop your mother in the water if you keep up this dancing."

Rebecca had the embarrassment of their kiss kicked out of her by her excited son. She hugged him, laughing, "Yes, Benjamin, you get to have dinner with Levy."

Lewis stood, picked Benjamin up and reached a hand down for Rebecca, and became gratified at how willingly she accepted that hand. He felt the heat rise in him as the delicate softness of her fingers lay in his rough palm.

*   *

Rebecca was unused to the warmth of her body's response to his kiss. The protection of his hand uncovered a desire for the protection of his arms. She surprised herself.

If she began to give to him, would she be able to follow through as far as he wanted to take her? If she began and could not finish, how could that be fair to him? How would she know?

CHAPTER SEVENTEEN

Rebecca sat in the sauna with Benjamin. She knew that Lewis would be pacing the lobby before she could get them both dressed, but she needed the sauna to help clear her thoughts. She had wanted his kiss, wanted it more than she thought would ever again be possible.

No one had made her feel this way since those nights in the jail. And in the jail, only Zoltan had made her feel human – Zoltan and his request that she live freely in his stead. As soon as they yanked him out of her cell, she knew Zoltan's life was forfeit. Yet, his care in the face of evil sustained her. Soon after she'd been turned out of the prison, there had been Benjamin to think about.

And suddenly, Levy's care gave her new, wider focus. She wanted to be with him, wanted Benji to be with him, but she did not want to hurt him.

How will I know?

And what if he knew about those nights in prison? Would he still want me when he can imagine the ugliness of it all?

Rebecca noticed Benjamin's restlessness and realized that she'd stayed too long in the sauna. She put a hand on his wet shoulder, "Let's go shower, little one. Lewis will be waiting for us."

*   *

Lewis paced the lobby floor, fairly certain that he was out of the dressing rooms before Rebecca could have gotten Benjamin dressed. Yet, her reaction to his kiss left him uncertain. She might just throw on her clothes and bolt for home. Her apartment was directly across the street.

He hoped his kiss had not spooked her. How could he ever begin to know the parameters of her fear? He began thinking back to the times she'd gone ashen, and he realized that each time, he had come close, physically, or been too probing in his questions. And now, to kiss her! Stupid idiot!

She was so intelligent, such a wonderful teacher – to Benjamin, and also to her music students. He could see that intelligence and care in the way she planned their lectures about physics and music. He loved listening to her explanations to Benjamin's questions.

And he saw that she tried to shield Benji from her fears, giving him safety without smothering.

Until some nut like Lewis tried to walk off to the bathroom with the boy. Then, then, the fear surfaced.

However, there was also the underlying feeling that she would shatter if touched, or if the wrong innocent remark were made. Lewis was sure Abraham Friedenberg and his wife knew why. As his good friends, they might even tell him. But he believed he should wait until she told him. If she were able to talk about it, perhaps she'd be better able to accept his help.

But where was she now? In the dressing room? Or gone?

His relief must have been visible to Rebecca when she and Benjamin came out of the dressing room. She crossed the lobby quickly, greeting him with a hand on his arm, a gesture which startled him.

"I am sorry to be so long, Levy. I needed to sit in sauna and think a little. I didn't mean to make you so worry."

He enjoyed one of her rare mistakes in English and put his hand over hers as they walked toward the door. "Rebecca, I am sorry for what I ..."

"It was not you, Levy. It was of my own mind."

Benjamin grabbed Lewis' coat. "Lewis? Are we still going to dinner?"

"Yes, indeed, my dear sir. Hold my hand while we cross the parking lot."

*   *

They stopped in front of a large old home with a wide veranda across the front, a play space for Portland's rainy days.

"Is this the restaurant?" piped Benjamin from the back seat. "Look at the windows, Mama. They have pictures."

Rebecca sat in the front seat, not surprised that his home seemed so open and welcoming. She regretted that she could not be as solid and warm for him.

"Yes," Lewis said to Benjamin. "This is the restaurant and the chef has just arrived. Do you want to help him make dinner?"

"Sure!"

Lewis looked at Rebecca, "Rebecca, I want you and Benjamin to know my home and feel safe here. I want this dinner to be a time of quiet and freedom to roam for Benjamin."

Rebecca looked at her hands, smoothed her skirt and bit her lower lip. When she spoke, her voice was almost imperceptible. "Levy, thank you for asking us."

"It will be fine, I promise you."

Her shoulders straightened. Her face became a brave mask, put on for both Lewis' and Benjamin's sake.

He leaned a little toward her. "Believe me. You are not a lamb and I am not a lion."

Her mask fell, the look she gave him was a mixture of apology and selfreproach. When he raised one questioning eyebrow, she gave him the laugh he was angling for. "All right, Levy, let's go in, as long as you let me help cook, too."

"That's what I like to hear – offers of assistance." Lewis reached across Rebecca, winked mischievously at her as he unlocked her door and then straightened up, pleased at the warmth in her eyes. She was beginning to come out all right. It was about time. Her jasmine fragrance was driving him wild.

Once in the house, Lewis let his four-year-old Beagle out of his "home" to play with Benjamin.

"What's his name?" Benji asked as the dog pounced up and down with a tennis ball in his mouth.

"Burford," Lewis said.

Both Rebecca and Benjamin stared at him.

"Why?" Rebecca asked. Staring at the short-legged bundle of energy.

"Because that's what my brothers wanted to name him when they came to visit me two years ago. Never did find out why. Made 'em laugh, so it stuck."

Benjamin shrugged and grabbed the tennis ball. "Come on, Burf," he called as he ran out the back door to the fenced yard.

In the big oak-paneled kitchen, Lewis unloaded his groceries while Rebecca watched Benji out the window over the sink.

He asked Rebecca, "Do you know how to cook salmon?"

"I know how to set the table and boil the potatoes."

"Do you mean to tell me that the alltalented Rebecca Gregory does not know how to cook?"

"My mother said she would rather listen to me practice than try to teach me to cook."

"Well, it's about time that you learned to enjoy the making of food. It's man and woman's most basic need."

"Is it really?"

Lewis looked at her askance, not sure in this case exactly to what 'it' referred. He took the safe choice. "Yes, it is about time. Cooking can be a good way to relax."

Outside, they heard Burford howl as if he'd been stuck. They ran out to find both the dog and Benjamin both set up a howling racket. They sounded exactly like two unhappy dogs.

"What's up?" Lewis asked.

"Ball's in the neighbor's yard," Benjamin said. ""Ah-ooh! Ah-ooh!"

"Whoa," Lewis called, as Burford took up the howling again.

Both dog and boy stopped and gazed at him.

From across the fence, came a missile. The tennis ball landed at Benji's feet.

"That you, Frank?" Lewis asked, peering across the fence toward the invisible neighbor.

"Yup. Dog howls whenever he loses his ball under the fence. When did you get the second pup?"

Rebecca's hand covered her mouth to keep in laughter.

"Oh, second pup's on loan," Lewis said, "But we're taking them in now, so you won't have to put up with the racket."

"No bother," Frank said.

Lewis beckoned Benji and Burford inside. "Let's make dinner and see what falls on the floor for Burf," he said.

Inside, Burford followed the handwashing and aproning of Benji with Beagle attention.

Lewis finished tying apron strings and said to Benjamin. "Bring me those green onions, Benji. I'll show you how to slice them so they are a nice shape."

Forty-five minutes later, they enjoyed broiled salmon stuffed with lemon and onions, accompanied by New Potatoes and a tossed green salad. After helping his mother debone his portion of the salmon, Benjamin ate with gusto.

When Burford had cleaned around Benjamin's chair, he harrumphed and lay under the table, alert, but at ease.

Candlelight for dinner had been Benjamin's idea, Lewis and Rebecca acquiescing to his pleas with embarrassment. Late in dinner, their conversation became subdued. Lewis' eyes often sought Rebecca's. She felt his gaze, probing her feelings, questioning her acceptance of his friendship, of his home as a refuge. The air was tense with the newness of their relationship, the unknown limits, the unknown expectations.

For the first time in a long time, Lewis could think of no way to lighten the mood. Rebecca actually took over the conversation, complimenting him on the salmon and answering Benjamin's questions about the fish, about what makes fire, about dark and light and burning. About why dogs howl in packs or howl at the moon, or howl instead of bark.

As always, Lewis marveled at how clearly Rebecca could explain things on a level that a bright five-year-old could understand, without being misleading. She was a very good mother. A very intelligent and beautiful . . .

"Lewis?" Benjamin's voice caught him off guard. "Lewis, where is your family?"

"Um . . . My family is mostly still in Ireland. I have a few cousins back east, though. Why do you ask, Benjamin?"

"Why do you have a so big house and no family, 'cept Burford?"

Lewis looked pleadingly at Rebecca. She was not aware of the need to save him since she too was interested in his answer. So, he plunged into it. "I have such a big house because I liked all this woodwork." He turned to include Rebecca, "I have a big house because I want other people to enjoy it with me."

Rebecca watched his eyes flame with intense wanting as he looked at her. She had constantly underestimated Lewis' friendship until today. And for six years, no man, including Gabriel, had been allowed even to put a hand on her shoulder.

She looked up meeting Lewis' gaze again. What magic had he done to make her lose herself to him for those few moments in the pool? She had wanted it as he had. He was so patient, yet so insistent.

*   *

Benji watched them closely. Something was happening that he didn't understand. He didn't want to stop it or interrupt it. Maybe, if he just watched, the end of it would be easier to understand than the middle. His mother seemed so small next to Lewis. Lewis looked like his feelings were hurting. Benjamin hadn't heard her say anything that would hurt somebody. What were they doing?

Oh! This is like Gabriel when his feelings hurt!

"Mama?" he piped, "Lewis is not so sad usually. He's a lot happier than Gabriel, aren't you Lewis? It's okay if Lewis likes you, because he won't be a big cloud like Ga . . ."

"Benjamin!" She was stricken.

Benji went silent. What was the matter? He just wanted her to let Lewis be her friend because he liked Lewis and wanted to be with him.

Benjamin scrambled down from his chair and ran to bury himself under the warm blanket on the sofa near the fireplace. Burford followed right behind.

CHAPTER EIGHTEEN

Lewis sat open-mouthed at the little boy's revelation. Rebecca's hands covered her face. He touched her arm and asked, "Gabriel? Your accompanist? Do you love Gabriel?"

"No." She glanced up at him. "He thinks I should, but I cannot make myself." Turning her face away from him, she added, "I am not sure that I can ever love anyone again, physically. I love many people in other ways."

"Rebecca, the kiss we shared as you came out of the water today, was shared. You will be able to. I'm a patient man, and I love you deeply." He gave her hand a warm touch as he rose and couldn't stop himself from kissing the auburn curls that were just now drying from their swim. "I'll go talk to Benjamin."

On the way into the living room, he thought about that phrase, "He thinks I should." What did she mean?

In the living room, Lewis sat on the floor next to the sofa and peeked under the edge of the blanket.

"Benji," he whispered, "You didn't do anything wrong. We were trying not to talk about our feelings, but we needed to talk about them. It isn't easy, but you actually helped us. It'll be all right. Yup, it really will, Buddy. Now, why don't you come on out of your blanket cave and choose a book for your mother to read to you while I clean the kitchen?"

Benjamin pulled back the blanket and took the thumb out of his mouth. He looked at Lewis apprehensively, and then met Lewis' infectious smile with his own dimpled grin. "Lewis, do you have books with pictures?"

"I sure do. My favorites have beautiful pictures. Come on over to my picture book section and see for yourself."

Benjamin brought the ribbon-edged blanket with him, trailing the long plaid across the floor as he followed Lewis. They could hear Rebecca putting dishes underwater in the kitchen as they looked over the selection.

"Lewis! This is just like at the library. You have a lot of picture books!"

Lewis was pleased. "Some of these my mother read to me when I was little – nursery rhymes and the tales of Irish heroes, the King Arthur stories and the poems of Robert Louis Stevenson. These are my Pooh books and my Paddington books. When I came to the United States, I bought children's books to send to my little brother, Dicken. I usually bought two copies, one for Dicken and one for my children who aren't here yet."

"When your children come, will they all be younger than me?"

"Yes."

"May I be your boy, too."

Lewis felt his heart thunk, hard. Gazing down at this open-faced child, he swallowed several times. What hopeful answer could he give to Benji's beautiful candor?

"You are mommy's boy. That's a great honor for you. I want you to be my special friend, always. And when my children come, I want you to show them how to be as good and smart as you are. You'll be important to them and to me, just as you are for mommy. Now, let's choose a book and go get your mother out of the kitchen."

They chose several and took the stack to Rebecca. She was de-aproned, led back to the hearth rug and left, leaning her back against the base of the sofa, hugging Benjamin and reading to him in that almost American accent that Lewis loved to hear.

Burford snuggled into the group, but Lewis dragged himself back to the kitchen and set into the pots and pans with a clatter of taut nerves. The jasmine scent of her still followed him.

* *

When Lewis returned to the living room, he found his beagle sleeping on the sofa. Rebecca and Benjamin lay curled up on the floor in front of the sofa, also asleep. She slept on her side, her head lying on one hand. The child was backed into her lap. Under her protective arm he was sucking his thumb and using the bow of her blouse as a ribbon, fingering the satiny fabric.

Lewis wakened his sleepy dog and took him outside. While Burford nosed around the bushes, Lewis stared at the stars. Not so long ago, these same stars had shone over Ballybly as he tried to talk his neighbors into a search for Dicken and Molly. They had shone over the home in New York of Benji and Rebecca as they made the decision to move for safety to Portland, and now, his new family were here, safe, and asleep on his living room floor.

"God be with you, Dicken and Molly," he whispered. "And God help me protect my Rebecca and Benji."

His beagle reappeared, wagging his tail. Lewis smiled, scratched Burford behind the ears and took him into his little cave- home in the den.

When Lewis returned to the living room, he sat down near Rebecca and Benjamin. He fed the fire. The crackles of new pitch stirred the boy in his sleep. He turned a little away from his mother, pulling the ends of the bow with him. Her blouse fell open at the neck revealing the lace which curved around her breast.

Lewis stared at the pulse beating softly at the base of her throat. He was conscious again of becoming an unwitting watcher at the stripping away of her defenses. Her defenses were legion, and each new revelation of her soul seemed like the punishment of Tantalus to him.

His gaze pulled his mind to the rise and fall of her breasts while she slept, feeling safe in his house. He pulled his mind back from the inflaming details to the whole portrait of her at rest. The open blouse formed a frame for the most innocent and vulnerable beauty he knew. The line of her attracted his gaze over her slender shoulder and the arm which protected her son.

His awareness was drawn down the slope of her side to her waist and up the smooth curve of her hip. Her straight skirt hugged into the flat planes of her abdomen, where Benjamin had recently been hugged into her body.

She overwhelmed his senses.

He looked at the fire, feeding it he could not count how many little sticks, not looking at Rebecca for he did not know how many minutes. His thoughts brought him enough of her to maintain the attack on him begun by her presence.

What had made her this untouchable? How had she been mistreated, as Miriam had said?

Or mistaught?

How often he'd heard the mothers of his town teaching their daughters to be wary of the dishonorable intentions of men in general and certainly of men from the other faction, whichever faction.

In the same way, the factions in his home town had set each other up to be worst enemies. Expectations were realized, new lower expectations were created until they too were realized. And now, his family was in the middle of an intermittent and terrifying civil war where expectations were as low as they could get. And that was why his Protestant brother, and a wonderful Catholic girl were missing since last spring.

"Levy, why are you so sad?"

He didn't know when she had first whispered to him, but when she touched his back, he turned and realized that she was unaware her blouse was open.

"Why are you sad?" she asked again. "I have never seen you so."

He took a second to gather his thoughts. "I was thinking about my youngest brother, Dicken. He and his wife, Molly, have gone missing since early June."

"And that's why you were in Ireland? To find them?"

He threw the last of the sticks into the fire where they hissed and crackled. "I tried. Both families seemed more able to blame than to help."

"Your baby brother . . . it must have been very hard to come back here."

"It was." He twisted around to face her, a slow smile replacing his pensiveness. "You make it better though – you and Benjamin."

She colored and looked away. "I know you need more . . . more courage from me, more trusting. I'm sorry. I . . .." Her voice trailed off in a confusion of strong emotions and difficult English.

Lewis breathed deeply and took a chance. "Rebecca, you have those invisible fences filled with electricity all around you. I can't see where they begin and end, and I run into them headlong."

She began to sit up to her elbow, looking at the carpet pattern near the fire, her eyes glistening. "I am sorry, Levy. I should have put a stop to our friendship long ago before it was . . ."

He reached for her bow and began tying it. "Benjamin's ribbon blanket," he explained.

She allowed him to continue making a bow, even smiled and sat up straighter.

"End our friendship before it was too late?" he finished her thought. "It was too late on the first night. After that, you couldn't have put me out of your life. You might have delayed things a little, but our relationship would have reached this point sooner or later."

She looked into his eyes and asked, "What is this point at which our relationship has arrived?"

His hands lingered at her throat. "It's where I care very deeply for you and for your son. And in return, where you trust me enough to fall asleep on my living room floor and then without flinching, you allow me to straighten the mess your son has made of your clothing." He smiled, raising one selfdeprecating eyebrow, making her laugh at the absurd relationship he described so accurately.

"Now," he said, "please tell me why the fences are there. You've told me about the break-ins, and the attempts to take Benjamin. But there is more, and it is about you, not Benjamin."

Her breath stopped and then restarted with a speed he had only seen in caged and frightened animals.

"Please, Rebecca. Why?"

"Benjamin." she said faintly.

"Look at me!" he commanded.

Her eyes came back to his, trying to focus, trying to climb the fence. "He hears." she whispered.

"All right. Come with me. Put him to bed. Then we'll come down here and talk." He spoke to her slowly.

"Yes," she said. He stood, bringing her up with him. Looking down into her eyes, he watched her gather courage. Perhaps he'd asked too much too soon, but he was sure something evil had happened to her, and she had to have help.

When she was steady on her feet, he lifted Benjamin in his arms and led the way upstairs. In the bedroom, he left the light on next to the bed. She covered Benji and pushed the ribbon part of the wool blanket into his searching fist. Lewis looked across the bed at her when she stood to face him. He promised himself to take it slowly so that someday Rebecca would come to this bed for herself.

She seemed to see the promise of care in his look before she lowered her eyes once more to her son, then she turned and stepped softly down the stairs again. He stayed a moment, trying to match his breathing to the relaxed rhythm of her child before he followed her.

CHAPTER NINETEEN

Rebecca leaned her forehead into her balled fists on the mantel. Lewis knelt beside her and fed the fire, though it didn't need it. After silent moments, he looked up into her dark, troubled eyes and judged the time was right. He stretched out on the hearthrug and said, "Tell me, Becca."

She smoothed her skirt in the way he knew well and came to her knees next to him. Her face softened as she gazed down on him. So, he knew he'd been right to lie back, assuming the most unprotected position he could think of. He waited patiently for her thoughts to sort themselves.

"In Hungary," she began tentatively, "I taught in the University at Budapest. I was a recent graduate myself, but they hired me on the recommendation of my teacher and because of the offers they knew I had from other Soviet conservatories. I had many students, coached chamber groups and was given adequate leave to meet the demand for concerts in Yugoslavia and Czechoslovakia as well as Hungary. I was invited to play a Bach concerto at the festival in Sopron, Hungary and was practicing for that.

"And then, one afternoon, I was kidnapped. I thought at first it was secret police, because I am Jewish, or because I had applied for a visa to play concerts in France and Austria. That's how it used to be in Soviet Hungary.

"But I was wrong about the reason. They were thugs, working for another . . . for a man who wanted something he believed I owned. They took me in a van to a prison in the hills in the northern part of Hungary."

Lewis watched the color drain from her face. He could feel the tension rising in her as the story went on. He turned on his side and put his hand on hers where she pulled at her skirt. She grasped his hand as a lifeline. Her slender fingers grew warm with strain.

"They asked many crazy questions about where I had hidden the missing concerti of Johann Sebastian Bach. They were certain that Raphael Atemvoll had given them to me."

"So, he was your teacher, not this guy in Austria that you told Steinmetz."

"Yes, Atemvoll. But only Abraham and Miriam …"

"Nobody else will know any of this unless you tell them."

She nodded. "Raphael never gave me those concerti. I've looked."

"But he did give you some music?"

"Yes, many boxes. My Uncle Tobias came to Budapest, hoping to hear me play at Sopron, but found my whole family missing. When he went to the police, he was approached by a policeman who relayed a message from one of the gangsters. That was how he negotiated my release."

"So, they know you are in America?"

"No, they believe I committed suicide right after the concert at Sopron. I have now a different identity."

"No . . ." It took him a moment to believe, and then he asked, "Zolesku, Darya?"

She glanced up at him. "How could you guess?"

"Suicide, Sopron. On All Classical Radio, I heard a concert you played in Prague – the Brahms Concerto. I still have it on my computer." He remembered his deep sadness when he heard the final news, "I erased the concert at Sopron after I heard you had died. You left the stage so … Until that last movement, you had me, everyone, in your palm."

She stared at him. "This far away? People could have heard that night, even here?"

"People who were paying attention to your career."

It took her moments to absorb that idea.

"So," he brought her back to now. "So, you have boxes from Raphael Atemvoll."

She nodded. "Uncle Tobias suspects the boxes are the reason I was kidnapped. He had his friend pack and ship them all to New York, to a building he owns, but not where we live."

"And since becoming Rebecca, you have been through them all."

"Every box. And now I am cataloguing it all. Most of it still stored in New York. There is nothing with Bach's handwriting. There is only the music he used for teaching. No original manuscripts among them other than one piece by Corelli, and Raphael's and his teacher's own compositions."

"Why did this gangster believe he had them?"

"I am certain he didn't have them. He … he was like my mentor. He would have let me help him hide them."

"Perhaps not. Perhaps he knew they were dangerous to own."

"You mean, he wouldn't reveal them to protect me?"

He nodded. "Why else would he store so much with your uncle's friend?"

She sat there, silently thinking, or remembering. "Since my escape I have never heard from Raphael, Professor Atemvoll. They have …"

"And you love him."

She looked down, tears streaming. "He was … he is my beloved grandfather."

"You are not to blame for what they did," Lewis said.

Suddenly, Lewis noticed the touch of her hands became lighter. She absently traced her forefinger around the perimeter of his palm, never actually touching the heart of his hand. At the same time, her voice became more ethereal.

"Benjamin . . .," she had to gather new resources and start again, "Benjamin's father was one of the prison guards."

She stopped talking, her finger stopped tracing. Her eyes moved a fraction of an inch, not looking at anything in the present, but held in the terror of days and nights six years ago.

Lewis carefully picked his way through her emotional barricades, conscious of the threat to her stability which he'd created. He moved his face into her line of vision again and spoke softly. "This guard raped you, Rebecca?"

She came back to his time and his living room a little, answering, "Not him. He was their victim. They dragged him out of my cell. He was not guilty. I choose to think of that guard as the real father even though . . .."

Her forefinger began to trace the perimeter again. Lewis didn't understand what had happened, but he now understood that she was searching for a way around the ugliness of the time, for the least painful way. He waited, holding his palm very still in her lap.

"That night, they whipped him. He knew the danger. Still for those moments before they discovered him, he gave me food, a coat, and talked to me about breaking the cycle of hate with love. And then they caught him. They probably killed him."

She stopped. There was more, but it was beyond her power to tell him. Lewis could feel it in the way she halted abruptly. Her hand let go of his, and her body tensed, willing him not to ask. Her explanation of Benjamin's paternity made vague sense, but the details were ugly and mattered only so he could help her get beyond them.

Instead of more talk, he wrapped his arms around her, drawing the tension out of her back and whispering to her of Benjamin. She was not going to crumble. She loved a small child who needed her.

He had to know more, yet, with every question he risked breaking her brittle, selfprotective wall. At last, he asked the critical one. "Darling. Why can't you go to the police about the attempts to kidnap Benjamin?"

"Levy," she pulled back to watch his face, "are you a citizen?"

"Of the United States? Yes. I have been one for eight years."

She took a deep breath, seeming to gather courage. "I am not yet a citizen, and I am not Rebecca Gregory. I am here under false pretense, illegal."

Lewis willed himself into control of the knot of fear which gripped his heart as she continued.

"If the police find the truth of my situation, Tobias, Gabriel, Benjamin – we could all be sent back to Hungary, or separated in jail."

She trusted him with her most dangerous secret. Her body went rigidly still, the blood drained from her face. He knew he'd asked the last safe question for tonight.

"I won't betray you," he whispered. "We have to find a way to get help without endangering you." He spoke firmly, hoping to give her strength. "If anything happened to you or Benjamin, I could not . . . I could not go on."

His hands moved up and down her back and neck, willing her to relax and trust. At last, her arms came around his shoulders, her hips leaned into him for support and he knew he'd won. He buried his face in her shoulder, silently weeping because she could not.

When her taut control had been conquered by sleep, Lewis held her in his arms on the hearthrug. He reveled in the feel of her as she let him protect her, warm her. His lips caressed the tendrils of auburn that fell over her sleeping features. He raised up on his elbows with his upper body hovering over her as she slept. He pillowed her head on his forearm. Her face relaxed, the peace of one who has thrown off a burden.

There was more of her burden to be gotten rid of, but she had earned this sleep. He put his own head down next to hers and drifted into dreams.

*   *

As the sun rose, Lewis rose, covering Rebecca with the sofa blanket. He went upstairs to check on the child who slept peacefully. Lewis allowed himself to daydream as he watched the child. He imagined Benjamin in his office, playing with his old tinker-toys, practicing on the piano in his living room, aproned and flourcovered helping make breakfast in the kitchen. He imagined Benjamin as his son.

No matter what his genesis had been, it was Benjamin who kept Rebecca whole. If anything happened to this child, both Lewis and Rebecca would suffer. He had to know what could be done to stop the threat of kidnapping.

Lewis started down the stairs to the kitchen, letting the questions flood his mind. Why would anyone try to kidnap Benjamin? If she didn't have what they were after, how could they be convinced? How could they make her legal in the U.S.? Could he discover who threatened her?

Lewis' concern for her emotional health brought numerous questions to mind. How had Rebecca escaped the prison? What else had happened there? How had she come to America? Why couldn't she contact her family? And who was Gabriel that she should love him, but could not?

He reached the kitchen phone and dialed the doctors Friedenberg. Glancing at his watch, he realized how early it was. He was impossibly impatient.

"Abraham? This is Lewis James. I am sorry to wake you."

"You didn't," the man's baritone boomed through the phone. "You saved me from having to clean the parakeet's cage, my dear boy. Now,

Miriam will become frustrated and do it herself before I get off the phone. What can I do for *you* on this rosy morning?"

Lewis enjoyed this man's optimism. He looked out the kitchen window to see that Abraham was right about the morning. "I called because I ... because ..."

"Is Rebecca all right?"

How could the man know so much? Was Lewis' interest in her that obvious? "Rebecca is asleep on my living room floor. She told me many things about her past last night. Telling me has left her worn out and I need more information."

After a long pause, Abraham said, "Before we get any further, young man, I need to know just what she did tell you. I don't want to be telling things for her inadvertently."

Lewis understood. "She told me about the attempts to kidnap Benjamin, about the breakins and the vandalism of her apartment here in Portland."

"Yes, that worries me considerably. What else did she tell you?"

"She talked about her kidnapping and about the prison, about the man searching for the Bach concerti, about the boxes of music and about Benjamin's father. She said something not quite understandable – that he was not guilty, but he was Benjamin's father. Then she said he was whipped for taking care of her. That's as far as she got."

There was a heavy silence on the other end of the line. Then Abraham spoke, deeply moved. "Lewis, you're the first person other than Tobias and us that she has ever told about the nights in prison. She must trust you very much. By the way, where is Benjamin?"

"Benji's asleep in my bed."

Lewis could hear Abe chuckle. "Putting the child in your own bed makes you less threatening, does it not?"

"I suppose it did," Lewis grinned at the picture of a clever and persuasive lover building up in the man's mind.

"Lewis," Abraham was suddenly serious again, "you're a sensitive man. Be very careful about how you show your love for her. Please."

"I am aware of the dangers, Abraham."

"And Benji ..."

"I want him safe wherever he is. Is it possible she has these concerti?"

"I've asked her Uncle Tobias that. They have both been through every box many times, and found no sign. The oldest pieces are of Atemvoll's teacher, Batislav. Of Bach, only the known pieces and none in his handwriting."

"Is it true that her legal problems are grave enough to cause their deportation?"

"I don't know. I know fear of it circumscribes her life. Last year, I tried to get her to go with me to the immigration office. When she refused, I even introduced her to a friend who is an immigration officer. I told him nothing, but they dated a few times and I was hopeful she would talk to him – nothing."

"Supposing," Lewis thought out loud, "Suppose I went to the immigration agents for advice for an unnamed friend? I'd get her permission first ..."

Abraham's normally booming voice was subdued, thoughtful, "I think you'd better get advice from her rabbi, Elijah Stamps – a good man. Dealt with immigration problems before. Also, he'd keep her identity confidential. Priests and rabbis have that right."

"I'll give him a call right after I talk to her."

"Right."

"Thanks. Abraham, when is her first class today?"

"Eight o'clock – a lecture class. Won't she make it?"

"I don't think it'd be a good idea. Can you take care of it?"

"Of course. And Lewis, she's been living on thin ice. She's had an impressive skating record for six years but be careful."

As he hung up, Lewis considered what "careful" meant for Rebecca. He was certain she needed to throw away the rest of her burden, and that she needed help doing it. But how fast should she be encouraged to face the effort it took?

While he mixed pancake batter, he came to two conclusions. One, she needed more laughter in her life. Two, she could get over what had happened if she were not imprisoned by fear for Benjamin and by fear of vandals.

The fear of deportation was the first one to tackle. It kept her from getting the protection she needed from the police. He would try to get her permission to sound out Rabbi Stamps . . . Perhaps when they worked on their lecture series tonight in her office.

*   *

She awoke to Lewis' infectious grin. "What is so humorous?" she asked.

He knelt beside her. "Only six weeks ago, in the Denver airport, I met the most beautiful woman. At the time, I never dreamed that I'd be picking her up off my living room floor." Smugness crept into his voice. "At least, not so soon."

"Oh, you!" Laughing, she shoved away the arms with which he was offering to lift her. "You let me fall asleep here just so you could tease me with it. I will not be allowed to forget this for some time, I'm sure."

"Right."

"Well, go back to your lair, you lion, and let me wake up properly." She began to stretch her arms above her head.

"Oh no! I like to watch you stretch as much as I like to tease."

She stopped stretching immediately. A gleam of mischievous idea flitted across her features. She pushed up onto her knees and then suddenly threw the blanket over his head. Pulling the ends around him like a net, she captured his arms inside. He flailed, made as helpless by his mirth as by her trap.

Suddenly, he rolled over taking her down to the rug under him, blanket and all. He pulled his arms out and pinioned her. Static made the blanket cling to her and to him. Lewis had to blow a little to get the last of the blanket out of his mouth. They were both unable to stop laughing. She kicked and squirmed to get out of his grasp, but was as effective as a small mouse under the paw of a cat.

When his lips sought hers, he felt the sparks of the static in her hair and on her blouse. The tenderness of their kiss set off new electricity, invading him. She arched her back toward him, offering the softness of her breasts to the hardness of his own. Her unparalleled gesture of giving aroused him more than their playful laughter. His hand came between them, exploring her body. Their kiss became more insistent.

The thud of little feet hit the floor above and took off running toward the stairwell. Lewis pulled away from her with difficulty.

"Damn! I do love children!" He mocked himself.

When Benjamin of the perplexed eyebrows peeked around the corner, he found them on the floor next to each other, laughing. Benjamin ran to be part of the fun, plopped down next to Rebecca. His right thumb was still in his mouth. Lewis rose to greet him, lifted him off his mother and wrapped Benjamin's legs around his waist. His laughing mother rose and wrapped her arms around both of them. It was wonderful to be in the middle of a hug.

*   *

Rebecca hugged her son and Lewis, marveling at how good it felt not to have escaped into her darkness. Lewis James created a magic she'd never thought to know.

When he lifted Benjamin and asked about pancakes for breakfast, the simple domestic art of him, awed her.

"Yeah for pancakes!" Benjamin shouted.

CHAPTER TWENTY

BUDAPEST, HUNGARY

1939

Twenty-five-year-old Raphael Atemvoll hovered over the small man on the sofa-bed in their apartment. "Grandfather, please let me take you to the hospital."

"No, Rafe," Anton Batislav, his grandfather and guardian, spoke in a hoarse whisper. "Lead me to the piano."

"But you are too . . ."

"Rafe, lead me. This is important to your father."

Raphael jerked. Grandfather had not mentioned father in many years.

"Come, son." Grandfather said, lifting his arms in a gesture familiar to both of them.

Raphael picked up his eighty-eight-year-old grandfather and carried his frail body to the piano bench. They had long ago constructed this bench to have a back that supported Grandfather, allowing him to play the piano in spite of his failing health.

Grandfather took a deep breath, raised his hands from his lap to the keyboard and closed his eyes. "Listen carefully. Tell me who wrote this piece," he said.

Raphael watched Grandfather's gnarled hands. He recognized the sudden change that came over his beloved old guardian every time he began to play music. Age fell away. The tight look of pain receded. Grandfather sat up straighter on his deteriorating spine.

And then, Raphael heard the contrapuntal opening, a melody woven into a harmony that contained another melody, and another melody, each voice a song contributing to other songs, as if all the birds in the forest sang separately and together, moving toward and away from each other in joy.

"Ah, this is Johann Sebastian Bach."

"And what is it?"

"I've never heard it before. A piano sonata, perhaps? When did you learn it?"

"Bring me my old satchel, Rafe. It is in the cedar chest."

Raphael saw that his grandfather seemed stable in the piano bench, but there was no telling how long the old man could sit up this way, so he hurried into the back room, lifted the lid on the cedar chest and grabbed out the old satchel by its worn handles.

Back in the front room, he handed the satchel to his grandfather. Twisted fingers reached inside and pulled out an old manuscript that Raphael recognized as court dances Grandfather Anton had once written, back when he was young and lived in that other country – a country Grandfather rarely named when they talked, saying, "Oh, Rafe, that country was so unimportant, it no longer exists."

Raphael reached out to help Grandfather settle the music on the music desk. Anton pulled his penknife from his pocket. To Raphael's surprise, Anton slit the endpapers of the notebook. Gently, he pulled out a strangely thin set of pages and handed them to Raphael.

Raphael felt the age of the paper, saw the fine handwriting and the few corrections on the page.

"Sit next to me," Grandfather said. "Play the upper voice."

Raphael sat.

Grandfather turned back to the first page of the ancient papers. "So, play, already." He said.

When Raphael glanced at him, Grandfather raised an eyebrow and smiled in his enigmatic way. Raphael knew he would get no explanation until they had played the piece.

By the second measure, Raphael knew. "Violin," he whispered, entranced by the loveliness of the soaring upper voice.

"Yes," Grandfather said and continued the lower voices. They played to the end of the first movement.

"Bach," Raphael whispered. "One of the missing."

"Yes."

Raphael could not wait to know what came next. Bach's middle movements were famous for their exquisite melodies. He turned the page and began with Grandfather, but soon, the older man let Raphael play all the parts while he watched. They turned pages and played more.

"Ah," Raphael said once, "This one also became the harpsichord concerto."

"Yes," Grandfather Anton said. "Bach re-used it. But clearly it was first a solo instrument with accompaniment."

Over an hour and three concerti later, Raphael let the last notes ring from the ceiling of their small apartment. In a trance, he turned to his grandfather. "The missing," he said. "How did you find these?"

Grandfather seemed subdued. "Your father gave them to me. He had them from his father and he from your father's great-grandfather who bought them from Bach's other inheriting son."

"Wilhelm Friedemann."

Grandfather Anton nodded. "Your great-great grandfather knew enough to make his way to Leipzig as soon as Bach died. He had heard the music, and he understood the rivalry of sons. He hoped to parlay human nature into a purchase. He left Leipzig with more than these, but only these have been kept from the plague of need."

"Father gave them to you?"

"Along with something even more valuable."

Raphael looked at his grandfather, his guardian, "But these are priceless. What could possibly be more valuable than these?"

"Yourself."

Raphael closed his eyes and absorbed all the feelings, all the memory of fear, a three-year old's memories of loss, of grueling tiredness, of rough border guards, the death of his friend the painter in a field of bullets, of running until he could no longer run, of falling into a ditch with his grandfather Anton, and sleeping the sleep of aching shivers while his grandfather held him to his wet chest.

At the piano bench, his grandfather touched his arm and whispered. "Raphael, until you can make certain they are safely cared for and available to all in the world, these pieces must be kept hidden. Men, careless and greedy men and women would sell them to Hungary's stupid Nazi leaders. The Hungarian Nazis would send them as a gift to that troglodyte, Hitler. And then they will once again be lost."

"Yes, Grandfather. I understand. Even a year ago, when we were so hungry, when we had to play all those long nights in the movie theaters, even then, I would have sold them myself."

His grandfather smiled at him. "You have become a man, and I trust you with your father's gift."

"Thank you."

"And now, my boy, in the closet, I have a roll of old wallpaper. We must hide these in the notebook covers once again. Then, please take me to the Széchenyi Baths. My bones ache."

CHAPTER TWENTY-ONE

"**M**r. James? This is Elijah Stamps. Sorry it's taken so many days, but at last I've been able to set up a meeting with an immigration agent – Mr. Joseph Selig. I've worked with him before."

"I'd like to meet him. Does he know who we're talking about?"

"No. Rebecca should reveal her identity only after we know it is safe. That way, there are no ethical dilemmas for Joseph."

"Good. Rabbi Stamps, do you think I should bring a legal adviser?"

"Sometimes that's a good idea, but in this case, I believe we can wait. Can you meet us at my office this afternoon at 5:30 in the evening?"

"Let's see . . . I can postpone my tutorial students for a day or so. If I come a little early can we discuss how much I should let her tell him?"

"Lewis, if there are some things about her situation you don't know yet, yourself, we could be opening Pandora's box here. Try to talk to her again before you come this afternoon."

"We're having lunch today. Thanks, Rabbi Stamps."

*   *

Lewis had brought sandwiches from the nearby deli for lunch. He'd made efforts to organize his books and papers for her arrival. Glancing at the clock, he realized he had time to greet her as she crossed the quadrangle, so he started down the stairs. From the big windows on the stair landing, he looked out and saw her coming around the corner of the library.

The skirt of her lavender dress whipped around her legs as the wind blew. Leaves of the Sweet Gum trees swirled around her, flashing yellow, red, purple in the sunlight. Her hair caught the sun and the wind and played with them both, flying about her face, teasing her eyes, her throat, her shoulders. Lewis was transfixed by the sight of her. She was so small, yet so proud. She could be so distant, yet so warm. She had been afraid for too long. He ached to release the spirit hidden inside her.

When she turned from the main path toward the physics building, he pushed himself away from the landing window and continued down to open the door. The autumn freshness came in the door with her, the wind giving her hair one last whip as Lewis took her hand.

He led her toward the stairs. While they climbed, he reached up, magicianlike, and produced a bright coral Sweet Gum leaf from the curls behind her ear. He handed it to her with a flourish, and an illconcealed smile.

"Ah" he said, "a gift from the Gods. Sweet Gum to take away your worries."

Rebecca laughed and chided him. "You cannot *will* the plants of the earth to have the powers you need at the moment."

"Your worries can be laid to rest if you have faith and let yourself trust the goodwill of those who care about you."

She took the leaf and returned it to her hair. So, she wanted to believe his optimism.

*   *

Rebecca entered his office tentatively. She realized immediately that he'd gone to some trouble to create an oasis of neatness in the midst of papered chaos. A casual visitor wouldn't have noticed the difference, but she'd been here often enough to know he'd put a lot of effort into rearranging stacks. It amused her to contrast the whirlwind appearance of his work place with the impeccable order of his lab.

When they worked on lectures and discussed ideas, his mind was like his lab – orderly, clear thinking prevailed. Yet, at play and in relaxation, his mind could leap from idea to idea leaving behind it a conversation as strewn with vivid imagery as his office was strewn with papers and books.

Rebecca believed Lewis was a good physicist and teacher precisely because he was able to let both the orderly and the imaginative parts of his mind have free rein. This room showed the part it played in his intellectual life.

"Sorry about the mess, Becca," Lewis shrugged and grinned at his beloved stacks.

"I'm not." she said.

"Not what?" he asked.

"Not sorry about the mess. I think all this paper would be good insulation on a cold day. It's probably just what an office on the northeast side of this building needs. What have we for lunch?"

"Turkey on rye, potato salad and a Henry's ale to share. I have no classes after lunch today, but you have five more students if I remember correctly, so I also made hot tea if you'd prefer it to the Henry's."

"Thank you. A half of a beer will be fine. Potato salad is very Irish for Weinstein's deli, isn't it?"

"It was very Irish until they added Mrs. Neushin's pickles. It is a cultural composite now. You willing to mix cultures?"

She looked up quickly to see how much twinkle she'd find in his blue eyes. His face was alight with fun. She smiled, but answered noncommittally, "Let's wait and see how well it works. We should give it a little time."

Lewis blew a theatrical sigh, "In that case, here's your sandwich, my lady, and your culturally mixed potato salad." As he dished up lunch, he added nonchalantly, "Could I ask you another important question."

"Fire away, as you Americans say."

"Rabbi Stamps has arranged a meeting with an immigration agent. Stamps suggested I should know more. Can you tell me what he thinks I don't know?"

Rebecca set her sandwich down carefully on the desk and wiped her hands on the napkin. She wiped her hands several times before one hand covered her mouth in the gesture he'd learned to read as fear fighting with courage.

He reached out, touching her cheek and taking her chin in his hands. "I will preserve your anonymity until you decide to talk to them yourself. But I can't ask the right questions and get the right answers if I don't know all of it. These kidnappers obviously believe they've got something heavy to hold over you. I'm going to love you no matter what. I just don't want to be taken by surprise. So, let me have it. Did you murder someone? Are you a communist? What do they know that prevents you from getting police help?"

At first, she flushed with puzzlement at his suggestions. Then, she looked into his loving eyes, his laughlined warmth and admitted that she should trust him to the last. She put her hands on his at her cheeks and turned her head to kiss his rough strong fingers.

"Levy, you know that in Hungary I am believed to be dead."

"Yes," he said, "and the concert at Sopron was the set up for apparent suicide. I heard it. All Classical Radio. That last movement was to create the idea that you were . . ."

". . . I went nuts on stage, playing so fast the orchestra couldn't possibly keep up, and . . ."

"The announcer left speechless on-air silence when you ran off-stage before the end of the movement."

"Uncle Tobias met me backstage. We drove into the hills on the old road leading back toward Budapest. At a very high point, we stopped. Uncle Tobias went into the woods a small distance and returned with a canvas bag. Out of the bag he took the dead body of a woman about my age . . ."

When Rebecca stopped, Lewis found himself breathing hard. Through empathy or a desire to take half her burden, his body mirrored hers in its response to her story. Now he felt sick to his stomach as she did. They sat silently holding tightly to each other's hands, fighting down her nausea.

She said, "She was to have been . . . for students. Instead, she became my suicide."

Another silence followed. Just as Lewis was about to ask a question, she began again. "We hiked about forty miles to FertöTö, the Neusiedler See . . . the lake that borders Austria."

Lewis nodded, "And then?"

"Tobias had hidden two wet suits about a mile inland. With grease to darken our skin and with the wet suits, we were well hidden. We crept to the lake and eluded the border patrols."

Lewis felt the tremors of remembered fear as she continued, "The patrols came very near us three times as we swam, but the darkness of the night kept our secret. It was so cold . . . so cold, even through the suit. Gabriel Kolya met us some way out with a small boat and took us into Austria. In Austria, we changed my identity and applied for an immigration visa.

"Levy, the problem with my visa is not just that I changed my name and identity papers. It is that some of my papers are not very good. If it is found out who I am, there are many people who will suffer for my escape."

"And if you are discovered not dead, the Hungarian gangster would take it out on your family."

"If they are alive," she said, "and they will again be after Raphael Atemvoll as well." She didn't add the obvious.

"Maybe the gang already knows," he said. "Maybe they are here."

She shivered deeply before speaking again. "In New York, I no longer played in the back of the symphony. I became too public. The news people were not satisfied with the false poster photo that my agent sent them. They began following me around to get photos. The photographers and the attempted kidnappings are why I came to Oregon. *The Oregonian* is not likely to be seen in Budapest. Here, I thought I could still play music and not be famous."

Lewis feared he had opened a box of evils after all. "Becca, which of your papers are not good?"

"The marriage license is very bad for instance. There is not even a Rabbi by that name and none who would say that he married us. Yet, I am listed as `Mrs. Lemuel Gregory, born Rebecca Sospiro Tsigane'."

Lewis froze. Then his mind heard all that she had said. "It is a lie. You were no one's wife?"

"I'm not. But to have lied on your visa application is grounds for denial of naturalization, of citizenship."

"Why was it filled out with this lie?"

She looked away at the stacks of papers, "I was pregnant. Gabriel tried to convince me to get rid of the baby." She looked at Lewis defiantly, "When I would not, he convinced me and Tobias that the only way I would be allowed into the United States was as a married woman. Otherwise, my visa would be denied on the grounds of moral ... moral what is it?"

"Probably `turpitude' since it's legal jargon." Lewis was impatient and angry with how she had been maneuvered into this situation.

"Yes. Well, Gabriel offered to marry me, but I refused. When Tobias' friend in Austria created false identity for me, he gave me the name of an American-ex-patriot who had recently died. I knew it was a lie and I signed the papers."

"Gabriel wanted you to be his wife?"

"But, I cannot ..."

"Good."   Lewis whispered. He leaned down and kissed her forehead gently. "Anything else I should know about the papers?"

She shook her head. "No."

He thought she had been through enough for one day. He took her face in his hands. Raising one eyebrow at her to signal the end of heavy thoughts, he said, "Now, turn up the corners of your mouth," he raised both eyebrows, "and smile at me." He kissed each corner, teasing it with his tongue until she was laughing. He knelt down in front of her to plant his next kiss very solidly on the softest part of her mouth. He could feel her surprise and then the warmth of her surrender to his touch. He gloried in the smell of jasmine and her tender giving gestures. He knew the small flicker of her desire was growing stronger each time he tested it. He felt wonderfully powerful.

But then she whispered. "Don't talk to Rabbi Stamps. Please don't."

Lewis felt a chill on his neck.

CHAPTER TWENTY-TWO

For many days, now, Lewis had been picking Benjamin up from his school. On Wednesday, he and Benji planned to go to a high school soccer game.

Benji called him in the morning, excited about their plans. Through the phone, Lewis could hear him jumping up and down as he talked.

"Lewis, do you know how to get me at my school?"

"Sure do, little buddy. I found you yesterday, didn't I?"

"Oh, yeah. Well, I'll be out front."

"No, you won't. You'll be in the classroom helping Mrs. Johnson set up for tomorrow. Don't leave her alone, buddy. I won't be able to find you if you aren't with her."

"Oh, yeah. I'll be with Mrs. Johnson. Lewis?"

"Uhhuh?"

"My school is over at threefifteen. Do you remember that?"

"I plan to be there at threefifteen and then we'll go to Grant Park for the game. Don't you worry. You'll get to see the world's fastest soccer players. They're fun to watch! See you in Mrs. Johnson's room, Benjamin."

"Okay. Bye Lewis."

*   *

Worried that Benji might actually forget and wait out front after all, Lewis arrived fifteen minutes early. He bounded down the stairs toward the kindergarten wing of the school. Even before he turned the corner, he knew something was wrong. A heavy scuffling sound echoed from the next hallway. As he flung around the corner, a small, weasel-faced man hit Mrs. Johnson with a resounding upper-cut. Her grip on Benjamin dropped as her legs crumpled beneath her. The short man made a grab for Benjamin's arm.

"Benji!" Lewis shouted.

Benjamin was already dancing backwards from the man, crying, "You hurt my teacher! You hurt my. . .! Lewis!"

The man looked up, watery blue eyes bulging as Lewis lunged toward him. The man's lank hand dropped Benjamin's as if it were a live electric wire. At that moment, the classroom door opened. Benjamin's classmates poured into the hall, tumbling over each other in naive curiosity. In his headlong gallop after the weasel, Lewis nearly ran over one of the little girls.

The kidnapper slithered away from Benjamin. He glanced over his shoulder as he gained the head of the stairs. Lewis caught and memorized that one glimpse of the man's menacing hatred.

"Stay with Mrs. Johnson, Benjamin! I'll be right back." Lewis shouted as he ran.

On the way by, he banged and wrenched open two classroom doors, hoping those teachers would come out. When he arrived at the playground, the man was climbing the fence with the speed only fear can give.

Seconds later, Lewis vaulted the fence too. The wretch had disappeared.

Lewis debated running through neighboring yards to find him. His chances were slim. Benjamin was frightened, and Mrs. Johnson needed medical attention.

He re-climbed the fence and darted back into the building to be greeted with children crying and teachers attempting to gather them into classrooms.

In the middle of a crowd of crying children, Benjamin comforted the little girl that Lewis had bumped in his haste.

After medics cared for Mrs. Johnson, Lewis, the, teachers and principal had given their stories to the police, and the children's parents had been informed of the fracas, Lewis left a voice message for Rebecca that he was on his way to the Reed campus with Benjamin. He was afraid she would hear about the kidnapping attempt from someone else before he had a chance to reassure her.

They met Harald Steinmetz in the hall outside Rebecca's classroom. The man glanced at Benjamin and frowned. Then he seemed to adjust his face and said, "Lewis James isn't it? And isn't this little Benjamin?"

Lewis thought, another one who believes she shouldn't have an encumbrance. These types miss the best things.

"Yes," Lewis said. "Hello Steinmetz. Haven't seen you since Friedenberg's party." Lewis felt Benjamin grab onto his leg and duck behind him as he did sometimes with strangers. Reaching around, Lewis lifted Benjamin up. The child's warm, round head snuggled into Lewis' shoulder.

Lewis felt a pang of grief deep in his stomach. He'd nearly lost this wonderful child. Only a minute later and the man would have . . .

Steinmetz's voice caught him in mid-shudder.

"I'm just a little surprised to see nonmusic faculty in the building. But, I can see that you've been taking care of young Mr. Gregory, so that explains it. Do you have Benjamin very often?"

"Sure, Benji here is one of my most curious students. He gets top grades in curiosity."

"Well, that sounds like the kind of student everyone would like to get their hands on. Is he with you every day?"

Lewis thought Steinmetz's questions a little nosey. He gave an evasive answer. "I get him whenever I can."

"How nice of you," Steinmetz said. "I'd better be going now. Nice to see you again Lewis, Benjamin." Harald Steinmetz picked up his briefcase from next to Rebecca's classroom door, nodded and went down the hall. Lewis stared after him. He could have sworn that Steinmetz was waiting for Rebecca, until Lewis showed up.

Well, thanks buddy. I don't mind having the field to myself.

Benjamin pulled tighter into the crook of Lewis' shoulder. The little boy was very quiet until his mother came out of the classroom. Then, all of Benjamin's tension broke in a flood of tears and incoherent efforts to explain what had happened.

After dinner at Lewis' home, when an exhausted Benjamin went to sleep in Lewis' bed, Lewis found the time ripe for a talk. She sat on the sofa as he came in from the kitchen. He found her leaning her head into her palms.

"Becca, we need to involve the police. They can't help you if they only know about today at the school."

"No police. We need to guard Benji better. I'll find a way to send him to a private school where no one will find him."

"Mrs. Johnson soon will tell the police that it is Benji the man tried to take. And I'm certain this was the weasel you saw at the airport the day we met."

"We will hide."

"They can find him, and you, right at home every day."

"I'm moving."

"When? Where?" He hovered over her, trying to hold his fear inside.

She moved away, plucking at the fabric on the sofa with nervous fingers. "As soon as I find a place."

He leaned over her on the sofa and spoke harshly. "You're going to give Benjamin a closet to sleep in and no friends because you fear the police?"

"The police will only be the beginning," she yelled up at him. "Then there will be immigration."

He tried to back up and calm his voice. "You won't talk to Rabbi Stamps. He has an idea, but you're too afraid even to explore a solution."

She turned from him and whispered. "They will take Benji from me."

"That's what someone told you six years ago. You don't know that person was right, even then."

She seemed to freeze. "Even then? You mean Gabriel could have been wrong?"

"Isn't he the one who wanted you to get rid of Benji?"

She nodded slowly.

"Get your information from someone who cares about you."

She breathed. "But Uncle Tobias . . ."

"Let's call your uncle and run this idea past him."

Rebecca looked up at him. "The guy had greasy hair?" she asked.

"The same little buzzard that came through the revolving doors the day you arrived in the airport."

"Where is my purse?"

"Right here," he reached down next to the sofa and lifted it.

"I'll put Uncle Tobias on speaker phone," she said.

* *

In that one conversation, Lewis learned to love Uncle Tobias.

"Becca," Tobias had said, "You might be right about wanting to hide, but I don't want that life for you or for Benjamin. That kid's curiosity needs a free, safe world to roam in."

"But Uncle what safe world? That world doesn't exist."

"Darling, you are suffocating in fear. You want that for him, too? Go see your rabbi."

*   *

Within an hour, they had an appointment for Lewis to sound out Rabbi Stamps about the immigration agent. If Lewis felt the guy was safe, Rebecca would meet with him, too.

CHAPTER TWENTY-THREE

Rabbi Stamps couldn't help grinning whenever he thought about Lewis James – the young man was so obviously afire with love for Rebecca. Last spring, Elijah Stamps wouldn't have bet two pfennig on her chances of finding anyone patient enough for her. But last spring he hadn't known this young Irishman. The man's exuberance and joy in life were the perfect foil for her more tentative acceptance of the world's pleasures. Stamps could also imagine the kindred feeling young Benjamin would have for Lewis – they would be two curious boys on an excursion through the physical world, questioning the how and why of everything they bumped into.

Thus, a smile wreathed the rabbi's face as he opened the door to his next visitor. "Come in, Lewis. Did you get a chance to talk to Rebecca?"

The diffident grin told Elijah that Lewis had enjoyed a chance for more than talk. Elijah thought that was good, too.

Go with care down that path, my boy, He thought, but do go down it.

"You were right, Rabbi Stamps. There were some things I didn't know, but how can I be sure this immigration agent won't have me followed until he figures out who it is I'm inquiring for?"

The Rabbi's big palms came up as his head cocked to one side in a clear gesture of fatalism. "We have only his word for it. He tells me that he won't divulge the information you bring him to anyone else and he won't act on it until the person we're discussing comes forward of her own accord. But, I do know this . . . Joseph Selig is a good man, a member of my congregation. I've worked with him before. I would take his word."

Lewis warmed with relief. He took the chair Stamps offered and they began a discussion of strategy that wandered into religious and moral paradoxes. After a time, Joseph Selig joined them.

Foreshortening the preliminaries, Mr. Selig began with a rapid series of questions. "Mr. James are you a citizen of the United States?"

"Yes, I've been a citizen for eight years."

"You came to study and stayed to teach?"

"Yes."

"So, it's not you we're discussing here but, in truth, a friend?"

"Yes."

"Does this person know you're talking to me?"

"Yes."

"And you've tried to get your friend to accept legal assistance?"

"Tried, but not yet succeeded."

"Tell me, then, what is it he fears."

"She fears denial of citizenship because of the manner in which she entered the country."

"What do you mean, 'manner'? Did she stow away? swim the Rio Grande? What manner?"

"Her visa application lied about her identity."

"Why?"

"She was convinced by her rescuer that she wouldn't be able to enter this country unless it appeared that she were married. Her passport and visa say that she's a widow. She is not."

"There has been no marriage ceremony?"

"No."

"Has she been living with her rescuer?"

"No. She lives here on her own."

"As far as you know, at any rate ...."

"What do you mean?" Lewis felt his anger rising and at the same time felt Elijah's hand on his arm, forcing him to stay in the chair.

Elijah interrupted the flow of the questions to speak quietly to Mr. Selig. "Joseph, the lady we are discussing is one I would trust to be telling the truth."

"All right, Elijah. I'll accept that she is not married or living with this fellow." Turning toward Lewis he began the machine gun approach again.

"What extenuating circumstances would account for her accepting his judgment in lying on her application?"

"Thugs – what appears to have been a lawless gang stole her off the streets in her home country and . . . imprisoned her for a time. They want something they believe she has, but she doesn't have what they want. During the imprisonment, she'd been . . . she was raped."

Lewis had to stop a moment. The memory of her hand tracing the pattern of her story on his palm brought numbing sorrow.

After a long silence, Rabbi Stamps continued telling what they had agreed on. "By the time she fled, she knew she was pregnant, yet refused to have an abortion. The man who helped rescue her convinced her that she wouldn't be allowed to immigrate to the U.S. if she were unmarried and pregnant."

Selig turned to Elijah, speaking angrily in a language Lewis did not know. The meaning of the words escaped him, but the disgust was unambiguous. Elijah answered, also obviously angry, but there was at least forgiveness in his tone.

Eventually, Elijah turned to Lewis to explain. "Joseph is saddened, in Yiddish, yet," his eyes flashed at Joseph. "He sees too much how people get themselves into trouble unnecessarily. In this case, your friend would have been eligible to enter our country by asking for the right to asylum, fearing persecution in her homeland based on her experience with the gang. A conditional entry would almost automatically have been granted. Any U.S. consular office would have helped her apply."

Lewis slumped down in his chair. "Six years, she has been afraid! And that's what the kidnappers have been holding over her!"

"Kidnappers? What's going on here?" Now Selig was leaning forward in his chair.

"The child she had is now five years old. For the past several months, someone's been harassing her and breaking into her home. And three times, someone has tried to take her son. The most recent was yesterday, when a man beat the boy's teacher in an effort to take him from the school. Because of her false citizenship, they've been too frightened to get help from the authorities.

"Who is they? I thought the fake husband was not in the picture."

" 'They' is the woman and her uncle who lived with her in New York." Lewis saw Selig shoot an incredulous look at Elijah.

Elijah answered the implied question. "The uncle is an uncle."

Selig came back to Lewis with his attentive black eyes.

Lewis went on. "The man who convinced her to take this path is still in the picture. He would like her to marry him in truth, but she cannot bring herself to do so."

"I should hope not. He's either an imbecile or a manipulative brute. She's been under this threat for six years? How sane is she?"

Lewis grew heated again until he saw Elijah shake his head. Trying to keep the anger out of his voice, he answered, "She's remarkably sane, considering. The son is a wonderful child. Until recently the boy has been kept unaware of the threat to him."

Selig let out a low whistle. "Do you know anyone who might be a party to these threats?"

"Firsthand, I don't know most of the people in her life except people she works with here and they met her only last spring. In New York, there's the uncle, whom she trusts implicitly, and the other man. Her friends in her homeland, all believe that she died in a suicide car accident. That accident covered her escape. Frankly, I don't see how anyone there would have known how to find her to threaten her."

"Do you have any other ideas? I mean about who might be guilty?"

"One other wild thought has occurred to me." Lewis began. "But this is purely speculative thinking, you understand."

Selig looked interested, "Go ahead and speculate."

"The breakins have netted them nothing. That strikes me as very odd since there were a valuable violin and lute sitting out for the taking each time they came. The gang in Hungary claimed she had hidden several valuable documents. These break-ins and kidnap attempts are most likely related to the gang's beliefs. Thus, it is possible this is the work of that same gang.

"However," Lewis continued, "Suppose this man who wants her to marry him is trying to convince her to seek his protection by scaring her."

Lewis glanced at the other two men and was struck by a marked change in Joseph Selig's demeanor. Joseph became flushed and no longer looked at either of them. "She has a lute and a violin," he said, almost to himself. He'd sunken in upon himself and was looking only at the floor. It was as if someone had pulled the plug and let all the air out of him.

"Joseph," Elijah too had noticed the difference. "Joseph, is Lewis saying something wrong?"

Joseph pulled himself a little more upright and tried to reenter the conversation. It was obviously an effort. "No, nothing is wrong. In fact, what Lewis is guessing may be the truth of the matter. Perhaps it is this man. Yet, perhaps there is some other explanation. It is difficult to find out how it's being done unless the victim will come forth.

Is your friend and her child living with you?" Selig seemed almost afraid of the answer, even as he asked the question.

"No, they're living in an apartment."

Selig appeared relieved by the answer, although Lewis couldn't see what bearing it had on the case. Joseph's next comment was delivered more in the clipped tones of his earlier questions. "I would like to see the child get protection, but I can only arrange for that if the mother will come to me and file an official complaint."

"What should I tell her about the false visa?"

"Tell her to come to me, with a lawyer if you like. We can work out something about the visa. There are some new amnesty rulings which will help her. She need not fear punishment. Nor will she be returned to her homeland."

Lewis asked more questions. An hour later, he decided he knew enough to convince Rebecca and reached to shake Selig's hand.

"Thank you, sir, and you Rabbi Stamps," Lewis rose and began moving toward the door. "I appreciate your help. I'll let you know what she decides."

While Lewis watched, Joseph Selig sagged again, as if he were suddenly very tired. Lewis had an inexplicable urge to comfort the man, although he didn't know why. Instead, he said. "I'm sure we can work something out. I'd like her to be free of this fear before the holidays. "

Selig glanced sharply up at the Irishman. "Before even Chanukah, if you bring her soon."

Lewis raised his brows in recognition of Joseph's small barb, nodded to Rabbi Stamps and left.

After Lewis had closed the door, Joseph turned to Rabbi Stamps. "Elijah, could you answer one question for me?"

"If I think it's appropriate."

"Were we discussing Rebecca Gregory?"

Elijah was very quiet for a moment. "You too, Joseph?"

"Me too?"

"If I'd known you were one of the congregation who had formed an attachment to her, I wouldn't have asked you to handle this. I'm sorry, Joseph."

"It's all right, Elijah. Abe Friedenberg introduced us."

"Ah yes," said Stamps, "I remember Abe had plans to create happiness for Rebecca."

Joseph glanced at his rabbi ruefully then down at his shoes. "I wanted it as much as Abe, but . . . well . . ."

The young man slumped silently for a moment and then sat up a little straighter. "I guess what I learned about her today answers a lot of questions I had about myself last year – about my ability to care for a woman." He glanced up at Elijah. "One more question, Lij?"

"Ask."

"Why him?"

"I don't know, but I have formed an hypothesis."

"Any idea would help."

"Before she met him, her life was dark with fear. Last spring, here, she began to 'see rainbows' as she put it. This Lewis James is a man of exuberance, of volatile imagination. Instinctively, he brought an intense light to her darkness."

Elijah put a hand on Joseph Selig's arm. "She is a lovely lady, Joseph. But you are too much darkness yourself sometimes. What you need is a woman of sunshine."

Joseph nodded slowly. "Thank you, Elijah." His smile came at last. "I do need that imagined one."

Stamps chuckled, "Yes, but she will come only when you are ready."

CHAPTER TWENTY-FOUR

Rebecca laughed at herself for daydreaming about putting Joseph Selig's prepaid cell phone to work rescuing her from another December evening with Harald Steinmetz.

Joseph had given her the cell in case her phone number was monitored in some way. He transferred her contact list and then took her phone to have it debugged.

He wanted her to call him anytime she needed help. His help had made a difference in her life. One of the most apprehensive times she'd known was the morning in November when Lewis and his lawyer had escorted her to Joseph's office, and she'd realized just who this immigration officer was.

But he'd greeted them warmly. Toward her he was very courteous and correct. He'd prepared carefully for her case and had everything they needed at his fingertips.

By the end of that afternoon, Rebecca had been well on her way to becoming legal, preparing to become a citizen. Joseph had taken her to the police station and introduced her to his friend, the blustery Sergeant Hardy. She'd filed reports on the breakin and on the kidnap attempts. Sergeant Hardy had taken her case very seriously, assigning

June Williams, a veteran policewoman, to investigate the situation and to coordinate with the New York police.

Afterward, Joseph had brought her home. It was close to sunset when he parked on her street, facing the Willamette River. Turning off the motor, he'd stared quietly at the gray and peach surface of the river, not able to say what he needed.

Rebecca broke the silence. "Joseph, you have always been kind. Today . . . today you lifted a great weight from me."

"I'm glad Rebecca. Right now, I . . . I've been trying to find a way to tell you that I finally understand about last year, about why we couldn't make love happen for us. The feeling I have for you is the same. But now, I'm at peace with caring for you and with anticipating nothing more."

She felt the sting of tears in her eyes. They'd both been hurt by their encounter last year. She had suffered from undeniable evidence that she wasn't able to accept physical love. His wound was from witnessing the fear his sexual advances had caused in her.

Rebecca's voice was choked. "Joseph, I tried to tell you, it is my emptiness."

"You tried to tell me. But last year I couldn't understand what you meant. When that part of life changes for you, I'll be there to wish you happiness. I want to dance at your wedding." He couldn't stop the escaping sigh. Laughing at himself he went on, "It will hurt, but not overmuch." He looked sidelong at her and managed a wink.

They both laughed and began remembering the fun of their better times. Then he gave her the cell phone and taught her how to call him in an emergency.

*　*

Tonight, in cold December, she wished some emergency would come up, because, while Benjamin had the fun of a high school soccer tournament with Lewis, Harald wanted to spend another evening reading through her 'fascinating' old manuscripts.

Harald, who was charming and had a trove of history stories, became less than interesting when they played music together. It wasn't that he didn't read and play well . . . it was that he didn't have any fun at it. He rarely showed a desire to polish a duet or see how much more music they could get out of it. Instead, like a dour soldier going through the manual of arms, he was determined to get through all her boxes and then help her catalogue them. She always had more fun playing duets with Lewis.

The only time she'd seen Harald daunted by the thought of plowing through music was when he came upon a particularly fat piano part to one set of Maestro Raphael Atemvoll's songs bound together with the lovely, but more pedestrian dances written by Atemvoll's teacher, Anton Batislav. Without finishing even half the book, he'd set it on the stack with those they'd already read and accepted a glass of wine to top off the evening.

She had never again shown him any of the Atemvoll and Batislav collection. They had been put into her book shelves where they appeared to be three books on music theory.

She wanted to savor the memories of Raphael Atemvoll that these pieces brought back. Reading reams of music without savoring any of it was artistic rigor mortis. She'd do it no more. She couldn't call for rescue from the heavens, or even from Joseph. She had to rescue herself.

She hopped up from the couch, put on her rain coat and grabbed her umbrella and purse. Turning on the alarm system and locking the door behind her, she struck out at full tilt down the hall. By the time she met Harald, she was going her legal sixty miles an hour, and wasn't to be stopped.

"Hi Harald. I'm gonna walk downtown 'n see the `Rocky Horror Picture Show'. Ya wanna come?"

Harald whirled to catch up with her, his handsome mouth agape in disbelief. His longish straight hair flew stiffly about as he turned to catch up.

He had to shuffle pretty fast to keep up with her. She hoped she could find the theater after he was soaked and before she was. She was amazed that he was sticking with her through this craziness. Marks for persistence. Well, Gabriel would probably get rid of him in the usual way when he came for their concerts next month.

In truth, that wasn't a very comforting thought. Gabriel would probably try to get rid of Lewis in that same manner.

CHAPTER TWENTY- FIVE

JANUARY, 2001
PORTLAND, OREGON

The rains of December had become snow flurries by the day in January when Rebecca drove to the airport to meet Gabriel. In spite of the blustery weather, there were quite a few fans at the gate to meet his plane. Rebecca turned her back on the television camera and wished she'd asked Abraham and Miriam to come to the airport with her. Last fall, she'd been grateful that no reporters had known she was coming on the night of her arrival. How did they know tonight about Gabriel?

Probably this crowd was created by his agent. She could imagine the huffy, round agent protesting now, "But Rebecca, Sweetheart, how's anybody going to know about you? Just one little talk show, Sweetie – maybe NPR, and maybe . . .."

In New York, she and Gabriel had become the subject of news reporters' curiosity when they played but being followed around by a cameraman while awaiting Gabriel's arrival seemed particularly invasive tonight. Rebecca could hear the reporter warming up her voice and testing the acoustics.

"The beautiful and talented Rebecca Gregory anxiously awaits her colleague, Gabriel Kolya, who arrives this evening for a series of recitals. These longtime friends have not seen each other for several months. This is an anxious time for Miss Gregory."

Rebecca wished she could retreat to the restrooms. She was anxious, but not in the way being imagined by news fans tonight. She had to thwart Gabriel's spell. Uncle Tobias' call last night had made her even more concerned about the spell of Gabriel's smooth logic. Tobias had warned that Gabriel intended to bring her back with him.

"If you let him convince you to give up," Tobias said, "you'll lose everything you've been doing for yourself. Play duets with him and let that be all he gets for his persuasive pyrotechnics."

Rebecca felt emotionally stronger after almost five months away from Gabriel. She knew she could resist his entreaties and logical arguments. What concerned her more was that the reporter was already setting the stage for how Gabriel might influence what happened to Lewis James and Rebecca Gregory.

News people gushed over how well Gabriel looked with Rebecca at his side. They assumed a romance was the natural outcome of collaboration between two nice looking people. Their expressions and gestures would be interpreted in the light of that assumed romantic attachment. Lewis was going to have difficulty not believing the attachment was there when the overwhelming vote of the news media was for its existence.

"Miss Gregory, would you move on up to the passenger door? He'll be coming out first." The cameraman talked to her but kept a sharp eye on the door.

"What? How do you know that?"

"They radioed ahead." he explained. "That way, we can get our footage and get out of everyone else's way. So, if you'll just move on up there we'll all be set."

Rebecca grew hot and angry. How dare these people orchestrate a greeting between friends! She spoke to the camera man directly.

"No. I stay back here. You greet him. Get your footage. When you have interviewed him, I'll take him to his hotel."

The reporter pushed in front of the camera. "But you're important to this story, too. We want the two of you together." He prodded her toward the passenger entrance with his hand on her shoulder.

She turned aside from his guiding hand and said heatedly. "Come to the concert. We get together on stage. You can even bring a camera to one of the rehearsals. That is what we do best. You really ought to see us play music, we're pretty good at it."

Just then, a flight attendant banged open the door to the airplane access ramp. The cameraman and crew surged toward the opening. A few seconds later, Gabriel Kolya appeared in the spot lights, smiling and greeting well-wishers. Rebecca sucked in her surprise at the sight of him. She'd nearly forgotten how very handsome this man was. His soft dark hair and attentive brown eyes contrasted with the granite strength of his forehead and jaw, giving just the right combination of steel and velvet to set women's hearts on fire.

In Lewis' home, pray God that Benjamin was not watching the evening news. He would be jolted by the sight of this formidable man. Benjamin knew Gabriel was coming to visit for two weeks, but the sight of him on television greeting Rebecca would worry Benjamin unnecessarily. In his small boy way, Benjamin knew what Gabriel wanted of Rebecca.

Rebecca pushed backward through the crowd and started down the concourse intending to wait for Gabriel at the baggage claim area where the television people might not have the patience to follow him. She had almost reached the main lobby when Gabriel's strong hand caught her shoulder and pulled her to his chest. He bent to kiss her.

"Darling, you don't need to hide from your public. I'll take care of you." He turned her toward the camera. "Let me talk for us, I know how overwhelming all these lights and questions must seem to you."

Rebecca tried to push away from his embrace, "Gabriel, I can talk for myself. Let me go." His arm tightened about her shoulder and his other arm with the briefcase came around her waist. His mouth came down, hard and insistent on her lips.

When she came up for air, he whispered hoarsely in her ear, "Don't pull away from me, Rebecca. You can't know how I've missed you all these months. Give to me, just a little, Darling."

He had never shown his passion in public, rarely in private. What would Benjamin think? And Levy . . .

"Mr. Kolya," the voice of the lady reporter broke through Rebecca's whirling thoughts. "Sir, before your arrival, Miss Gregory said that the two of you make beautiful music together. Would you say that you might become a permanent duet?"

Gabriel turned Rebecca to face the camera with him. He leaned down to kiss the top of her hair. "She said that?" He looked at her incredulously. "How nice of her."

"I was quoted out of context, Gabriel," she said. "Don't take it the way she said it."

He didn't hear her, but went on talking to the reporter, "Someday, perhaps we'll sign a permanent contract. For the immediate future, we'll play it by ear."

Rebecca did not smile, and tried very hard not to look as close to Gabriel as he was holding her. If she jerked her waist from his grasp it would make him look pretty foolish and might make it look to her son as if Gabriel were using force. Well, he was . . .

This night his actions worried her. She'd never had to ask him to let go of her before. Was it really the effect of five months absence? or was he taking some new tack in his pursuit of her?

Dear Levy, please keep Benji away from the television set.

"Gabriel," she said loudly, "we have to get your luggage and get you to your hotel. It's late. I have to pick up Benjamin and get him to bed."

"Hotel?" he whispered harshly. "Why a hotel?"

"I'll explain later. Let's get away from these lights."

He kept an arm firmly around her waist as she led the way down to the luggage area. When they were finally away from the reporters and settled in her car, he turned his hurt eyes on her. "A hotel, Rebecca? Do you no longer trust me?"

"After this greeting, no. I don't trust you. Plus, for two weeks you'll need a real bed, not a sofa."

He jerked but came back strong. "Can we stop off somewhere on the way and have a drink? I want to talk to you."

"I need to put Benjamin to bed."

"Can't we have a drink at your place and then I'll walk to the hotel? I only have the one suitcase."

"I need to get to sleep, too, Gabriel."

"What is the matter darling? Why so much distance?"

She didn't answer him for a moment. Doing something made her feel safer, so she started the car and began the drive home. "Gabriel, why were you doing all those things to me in front of the television cameras?"

"Oh, so that's it. I missed you terribly, Rebecca. I guess that was just the accumulation of all the small contacts we could have had if you'd been at home since August. I've been stowing up the need for you all this time. I saw you practically running away from me down the concourse and my control broke."

"Don't do that to me, Gabriel." Her voice choked with anger.

"I thought you responded rather well . . ." the silk smooth taunting suddenly infuriated her.

"Charitably. I responded charitably. I didn't want you to look like a fool when I slapped you."

"That was kind of you, princess," his jaw muscles were grinding, "I'm beginning to think that some man ought to take you over his knee and then make love to your soft body until you are no longer so spoiled."

Her vision blurred, the darkness of the past closed in and the heavy iron doors of her memory banged shut.

Gabriel grabbed at the steering wheel and slammed his left foot on the brake. They ended up facing a large expanse of snow covered lawn near the entrance to the parking lot. When the nightmare had played out, she woke, drenched in fear and sweat. Gabriel sat next to her, watching. He heard the sigh that signaled her release from the demons of the past.

"Rebecca, it's just that I want you with me. This last few months were shear torture to me. I built it up in my mind that you'd missed me as well. Does any other man make this nightmare happen to you?"

Suddenly she realized that he prided himself on his ability to cause these episodes.

"No other man tries so hard to do it." She was silent, gathering a kind of strength she hadn't thought she would need to use. Finally, she was ready. "We are still in the airport. I will take you back to the lobby and let you off to buy a ticket home."

His surprise was complete. "What about our concerts?"

"I'll cancel them. You became ill or something. They are not so important that I have to put up with this nightmare as often as you choose to provoke it. I never realized until tonight that you do try to make it happen to me, to put me in the role of a sick person who needs your care."

His eyes widened with surprise. "You really believe that? Or is it just that I'm the only man who is close enough to make you think about acting like a woman?"

Rebecca saw for the first time a dim outline of what he'd done to her for the last six years. Her answer grew in strength as she spoke and as the blurred lines of his method became sharper in her mind. "No, you are far from the only man who makes me feel like a woman. But you are the only one who constantly reminds me of how it feels to be a victim of men. You have dwelt on that memory for me, kept it alive and used it against me for a long time. I should be well by now. You've kept me a little bit sick so that you could feed your own hatred of what happened over and over and over . . ."

His eyes suddenly glittered with that very hatred, "You made yourself a victim by keeping him. Every time I see him I am reminded of what they did . . ."

"You are reminded, not me. When I see Benjamin, I am reminded of how wonderful any human being can be if he is loved. He reminds me only of himself and of the goodness of new life, the renewal of hope."

Gabriel's eyes narrowed. "Hope? You have always been blind when it comes to that child – the same misplaced . . ."

Rebecca whispered, "Shut up, Gabriel."

He shut up. She started the car again and backed out of their awkward position. Then she turned abruptly left and drove back toward the airport. Gabriel sucked in a quick breath. "You wouldn't!"

"I am. You will leave."

"I don't understand . . ."

She pulled up in front of the airport. "Goodbye Gabriel."

There was panic in his eyes. "Rebecca, I . . . What can I do to make you change your mind?"

"Nothing."

"Rebecca!" He leaned toward her, but his hand reminded itself to stop before he touched her. "I don't want to leave you like this, not after all our years together. What can I do?"

"It would be too difficult for you."

"Please . . . what?"

Rebecca watched the emotions that played over his face. All these years and he still didn't understand what made her able to function normally.

If he stayed and was forced to live with her new strength, she would grow even stronger. She wanted to prove that strength to herself.

Rebecca moved the gear shift into park.

"If you want to stay for the concerts, you'll have to say nothing to or about Benjamin which even hints that his life is a mistake."

"But . . ."

"Not one thing."

He sank back into the seat. "All right. I'll say nothing."

"Furthermore . . ."

He glanced sharply at her as if complying with the request she'd already made was tough enough.

"Furthermore, I don't want to spend two weeks escaping from your physical attentions. You will keep away from me except when we are practicing, and you will keep your hands off me. Tonight was . . . I have not changed that part of my life."

"If I promise to keep our friendship completely on stage, will you let me stay? We really do make beautiful music together."

Rebecca still pondered the advantages to kicking him out of the car. When she answered, her response was a surprise to her. "Yes, Gabriel. We'll play our duets, but that is all."

As soon as she said it, she knew it was right. There was no other way for her to grow beyond what Gabriel had made of her. She had to face him and make him become a colleague instead of him pretending to be a hovering protector.

"Make one mistake and you are in a taxi back to the airport," she said.

"What has happened to make you so hard?"

"I have lived for five months free of you, and will go on living without even your piano playing, if you screw this up."

She started the car again and backed out of their awkward position. On the way to the Heathman Hotel, she kept the conversation on a businesslike plane. "Our first concert will be at the Commons at Reed, two days from now. We'll do the Franck, that Mozart we always do so well, you do the Bach prelude and Fugue in D or whichever solo you like. I'll play the E major Partita. We can finish the concert with Didon Abandonatta and a couple of flash encores – maybe a Sarasate. How does that sound?"

"Do we get to do the Brahms G major Sonata at some point along the way?"

"Of course. I put it on our last concert program. The programs for that concert have already gone to the printers, just as we planned it over the phone."

She was certain that Gabriel misread her decision as a capitulation. He would be with her for most of the next two weeks, even if he were not staying in her apartment. He inevitably would try again to take control of her emotions. But she had grown strong and independent in ways he could not yet believe. And these two weeks would let her prove that to herself as well as to him.

CHAPTER TWENTY-SIX

Lewis couldn't believe how much the sight of her in Gabriel's arms affected him. Ever since the newscast, he'd been wandering aimlessly around his house banging things. When the doorbell rang, he slammed the last cupboard door on his nervous energy and answered the summons.

Through the beveled glass windows, he saw her, alone on the porch, looking at the daffodil leaves which stood bravely in the snow. He opened the door and looked around.

"Hello, Levy." She sounded almost happy.

"Becca. Where is he?"

"I took him to his hotel." She noticed how tired Lewis looked. "Did Benji wear you out with his ideas for things to do?"

"No. In fact, he went to sleep rather early. Then, I sat down to watch the news." He added the last out of spite, though he tried to soften the effect as the sentence spilled from his mouth.

She didn't hear the spite, "I'm glad Benjamin didn't see the news. Levy, I'm going to invite Gabriel to visit my class tomorrow and then go out to dinner. Would you come with us? I'd like him to meet you."

"Why are you glad Benjamin didn't see the news?" He knew that he, too, was listening selectively.

She looked down, her cheeks colored deeply. "I don't want Benjamin to worry about Gabriel. Gabriel is so . . . so . . . .."

"Yes, I can tell by the way you kiss him just how `So' he is."

She was startled and angry. "I kiss him? How could you think…?"

"I didn't even have to imagine it. It was on the screen in digi-color." His frustration and despair wouldn't let him stop. "I was led to believe that this was a man you couldn't make yourself love. It seems to have gotten easier."

Her eyes were wide, their almond curves rounded in disbelief. "Levy, do you believe what you're saying?"

"I believe what I see."

She took a deep breath and looked away for a moment. When she replied, her voice was shaking. "And I suppose you would believe that the source of your echo is the rocks across the valley."

She didn't wait for him to respond, but walked into the house and up the stairs to pick up her little boy from Lewis' bed. When she came down, he was on the stairs to help her, but she swept past him and out to the car. He opened the car door and stood back while she buckled Benjamin's seat. Lewis wanted to put his hands on her waist, hold her close and hope that the scene he'd witnessed with Gabriel was nothing more than a greeting between friends.

But his experience of friendly greetings didn't include anything as passionate as what he'd seen tonight. And his experience of Rebecca was completely unlike it, too.

Suddenly he felt the fool. "Rebecca, I'm sor . . ."

She interrupted, "Levy, when I was setup tonight by Gabriel and his clever agent, I worried that perhaps Benjamin was watching and would misunderstand. I did not think that you would be so gullible. I believed we knew each other better than that. Goodnight. Benji thanks you for all your care."

She shut the car door and left him standing, arms akimbo, heart pumping in his throat.

Rebecca made it around the corner before she had to pull over to the side of the street. The hurt and anger in Lewis was the very thing she'd feared when she heard the reporter romanticizing about Gabriel. Why hadn't she told him before about Gabriel's way of clearing the field of rivals? Tonight, Gabriel was at his most effective. Why, then, was she so surprised that Lewis fell for the tricks?

Tomorrow as they crossed campus, she would apologize for not warning him. She wanted to turn the car around and go back to him now, but he'd seemed too angry to listen.

CHAPTER TWENTY-SEVEN

Dick Street turned his wheel chair, so he could see the clock on the Commons wall. "Aren't you going to be late, Dr. James?"

Lewis came abruptly out of his daydreams, "What? No, I have a lab class next. I found a new route that's fast. Let's finish our coffee."

"This is the third day in a row that you've left late." Dick didn't want to come right out with his thoughts, but he believed he knew the mistake Lewis was making.

"You wanting to get rid of this old man, so you can keep an appointment with a sweet young thing, Dick?"

"Me? I don't know any sweet young things. Not likely to either, not from down here." Dick could feel the red creep up his neck.

"Why not? You think they all go for the football heroes? This college is short on football heroes. The ladies didn't come here for that."

"They didn't come here for this either," Dick slapped the bony protrusions his mother called knees.

"Dick," Lewis put a hand on Dick's knee, "Give the ladies a little credit. They see all of you, and all of you adds up to a lot more than most big brawns have got to offer them. You're a thoughtful and exciting person to be with. Why do you think I keep lingering over our coffee, here?"

Dick snorted, "You linger because you're avoiding Dr. Gregory since that big piano player got here." Dick knew he'd stepped over the fine line between student and friend. He looked out from under his pale blond brows to see if he was going to be accepted.

Lewis sat up and stared at Dick in disbelief. "What do you know about Dr. Gregory? Let's have the rest of it, Dick. Too late to be reticent now, man."

"A guy sitting all day in the central building of a big school hears a lot of things."

"And you have heard . . .?"

"That last year, when you were on sabbatical, her stiff-arming tactics with amorous guys were legendary, that you're the only guy who gets anywhere with her and that you see her every day after my tutorial."

"That's a lot of things, all right. What makes you think I'm avoiding her, now?"

"I copied the news on the night the piano player arrived. My roommate is a real news nut, but he had a hot date that night, so I got it all on film. It doesn't look the same the second and third time you watch it."

Lewis played with his coffee, sloshing the dregs around in the cup for a while before he could look at Dick. "What *is* different the second time?"

"It's pretty clear he's pushing her around. She doesn't want to make him look like a fool, but she isn't liking the contact either. By the third time, I can tell pretty much what she's saying to him."

"How can you tell that? She didn't say anything you could hear."

"Dr. James," said Dick patiently, "you know I don't hear much at all."

"Part of the congenital problem?"

Dick nodded.

Lewis smiled, remembering their conversation in the hall of the physics building. "I forgot. You read lips and keep secrets."

"I'm pretty good at it – the lip reading – even when you're not looking directly at me. I spent several years doing wheelies at Tucker Maxon Oral School, so I could carry on conversations with real folk."

Lewis flinched at the 'real folk', but he asked, "So you read her lips?"

"His too. In fact, he was the one facing the camera the most. He was asking her not to pull away from him. She was asking him to let go of her. There was other stuff about getting her son to bed, taking Kolya to the hotel and the like, but that was the basic conversation."

Lewis spent several seconds staring into his coffee cup while leaden regret spread through his body. He'd let her down. How could he expect her to trust him if he so easily backed out of her life?

Dick's voice stopped Lewis's selfreproach. "If that guy is going to be around for another week and a half, I think she could use a friend."

Lewis dragged up a smile, "Dick, thanks for doing 'friend' duty for me. I'll go find her."

"Good. She's really something. Be a shame to lose her."

"You're right there." Lewis stood up.

He turned back to take care of a nagging thought. "By the way, tomorrow I want to know why you call the rest of us 'real folk'. I know people with two working feet who are no more real than a bookcase."

Lewis could see that Dick's laughter was partly at Lewis' imagery and partly a release of tension.

"For you, Real Guy, I'll butt in anytime," Dick said.

*   *

"Hello?" Rebecca answered her office phone.

"Becca, forgive me for being a jealous fool." Lewis' voice sounded tense.

Rebecca glanced through the window on her office door. Out in the hall, Gabriel positioned himself between her line of sight and

Harald Steinmetz. She sighed, "Levy, you are not a fool. And thank you for being jealous."

"Rebecca, I've left you alone too long. It's my afternoon to pick up Benjamin. When I get him from school, he and I can make dinner for you and Gabriel."

"I'd like that. Would you mind inviting Abe and Miriam? I think conversation would be easier."

"Is conversation that tough, Becca? I'd be glad to invite them."

Out in the hall Harald's face grew stiff as he listened to whatever Gabriel said. Harald's eyes caught hers through the glass door. He looked away.

"Yes, Levy, it is tough. Music is good, but the rest stinks."

"Why Becca! You're usually such a lady."

"I keep reminding myself that he does all this because he thinks he loves me."

What is Gabriel saying to Harald out there?

Lewis' voice was strong and clear. "Remind yourself that selfish love is different from giving love."

"Thank you. You've given this situation perspective."

"I love you, too. I sometimes throw jealous fits, but otherwise I'm a swell person to be with."

She laughed. "That's the truth." She'd known he loved her, but it gave her strength to hear it. "I've missed you, Levy. Please be patient with Gabriel's jealousy."

"Rebecca, how do you feel about him?"

"I want these two weeks to prove to myself that he cannot influence my life anymore. He doesn't know it yet, but I'm practicing emotional weightlifting for two weeks and then, he and I will no longer be musical partners."

"Good for you. You're right about the two of you making music together, but there are many pianists in this world. I was there last night. You are wonderful."

"What was your favorite?"

"Favorite is hard, but I tell you that's the first time Beethoven's Kreutzer Sonata has sounded like a unified piece. Usually, it comes off as several ideas pasted together."

She warmed to his praise of the most difficult work they'd played. "I thought I saw you lurking in the back."

"I hated him." Lewis' teasing voice was soft.

"You need not have. I . . . I'm glad you came. See you tonight."

Gabriel came into the office as she hung up. "What was that all about?"

She picked up her violin case to head out the door. "That was a friend who has invited us for dinner tonight. He said our Beethoven was wonderful last night."

"He's right." Gabriel tried to take her by the shoulders and smile down at her, but she moved away from him. He pretended not to notice. "You are even better than last year. You take more risks and are ... I don't know . . . freer. The tempo of that Sarasate was wild. I thought the audience was going to start dancing in the aisles – like fiesta night in a dark taverna."

"Gabriel, such eloquence!" she laughed. She hugged her violin case and walked to the door of her office. "Have you danced in dark taverns on such a night?"

He looked away, a boyish embarrassment on his face. "My taverna days were long ago, before you, lady. I am not so wild as I once was."

"Why not? Was it not crazy fun?" she asked. Jealous women had sometimes hinted to her of Gabriel's reputedly reckless youth. He'd been carefully a gentleman all the time she'd known him.

"I've heard that you are an exciting dancer," she pushed on. "You should go to such places and enjoy."

He strode to the door, but she opened it and stepped into the hall.

He said, "While you're in my care, I would never be so uncontrolled." The heat grew. His eyes became dark with hunger.

She started down the hall. "I'm not in your care. We need to go out on the stage and rehearse for tomorrow night."

"I see. The stage again."

"Yes. We'll use the bigger auditorium. The chapel was too crowded last night."

He moved to catch up with her. "Do we have to be with this friend tonight for dinner?"

"I think you should meet Levy James. He's a good friend of Abraham and Miriam, and quite knowledgeable about music."

"When do I get to talk to you alone?"

"We're alone quite a lot. And you are trying to forget the conditions of these two weeks."

His exasperation was clear, "On stage only. This conversation in the hall is the most alone we've been for three days!"

"Gabriel, you promised to keep our friendship on the stage. This other is not for us. Last night there were women dying to meet you, some very intelligent and exciting women. You need somebody more like your real self, a little wildness – a lot of intelligence . . . look around."

"I cannot. It's you I want, always, from that first night on the lake."

"It's not me you want. I'm not the helpless princess you created. You're right, I am becoming freer here, and I won't go back."

"But Rebecca, your career suffers the longer you stay away from New York. The recording studio is after you to come back, too."

"I can record without living next to the studio. Here, I am making better and better music. Columbia Records knows where I am. They write to me all the way across the country."

"Don't put me off, Rebecca." His frustration shortened his patience. "You know it would be easier to get recordings done if you were there with me. And there would be concerts."

"Gabriel, I read *The Times*. Your career is not suffering because I'm gone, and I'm not hurting either. New York won't forget me. And

New Yorkers aren't the only audience in the United States. I will solo with the Oregon Symphony in March and the San Francisco Symphony next fall."

"The Oregon Symphony!" his disdain was evident.

"One of the few fulltime symphonies in the United States . . . and high-quality recordings, too."

"How could they . . .?" disbelief was in every syllable.

"Oh, Gabriel, don't be so provincial! You've lived too long in the same insulated town. Let's go rehearse."

She started past him, but he grabbed her upper arm tightly in one hand, his face arrogant. "Even in Oregon, you seem to be in danger from vandals and kidnappers."

His arrogance softened with real worry. "I can't leave you here. God knows what might happen."

She yanked her arm away. "Yes, there's danger, but here I have many friends who help me. In New York, you drove away any who wanted to befriend me until I had only you and Uncle Tobias. And only Tobias cares about Benjamin."

He exploded with fury. "I drive away your friends? You, with your coldness – how can you think that I drove them away?"

She wouldn't take that coldly. "That's what you were doing just now with Harald Steinmetz."

His voice was condescendingly smooth. "You've such an imagination to see enemies in your best allies. No wonder you are afraid so much."

"I don't need to imagine. I know you." She straightened her sleeve and held her head up. "I'll be on the stage until two o'clock if you want to rehearse. And I've invited my students to hear our rehearsal."

*   *

In the hotel near the downtown concert hall, Harald Steinmetz pulled a cigarette out of a blue and white package. Russmann lit it. Harald dropped the empty package into a nearby bowl and then slouched onto the window frame, leaned on the glass and studied the leafless trees of Portland's winter.

The package lay in the bowl, its famous dancing gypsy face up in her traditional design – a waft of smoke.

Steinmetz turned only enough to be sure Rossman was standing at attention, then he said, "The child is definitely mine."

"Yes, sir. Very bright."

"And handsome."

"And five years old."

"Young enough to be trainable, nein?" Steinmetz said.

"Ja. Yes. Trainable."

"We have to stop playing around. She is barren and frozen, so I'm taking a new tack."

Russmann glanced at Steinmetz and then returned to staring at the wall like a sergeant awaiting orders.

Steinmetz returned to his study of the frozen streetscape. "He has to be taken and sent to Hungary for retraining as my son."

"Frau Rossman can bring about wonders, there," Russmann said.

"For a time. And then tutors."

"Yes, sir."

"Her uncle has shipped more boxes and she doesn't keep them in her office."

"You want the boxes?"

"All her music, anywhere, office, home."

"We will find them."

"I've decided," Steinmetz said. "She will not be pleasure. So, we just take."

Russmann nodded.

Steinmetz stumped his cigarette out on the package. The dancing gypsy writhed in the fire.

CHAPTER TWENTY-EIGHT

That evening, in his master bedroom, after dinner with Miriam, Abe and Gabriel, Lewis helped Rebecca put on her coat. Downstairs, he heard his other guests still talking and waiting for him to bring the coats downstairs. Standing behind Rebecca, his hands rested on her shoulders, lightly pulling her back into his body. He leaned down to whisper in her ear. "I love you, Becca. I think he's going to grill you about me."

She smiled and turned to see the twinkle she knew was there. "Do you blame him?"

He glanced at the stairwell to see if any guests were coming up. "No. He has every reason to be jealous. No reason to worry about your safety with me, though. And that's probably what he will grill you about."

"Well, then, let's avoid that awkwardness. You take his coat and I'll take Abe's and Miriam's. Let's get back down there in a reasonable amount of time."

"How long is reasonable?" he asked, already missing the feel of her winter coat beneath his hands.

"Five minutes ago might have been soon enough." she grinned as she reached across his bed for Abe's overcoat.

Lewis caught her as she came up with the coat. Putting his arm around her waist, he pulled her toward him. He captured her wild curls and held her head in his hand while he studied her in the light of the bed lamp.

"Come back here soon, Becca. Come back here whether he thinks it's safe or not." His kiss was gentle, a promise of more for the future.

She wanted more, now. She reached up to kiss him again, dropping the overcoat to free her hands. The fire he felt in her kiss jolted him. He hadn't expected it, not yet.

What happened? What ignited this passion at last?

When she released him, he drew her close again. Jasmine and soft hair made him oblivious of time and place.

Rebecca pushed from him gently. "We must go down. I'm sorry I did that to you."

He was staggered by the passion she'd set loose in him. "What's happening to you, Becca?"

She hesitated, as shaken by this new sensation as he. "Uncle Tobias was right. He always said I would want again someday."

Lewis stared after her as she took Abe's coat and hurried downstairs. He followed more slowly, trying to clear his head for the last sparring match with Gabriel before they went home.

Downstairs, Gabriel glowered. "Thank you for bringing my coat. I didn't realize you both had gone up for them." Gabriel glanced significantly at Lewis who was just coming down.

Lewis saw that Miriam turned her back to conceal a fit of the giggles. He decided to ignore the high moral tone of Gabriel's implied question.

"Mr. Kolya, it was good to meet you at close quarters. I admired your playing last night and am looking forward to your last concert."

Stepping between Rebecca and Lewis, Gabriel offered Lewis his hand. "Mr. James, perhaps we could have lunch together tomorrow."

Over Gabriel's shoulder, Lewis saw a look of fear cross Rebecca's face at the mention of lunch. He paused to figure out the cause and decided to postpone the lunch until he could ask her. "I'm afraid I'm engaged tomorrow. Perhaps on Friday. Isn't that your last day in town?"

Rebecca's relief was just as evident to Lewis as her fear. He knew he'd done the right thing. He'd call her tomorrow morning before classes and find out what worried her about this lunch.

*   *

Rebecca felt numb. When Gabriel invited a friend of hers for lunch, it almost always signaled the end of close ties to Rebecca. She had a reprieve until Friday. She had to call him and forestall Gabriel's effect.

She bent to put a coat and hat on sleepy Benjamin. It had been the evident closeness between Benjamin and Lewis that made Gabriel jealous. From the moment Benji rode into dinner on Lewis' shoulders, ice had formed. The fact that Benjamin obviously was a great pal of Lewis's beagle had put another layer of ice on the wall between the two men.

When she'd buttoned Benji's small coat, Lewis moved her aside with one hand on her waist. He lifted Benjamin, saying, "I'll buckle him in the car. He's getting heavier and longer this year."

After Benjamin was bundled into the car, Gabriel took the keys from Rebecca's hands.

Surprised, she grabbed them back and opened the passenger door for Gabriel. Once seated in the passenger's side, he rolled down the window and said goodnight to Lewis. Before the window rolled up again, Lewis heard him say, "Where tonight? My place or yours?" He shut the window before Rebecca's reply.

Lewis stepped back as if struck. What does he mean? Is he staying with Rebecca after all?

Don't be crazy here Lewis. You jumped to such conclusions once before and were entirely wrong. It was you she kissed that way in the bedroom, not him. Call her later tonight and ask what bothers her about the lunch with Gabriel. Then you'll know what's going on.

No! Don't check up on her like that! Call tomorrow morning.

After he calmed himself, mostly, he went inside to let his Beagle Burford out of his cave and into the back yard.

*   *

Angry over the deliberate deception created by Gabriel's last remark in Lewis' hearing, Rebecca drove around the corner and stopped.

"Get out," she said.

"What?"

"You heard me."

As soon as he stopped talking, she said, "You walk to your hotel. And you know exactly what you did to deserve this."

"But . . ."

"I'm not interested in your excuses. Get out and walk to the hotel."

He rolled down his window and slowly ducked out of the car, leaned back in and started to talk, but she rolled the window up again and drove away. A few minutes later, she returned to her apartment with a sleeping Benjamin.

Once in the elevator, she grew uneasy. She hoisted Benjamin higher in her arms and stepped out of the elevator at the fourth floor. Precariously balancing her long five-year old, she walked down the hall. One of the hall lights had burned out near her door. Dark shadows made her uncomfortable. She slowed down before approaching her apartment.

A flash of light came from under her door, running across the darkness of the hall carpet. Someone shuffled on the inside.

She stepped back and watched the flash pass across the carpet once more. Her heart thumped and her arms stiffened around Benji.

A scraping sound came from inside the apartment, as if someone dragged cardboard across the floor. The doorknob turned. Rebecca turned and fled around the corner to the stairwell. She stopped at the head of the stairs, unwilling to descend. Benjamin had grown so much since August that carrying him downstairs was dangerous.

Footsteps in the hall plodded toward the elevator.

She'd brave the stairs for one flight. Whoever had invaded her apartment would probably take whatever he dragged directly outside. After the invader stepped into the elevator and the door closed, she opened the heavy fire door by reaching both hands around Benji's legs to grasp the knob. Quickly, she stepped into the concrete well of stairs. She stopped the door with her hip and let it shut smoothly, so as not to telegraph her location to anyone who might be on the next floor. Leaning against the wall and handrail, she descended the stairs. Once in the hallway of the third floor, she listened for other interlopers. Silence greeted her, so she lay Benjamin down on the carpet.

In her purse, she found Joseph's' prepaid cell phone. She turned it on.

"Joseph, this is Rebecca." *Be near the phone. Oh, please answer.* "Joseph, this is Rebecca."

Joseph's voice came through, clear and worried. "Rebecca, I'm here. What's happening?"

"I'm at my place, but I'm on the third floor. Upstairs, someone was in my apartment with a flashlight. They dragged something toward the door as I came down the hall."

"You're on the floor below?"

"Yes."

"Is Benjamin with you?"

"Yes."

"Did this person see you?"

"No."

"I'm calling Officer Hardy right now. Hang on."

The crackles from his end went on for several moments before he came back. "I got Sergeant Hardy. They're on their way. They said for you to stay where you are and knock on a few doors to let your neighbors know you might need help. If you know someone on that floor, go into their apartment. Do you know someone?"

"Not on this floor, only on mine."

"Then stay in the hall but wake somebody up just in case. I'll be right over."

Rebecca looked at her watch. Eleven thirty. She was afraid that knocking on anything might be heard upstairs by the thief. She lifted Benjamin and moved down the hall away from the stairwell and near the window overlooking the river. Benjamin began to awaken as she sat next to him on the floor.

"Hi Mama." He smiled and stretched. "I love you." His dimple deepened as he turned into her and found his thumb again. "I love you too, Benji."

Please sleep. I don't want to scare you.

From the floor, she could see out the long window. Her car was a little to the right outside of the frame of the window. Below her sat a large red car and several smaller cars. Off in the distance the lights of the bridge and the east side streets reflected on the river. The scene was a calm contrast to the thumping in her ears and the tightness in her throat.

A balding blond man came out of the shadow of the building below her, carrying a box. She moved quickly away from the window.

Did he see me?

She heard the man answer his own cell phone. Moments later, she heard him open the main door again.

CHAPTER TWENTY-NINE

She scrambled to her feet and picked up her son. Wishing she already had knocked on doors, Rebecca kicked on the first door she came to.

"Fire. Wake up! Get out!" she shouted. She kicked each door, yelling as she ran down the hall carrying her sleepy burden. Behind her, the doors opened. People in night dress milled around.

"Go down the stairs," she yelled.

If she descended with all these people, she might get past the man. Once outside, she would decide whether to hide or stay with the crowd.

"What fire, Mamma?" Benjamin was wide eyed though still partially asleep.

"I'll explain later, honey."

The tenants filed into the stairwell, everyone talking, asking questions. Rebecca reassured them that the firemen and police were on their way.

As they rounded the second-floor landing, the blond man pushed his way up through the crowd.

His lips formed a grin – the creases next to his eyes moved, but the effect was chilling. She recognized him. The man with the fedora who'd been on her airplane from New York.

"You," she shouted, "stay away from me."

The people with her shouted, "What the hell." What's he?" and "Fire. Get out of the way."

The man rose close to Rebecca and turned, grabbing her elbow. Her throat constricted.

"Let go of me." Her voice was a forced whisper. She forced it harder. "Get away!" This time it was a yell. "Leave us!"

The people in the stairwell pushed around them. "Hey there, what is this?" The neighbor behind her was indignant.

"You leave them be," the neighbor hollered. "Get out of my way. There's a fire behind us."

But he kept his grip on her pulling her down the stairs with everyone surrounding him as if they were mere flies to him.

The neighbor behind kept yelling, and then pushed on the blond man. The man stumbled, pulling Rebecca and Benji with him. The three of them surged forward, tangling their feet in the robe of the lady on the stair below.

Rebecca screamed. They all fell. Instinctively, she pulled Benjamin's head to her chest and turned to her right as the stairs came toward her. Her shoulder and then her head hit the bottom landing. She was only aware that the blond man's hand was no longer grabbing her elbow and that the woman's robe ripped as they fell in a crushing heap. Then, for a moment, all was blank.

You can't do this! Open your eyes and take care of Benji!

Sirens blared in the distance. Her eyes opened. The lady with the robe sat on the bottom step, her head in her hands. Benji was on his knees bent over and crying into Rebecca's arm. "Mama. Mama."

"I'm all right Benji," she whispered. "All right."

But she couldn't make herself move. Through the long window at the bottom of the stairs, she saw the streetlamp and the big blond man, crouched on the walkway, using a revolver to hold at bay the half circle of pajama-clad neighbors.

The man's balding head shown in the light as he searched for the source of the sirens, glancing up and down the street. He glared toward Rebecca, then again up the street. Coming to a decision at last, he ran to his car. After a moment's silence, he revved the motor, and, with his tires squealing, he swerved across the street into the parking lot of the Athletic Club.

The police cars turned down her street. The big red car flashed beyond the swimming pool building and headed for the far driveway out onto Macadam Avenue.

"Mama! Get up!" Benjamin's anxious face came into her line of sight. She struggled to her knees, trying to hide her dizziness from him.

The door to the stairwell banged open. Police Sargent Hardy stood silhouetted against the light of the street lamp, his feet wide apart. His hands clamped together on a gun pointed at Rebecca. Next to her, the lady with the torn robe, prayed. "Lord 'a mercy!"

Another police officer, gun drawn, and body motions taut, hurried up next to Hardy. It was June Williams, who'd been assigned Rebecca's case back in the fall – three fruitless months of communication with New York. No leads, no suspects.

"Miss Gregory," June yelled. "Is he still upstairs?"

"He's gone. Red Buick," a man said.

Rebecca tried to look all right for Benjamin's sake, but her head throbbed, and her shoulder ached. Pulling herself up, she pointed out the front door where now the neighbors were huddled, talking and gesturing.

"He drove south down Macadam in a large red car," Rebecca said, her voice a wisp of sound.

The neighbor lady pulled her robe close about her and said, "I gots his license number."

June Williams whipped out her radio, "Give me the number. We'll give chase."

As Officer Williams dispatched chase cars, Hardy broke in, "I'm going up to the apartment to see if there's anyone else there. Give me your keys."

As she fished in her pocket, he asked, "Did this guy see you?"

"He started to come up and get us. I woke all these people. In spite of the crowd, he came up the stairs and grabbed me."

The lady with the torn robe nodded, "He did, too, that Bas . . .!" she glanced at Benjamin. "Bold as brass and mean looking!"

Benjamin cried, "He pushed us on top of Mama."

"You can't stay here tonight," June said. "So where?"

*   *

At that moment, the door to the second floor flung open behind Rebecca. Joseph Selig raced down the stairs, pale with fear. He glanced at Benjamin and then at Rebecca. "You're both safe!"

She nodded, grateful to hear he cared about Benji, too.

"I went to third floor," he said, "and couldn't find . . . Thank the God you called me. I hoped there'd be no need for that phone."

"I know the man," she said. "He flew out here on our plane from New York, six months ago."

"Damn," June Williams said, "So, he's known where you were from day one."

Sergeant Hardy said, "Let's go up and see what he's done."

"Just a moment," Rebecca said, then she opened the door and talked to the crowd.

"I'm sorry to have lied to you. There was no fire, but you all helped keep that man from stealing my son. I want to thank you for trying to stop him and," she turned to the neighbor on the floor, "And for getting his license number."

"Can we go back to bed?" one man asked.

Officer Williams said, "I'll need your descriptions of him, and what he did, then you can all return to your lives."

They crowded around her, all talking at once until Officer Williams said, "Let's do this by age, so we can get the older neighbors to bed soon."

* *

Joseph looked carefully at Rebecca. "I can take you to Rabbi Stamps or to Friedenberg's for the night. He'll not try to get at you there. I'll make arrangements from your apartment."

"Thank you, Joseph, I can make arrangements." She glanced at her silent son who still shivered in fear. Remembering the blond man's face she shuddered.

Officer Hardy came noisily back down the stairs. "The phone rang when I got in there. I'm sure the caller heard my voice, but he didn't say anything, just hung up. Might have been an accomplice. Nothing in the apartment seems to be upset, but you'll have to look around carefully to tell for sure."

While Officer Williams interviewed the neighbors, Officer Hardy and Joseph accompanied Rebecca as she carried Benji to their apartment.

Everything seemed too immaculate. Officer Hardy followed her around the apartment asking her not to touch anything so that they might get finger prints when the crime lab team showed up. The music instruments were where she'd left them this afternoon. Only the four boxes of Raphael Atemvoll's music were gone.

"Why?" she whispered to herself. "Senseless."

"What's missing?" Hardy asked.

"Four boxes of music by my violin teacher, but not of value to anyone but me."

Benjamin pulled on her shirt tail to interrupt. "Mama, where is the fire?"

Rebecca knelt next to him. "I'm sorry, honey. I'll explain. I used the fire excuse to wake up all those people so we'd be safe from that man. Now, we're trying to find out why that man was in our apartment tonight."

Benjamin's eyes grew round with fear. "Mama, was the little man here, too? Was it the one who hit my teacher? . . . the one who wants to steal me?" He tumbled from the sofa, shaking, and clung to his mother.

"No Benjamin, this one only wanted my old boxes of music."

As he clung to her, Benjamin cried, "Mama, let's go home to Lewis. He'll hide me from the bad man."

Over Benjamin's shoulder, Rebecca saw a sharp grimace cross Joseph's face.

"I can sleep in Burford's cave-home. That would be safe."

"Levy will be asleep, little one," she said. "We'll go to Grandma and Grandpa Abraham. We'll be safe there."

"We can call Lewis," Benji insisted.

"Tomorrow will be soon enough, Benji. You may call him during breakfast."

Officer Hardy broke in, "Miss Gregory, we're going to have to ask you to come to the station tonight to file some papers. We'll make it as short as possible."

Rebecca glanced at Benji's tired, scared face. "Maybe Abe could meet us there and take Benji home while I work with you."

"That'd be fine. Are you sure there's nothing valuable in the boxes?"

She shook her head. "Valuable only to me. Beautiful music the world should have —I want them back, but they're not valuable to others, yet."

She took Benjamin with her. In the bookcase near the piano, she found the stack of music she and Harald had already played, and the three notebooks of Batislav dances and Mr. Atemvoll's theater interludes and sonatas.

"These are the ones we've read through. In all that stack, there was beautiful music, wonderful songs, but nothing worth stealing."

"Officer, can we take these with us tonight?" Joseph asked.

"After they've been dusted for prints."

Rebecca spoke to Joseph in Yiddish so that Benjamin could not understand. "His eyes, Joseph, they were the eyes of the evil one."

Joseph put his hand up to his mouth and she knew he was spitting at the name of evil. She herself felt the urge to do so. Old superstitions die slowly. She smiled at their shared habit. He caught himself and shrugged, a gesture as fatalistic as any Rabbi Stamps had ever made.

*   *

Officers Hardy and Williams let the crime lab team into the apartment, while Joseph and Rebecca made arrangements with a sleepy, but worried Abe and Miriam to meet at the police station. The lab team finished up quickly. She left the apartment taking her violin, her lute, her stack from the bookcase and Benjamin's favorite Boo Bear and ribbon blanket.

Five minutes later, at one o'clock in the morning, the phone in her apartment rang again. After twelve rings, it ceased jangling.

*   *

Hearing the masculine voice answer her phone at midnight had knocked Lewis sideways. An hour of prowling around his apartment and arguing with himself convinced him he must have dialed incorrectly. The voice was neither Gabriel's tenor nor Abraham's base. There was no one else she would have in her apartment at that time of night. Yet, when he dialed again at one o'clock in the morning, he got absolutely no answer. He let it ring many times, hoping that she was just asleep and would take a long time to hear it.

At last, worried that something had happened to her, and unwilling to think she might have gone to Gabriel's hotel, he dressed and drove to her apartment building. And there he found the police tape on the door, telling him all hell had broken loose.

He unearthed his phone. He tried to call Abe and Miriam. He tried to call Rabbi Stamps. At last, he called 411 and asked the operator for the number of the Heathman Hotel.

Gabriel answered his room phone, a deep roughness to his voice. In the background, Lewis could distinctly hear the sound of Rebecca playing the E major Partita by Bach. He hung up.

Lewis knew instantly that he'd been hearing a recording – he had that recording himself with the odd little rococo flourish that Rebecca had added to the opening of the main theme – an embellishment the recording studio had left in even though it was entirely un-Bachian.

He started to dial the police station and ask for Officer June Williams, but a different police officer came around the corner into the hall where Lewis stood outside her apartment. The officer's gun aimed at Lewis.

"You didn't get everything the first time, fellow?" the officer said.

"Where are they?"

"Buddy, put your hands up. My partner is behind you."

Lewis raised his arms. "What has happened to Rebecca and her son?"

"You're coming downtown with us."

Fear for Rebecca and Benji jagged down Lewis's backbone.

CHAPTER THIRTY

After two hours of interrogation, the officers who took Lewis to the station seemed partially satisfied. They finally called in Officer June Williams to verify his story. To his relief, Officer Williams told him that Rebecca and Benji were safe at Abe's with police guard.

He caught a cab and went to Abraham's for breakfast. It took a little talking to get the officers there to let him knock on the door.

Abe answered. "Come on in."

"How are they?"

"Rebecca and Benji are sleeping and Miriam, too. It's just me and Miriam's Parakeet. Blue Boy is barely clinging to his perch, himself, after the flurry of last night."

"Officer Williams says the red car showed up on the street about two this morning. No boxes. The car was reported stolen six months ago in Philadelphia."

Abe's chipper façade fell. "Damn. I thought we might get him and put an end to this."

"I suppose Rebecca still plans to do the last concert with Gabriel."

Abe nodded. "There will be police backstage and in civies all over the auditorium."

"I'll be there too. And Benji?"

"Backstage with Sergeant Hardy and Officer Williams."

At that moment, a dog howled from somewhere in the downstairs hall.

Both men stood. Abraham strode to the hall with Lewis on his heels. Abe said, "Did you leave Burford in your car?"

There stood Benjamin, grinning. "I howled."

"You scared us," Abe said.

"I can make a police car siren, too," he said. "Want to hear?"

Lewis picked Benji up. "I think we want your mother to stay asleep. So, no more sirens and dogs until she wakes."

Benji put his head on Lewis's shoulder. "Mama cried. That man hurt her. I hate him."

Lewis held him tight and whispered, "But the neighbors helped, and the police came, and you are safe now."

Benji lifted his head, tears now streamed down his cheeks. "It happens when he's here," he sobbed to Lewis.

"Who?"

"Gabriel. Bad things come with him."

Lewis glanced at Abe.

Abraham's face hardened. He nodded but held a finger to his lips.

Lewis held Benji tighter. "You are safe with us, now, and Gabriel soon will be going home to New York."

* *

That evening, Thursday night, Lewis sat with Dick Street in the back of Civic Auditorium awaiting the last in the recital series. He'd had updates from Abe during the day. Rebecca had awakened in time to get dressed for the concert and to make sure Benji would be in a safe room backstage with Officers Williams and Hardy. Abe assured him she was ready for this concert.

Lewis couldn't see how she'd be at all calm, after the terror of her night and the knowledge that the man who took her music still roamed free.

When Rebecca's small figure came on stage followed by the dark imposing body of Gabriel, Lewis could feel fear for her in his gut. He sagged forward in his chair so abruptly that Dick looked sharply at him.

Lewis straightened himself in the chair and watched the audience for any signs of the man. He knew now, from Abe, that it was the same man in the fedora who had been on their flight from Chicago, the same who had called from a phone booth that night near her apartment. He thought he could recognize him, but discovered from the balcony vantage, that the audience contained many blond men with thinning hair.

He spent most of the concert not looking at the stage, but scanning. Even so, he could hear the oneness in their playing together. And he could hear the drama of her phrasing and the beauty of her tone.

At last they began their finale, the Vitali Chaconne. The great organlike chords of the piano seemed to underscore the power of Gabriel. But when her first chord filled the hall, Lewis looked up. She filled the stage with her own strength, dwarfing the big man behind her with an aura of control and spirit all her own. She led the way in creating a structure of darkness and light, a cathedral of sound.

Lewis remained transfixed. Through the piece and the applause that followed, he gripped the arms of his chair and watched her every move. Her encore was a Gypsy dance he'd played with her one evening. Her newfound abandon made the dance take on fresh life. It was wild and tender, loving and grieving. It was reckless.

When it was over, he knew she had found life in spite of fear. He celebrated her new powers. She should live as she had played it tonight.

During the wild applause, Dick turned to him, shouting into Lewis' ear, "Even I can see that she is more lively, more present than at concerts last year. And through my feet, I can feel the wildness of that last dance. Last year, she was great, but not like this."

"Yes," Lewis nodded. "She always had this promise. Tonight, it bloomed."

*   *

Police and plainclothesmen swarmed the reception in the main lobby. Lewis and Dick watched the edges of the crowd for anyone who might be related to the man in the fedora. No one tipped their hand in any way.

Harald Steinmetz came by Lewis's position at the edge of the crowd. "I'm sure you realize what happened tonight, professor."

Lewis started to answer, but Dick spoke first. "Mr. Steinmetz, I assume you refer to the huge audience."

Harald laughed but didn't look at Dick at all. "I refer, of course, to the fact that Rebecca has outgrown her Reed College teaching job and her local concerts. She will be the international star she always should have been."

Lewis admitted to himself that her talent might, indeed, take her from him, but not, he hoped, until the mystery and danger were solved. "Yes, she can be," Lewis said. "She has choices to make."

"The musical world will clamor for more of the quality she gave us tonight."

Lewis nodded. "I'm sure you're right, Harald. It will be interesting to see what she does about that."

Harald smiled. "It will indeed." He drifted off toward the center of the circle that surrounded Rebecca. Lewis noticed that he leaned in to whisper something to Abe, but that Abe shook his head. Afterwards, Harald Steinmetz spoke to Rebecca. She seemed startled, put her hand on Abe's arm, and then she too shook her head at Harald.

Dick said, "Wanna know?"

Lewis chuckled. "Okay, Lip-Reader. What's up?"

"He offered her a ride home. She declined. He's got no idea what happened last night, or where she's staying now."

"Good."

Late in the evening, Officer Williams and Officer Hardy brought Benji to Lewis.

"He asked to go home with you," Officer Williams said, "but I just promised he could come visit you until his mother is ready to go home."

Lewis lifted Benji in his arms. "Benjamin, I want to introduce you to my friend, Dick Street."

Benji took his thumb out of his mouth, offered wet fingers to Dick for a handshake and said, "I am Lewis's friend, too."

"Are we lucky, or what?!" Dick said.

"Lucky," Benji decided.

CHAPTER THIRTY-ONE

On the morning after the police interrogation and Rebecca's concert, Lewis' hands hovered over the keyboard of his old Underwood, waiting for his thoughts to straighten themselves. He'd neglected this article for too long. He'd nearly forgotten the thrill of discovery about rocket fuel that this article would reveal to the scientific world.

Nothing but his fear for Rebecca and Benjamin seemed to touch him. Not even the cold he was developing could add to his misery. He knew they were safely at Abe and Miriam's, but he also knew the police still had not found the suspect.

He knew she was being protected and guarded, but he couldn't be satisfied unless he did the guarding. And as long as the officers still hadn't caught the man, she needed more than his one-man care.

He couldn't even get started on work. The article sat, barely begun in his ancient machine. But if he gave into this cold and went to bed, he would only get worse, closing his eyes and dreaming.

Come Lewis! Think of waves and stars and energy . . .

Oh, the energy of a five-year-old . . . and the questions, the endless questions. How quiet he is when they're with Gabriel . . . how round eyed and sad. His mouth is sad at the corners like Rebecca's.

Funny, I never noticed that before. Before, I only noticed his excited laughing, his twinkle, his optimism.

"Mr. James?"

Startled, Lewis looked up into the handsome, dark face of Gabriel Kolya. The man stood in the doorway to Lewis's office.

"Uh . . . Gabriel. Come in. Here I'll find you a chair." Lewis cleared a stack of neglected books off of his second chair, plopping them on the wide windowsill. He turned to face his visitor, perplexed.

"I'm leaving this evening, Mr. James . . . Lewis. I hope you'll have time to go to lunch with me." Gabriel stood next to the chair, one hand on the back, as if he might actually deign to sit in it sometime.

Now, Lewis grew truly puzzled. Why was this man bothering to visit him? Was he aware of what had happened at Rebecca's the night before? Was Gabriel part of the cause?

"You once mentioned lunch together," Lewis said, "but you must have uh . . . friends you need to visit before you go."

"There are some things I wish to talk to you about before I leave. Perhaps a quiet meal is the setting in which we can listen to each other. There are some things I hope you'll be able to understand about Rebecca and myself."

"I'm game." Gabriel's arrogant possessive tone bugged.

Gabriel seemed to relax a little now that he had hooked his quarry. "Let's go to Papa Haydn's. It's a little place Rebecca showed me."

He neglected to mention that Rebecca had also taken Abraham and Miriam there that night, but Lewis knew it.

Lewis grabbed some nose tissues from a battered box and his jacket from the doorknob and followed Gabriel out. On the way down the stairs, Lewis decided to take charge of the situation. He fished out his car keys and at the bottom of the stairs, turned toward his parking lot rather than the visitors' lot where Gabriel's car must have been.

"I'll drive and then bring you back to your car. I know the town." Lewis did not look back. He jingled his keys, blew his nose, and kept on walking.

Gabriel shrugged and followed him, making an attempt at friendly conversation. "This is a very impressive building for a small college," he said.

"Small, but well endowed. Our alums are successful."

"I know about Reed College. I did quite a bit of research on the school before I let Rebecca come."

"I thought Rebecca signed this contract."

"I advised her to do so. I believed that she needed to make a change for a year. She will appreciate New York cultural life more when she comes back."

"Was she finding New York cultural life tedious?"

"No, Mr. . . . Lewis, she was quite well accepted there. She had many students and important concert engagements which I was able to work out for her. But she is a highly-strung girl and the pressure of being a mother and a musician was becoming too much for her nerves. She can arrange to spend more time on her talent when she returns to New York. By that time, the boy will be old enough for one of the many fine boarding schools that the east offers such children."

"Such children? What kind of a child is Benjamin?"

"Oh, he's bright enough, but in need of discipline which his mother finds difficult to administer."

Lewis looked at Gabriel incredulously. "*What* about Benjamin needs disciplining?"

Gabriel raised one eyebrow imperiously and explained with illconcealed impatience. "The boy's too dependent on his mother. He's always in her way when opportunities arise. She considers him above her own needs and doesn't accept that he can do without her. He is quite old enough to be more independent."

Lewis opened the passenger door to his car, letting Gabriel in. He walked slowly around the car to simmer down. He knew he didn't like this man, now he knew exactly why. The man was beyond selfish.

As he began the drive to the restaurant, Lewis asked, "What about the kidnapping threats? Don't you think that Rebecca keeps Benjamin close out of fear for his safety?"

"Unfounded fear." Gabriel dismissed the possibility with a flick of the wrist. "The only time there was an attempt against him in New York was when Tobias foolishly decided to take him out in public transportation. He won't do that again. There's no danger."

"Gabriel, you're ignoring two other attempts on him."

"Very unsuccessful, puny."

"Besides," Lewis continued, "why should they have to barricade themselves into their apartment and private car? Now that she's becoming a citizen, she can rely on the protection of the police."

Gabriel's answer sounded well practiced, "She must rely on the protection of her fellow exiles. The government of no country will take care of her as well as those of her race. She can rely on no outsiders. They've betrayed her before and they will always betray us."

Lewis pulled into the restaurant parking lot. He opened his door and got out without replying to Gabriel's implied accusation against him as an outsider.

Gabriel had no idea that Papa Haydn's wooden booths were a favorite place for Benji as well as Rebecca. That's the kind of thing the grown jerk would never have asked.

Lewis wanted to keep Gabriel talking to him. The man thought he was talking Lewis out of pursuing Rebecca. The more he talked, the more Gabriel fed him the very information Lewis needed in order to help free Rebecca.

Lewis pushed off of the car and led the way into the restaurant.

As they finished up their lunch, Gabriel also finished a long soliloquy on Rebecca's talent and why only New York would do justice to her, financially and artistically. He expounded on her supposed emotional deformities and on how he, Gabriel, often had to save her from self-destructive decisions.

After their bill was delivered and ceremoniously taken care of by Himself, Gabriel leaned toward Lewis and said in a dramatic stage whisper, "You must come to realize, too, that she will never again be able to respond to a man. I expect you are already aware of that fact."

Lewis attempted to keep his face unemotional.

"Why do you believe that?" he asked at length.

Gabriel's eyes narrowed as he leaned back, "She was physically abused. Did you never ask her how she came to have that child?"

"Yes, she told me about Benjamin's father."

Gabriel straightened, anger flashing from his dark eyes . . . anger and hate. "Father! Father!" his voice sneered at the word. He leaned forward again, his intense hatred making him shake. A deep whisper struggled to rip out of the angriest part of his being. "It was fathers! Four terrifying days and nights. She was nearly dead when her uncle rescued her."

Lewis was knocked back in his chair as if hit.

This is another lie from Gabriel.

Gabriel's voice broke through Lewis' inner torment. "And she still chooses to believe the child is the son of the one man who opposed the rest. She claims he inherited that man's characteristics. She is both unable to face what really happened and unable to get rid of the memory. She will be unable until that child is no longer there to remind her of it. Even then, it may be impossible. She is not a whole woman. She feels the terror of it too clearly to . . ."

"No!" Lewis shouted. His fist slammed the table, sending dishes to the floor. He rose, knocking over the chair. His legs carried him to the door and out to the parking lot where the freezing afternoon downpour soaked him. He leaned his head on the car, letting the rain wash away the picture in his mind, replacing it with the image of Rebecca as he knew her.

There! See her? She's walking toward me on the campus, free strides, open smile, her hand holding that of a small child, a violin under her other arm. Rebecca sane, warm, exciting . . . the Rebecca I really know, not the walled off Rebecca that Gabriel created. She will be whole, given time and a persistent love.

She had overcome those nights by loving the child who was the product of them. She could move on beyond her fear because the child himself now had nothing to do with that memory.

Gabriel appeared beside him. "Well, I thought for a minute that I was going to be taking a taxi back to my car. Do you think I should drive for you?"

Lewis refused to look at him. Keeping the image of Rebecca before him, he took the keys from his pocket and inserted them into the lock. "No, I'll have you back to your car in a minute."

After they were out of the parking lot, Lewis spoke in a very controlled voice. "You are wrong about Rebecca. She's grown beyond those nights, and she's done it in a way you'd never be able to understand. She's been able to sow love where there was hatred and hope where there was despair."

Gabriel's' reply was glib. "Perhaps she seems well to you on a short-term basis. You've only known her since the end of August. I have known her since before she came to the United States."

Lewis no longer wanted to hear Gabriel's opinions about Rebecca's mental health. He knew that those opinions were warped by the man's view of life. Gabriel Kolya seemed incapable of trusting the judgment of the woman he thought he loved. When Rebecca made decisions contrary to his wishes they were, to him, a sign of her mental illness.

One of the decisions she'd made was not to love Gabriel Kolya no matter how grateful she had once been. She practiced enough logic to know that gratitude and love are not equivalent emotions.

CHAPTER THIRTY-TWO

After dropping Gabriel off at his car, Lewis turned toward home. His cold and his anger made him shiver. An ache built in his shoulders and back. He pulled up in front of his house, but the images Gabriel had built up and his own whopping cold subjected him to increasing nausea. Slumping over the steering wheel, he tried to shake sickness. He'd held it in check while driving, but his emotional reaction to Rebecca's ordeal left him at the mercy of a dark dread.

He had to keep showing her what life outside protective walls could be like. When he arrived home, he pushed open the car door and dragged himself to the house, trying to think of what to say when he called her on the phone.

A fresh chill of horror drove through his body. What if Gabriel hires someone to do these things to Rebecca? What if he is the cause?

Once inside, he leaned against the sunlit wall and closed his eyes. The nausea and the cold came over him again before he could reach the phone.

But at her touch his eyes flew open. Instinctively, he put his arms around her and pulled her to him. "Becca! Becca! I thought you were safe at Abraham's . . ."

"Never mind about that. I . . . ."

"How did you know to be here?"

"I was coming to your office . . ."

"With police?"

"Yes. Officer Williams is in her car. Another officer is in the driveway here."

He blinked. He'd seen none of this.

"Anyway, I saw you leave with him. I wanted to be where you could talk to me afterward. You're soaked!" Rebecca led him, peeling off his dripping tweed as she urged him up the stairs. At the second floor, she propelled him into the bathroom.

"Take a very hot shower. I'll be back with your robe in a minute."

Lewis stopped her. "Where's Benji?"

"With Miriam and Abe until I get Gabriel off to the airport. And Sergeant Hardy will come to the airport with us. Now stop worrying and take care of yourself."

She turned on her heel and strode into his bedroom.

* *

Standing in the hall, Rebecca heard the shower turn on and the click of the shower door. She went into the bathroom, intending to hang his robe and leave.

"Becca," he called over the roar of the shower. "Becca are you there?"

"Yes, Levy," she turned away from the shadow of his shoulders and taut thighs on the other side of the pebbled glass.

"Becca, thank you for being here." His tense voice came slower than usual. "I want to talk with you before you take him to the airport. Please wait for me."

"Are you warm enough, Levy?"

"I'm getting warmer. Will you wait?"

"Yes, I don't have to leave until seven tonight. Why were you so wet? Did he leave you somewhere?"

"No. I just stood in the rain to get rid of his ideas . . . Becca, I can't talk like this. Please wait for me."

"I will wait. I'm going to turn on the furnace and make you something warm to eat."

From downstairs in the kitchen, Rebecca heard him leave the bathroom. She poured the soup into a heated bowl and placed it on a tray next to the spoon and a small vase with narcissus. She'd taken a quick excursion to the porch planters where, last week, she'd seen the brave bulbs promising to bloom. Outside, she told Officer Williams what was going on.

Then, carrying the tray upstairs, she met him as he started to come down.

"No sir!" she said to him. "You go to bed at this time. A short talk and a good stiff sleeping are what you need. And then, I hope you will not be too sick to help me put Gabriel on the airplane."

Her mother-authority voice and misplaced English presented the best bluff she could use to cover her anxiety. She grew fearful thinking what idea Gabriel might have given to Lewis that he would want to stand in the rain to get rid of it. Last year she'd begun to guess what kinds of things Gabriel said in order to get rid of people he felt were undesirable for her.

She didn't look at Lewis, but kept climbing the stairs, fearing the face of disapproval she might find there, or worse yet, the pity – oftentimes it was pity on the face of someone Gabriel had singled out for revelations about her.

She nearly bumped into Lewis. He hadn't backed up the stairs as she expected. He simply waited and took the tray, turning in one smooth motion to let her walk up the stairs ahead of him. Nudging her waist with the tray, he guided her into his room. He set the food down on the night stand next to his bed and folded back the covers. Motioning her to sit at the end of the bed, he sat down where the sheet was exposed and took the tray into his lap.

"Thank you, Rebecca." He smiled at her briefly and began eating, beads of fevered sweat forming on his forehead. Within a few moments, he had nearly finished the soup. He set the tray down on the night stand again, leaning forward.

The top of his robe fell open to reveal that he hadn't found any pajamas to wear under it. Rebecca looked away from his body. She quelled the urge to watch his smooth muscles fill the robe as he straightened. She was surprised by her body's response to the sight of him. When he looked at her again, she felt her defenses going up.

"Look at me Becca. Please, look at me and talk to me. I can't leave it as he painted it. I want to hear it from you."

She looked up at him, still not finding the pity she expected – only the drawn look of a sick man who desperately needs to know something before he can recover. "What do you want me to tell you, Levy?"

"First, I want you to pull these covers up around my chin because I'm starting to get chilled again." He slipped his feet under the covers and tried to wink at her as his feet pushed against her leg.

Rebecca stood to pull the covers up to his shoulders, gaining self-confidence with each layer.

He smiled.

"Do you have a hot water bottle somewhere?" she asked. "I think you would stay warm longer if you had one."

"That's a very good idea," he gazed up at her, half tired, half sick and all gentle. "There's an electric heating pad in the top of that linen closet out in the hall."

She was back soon, plugged it in and set the dial. Reaching under the covers, he slipped the pad onto his chest. As she leaned over him, she saw the questioning look in his eyes. Here she was, treating him as if he were her child one moment, then made suddenly aware of his desire for her. Flustered, she backed away.

"Sit down, here, Becca." He ordered quietly, reaching out for her hand. She sat down out of reach. He lifted his hand, waiting for her to take it. Studying his graying face, she moved toward him, not taking the hand but covering him again and sitting close with her hands on the blanket at his shoulders.

"How could you become so sick in two hours?" She whispered.

"I was already getting a cold – ignoring it as usual, and feeling quite sorry for myself, because I believed I had no right to protect you and Benjamin."

She gave a start. "Why would you believe that?"

"Because Officers Bailey and Schmidt arrested me for coming back to the scene of the crime on the night before your concert. They thought maybe I had broken into your apartment, questioned where I was when your apartment was ransacked. By the time June Williams got them straightened out, you and Benji were asleep at Abe's. I think some policemen still can't believe I'm not their man."

"You were also at the police station?"

"In an interrogation room."

"How did the interrogation make you this sick?"

"Not the interrogation. But I didn't get out of there until three in the morning. When I went by Abe's, he said you were safe and asleep. I went to your concert last night – wonderful concert, by the way. My friend Dick Street and I waited until you were safely on your way to Abe's again and then we went home. By that time, I knew I was getting this cold."

She smiled at him. "I saw you and your friend checking out everyone at the reception. Thank you for your care."

"Yeah, well nobody could get anywhere near you, except that Steinmetz fellow. Glad you turned down his offer of a ride."

She laughed. "That Steinmetz fellow is pretty benign, you know."

Lewis smiled. "Not in my book. For my taste, he likes you too much."

"No threat." She said, glad for his jest at jealousy.

"Good." He snuggled deeper in his covers. She noticed he let one foot rest against her back as if by accident.

"And then," he said, "I went to lunch with Gabriel. It was work not to punch him in the face. I was already sick from his talk when he went one step too far and told me something I should have heard only from you. After that, I had to be taking myself outside, away from him. The rain felt good. Really. It helped me clear out the image of you he was creating and replace it with the Rebecca I know."

"What did he tell you that I should have told you?" She asked, looking at her hands on his shoulders, kneading the blanket. She couldn't look at his eyes.

"Becca, look at me. We are talking together. I am not judging you. There. That's better. Keep looking at me and tell me about the nights in prison."

She pulled her hands away. Suddenly they were very hot. She stared at him, horrified, waiting for his eyes to change. "How could he tell you that? How could he?"

Lewis reached again for her hands, keeping her close. "Tell me, Rebecca. Something about those nights gave you a strength that most people could not have."

She raised her gaze to his again. Here at last was one who guessed the truth. Yes, something good had occurred – a good something that had been covered with guilt in her heart ever since.

She began in a soft voice that grew stronger as she found her way. "I was blind folded. There was one man in a very fine wool suit. He smoked strong tobacco."

She stopped suddenly. Lewis knew the cigarettes meant something, but he wasn't going to ask. He merely nodded to encourage her.

"I won't forget his accent. His Hungarian was actually very German and harsh. He wanted the concerti and to get it, he decided to break me. When he got bored, he gave me to the head guard."

"And there was one who stood against them?"

She glanced up, surprised that he knew. "Zoltan Nagy. He was one of the guards, but also a prisoner of the gang. He had been a student of mine. Zoltan brought me food and his coat. He gave me a moment of sanity in that Kafka nightmare.

"He said two things that night that I have needed ever since. He said not all men are like the men at the prison. And he told me to be his freedom."

"Thank God he came to you."

Lewis began to see where her inner resources came from. She sat in his room, but her mind focused on the words. He wouldn't ask her any questions. The story as she told it was controlled by her own need to understand what had happened.

Questions would ask for facts. Facts were not what had happened to her. During those nights, what took place happened inside her mind as much as outside.

Rebecca took a stronger grip on Lewis' hands and finished the story. "The other guards came moments after he arrived."

"And you don't know what became of him." Lewis stated.

"No. I know they whipped him unmercifully that night. Friends of Uncle Tobias tried to find out for me if he lived, but he disappeared." She looked at their hands for a long time, watching her fingers entwine with his over and over. Finally, she gazed into Lewis' eyes with sadness. "I will never know. I will never know about any of them."

They were silent, both of them facing the probable truth of her permanent isolation from those she had loved.

"His name was Nagy?" Lewis asked at last.

She roused herself from the past. "Zoltan Nagy."

"Ah, yes, Benjamin's middle name. Benji put it into our guessing games once. Zoltan. I am grateful to Zoltan for his defense of you. Your strength is in replacing hatred with love. He knew you well to give you that."

"I pray that he had the strength to do it, too. His life must be very difficult since. . . . if . . ." Rebecca's voice broke.

They were both very quiet. There seemed to be nothing to say. Zoltan Nagy's prospects had been very dim. It seemed impossible to imagine any but the worst outcome.

After a moment, Lewis whispered, "and you have no way to find out – no contact with friends or family for six years."

"None," she looked at the ceiling, blinking quickly to stop the tears that threatened. "Uncle Tobias has tried all the avenues he can think of, but for all of them, direct contact from me would be dangerous. I'm supposed to be dead."

"I am sorry it's been like that for you, Rebecca." As Lewis spoke, he turned his hands to cover hers, smoothing her wrists with slow strokes of his thumbs. "It must feel as if the foundations of your life have been torn out from under you."

"It has. But here in Oregon," she said, and then she straightened her back and whispered, "I am building new foundations. I could have done so in New York if I . . . if I had not had the threats against Benjamin."

Lewis moved his hands to her arms, feeling the tightness in her. "Those threats must be gotten rid of. I want to talk to you about them soon, but you've been tense this whole time. You need to relax a while. And Rebecca, I'm in need of sleep."

He pushed himself up a little, looking down at the sadness in the corners of her mouth. "This afternoon has been hard on both of us," he said softly. "If you'll grant me the boon of lying down here, where I can see you, I promise to be a gentleman. We can sleep for four hours before it's time to take Gabriel to the airport. Will you do that?"

"Yes," She answered so quietly that he wasn't absolutely sure she'd said it. Nevertheless, he opened the covers on the far side of his bed. When she slipped between them with her back to him, he pulled the covers around her shoulders and lay down facing her incredible auburn curls.

Lewis, aware of how far they had come together, felt a deep happiness spread through him. Thinking about where he hoped they soon would be, a smile crept over him. He closed his eyes eventually and slept, and he kept to his promise. He was the epitome of a gentleman, except in his imagination.

*   *

That evening, after Gabriel Kolya's stiff and chilly departure, Lewis and Rebecca returned to Friedenberg's to enjoy dinner and a game of monopoly with Benjamin, Abe and Miriam.

Lewis's cold was miraculously better – a cure he silently attributed to Rebecca's warm presence during their afternoon nap. After monopolizing the railroads and all of what he called the "purple streets", Benjamin's head drooped to the table. Abe announced his intention to put a quick end to the game and to everyone else's fiscal misery.

Abe magnanimously bought out all of Benjamin's real estate and allowed Lewis to carry the little boy upstairs to bed while Abe planned the `Friedenberg financial strategy'.

Having followed upstairs, Rebecca watched from the guest room doorway as Lewis covered her son.

Lewis said, "He feels safer here at Abe and Miriam's, Becca. I'm glad you've decided to give up the apartment until we get this guy behind bars."

"I'm more comfortable here as well," she said. "With the security system and all those extra locks on the doors, the apartment began to feel like a . . . like a . . . "

"Like a prison?" he asked gently.

She bit her lower lip and nodded almost imperceptibly.

He wished she wouldn't stand in the doorway – as if she needed an escape route.

Rebecca seemed to read his mind. Crossing the room, she busily closed the curtains and turned on the night light. "It's very generous of you to have my piano moved into your house, Levy," she said as she returned to the doorway and flipped off the overhead light.

Lewis stood to look at her silhouette. His answer was quiet, tense. "There's plenty of room in my house to care for anything you need." He bent to tug again at the same blanket he'd fiddled with for two minutes. His voice took on a more teasing tone. "I'm hoping you will come visit your imposing Mason and Hamlin and stay to say a word or two to me. We could play duets on our two facing grands."

She smiled. "That piano is very heavy. Will the movers protest?"

"Not after I pay them."

She laughed and shook her head. "I'm glad Benji is asleep. You say things like that in front of Benjamin and I hear him quoting you later. He takes you quite literally you know."

"He should." He grinned down at his biggest fan. Benjamin's thumb was being worked overtime. Since their escape from the thief at the apartment building, Benji needed extra hugs from everyone.

Rebecca watched Lewis' last careful tucking and said, "I'm curious to see how you will manage to get both pianos in the same room."

He stood abruptly, facing her. "Come here. I'll show you."

Rebecca stepped a little closer in the darkened room. The look on her face grew expectant, puzzled. Lewis took her hands in one of his. "My piano has always sat with its back to the window." He jabbed his thumb over his shoulder toward the window wall behind him. "Now your piano on the other hand . . ." his hands positioned her directly in front of him, ". . . yours will face the window. In that small room, the two pianos have to be close together." He drew her slowly toward him, carefully watching her reaction. "It's good thing pianos are built to work in that way. The curves of one fit very neatly into the curves of another."

He put his arms around Rebecca, gratefully recognizing her willingness. As her body leaned into his, he nuzzled her hair and whispered into her ear. "It's really a very nice design – and a pleasure to look at. We should be quite thankful to whoever decided to make pianos in that shape."

She lifted her face to him. The corners of her mouth turned up just before he kissed her. He was not hoping for the sensuous abandon of her last kiss. That wildness had been borne of desperation in the face of Gabriel's domination.

He did not get the sensuous abandon, but a bittersweet tenderness that warmed as he moved into her. Her hands moved up his chest until she caressed his throat and jaw line. Her soft lips followed the line of his throat down to the hollow where his pulse beat wildly. His body yearned for that moist contact to continue moving down the front of his shirt. He held her loosely in his arms kissing the top of her hair, waiting. It was an exquisite sensation just to hope she might become so intimate.

Her fingers pushed aside the button front and caressed his chest. Her mouth trailed after her fingers. He closed his eyes.

Abraham came to the bottom of the stairs. "Is my little boy all bedded down?" he called.

Lewis collapsed against the wall, holding her tightly into him, his breathing ragged and deep. Hers was no more controlled. They heard Abraham's footsteps on the stairwell. Then Miriam's voice called from the music room.

"Abe, I need you to hold this, quickly."

Abe's steps receded. Lewis took a deep breath and massaged Rebecca's back firmly, helping her back to normal. If stopping was hard for him, how much harder it must be for her. She had to come so much farther to get to this pitch. He held her head in one strong hand and sought her lips, needing at least the fulfillment of a probing kiss. She responded as he hoped she would, opening her lips to his questing tongue.

When she rested against his chest, he chuckled. "Abe just about became one very shocked man. I, for one, was not going to be able to gather myself together by the time he reached that top step."

Rebecca smiled up at him. "What were you going to say when he came in here?"

"You mean if I could speak by that time?"

"Yes, If."

"I would have told him the truth. It would have been pretty obvious anyway."

"What truth?"

"That I was showing you how to get two pianos into one small room."

He loved her full-throated laughter.

*   *

Downstairs, Miriam handed Abe the rescued stack of Rebecca's music. "Abraham Friedenberg! Where are your senses! When those two are alone anywhere in the house, you stay away. Now take this. Lewis wanted to go through it looking for codes, or puzzles or any other possible clues as to why the rest of the music might have been stolen."

Abe took the music, his eyebrows beetling as he frowned down on the yellowed papers. "The thief was pretty thorough," he said. "If he left this batch, he didn't want it. Why would it tell Lewis anything?"

"I don't know. You know how Lewis' mind works."

"All the time," Abe chuckled wryly.

Miriam gazed at the tattered collection of pieces and shrugged. "I suppose it's the only thing we've got, and Lewis just wants to test a few theories."

"All right. Where do I put it?"

"On the piano."

Abe started past the stairwell with the stack, then glanced up into that darkness. "Miriam, they've been up there a long time. What if he . . ."

"He won't. And if he does, it will be because, at last, she wants him to. Don't you see how careful he is? Stop worrying."

Several minutes later, Lewis came clattering down the stairs by himself. He accepted a cup of tea from Miriam and headed for the piano where he had to play Brahm's variations on a theme by Schumann just to clear his head. At last he reached for the stack of music and began playing through the pieces. In the middle of the stack were three empty mailing envelopes and three notebooks.

Lewis turned the envelopes around and read the address. "Tobias Kossuth, Sheet Music Service of New York." The return postal stamp read "Feodor Sospiro, Box 542, Király Ut, Liszt Ferenc Tér, Budapest, Magyarország."

The name meant nothing to Lewis, though it seemed familiar. Probably a common Hungarian name.

Across the face of each envelope the sender had written "Incorrect Copies" in English.

There was no telling what had been in theses envelopes, or why the envelopes had been kept. So, Lewis put them aside and began playing the music in the stack.

He soon began to recognize her teacher's lyric style and calligraphy. Another, more cramped hand, had penned little marches and dances on older paper. There came up some very lovely violin and piano duets in her teacher's hand, followed by orchestrations of organ pieces and songs for some long-departed soprano, perhaps the love of Atemvoll's youth.

Lewis played them, wondering if he needed to be a cryptologist or a musicologist to find whatever they might reveal about Rebecca's pursuers. In the role of cryptologist, he tested out the idea that perhaps the notes of a tune, corresponding to letters in the alphabet, might carry a message. None of the tunes left him with anything but nonsense words, though he'd have to ask Rebecca about possible words in Hungarian or Russian.

At eleven o'clock, Miriam came in with some cookies and a fresh pot of tea. "How's Rebecca doing?"

Lewis glanced at Miriam. "I sent her to bed. I didn't want her here when I did this. She's too close to these pieces to see anything other than her teacher in them. If there's a hidden message here, someone unrelated to Atemvoll will have to find it."

"That isn't what I meant. How is she holding up, Lewis?"

He took a sip of the tea while he considered the answer to her question. "She has remarkable strength. Now that Gabriel's influence is removed, she'll be even stronger."

"And those walls – is she still putting up those walls?"

He looked over the rim of his cup. "She has stopped building them and she's scaled a couple. But there are many between us yet."

"Time. It will take time. Well, it's getting late. You don't have to go through all of these pieces in one evening you know. Since tomorrow is Saturday, why don't you let me make the couch into a bed. You can get up and look through the rest in the morning, when Abe is available."

Lewis knew he could go on playing through the night, dreaming about that kiss and laughter, but decided that Miriam was right to hint that he quit. He let her fix him up with some of Abe's toobig pajamas and then he slept with the stack of music next to him on the floor, reluctant to let anything of Rebecca's out of his sight.

CHAPTER THIRTY-THREE

Paper covered every surface in Harald Steinmetz's Heathman Hotel room. In the middle, stood Russman, holding a manuscript of yellowed paper.

"No," Steinmetz yelled. "Old Corelli, but not Bach."

"Isn't Corelli just as well-known as Bach?" Russman asked.

"Yes, and valuable, but nowhere near the value of Bach's missing creations. Nowhere near!"

Russman stared at the calligraphy of the Corelli. "How did she even get this?"

"You missed something in that apartment. It has to be there."

Russman said, "It has to be in her violin case, then. A false bottom, maybe, something …"

"You shook the lute?"

"Of course, and the violin and its case. Nothing seemed loose."

"They must be there. The old man sent her everything else – that Corelli shows he collected."

"But he never broke, and I applied everything."

"There's only one way," Steinmetz said. "Force her to look deeper."

Russman glanced at Steinmetz. "The boy."

"He is rightfully mine anyway."

"How do we get at him?"

CHAPTER THIRTY-FOUR

Before dawn on Saturday, Lewis seated himself at the piano again. He found a fat manuscript book which seemed to have the handwriting of several composers in it. At some point in the long past, someone had sewn the pages together into these notebooks.

Suddenly, Lewis realized there was something very odd about the covers. The endpapers had a pattern that featured small roses. The roses were in rows, but the paper on the back cover had not been cut exactly on the square. The rest of the notebook had been very carefully sewn, and the endpaper on the front was elegantly cut so that the roses lined up with the notebook edge.

Lewis took his pocketknife out, lay the notebook on the piano bench and slit the edge of the back endpaper. Almost immediately, he could feel extra pages loosening up, as if breathing. He proceeded with great care, retrieving pages from both the front and the back cover of the notebook.

In minutes he held very old music pages in his hands. Lewis had seen Bach's handwriting in many reproductions and this one was not like Bach's writing. But these were hidden. Something about them made hiding necessary.

He returned to the other pieces in the notebook. Reading through these, Lewis began to recognize the two songs for violin that Rebecca had been playing on the afternoon of the party, five months earlier. The piano accompaniments were quite different from what he'd imagined, rhythmically more creative and playful, so he played through all of them, humming the violin part to himself. They were among the loveliest pieces for solo instrument that he knew – delightful gems.

He recognized that he was postponing the real discovery. At last, he returned to the hidden and oldest papers. He had to lean very close to the music desk to read the fine, almost feminine script. This was a solo concerto in the key of D minor. He used his left hand to follow the faint notes as his right hand played the solo line. At the end of the first page, he glanced at the whole notebook. Some memory nagged at him.

The notebooks held another clue, he was certain. He studied the fluid handwriting of Raphael Atemvoll. His sure italic print and clear notation caught Lewis's attention.

Lewis grabbed the discarded yellow envelopes. Yes, the handwriting on the envelopes was Atemvoll's, and the sewn notebook fit inside one of them. He glanced at the stack. There were three similar notebooks along with the remaining music. He pulled them from the stack and found the same set-up. Atemvoll's pieces and Batislav's laendler and dances. And the covers carried carefully cut and glued endpapers – all small roses.

Three manuscripts. Hidden manuscripts.

Bach's handwriting or not, the coincidence of three and the disguised method of mailing suggested more than coincidence – a lot more.

Lewis played the lively allegro in the first folio. As he played on to the end, he realized that someone else was in the room. He turned to find Rebecca staring, transfixed by the manuscript.

"That's it," she whispered.

"That's . . .?"

"The Bach they are after. Turn the page." She still had not looked at him, only at the faint notation.

He turned the page and began playing the adagio movement, her soft clear voice preceding him in the violin part. He stopped playing the upper line and supported her voice with the counterpoint in the orchestral part. Her unaffected soprano flowed in a finely spun reverie. Her intensity was so great that she seemed totally unaware of him.

At the end of the *Adagio*, she turned the page and sat next to him on the bench. He moved slightly and said, "I'll play the viola and cello parts. You're the violin, of course."

They played recklessly through a lively allegro, dropping a few faintly written notes along the way, but too enchanted with the fun of it to care. After the violin's last ascending flourish, there was an unanswered question in the air.

He laughed. "That was wonderful."

"Oh," she cried, "What has he done?"

Lewis showed her his cuts on the endpapers of the first notebook. "He hid them carefully and mailed them in these envelopes to your Uncle Tobias."

She reached up and took the next notebook from the stack and turned to the covers and then handed the notebook to Lewis.

Lewis cut each cover carefully.

"This is the G minor," Rebecca whispered.

Setting it on the music desk she reached for the third. And then, she sat staring – staring so long Lewis worried about her.

At last, she whispered, "And this is the other double concerto, in C minor. That damned gangster knew they were somewhere. How did he know?"

Then she touched the music. "Raphael hid them in these, got rid of them to Tobias because he was afraid for them." And then, suddenly, she put her head on her arm. "Where is he? Where are they?"

Lewis knew she meant her family, her teacher, and Zoltan. He knew finding them would free her, and he knew the search was his to make because she could not return to Hungary.

At the other end of the hall, they heard Abraham and Miriam stirring in their room.

She sat up and glanced at her robe. Pulling it closer, she looked up at him, tears streaking down her cheeks.

"These are here," he said. "We have to protect them and you. You change, and then we'll plan."

She touched the music one more time, smiled sadly and rose. "This was lovely. Playing it was fun, no?"

"It is fun, yes. And now we know."

She took a deep breath. "Raphael would never have told them, no matter what they did to him."

Lewis nodded. "He wanted you safe, and he had a duty to these as well."

*   *

As she climbed the stairs, he returned to study the first piece they had uncovered. She had said that this music was what the thieves wanted. How did she know that so quickly?

It was a great piece – he knew that.

He sat up and began looking at the first movement again. She had known its significance right away. What was there about it that told her? As he played through it, Abraham came in with two cups of fresh coffee.

Abe stared at the music.

Lewis kept playing and asked, "What do you think, Abe?"

"It's the first movement of a Bach concerto that Rebecca played for me last year. You know it as one of his harpsichord concerti. Her teacher taught it to her when she was very young – a piece he wanted her only to know by memory. Not many people know it as a violin movement, because that's the only movement that has ever been found."

Lewis finished the first movement and turned to Abe. "Did you hear Bach's smooth transitions to related keys?"

Abe nodded, still staring at the manuscript. "Look how the accompaniment is slightly different from the harpsichord and piano transcriptions. Clearly written for orchestra."

"Becca came down this morning when I played this. When we turned the page, look what we found."

Abe set down the coffee, and leaned closer, reading the second movement in his mind. Carefully, he turned to the final allegro. Lewis watched Abe's eyes follow the counterpoint from voice to voice. He saw him swallow hard as he turned to the last page. The older man straightened up.

"If that isn't it, it's a damn good imitation! But the hand writing is all wrong. It isn't Bach's and it isn't Altnikol's."

"Who is Altnikol?"

"A friend. Bach sometimes dictated to him when his weak eyes gave him trouble."

Abe took the book to the chair by the window for better light. "Sometimes in the end, his eyes bothered him so much that he wrote in the near dark. His last manuscripts were often of watery ink like this . . . hard for him to tell the difference I guess, since he was in the dark anyway. But still, this isn't his handwriting."

Abe turned the page to the following yellowed papers. As his eyes followed the notes, he sat up, intensely concentrating on what he saw there.

"Look at this," Lewis said. He reached for the stack of music he had already been through, thumbed through the edges until he came to the tan envelopes. Holding them out to Abe he said. "This is the same handwriting as the pieces at the front of the notebook."

"Sheet Music Service of New York?" Abe read. "Tobias Kossuth never ran a sheet music service. He's a coroner."

"The handwriting is the same as the pieces in the beginning of each of these notebooks – the composer, Raphael Atemvoll," Lewis said.

"But, three envelopes? And Feodor Sospiro?"

Lewis sat up like a rod, "God! She used that name as well. Rebecca Sospiro Gregory, né Tsigane – the false name on her papers."

Abe frowned, "It must be a symbol between Rebecca and Raphael."

"And look at this." Lewis fit the notebook with the Bach piece into the first envelope. "The notebook fits. The creases on the envelopes indicate that this is exactly what was mailed in it."

"Abraham," Rebecca whispered from behind them. "Let me see those envelopes."

They both turned in surprise. Rebecca, barefoot, dressed in slacks and a barely-tucked-in blouse, had come silently into the room.

Abe handed her the envelopes and pointed to the return name.

"Sospiro," she whispered. "That is Raphael. I assumed they were from a hospital to Tobias." She looked them over carefully. "What made him send them to Tobias?"

Lewis watched her face as she studied the handwriting. "It is Raphael's, but very hurried. Most of the time, he wrote a neater italic print."

Then, her gaze went to the stamps. Her eyes widened. Her cheeks lost color. "My God," she whispered. "The post office cancelled these stamps on the day I was kidnapped." She looked at the other two envelopes. "Yes. The same." She swayed.

Lewis stood up and urged her onto the piano bench.

She said. "They knew he had them, but he got rid of them before they . . ."

"All three?" Abe asked.

"They are all there," she said. "The double concerto, too."

Abe looked at her.

She answered his unspoken question. "The g minor, the d minor and a double concerto in c minor. That bastard insisted I had them. I never believed him. Then this morning, Lewis played Raphael's songs and then the first movement of the concerto soon after. I began to understand.

"Raphael Atemvoll had told me that his pieces were not important enough to bother with. Yet he bothered to teach me the first two songs in that first notebook just before I graduated from the grammar school. And that was the year he taught me the Allegro – the one movement known from the D minor concerto – and all taught to me by memory. 'This will enhance your mind. Always remember these in your heart,' he said. He was giving me a message, but I didn't understand until Lewis played them together this morning."

"Why would he send them to your Uncle Tobias?" Lewis asked.

"The date he mailed them," Abe said. "Probably he didn't know you were being kidnapped, but he knew someone was coming for them."

Lewis said, "If someone threatened him, he couldn't give them to Rebecca. She would be in danger. But he had to get rid of them."

Abe frowned, obviously puzzled. "Becca, how could he have had them?"

Rebecca leaned on Abe. "After we played that first one this morning, I figured out the history of where it must have been before him. Batislav gave Raphael all his music in his will."

Ah," said Lewis. "Batislav of those little dances and marches."

Rebecca smiled. "Yes. They were composed for the social affairs of the St. Petersburg aristocracy."

Lewis grinned. "That explains why they were so . . . well . . ."

Rebecca said, "But Batislav was far from boring when he played violin or piano. He taught the famous pianist, Count Feodor Czigler, who died during the Russian Revolution."

"Feodor," Lewis said, pointing again to the name on the envelope. "Another hint?"

Her eyes widened. "It couldn't . . . but it must be."

Abe filled in the next part of the story. "Count Czigler's grandfather, as well as Anton Batislav, studied with a Mr. Kreinstat. What's the connection to these?

She said, "Kreinstat was a nephew of the great musicologist Georg Polchau."

"Polchau!" exclaimed Abe. "Now I get the connection!"

"But I don't." laughed Lewis. "Enlighten me please."

Abe was on his feet pacing and hugging the music to him. "Polchau was the one who collected the Bach manuscripts after the death of Carl Phillip Emmanuel Bach. Polchau also discovered Bach's Sonatas and Partitas for violin. They were on their way to becoming wrapping paper in a butter shop."

"So Polchau, or later Kreinstat, or Czigler knew to find or buy the concerti" Lewis guessed.

Rebecca smiled. "All this long tale tells you how these pieces might have come to Batislav, and then to his student, Raphael, but it still doesn't tell Lewis why all three violin concertos were there together."

Abe took up the story again. "When Johann Bach died, his music was divided among his two musical sons Emmanuel and Wilhelm Friedemann. We have the violin concertos that Emmanuel inherited. He was very careful with his father's music. Those that Friedemann inherited were lost because in a moment of pecuniary panic, he sold them all to some unknown for twelve thaler – a pittance! We knew they existed, but we've only seen the one movement of this one that Becca knows and piano transcriptions of the others."

Lewis suddenly saw the whole picture. "So, Rebecca believes that Friedemann Bach had sold them all to the same person, a Russian."

Abe, his eyes bright with excitement, nodded his agreement.

Rebecca laughed, a vibrant sound that warmed Lewis. He glanced at her, pleased to see the rose in her cheeks again.

"What's the joke, Little Mother?" asked Abe.

"Harald Steinmetz would be astonished," she said. "We almost found these before Hanukkah."

Abe's forehead wrinkled. "Steinmetz? You mean when he played duets with you?"

"Yes. We started through this notebook that evening, but before we finished Batislav, he got bored, set it aside and we took a break. Oh…" she tried unsuccessfully to subdue her mirth. "He would never forgive himself."

Lewis smiled. "I know what turned him off."

Abe nodded. "The Batislav dances were planted there especially to discourage stuffy academics."

Her sad laughter stopped. "Abe, they know who I am, that's clear, but how did they know so quickly that I came to Portland?"

"Someone must have told them," Abe said.

"Never Tobias," she said.

"No. But Gabriel knew." Abe said.

Rebecca's face grayed, and her gaze became glassy. "Not on purpose."

"Maybe not," Abe said. "But Gabriel's greater purpose has always been to own you. He may have said something he thought harmless, but enough of a clue for them."

Lewis said, "The biggest problem now is how to protect you, Benjamin and the music?"

Lewis saw Rebecca shiver. He handed her his warm coffee. "Drink this."

"Abe," he said, "the thieves have got to know a lot about music even to suspect she has these pieces."

"Yes, and enough about musicians to have recognized Darya Zolesku." said Abe.

Lewis sat on the bench and took her hand. "To these men, the blond who invaded your apartment, the dark little weasel who knocked out Benji's teacher, and the curly haired one who tried to walk away with him from your apartment playground in New York – to them, you are a meal ticket, and we have to figure them out right away."

Rebecca's voice showed her fatigue. "Wouldn't it be easier to figure out what they want to do with the concertos and foil that?"

"Isn't it obvious?" said Lewis. "If they get the concertos, they want to sell them to the highest bidder."

"They could just want to own them," Rebecca interjected, hugging his warm coffee mug to her.

Lewis said, "Isn't kidnapping a little drastic for someone who merely wants to own old music?"

"Some people are that crazy," Abe interjected.

"I disagree," said Lewis. "They've spent a lot of time and money tracking the music, and then finding Rebecca. I think they're hoping to make a lot more money in the long run."

Rebecca shook her head, "Where do people sell such things, if they have them illegally?"

Lewis whipped back to face her. He broke into a grin.

"I think you've hit the solution, Becca!" He turned back to explain to Abe. "We have to let the world know that these have been found. If the whole world knows that they tried to steal the famous Bach concertos from the famous Rebecca Gregory, the thieves won't be able to sell them to the big collectors – the people with the real money. Those people wouldn't want to be caught making such a deal or holding the merchandise afterward."

"Lewis," Abe said, "I see your reasoning, but what solution?"

Lewis's grinned. "We make the rightful ownership public!"

"Yes," she said. "In concert. The sooner the better. They've counted on my fear of immigration for long enough."

Lewis nodded. "Time to surprise them by being on the offensive. Have you started rehearsals with the Oregon Symphony?"

"We start Monday. The first concert is the second Friday after that." Rebecca said. "I believe you're right. Mr. Tovey, the conductor, would help us. But we'd have to make good copies right away. The copies will have to be disguised so that the real composer is unknown until opening night, or they'll try to stop us."

Abe burst into their plans, "Whoa up. . . whose handwriting is on this music? Until we know that, we don' know for sure if we have the real thing."

Rebecca smiled at him. "Abraham, you should know her hand as well as his."

"As well as Bach's? It's similar, but why should I know it?"

"Because she copied much of his work. She learned from him to write music. It's Anna Magdalena's hand – Anna Magdalena, Bach's student, and then his second wife."

Abraham Friedenberg made a properly humble face and sat back, waving them on with their plans.

CHAPTER THIRTY-FIVE

The help Abe rounded up for the morning amazed Lewis. Francis Tovey, the conductor of the Oregon Symphony, was brought into the scheme. Through Tovey's contacts, music editors of three key newspapers in the U.S. and Europe were alerted that something extraordinary would be happening in Portland on the concert date, but they were warned to keep from speculating in print or gossip because of danger to the participants. Amazingly, the media agreed. They smelled a story too good to ruin by trying to scoop each other.

More importantly for Rebecca, news editors were told that the discovery to be unveiled was made by the well-known musicologist, Abraham Friedenberg. The hope was that the news focus would thus be on his music researches in Europe and Asia. Rebecca's part in the discovery would be played down for the sake of any friends and relatives left in Hungary who might suffer if her background and escape were investigated by some curious reporter. The conductor, Tovey, called a friend in Austria who was willing to claim he'd taught Rebecca Gregory in that country before she moved to the United States. Rabbi Stamps had a friend in Leipzig who put nuptial papers into his synagogue archive for Rebecca Sospiro and Lemuel Gregory on the appropriate date.

At breakfast that first morning after the discovery, some doubt, or perhaps jealousy, made Lewis insist to Abe that neither Gabriel Kolya nor Harald Steinmetz be a part of the inner circle.

When Rebecca heard their conversation, she seconded Lewis. "Steinmetz's interest in music is superficial," she said. "He could not appreciate Atemvoll's songs, and had no sense of humor about Batislav's dances."

Lewis, grateful, let her assessment stand, but he saw and wondered why she kept wiping her hands on her jeans whenever Steinmetz's name came up.

Abe shrugged, "Okay, I was wrong about him, eh?"

Miriam smiled at Abe. "You want the right things for Rebecca, but you're no matchmaking Yente."

At Rabbi Stamps' suggestion, Joseph Selig was asked for help. For the safety of her family and teacher, Selig sped up the creation of better forged documents which would support Rebecca's claim to have grown up in Austria instead of Hungary. Lewis noticed, with some amusement and compassion, that Joseph could actually lie for a good cause, but it made him sweat a lot.

Her citizenship papers were in process. Joseph believed that Rebecca Gregory would be a citizen by the concert.

*   *

By that afternoon, most of the details were pinned down and all the musicians in the conspiracy got down to the business of copying music for Monday's rehearsal. Lewis worked quietly, first on the cello part, then the bassoon, flute and oboe parts for the orchestra. Tovey, Abe and Rebecca worked near him on the dining table and buffet, making fair copies of all the other parts. They agreed to use the name

Jan Dismas Zelenka, the name of one of Bach's contemporaries, to identify the composer.

All the time they worked, Lewis and Rebecca kept Benjamin supplied with paper, so he could draw "music" too. Miriam kept them all supplied with chocolate chip cookies.

For some reason, Rebecca grew more and more silent as the afternoon wore on. During a break before supper, Lewis saw Rebecca head toward the upstairs. He followed her toward Abe's study. She heard him on the steps and watched apprehensively as he approached. His heart lurched when her hand on the doorknob trembled.

"I'm not going to touch you," he said and could have kicked himself for cornering her. Still, he couldn't let the silence between them go longer, so he spoke quickly, "Please trust me."

"I do trust you, Levy."

He watched as she gave off waves of tension, reacting, he was sure, to his presence in this deadend space. He backed away from her.

As she watched him retreat from her, the tension increased rather than diminished, so he stepped down two levels on the stairs to allow her to feel safer.

Rebecca's hand rose and fell ineffectually several times before she could speak again. As her soft voice pushed itself past her fear, she gazed blindly toward the door jamb beside her.

"I had a dream last night," she said. "We had married, and . . ."

He waited, stiff with anticipation, glad that her dreams allowed the idea.

"And I . . . I disappointed you."

"What?" His whole face felt numb. "You mean I said that?"

She shook her head. "I hid from you." He saw her cringe at having to say it.

"Becca, this was a dream. Your mind testing ideas."

"I don't want to treat you so."

"Hold onto this," he whispered. "You dreamed we married. And I'm going with that."

"Oh, Levy. I have to be fair to you."

"Then dream that I am patient. You want me to hold you in my arms. The rest will come."

"But you deserve more."

"And so, my darling, so do you. Don't give up."

She stared at the door jamb. "I . . . I will try."

Downstairs, they heard Benji calling, "Grandpa, where's Mama?"

She glanced at Lewis, and then called "I'm upstairs, Benji. I'll be down in a minute."

He stood aside for her to go down. On the way by, she whispered to Lewis, "Please forgive me."

"I love you," he said. "And it was a dream."

Rebecca glanced at him, an apology and sadness in the downturn of her lips. Then she stepped down to the dining room. He heard her walk into the living room and greet Benji.

Moments later, slowly, painfully, he descended into the dining room where Abe eyed him warily. All the rest of the crew were in the living room with Benjamin and Rebecca.

Lewis, his back straight, his body cold, stalked into the kitchen. Miriam took one look at him and pushed him onto the high stool. "I'll get you a whiskey," she announced.

*   *

After dinner, Abraham prevailed on his banker to open the vault on a Saturday evening and take in the original manuscripts without knowing what they were. Box seats for his family at the affair encouraged his cooperation and his secrecy.

That evening, the team celebrated the discovery together, careful not to let their elation show to outsiders. Abraham began secret negotiations for transfer of un-named valuable documents in his possession to a museum and library they all trusted. They had a plan to foil the gang in Hungary and its representatives in New York and Portland.

Rebecca called on young B.K. Price, the symphony oboist. When he came to Friedenberg's, he was at first overwhelmed with looking at the manuscripts and learning that they truly did exist.

They all sat in the big music room and listened to the first rehearsal and sight reading of the double concerto. Lewis played a reduction of the orchestral parts on the piano.

Price was absolutely stunned to have become a part of this historic occasion. When Abraham congratulated him on his ability to sight read with such feeling, he ducked his head in pleased embarrassment, smiled a beautiful smile and pulled on his Padawan braid. Lewis felt they had found the right combination for delivering this music to the world.

Care and secrecy were tinged with joy in the music and grappling with the wonder of having found these beautiful pieces.

For a week following the discovery of the concertos, Benjamin was kept out of school, either with Abraham or Lewis at all times. Rebecca told the school that she was testing a home-schooling situation.

She wasn't going to give the kidnappers any chance of getting at him before the concert. It was possible that in spite of all their efforts, word of the concerti might leak out. If so, the efforts to get Benjamin would be renewed and vigorous.

While Benjamin was thus guarded, Abraham taught him to play chess. Lewis taught him how to play tennis or at least some semblance of it. He went with Lewis and Rebecca to the swimming pool, with Lewis to the fencing gym and with Abe and Miriam to the winter Disney movie.

*   *

Rebecca enjoyed Lewis's protection of Benjamin, but her heart ached with longing for Lewis's affectionate touch. Since the morning they had discovered the Bach, and she had told him of her dream, he touched her only to help her with her coat, or to guide her over the icy sidewalks. She didn't want to hurt him. He'd reassured her, but her dream must have repulsed him. Nevertheless, she was grateful that he took her to rehearsals and waited for her backstage. She was very quiet when they were together and always left him in Abraham's good company as soon as she could.

One evening, she turned back to look from the stairwell down into the music room and found his eyes on her. There was an open look of pain on his face. She knew then how deeply her dream had wounded him.

*   *

Lewis accepted her silence and distance – evident fear of the physical possibilities. He was afraid to cause her another concern before the concerts. Besides, his body was so frustrated by its brief knowledge of her that he thought it safer to keep his distance.

As Rebecca withdrew, Lewis's love for Benjamin was made even more painful. His enjoyment of their tennis games was tinged with a bitter edge. Lewis' dreams for their life together as a family seemed to be in long-term limbo.

But, on the next Friday night, a week before the concerts, sleepless and frustrated, he determined to begin again at the beginning. He couldn't give Rebecca up. She had mistrusted him when they first met, yet over the months he'd made that distrust become love. This time, it was herself she mistrusted.

He would wear her down again, until there was nothing she could do but trust him and her own reaction to him.

*   *

On Saturday morning, Lewis brought his old tinkertoys with him when he picked Benjamin up for their trip to his office. Miriam and

Rebecca were going to shop for a new concert dress, and then Miriam had to work in her office on campus.

When he arrived at Abe and Miriam's house, Lewis left the toys in the car and came up the stairs just as Rebecca came out of the house. She banged into him as she turned from the door.

"Oh! Levy, I'm sorry." Her eyes were round with surprise.

Attempting to keep her from falling, he'd taken hold of her shoulders, and held her longer than necessary. "Don't be sorry – about so many things. Don't apologize and pull away so readily, Becca."

"I just didn't want to hurt you." Her gaze wavered.

"Look at me. I can protect myself. The real question is what do you want?"

She was confused for a moment, but his persistent questioning look made her admit the true meaning of his interrogation. She swallowed hard and blinked away the pain of her answer. "What I want is not what I may have any more."

"I don't for one minute believe that is true. I want you. I want Benjamin. I want you to keep trying because when you give up like this, I go through hell."

Her eyes opened wide in disbelief. "I thought you . . . I thought my dream made you . . ." She couldn't bring herself to say it.

"You thought I was afraid of a dream? You're damned right. I'm afraid such dreams will haunt you, embarrass you, make you do just what you did – avoid me." He kissed her forehead just as the door banged open again.

Benjamin came out with Miriam. Miriam, mouth agape and mind paralyzed, let go of Benjamin's hand.

Benjamin tugged on Lewis's sleeve. "Lewis! Aren't we going to your office?"

"Just as soon as I hug your mother, little man. Please wait." He took her chin in his hand and made her look at him. His eyebrows rose a moment before the smile invaded his face. He'd seen the "yes" she was afraid to say. While he kissed her, Benjamin hugged both their legs and Miriam ducked back inside as if for some forgotten item.

* *

Entering the physics building, Benjamin and Lewis met Dick Street at Dick's least favorite moment of dependency. Every Saturday, three large friends carried his wheelchair up to the chemistry lab. Dick knew he ought to be grateful to these guys, but he didn't like having to coerce anybody into this kind of duty. Lewis and Benjamin came along just as he was running his chair up the sidewalk.

"Neat gadget you got there!" exclaimed Benjamin.

"Thanks kid. Where's your Go-cart?"

"I have Big Wheels, but it isn't so cool. Can I have a ride?"

Dick laughed. "Sure, up to the front door. After that I'm on a dangerous assignment, so you've got to get out."

"What's dangerous?"

"How I get upstairs – these fellows keep threatening to dump me."

"Oh, they're just teasing." Benjamin was sure because Uncle Tobias used to tease like that on the way up to their apartment. He hopped on where Dick showed him and rode in style while Lewis and the three friends followed.

They signed in at the front door logbook and navigated the two flights to the lab successfully. Lewis carried Benji up one more flight to the third-floor offices while Dick made arrangements for his friends to come back in four hours.

To Benjamin, Lewis' office was a wonderful place – a regular rabbit warren of chairs and tables and desks to hide under, no end of paper to draw on and the box of tinkertoys which provided Ferris wheels and houses for all kinds of imaginary people.

Lewis typed away between conversations with Benjamin. He had a rough draft of the long-neglected journal article hammered out, probably not a very coherent one, but at least the ideas were all on paper. When the phone rang, they had a little trouble finding it, but it kept ringing until the right papers were moved.

"Dr. James?" The voice on the line was muffled by crackling sounds. "This is security. There's a fire in your building. Please come down to the front door."

"We'll be right down." Lewis could smell smoke already. He grabbed Benjamin and explained as they ran down the stairs. Out on the front sidewalk, they looked back to see smoke and flames pouring out of the second-floor lab.

Miriam Friedenberg ran out of the science building at that moment, nearly colliding with Lewis.

"Grandma," Benji cried, hugging her legs, "were you in there too?"

"My teaching office is on the first floor Benji, but we're all safe now."

Benji glanced up at the windows on the second floor and shouted, "The wheelchair man, Daddy! He's in there still!"

"Dick!" Lewis looked around, hoping Dick had been brought out by some colleague in the lab. Many others milled about, but not Dick. Nearby stood the security guard, a gray-haired man about sixty years old and very small.

"Is someone still in the building, sir?" the guard asked.

"A man in a wheelchair, in that second-floor lab."

Some shouted, "He must have started this damn fire."

The security man said, "The firemen are on their way, no tellin' how long that will take."

"The chem lab," Miriam said. "It could become an inferno."

Lewis looked back and forth from the orange hot flames to the security guard. No sirens! No other people! He couldn't just let Dick suffocate up there. It might already be too late.

He thrust Benji's hand into Miriam's and turned toward the guard. "Mister, I'll go in after him. You watch over my friend and my boy here. Don't let them come in after me, whatever you do."

"I'll be here with them, but you get out of there soon. No tellin' what's burning in that place."

"Go," Miriam shouted.

Lewis raced for the stairs. He bounded up them two and three at a time, but as he reached the landing to the second floor, he faced a wall of smoke. He backed down to clearer air and took several deep breaths, hoping to get enough good oxygen in his blood to carry him through the lab. He took out his bandana-handkerchief and tied it around his face. The smell of the smoke was sulfurous. Lewis tried to remember what was in the lab that might explode.

Heading into the billowing smoke, his eyes watered and stung. The flames filled the left half of the room, the chemical storage areas. Orange and blue shot up the walls near the windows.

Lewis ran toward the heat and the flames by the open window, holding his breath. He dove right toward Dick's lab bench and fell over something in the aisle. He groped around searching for a familiar desk corner or piece of equipment. The heat was intense, searing his skin through his shirt.

Over the roar of the flames, he heard a faint clicking, repeated, regular. No. It was slowing down, like the click of a freely rotating bicycle wheel.

Dick's chair!

Tipped over. Where?

He crawled forward, eyes closed against the smoke, tears running down his face, hands groping.

Where? Where? Oh, don't stop clicking until I find him. Where is he?

Lewis kept his face close to the floor where the smoke was not as thick. He couldn't see anything. One cupboard, two cupboards, the reference bookshelf, the cloud chamber, the air track machine, a third cupboard, a desk chair. Suddenly, his forehead grazed the rubber of a rotating wheel.

He groped in the seat and found the strap which held Dick, empty. Wildly he climbed over the chair, feeling on all sides.

Nothing!

Quickly he crawled past two more cupboards until at last his hand rested on the thick shoe that covered Dick's leg braces.

In moments, he had Dick in his arms. He headed toward the back door of the lab. Five feet too soon, he ran into something solid. A cupboard had been pushed in front of the door. He couldn't even get at it without putting Dick down. How much time did Dick have? Was he breathing even now? Lewis didn't think so. Given no choice, he headed toward the flames and the one door he knew was open to the hall – the door near the chemical storage.

He ran as straight as he could down the aisle toward the light from the window and the fire. His lungs ached. His throat was seared. He could barely see the light through his eyes which refused to open more than a slit. His tears distorted everything he saw, and he bumped into the tables on his left several times as he approached the chemical cupboards. Knowing the cupboard could blow any minute, he lunged. When he reached the end of the desks, he veered blindly left toward the hall door.

Once in the hallway, he had to lean against the wall to keep himself from wobbling aimlessly across the hall. He had lost all ability to tell up from down. He was aware only of the heat, the craving of his lungs and the limp body in his arms. The stairs loomed as an insurmountable difficulty.

He rounded the corner to the stairwell. The light from the floor to ceiling window on the stair landing blinded him. Three large shadows stood between him and the exit. One of them tried to take Dick from him, but he wouldn't let go of him. They struggled. Lewis heard a voice somewhere shouting at him. "Dr. James, let me carry him down.

You've had it. Steve, help Dr. James out. Noah call an ambulance. Dick isn't breathing."

"Who?" gasped Lewis.

"It's us – Dick's friends. We heard the fire engines and came back to make sure Dick was out. They took your boy to the hospital just a moment ago."

"My boy?"

"The little fellow who rode the chair. Let's hurry out. I've got to try to get Dick breathing."

Lewis stumbled down the stairs. There was searing pain in every breath. He reached the front door in time to see Miriam trying to rise from the sidewalk.

A blue Impala worked its way around the entering fire engines. Benjamin crying, scrambled to look out the back window. His flailing arms knocked the gray wig off of the security guard. The thin dark hair of his kidnapper was all that could be seen above the back seat.

Lewis felt a stab of pain as he watched the man pull Benji down in the car seat.

"Take care of Dr. Friedenberg," Lewis shouted to Dick's friends, and took off after the car.

Lewis knew his own car would be blocked by the engines. He dragged his leaden body after the blue car as it headed out toward Woodward Boulevard and turned toward Laurel Street. Forcing his legs to run, Lewis made a right turn and headed across campus toward the intersection of Woodward and Laurel. His only hope was to cut across the hypotenuse of a triangle and gain a little time.

Let the traffic be with me. God, my lungs! My son!

And then he plunged on.

As Lewis raced toward the intersection, the blue car slowed down to stop before turning right on Laurel. The blond driver seemed unaware of Lewis until he saw him grab the door handle.

The driver jerked the wheel to the right, driving the car into Lewis and across the curb back onto Laurel.

The last that Lewis heard was the high-pitched squeal of the tires. He saw Benji's hand reaching toward the lock.

CHAPTER THIRTY-SIX

Lewis tried to postpone the pain that light and reality would give him, but a movement of his mattress and the warm evening scent of jasmine awakened him. Next to his arm, Rebecca's head lay on her folded hands. She must have leaned forward from the chair by his bed, rested and finally slept there. Behind her, looking out the hospital window at the sunrise, stood a bear of a man in a black overcoat.

Lewis frowned and moved his hand to caress her hair. He tried to speak, but found only agony instead of voice. The white light of pain cut him off from everything.

*   *

Uncle Tobias heard the wrenching of Lewis's body. He turned quickly to see the hand on his niece's head convulse once before it lay still in unconsciousness. The young man's face, so promising of humor when at peace, was now lined from pain and anguish. Tobias knew his own face mirrored that anguish. Nothing had been heard from Benjamin's kidnappers for eighteen hours. Rebecca had waited at the hospital for a call from Abraham.

Throughout Tobias' flight from New York, Abe had kept a text update going for everyone who searched for the kidnappers. Leads followed and petered out all day long.

Now, they were down to a region-wide search for the car. Miriam had gotten its make and license.

Tobias watched Rebecca's strength ebb as the hours stretched. He began to fear anew for her sanity. Yet, when she witnessed Lewis' nightmares of self-blame and seeking for their boy, she seemed to have strong resources within. She held him, forgave him, encouraged him – whatever she thought he needed. Tobias's entreaties to go home were gently pushed aside. She slept as now, in the chair next to his bed.

*   *

When the late winter sun rose high enough to shine on her back, Rebecca awoke and realized that Lewis had been awake during the night. She took the hand that had rested on her head, kissed it and held it. It was noticeably warmer than last night. As she stood over him, his eyes opened. He had trouble focusing. Rebecca took his face in her hands, trying to smooth away the lines of sorrow. He blinked and turned into her cool fingers. His mouth formed a word, but the effort to say anything around his seared throat stopped him.

Rebecca knew what he needed. She leaned over him and whispered, "We'll hear from the kidnappers soon. They'll let us know where he is and how we can get him back. You just get well so you can help me. Sleep now, you must sleep. The doctor said your throat would feel burned for several days. You have two broken ribs and a concussion from the car."

She stopped cold as Benjamin's face played across her mind. He must have seen the car hit Lewis. Benjamin's fear would be magnified by his grief.

She felt Lewis's hands pull at her arms. His eyes were asking her one more question.

What should he know to help him rest? Oh!

His student . . .

"Dick Street is conscious and getting better," she said, "but he doesn't know what happened. Someone hit him on the head from behind. His friends got him breathing again before the ambulance arrived."

Lewis' eyes closed thankfully, but in a moment, he was back at her with more questions. "Miriam is well and at home in bed. The students on the sidewalk said the kidnappers held a gun to Miriam so no one dared stop them. Then, they hit her and took off just as you came down."

He waited, holding Rebecca's arm, still. She cast about for what else he needed.

Tobias, realizing what Lewis was trying to say, leaned over her. "Young man, when the kidnappers call, we'll wake you up."

Rebecca was grateful for the relief her uncle's words brought Lewis. His face relaxed and his hands fell from her arms as healing sleep took over.

*   *

Hours later, Tobias left Rebecca resting in the chair and went to the cafeteria to get them both something to eat. He was gone only a little while when the nurse, Vera, came in.

"Mrs. Gregory, there's a telephone call for you. You can take it in the little office near the nurses' station."

Rebecca followed the nurse to the phone in the nearest small room. She took up the indicated phone as Vera closed the door. A harsh New York accent attacked her ears. "Mrs. Gregory?"

"Yes?" Her heart filled her throat.

"Listen."

There was a brief silence. The phone at the other end was knocked on something and then the sounds were muffled before she heard Benjamin cry. "Mama! They killed Grandma and Lewis!"

"Benji! Grandma is fine. Levy is alive. Where . . .?"

The phone was taken from him. In the background, she could hear him yelling for her. The New Yorker came back, his Bronx jarring her already frayed mind. "You know that voice? Sure ya do. Ya want him back?"

"Of course! How? Where?"

"Bring the manuscripts to Timberline Lodge. You know where that is?"

"Yes, on Mount Hood. I've seen it."

"Yeah? Well, if Abe or your uncle or anyone else knows about this, the kid's dead. So, you come alone. Come to the lodge and walk west along the Timberline Trail until you get to the signs for Highland Ski Trail. Go down Highland Trail and we'll meet you with your little brat here. Bring the concertos, ya got that?"

"Bring the concerto?"

"Don't play dumb, Betty Boop. Bring all the music and don't bring anybody else because there are enough of us to watch. The kid don't make it if we smell anything bad goin' down, you got it?"

"I understand, but I can't get the music until ten o'clock Monday. This is Sunday."

"In the bank, huh?"

"Yes."

"You figure it out. You and the music be there by one o'clock tomorrow or he's gone. And no one knows, verstadt?"

"I understand."

"Now pretend this was a call from some old friend who's very worried about your health. Not too far from the truth, nein?"

"May I speak to Benji again?"

"Tomorrow."

There followed a click and the drone of dial tone. Rebecca moved slowly away from the phone, she opened the door to the room and stepped into the hall. A moment later, she was able to walk toward the nurse's desk.

The nurse, Vera, looked up from her computer screen. "You all right, Mrs. Gregory?"

Rebecca straightened up quickly and forced a smile. "Yes, I'm fine. Just a little tired, I guess."

"I'm not at all surprised about that. A good sleep will help you be of more use to Dr. James, you know."

Rebecca knew the nurse was right. Also, she would need to sleep enough to drive up Mount Hood tomorrow morning. "Thank you, Vera. I think I'd better sleep now. Would you tell my uncle where I've gone?"

"Good. We'll tell him. The rooms for visiting families are up one flight. Ask at the nurses' station for room four twenty-four."

Rebecca couldn't go back into Lewis' room right now. She had to have time to think, to hide her fears so no one would know that she'd heard that threatening voice and the cries of her frightened son. Stumbling up the stairs, she followed an efficient nurse to the small bedroom where she fell to the bed.

* *

Lewis heard the door open slowly. He was surprised to see Harald Steinmetz.

"Oh, Dr. James! I'm glad to see you're coming out of your coma. I thought Rebecca was still here with you."

Lewis shook his head. He pointed at his throat and gestured helplessness. Steinmetz smiled. "I know – the fire. You were very brave to go back in after that fellow."

Lewis raised his eyebrows.

"They told me he's doing all right. Street wasn't it? A student of yours?"

Lewis nodded.

"Did he know who started the fire?"

Lewis slowly shook his head. He tried to ask Steinmetz about the science building, but his voice wouldn't come out.

Steinmetz seemed not to realize that Lewis wanted to talk. He was inching out of the room, asking, "Where's Rebecca?"

Lewis shrugged.

"Oh, well I'll let you get back to sleep. I'll find her. Glad you're doing so well."

Steinmetz didn't wait for Lewis' nod. He was in too much hurry to see Rebecca. Lewis frowned. Jealousy had gotten him into trouble twice in the last two weeks. He couldn't afford that emotion anymore.

But Steinmetz's presence felt odd and hurried.

Lewis' head felt as if a leather belt tightened around it. Burns left his back and neck raw. Gauze bandages protected the skin but did nothing to buffer the constant torment of fire in his flesh. Overall his physical pain, despair smothered his mind, and the image of Benjamin frantically fighting to get to the door lock on the blue Impala. He punched the nurses' button next to him. He had to think about something outside of himself. Where was Rebecca? When would the kidnappers call?

The nurse came in, ready to dole out his pain medicine.

"Need phone." His throat barely allowed the sound to form.

"I'm sorry, sir. This is Sunday. The maintenance crew can bring you one on Monday."

"I'll . . . use . . . one . . . down the hall."

"Oh no, sir," she said emphatically and added, as if to a dull child, "When Doctor comes back, you can talk . . ."

"Doctor . . . damned! Son . . . kidnapped! Need phone!" He could barely hear his own whispers, and he knew his eyes flashed frustration and anger at her. His mind yelled at him.

If she doesn't get the phone, check yourself out of here and look for him on foot.

Aloud, he shouted hoarsely, "Get it or not?"

"I can see why you would be upset . . . "

Lewis flung back the covers and started up out of the bed, heedless of the fact that the hospital gown hid almost none of his body. The nurse flung her arms out as if to stop him. "I'll get it, Dr. James. I'll be right back. You just stay there."

As soon as she disappeared, he fell back on the bed with a sharp groan. He couldn't have made it very far down the hall, but the nurse didn't know that.

She returned, plugged in the phone and remonstrated with him over the state of his bandages before he shooed her out. His first call was to Abe who said Miriam was fine, just nursing a bruised jaw. Abe had not heard from the kidnappers, neither had Miriam, but many people had called Abe about Lewis and Rebecca.

Lewis called the front desk. He found that Rebecca had gone to sleep upstairs directly after taking a phone call. Her uncle waited in the hall, thinking Lewis was asleep. Lewis asked that he be sent in.

When Uncle Tobias came into the room, he confirmed that no one had heard from the kidnappers.

The situation didn't make sense to either man. The kidnappers had taken Benjamin at about noon Saturday – almost twenty-four hours. Either they didn't want that music very badly or something had already happened to Benjamin. If there was nothing to exchange . . . Lewis hands clutched at the sudden pain in his head.

He had to think . . . The nurse said Rebecca had been called, here, today. And then she'd gone upstairs, before her Uncle Tobias had returned with her breakfast. Something made her want to be alone after that call. Perhaps she was just exhausted from the night in his room. But it was very unlike her to disappear without explaining to Tobias.

The call had been made to the hospital, where she could be reached by herself, and made at a time when Tobias was gone. Did the caller know that Tobias had stepped out to get breakfast? He had to have an informant in the hospital – or the call was made from within the hospital.

Lewis called Abraham again. The man's deep voice sounded tired.

"Abe?" Lewis forced his voice beyond a whisper, "Harald Steinmetz call there?"

"No, Rebecca said last week that she'd not heard from him much lately – nothing at all since Gabriel had one of his "talks" with him. Why?"

"He . . . here."

"He bored her, Lewis. Keep that in mind when you're feeling jealous."

"Check." God his throat burned right through his ears! "So why ... he here?"

"Damn," Abe said.

Off the phone, Lewis asked, "Tobias, you talked to Gabriel Kolya?"

"Gabriel's called my hotel several times," answered Uncle Tobias. "I've been trying to keep Gabriel out of this, but the man knows something is not right."

Lewis tasted angry bile in his throat, the flavor of his lunch with Gabriel. "Gabe know manuscripts?"

Tobias frowned, "Do you mean, is he the man behind it all? He's not good for her, that's clear. But, I think he truly thinks he loves Rebecca. And he doesn't know about the music."

"Maybe. Nothing about Benji?"

"Nothing. And I would tell you right away."

"Afraid Rebecca by herself," Lewis whispered.

The older man's eyebrows knitted and then relaxed. "If I hear, I will tell both of you, together." Lewis closed his eyes in fatigue and painful memory of little boy eyebrows.

To save Lewis's throat, Tobias made one last call for him, asking Joseph Selig to get police help watching Rebecca. Afterwards, Tobias went upstairs to check on her.

Lewis allowed himself five minutes to clear his head before he went to the closet for his clothes.

CHAPTER THIRTY-SEVEN

That night, Lewis had his street clothes on. Rebecca appeared in his doorway. She saw him sit up quickly, blinking as if it were an effort to see who was coming in.

"Levy? You should be resting." She put her cool hands to his forehead. He leaned against her so heavily that she knew getting dressed had been an ordeal. Why was he pushing himself? Her memory replayed last night's ravings, his guilt over Benjamin's loss.

Had her message gotten through to her son? Did he know that Lewis stilled lived? That would at least give Benjamin some hope. But she couldn't tell Lewis that she'd spoken to her son, and knew how to get him back. She couldn't let him know Benjamin lived.

When she brought Benjamin home, then Lewis would be able to get well faster.

Rebecca's fingers felt the taut muscles in Lewis' back and the back of his head. She massaged his muscles deeply, avoiding the bandaged burns. His head turned, bringing his face into her cotton dress. She felt his lips move against her breasts, his hands came to her hips, spanning her. He pushed further into her, held her tightly to him and wept.

"Who called you?" he asked, looking up at her.

Rebecca wouldn't look at him. "It was … Maria. The concert mistress. New York. She knows Tobias came for some emergency."

So, he thought, Rebecca doesn't lie well. They did call her here. She knows where he is.

"I've got to get out."

She bent over him, brushing his hair with one hand. Her own tears fell on his neck. Her fatigue and fear came out all at once.

"Levy! You can't leave here. You're still in danger from the concussion. You'll kill yourself – and besides, if you come after them, they'll kill him. You must not be seen by them."

"Is he all right?" Lewis grew alert.

"I … he must be afraid. But they wouldn't hurt him as long as there's a chance of getting what they want."

He pulled her down next to him on the bed. "Rebecca, promise me you won't meet them by yourself." He saw her hesitate. "Promise me, Becca."

"I'll do the safest thing at the time – safe for Benjamin as well as for me. You know that, Levy."

He nodded his assent, but his green eyes probed the dark hidden depths of her. "Have they told you when to meet them and where?"

Her eyes shifted away from his, just slightly. "Abraham would call here if he heard."

"Rebecca who called you here in the hospital?"

She looked down at his arms while she composed her answer. "I told you. It was a friend from New York wanting to know how I am. The … the concert mistress in the philharmonic."

He tried to regain contact with her eyes, but she evaded him. With a sigh, he reached for the nurses' button, and encouraged Rebecca to go back to her room for some sleep. When the nurse came, he asked that Tobias be sent to him. It had become obvious that he and Joseph would have to work out a thorough plan to keep track of Rebecca.

* *

Joseph brought with him a Marine, hand-held radio for each of what he called 'our team members'.

And then he showed them how to set the radio so they could all hear each other and follow what might be happening with the kidnappers and Benji.

"We can't let Rebecca meet these guys by herself, but they probably have told her not to contact the police or anyone else," he said.

Tobias nodded. "She'll be scared but determined to do exactly what they say in order to get Benji back."

Miriam added, "Vera, yesterday's nurse, says she had that call traced. It came from the lobby phones in the hospital and then was patched into a cell phone somewhere else. So, someone was here, watching, and they knew exactly when she would be alone."

Lewis determined to push off the fog that his concussion and pain medicine had put on him. He had stopped taking any pain medicine yesterday because he knew he had to be ready for action at any moment.

"Is she still in the bedroom upstairs where she's been hiding out?" he asked.

"Vera has the upstairs nurses watching that door. They promise to call down if she leaves the room for any reason."

"So," Lewis said, "How are we going to watch every place she might go?"

Abe said, "They are after the manuscripts, so I will make sure she can't get them from the bank without me."

Tobias said, "If she slips us, we better have people watching the car she's using. Isn't that your Volvo, Abe?"

"It is. Miriam and I are driving our Audi these days."

"Where has she parked?" Lewis asked. "Maybe we should disable that thing, so she has to ask for help getting it started."

"I know where we parked when she brought me here," Tobias said.

Miriam interrupted, "You want her to come to us, but you cannot give her zero options. We don't know what they've told her, or when they've told her to do anything. I'm going up there and let her know we know she had this call and she'd better have help."

Lewis swallowed hard. Here they'd been planning to thwart Rebecca, and good old Miriam knew to take the problem out in the open and deal directly with Rebecca. He should have thought of that.

The rest of them must have had the same feeling because as Miriam went upstairs, they kind of mumbled at each other and fiddled with the radios while Joseph called Officer June Williams for help.

Tobias left with Abe's extra keys to find the Volvo.

Half an hour later, near sunrise of Monday morning, they knew that Rebecca had not gone back to the room upstairs. Miriam had found the bed made and no note. The Volvo was not in the hospital parking lot.

Abe's banker said he'd had a phone message from Rebecca, but he hadn't known about it until the bank called him. He went to the bank to meet Abe and hope that Rebecca came there.

She was gone. She had avoided all of them by never going to the room upstairs, to Abe's home or her apartment.

Plus, either she wasn't listening to her cell phone messages, or she was simply not answering repeated calls.

"I just hope she hasn't turned off the GPS in the phone," Miriam said. "We may be able to get the officers to trace her."

Joseph was on his way to Abe's as they talked and would check back as soon as he knew anything.

Lewis pulled on the boots Uncle Tobias had brought last night from Lewis' house. Yesterday afternoon the older man had protested, but when Lewis explained Rebecca's sudden deceptiveness, Tobias had taken Lewis' keys and gotten everything he asked for.

They knew she was going to meet the kidnappers alone, but now, they had outfoxed themselves. Knowing that she needed the manuscripts to trade for Benjamin, Abe had taken them from the bank as soon before dawn as he could roust his banker. But she had not come to the bank or to Abe for the music. She was meeting the kidnappers and had nothing to trade.

Pulling on his parka and pushing his way past the protesting nurses, Lewis had a sudden flash of inspiration. The hand-written copies of the concerto were left at his own house. Orchestra members had only Xeroxed copies of those. What if she thought to use them for the trade? She couldn't ask anyone to give her the manuscripts, yet she had to have something to trade, and their handwriting might fool the kidnappers for at least a short time, especially if she put her feminine italic print on top of the pile.

Lewis found his van where Tobias had left it. At over the ideal speed, he roared down Hospital Hill and onto the Ross Island Bridge, coming up to his house the back way. Rounding the corner to his quiet street, he saw her grey Volvo two blocks ahead, turning toward the east-bound freeway entrance.

*   *

As she entered the freeway, Rebecca's right hand turned off Joseph's prepaid phone. Rebecca no longer wanted to hear the other voices trying to call her – Joseph's voice hoping she would answer him, or Lewis, frantically trying to establish where she might go. Her own fears harassed her as much as the voices of scared friends. The only sound in her car besides the drone of studded tires was the slap and squish of her limping windshield wipers. She did not feel better.

She glanced at the manuscripts beside her. She'd used dirt from the potted plants on Lewis' porch to yellow the edges of the parts and the front and back pages. The trick might give her a little more time to get away before the kidnappers realized how new these papers were. On top, she'd put Lewis' copy of the cello part. His masculine hand was more like Bach's and would be more immediately convincing than hers.

She peered through the windshield looking for the Wood Village turnoff to Mount Hood. As she reached the first stoplight in the village, she looked in the mirror. There were two log trucks behind her. Coming off the exit ramp, was a rust and tan Volkswagen van.

Lewis?

She stared at it until it disappeared behind the log trucks. The truck behind her blasted a horn designed to shred nerves. The light had turned green.

Rebecca drove through the village and onto the mountain highway, glancing frequently to catch sight of the van. If it were Lewis, she was afraid of what he might do – more afraid of what the kidnappers would do to Benji. With relief, she watched the van turned off at Heidi's German Restaurant. After all, she told herself, there were many such vans. Besides, last night when she'd tiptoed into his room to watch his restless sleep, he'd been far from able to drive a car.

*   *

Lewis waited until she'd driven a few hundred yards before he left the restaurant parking lot. Her driving had been erratic since they'd been close to each other in Wood Village, and he was sure she was trying to see if it was his van. He was afraid that if she saw him she would do something dangerous. For now, he would just keep her in his sights. From this point forward, there were few exits that he couldn't see at a distance. He knew all the roads to the back areas of the mountain. From his cabin near Cedar Meadow, he'd skied and hiked most of them.

The snow flurries were wet and sticky. Little prisms hit and stayed on his windshield – a series of unique hexagonal patterns. Benjamin would love to see this display. He would be one string of questions and expressive eyebrows.

Suddenly, Lewis cried out to the empty van, "Oh, Rebecca, be careful!"

Again, he took up the Marine hand-held radio Joseph had given each of them last night. It was set to call Joseph. "Selig, James here. She's still heading up Mt. Hood through Wemme Forest Corridor. No sign of the blue Impala. Do you hear me?"

Nothing.

Talking fed the fire in his throat – the flames reached into his ears and set off a new series of headaches. Still, he needed Joseph. He tried again.

Again, nothing. Through ZigZag and Rhododendron he listened to her dial tone on the phone and concentrated on driving. He willed her safely through every corner around the steep cliffs at Laurel Hill and breathed a sigh of relief when the highway signs at Multorpor Mountain indicated that chains were required ahead. Now she would have to turn off and he could catch her, make her take him into the plan.

*   *

Rebecca saw the sign warning of the need for tire chains, but she'd foreseen this possibility yesterday and had the studded tires put on at Abraham's favorite garage. She wouldn't be late to meet her son's captors, no matter how deep the snow. The going was slower though, because of the slush and the people milling around the side of the highway. Her windshield wipers threatened to stop several times, but she was able to roll down the window, reach out and nudge the nearest one back into action. The snow in Hungary had never been as full of water as this. This snow weight was many times greater.

Just past the village of Government Camp, she saw the turnoff for Timberline Lodge. She signaled and took the left turn as quickly as she could. From sightseeing trips with Abe and Miriam, she remembered this section of road as very steep and wanted to get a good fast run at it. Within seconds of turning, she was in a world entirely of snow walls. The plows had built up the snow at the sides of the road. There were no other cars in front or behind her as far as she could see. The noise of the slushy highway was gone, and the enveloping silence of winter closed in on her. She could see out of a few inches of windshield and only as far as the next hairpin turn. She kept a steady foot on the gas pedal and prayed she wouldn't be slowed by other vehicles. The drifts building up on the road were heavy, sodden hurdles.

*   *

Lewis couldn't believe his eyes when she turned left and took a run up the steep incline toward the first sharp turn. In his tall van, he dared not drive like a race car fanatic, but to keep close to her he had to try. Why hadn't she stopped to put on chains? Was she out of her mind?

Who could blame her? Benjamin was her life, the mirror of her real self when she'd been free of fear. To have him become a captive in turn – that was the deepest terror she could know. There was no doubt in his mind that the kidnappers intended to kill them both once they got what they thought were the concertos.

There was no doubt in his mind, as well, about who was behind it all. He had begun to recognize the signs on the evening he saw Harald Steinmetz after Rebecca's recital with Gabriel, only then, he hadn't put it all together. On that wet evening, the man's straight hair had begun to curl. The hair close to his scalp had grown in wavy. He was the man who had tried to take Benjamin from the apartment play yard in New York.

In the hospital, when Harald poked his head in the door, Lewis suddenly knew. Harald's hair had been straightened again, but his haste to find Rebecca was the give-away. And then, to find that the call to Rebecca had been made by someone in the hospital – that clinched it.

The man responsible for all the attacks had to be someone with a great knowledge of music, someone who would have had the opportunity to know what Rebecca looked like in her former life, someone who could travel freely among the Russian satellite countries and yet leave with everyone's blessings and enough money to live as if he had a job somewhere while he tracked her down. And yesterday, when Abraham had followed the trail of Harald's colleagues' credentials and found that most had been falsified, Abe had felt used – betrayed.

God damn! Ice! Hold the wheel against the spin! Not so sharp – too fast! You'll flip her! That's it, pull out slowly. Control, control. Over she goes! Pull back, right. No! The snow wall behind you – watch your head!

The back end of the van plowed into the wall of icy snow and crumpled. When the motor died, he sat gripping the wheel, trying to stop shaking. The bitter air made him take a quick deep breath. The reality of winter invaded his heaterwarmed cocoon. He glanced at the odometer. Three and seven tenths miles from the lodge.

Should he hike across country, knee deep in snow and try to catch her near the lodge? Or should he follow the road? Other cars on the road might also not have chains and be as dangerous as his van. At least his van now was mostly out of the downhill lane.

He grabbed his winter gear and the radio, climbed out of the van and took his toolbox from under the driver's seat. The claw hammer was the closest thing he had to an ice pick. It would have to do. He put everything into a pack on his back, put metal crampons over his boots and climbed to the top of the van. Then, he tackled the sheer snow wall into which his van had plowed. He created footsteps with the claw hammer. Several precious minutes later, he stood on top of the snow wall and looked across the snow field, up the road.

The steeply pitched roof of Timberline Lodge and the highest portion of the parking lot were visible from up here. Following the view of the road's switchbacks, he saw her Volvo climbing steadily, but slowly, toward the lodge parking. The drone of a large motor brought his attention to the left across the snowy plain on which he stood. He was surprised to see that the ski lift was operating on a Monday. His hopes rose. He might still make it! He struck out, cross country to the bottom of the TBar lift. That lift ended just below the newer, smaller WyEast Lodge and barely downhill from the historic old Lodge at Timberline.

His boots were the ones he used whenever he hiked into his cabin – good support and watertight. But at each step, he sank to his knees in the heavy snow. Frustrated by the need to take many, small steps so that his feet wouldn't sink so far, he found himself sweating soon after he began. He removed his parka and tied it around his waist. Within minutes, his hat and scarf were in his pockets with his mittens. He kept glancing to his right where the road zigzagged up the steep incline. The Volvo had caught up to a station wagon and slowed to the few miles per hour that its driver was willing to hazard. Lewis tried to increase his pace but had to return to the steady small steps demanded by the snow.

It took him an endless five minutes to cross the field. By the time he reached the lift operators' cabin, his turtleneck shirt was soaked with sweat. The operator was a young boy who balked at letting Lewis use the bar without a ticket or skis. Lewis, deciding that a peek at adventure was in order for this kid. He flashed his Reed Faculty library card, complete with picture I.D. "Young man, there's a kidnapping going on near the lodge. Lewis James. Radio the upper shack that I'm coming so they can be ready to assist me. I'll commend you for your swift reaction to the danger."

"But Officer James, how are you going to. . .?"

"Thank you for your concern. I would like to borrow your skis."

"My skis?"

"Any skis you've got, just hurry. That little kid is in danger, and so is his mother."

"Yes, sir. There's an old pair with cable bindings." The boy reached into the shed just as Rebecca's Volvo turned into the upper parking lot.

"Good man!" Lewis grabbed the skis and slammed his feet in them, snapping down the front lever. The boot cable was tight, but it would have to do. Lewis plunged into line for the next Tbar that swung around the pulley housing. In the middle of the run, he realized he had no poles.

From the top of the offramp, Lewis caught a glimpse of Rebecca, bent into the snowy wind, hurrying past the massive stone and cedar lodge toward the trails. She wore boots and a wool coat. On her back she carried his own hiking backpack. Under her arm was a manila envelope probably wrapped in plastic – no doubt the copies of the concertos.

Half a football field behind her, he skied off the ramp and struck out on a path that would take him around the WyEast Lodge. It would intersect Rebecca near the scrub pines at the beginning of Highland Trail.

Stopping long enough to put on his sweater made Lewis increasingly aware of his all too recent concussion. As his head came through the neck hole, his sight grayed over, unfocused. He stood very still, blinking. After a moment, he could see again, but he couldn't find Rebecca. He pushed forward, angling across the open area below the road which divided the imposing Timberline Lodge from the small WyEast Lodge.

Passing the few skis parked outside WyEast, he took a pair of ski poles and slogged on. His constantly refocusing eyes made it hard for him to see the terrain. Finding Rebecca in the snow flurries uphill from him was impossible, but he kept to his original route. He'd been sure she didn't mean to enter Timberline Lodge, but instead to head off into the twisted trees on the trail around the mountain.

He'd almost come to the top of the open area below the road when he saw her again, two hundred yards ahead of him. She turned, furtively, looking behind her. He ducked down, nearly losing his balance, dizzy at the sudden movement. He watched her enter the trees along the trail and then, in spite of his head, he burst into action, moving straight forward, deciding not to follow her directly, but to stay downhill from her in the woods. The skiing would be harder, yet it might give him a sight of the kidnappers before they met her and before they saw him.

She pulled her mittens and hat from her pockets and stopped long enough to put them on before moving forward again. At the sign to the Highland Trail, she squared her shoulders and turned downhill.

Lewis knew this trail from ski trips with longtime Oregon residents. It had once followed the abandoned right of way for the original Timberline Skid Road, Cedar logs had been hauled from a meadow near his cabin up this three-mile trail, and used to build the lodge. In the 1960s, a land slide had turned about fifty yards of it into a long cliff. The newer Highland Trail skirted that cliff and followed the terrain down to the back of the little village of Government Camp.

Lewis skied below her trail, following her – moving when she moved, stopping when she stopped. Suddenly, his senses told him to stop even before his mind registered the two dark forms near the trail. The smaller form stepped out onto the trail in front of Rebecca, the larger closed in behind her. Lewis froze.

*   *

Rebecca felt her throat constrict. This was the man in the subway. He noticed her recognition and smiled. "I oughta kick you in a kidneys, just fer old times, nein?" The harsh Bronx followed with the German was just as incongruous and sinister as she remembered it from the phone.

"Where is my son?"

"You'll see him." He glanced at his taller companion. "Anybody following her?"

"No cars – except for a station wagon with a family. That tall guy's nowhere. There was a phone in her car, but it was off."

The smaller man grinned. "You're on your own, Betty Boop. This the music?" He took the envelope opened it and pulled out the manuscript. "Cello? Where's the violin concerto?"

Rebecca reached for the papers, "That's one of the orchestral parts. The last section here is the violin part – the solo part of the concerto." She slipped the violin part on top and the cello part underneath, hoping that he didn't notice the new feel of the pages in between.

He took it back, stared at the violin part trying to read something on it. "Where does it say it's by Bach?" He looked accusingly at her.

"Bach didn't sign it because he dictated it to his wife. This is her handwriting."

"Why did she use French and German in the title?"

She stared at him, thinking how incredible it was that such a man would even want these concertos. "Musicians just did in those days – they used whichever language seemed best for the thought they had in mind at the time."

His suspicious eyes narrowed, but he slipped the manuscript back into the envelope. "Give her the skis, Ernst."

The taller man stepped off the trail and came back with a pair of boots and skis. "Put these on, we have a ways to go, yet."

"Is my son well?"

"Put these on."

She sat down and changed boots.

There has to be someone else, she thought, someone who really knows music. This Schlemiel wouldn't know a concerto from a symphony.

When she was in the skis, Ernst asked. "What's in the pack?"

"Warm clothes for my son."

"Leave it here. He has plenty and I don't want you slowing us down."

Rebecca hesitated. The little man backhanded her across the face. "Leave it!"

Her cheek stung, and her eye closed over the scratch his glove had caused. Blindly she shrugged off Lewis' pack and dropped it. The small man started down the trail. The bigger man gave her a shove. She grabbed the ski poles and followed the shadow of the big skier.

They will kill us both. I was a fool not to tell Levy. But what could he or the police have done? These men have watched my trail and would have killed us all anyway.

*   *

At the head of the trail, Lewis waited. The rock of anger in his stomach took his mind off the cold dampness of his clothes and the tightening pain in his head, turning him to cool efficiency. There was a remote chance that Joseph was within transmission range. When the men were down the trail a bit, He pulled out his radio and tried to raise Joseph.

No answer. They were on their own. As her captors moved out of sight, Lewis retrieved his pack from the trail, took the child's clothes and winter gear out, stuffed them into his parka pockets and followed Rebecca. He left the radio on and near the trail in case anyone came this way.

And he turned off all but the GPS on his cell phone in his pocket. A chance of being tracked.

CHAPTER THIRTY-EIGHT

Through thick flakes, Rebecca could barely see the back of the weasely, dark kidnapper. She skied clumsily because the eye he'd scratched wouldn't stay open. The big man pulled her up roughly each time she stumbled, and each time he taunted her with his knowing smile.

Little by little, she felt her eye healing from the scratch. At the same time, she realized that seeming to be clumsy might have some advantages, though she didn't see a way to use it yet. As her sight returned, she continued to ski like a novice.

The trail followed the contours of a low hill. Just beyond a sweeping curve, a cloaked figure stepped out on the path, holding a child by the shoulders in front of him. Benjamin broke loose and ran toward his mother. She stopped in a sharp christie and took him in her arms. His little body was very cold. His only coat was the light jacket he'd taken to Lewis' office last Saturday. Rebecca pulled him into her long wool coat and put her hat and mittens on him. She pulled the coat around them as much as possible – trying to give him warmth.

The man who'd been holding her son stood under the protection of the fir branches. When she glanced at him, he drew back his hood and stared at her malevolently.

"Harald Steinmetz! Why?"

He arched one eyebrow and drew off his leather glove. "There are certain investors in Bach's own country who want the concertos back – you know, to celebrate reunification properly." Steinmetz chuckled at his own joke. "They are willing to pay me handsomely to find them."

"I'm not asking about the music," Rebecca said contemptuously. "Why would you frighten a little boy? Why let him freeze out here?"

Steinmetz's lips smiled at her. "But my dear, it is the music. Nothing but the boy would have made you give it to me. And now that you're here, it won't matter much longer how cold he is."

He stepped toward her, reached down and lifted her chin so that he could watch her face. His thumb strayed to the wound near her eye, stroking it as he spoke. "When I first met you, you were so – well, shall we say, so promising, that I hoped to get the music simply by making you mine as well. I would have made you my partner, in the business and in my bed."

She shrank from him, covering Benjamin's ears with her hands.

His hollow laugh mocked her. "It doesn't matter if he hears. You're safe from that kind of attention. Gabriel Kolya was kind enough to inform me that you would probably always be cold to the touch."

The pain of betrayal cut deep, severing her finally from any worry she had for Gabriel. Rebecca's arms tensed around Benjamin. Only he mattered. She had to find a way to save her son, to get him back to safety, to Levy.

When Harald stepped away to pull a cigarette package from his pocket, she watched him and whispered to Benji inside her coat. "Benji, Levy is alive, in the hospital. You must get to him. Do you know where the lodge is?"

"Yes," he whispered, "up the hill and . . ."

Harald Steinmetz's voice went suddenly smooth. It stopped Benji's whispers. Steinmetz held out the blue and white cigarette package to gesture at her and spoke in Hungarian. "Darya, don't you remember me?"

She couldn't move. Still hunched over Benjamin, she heard the voice and knew, the nasty insinuation, the expectation of compliance.

"You were a bore," Steinmetz said. "So lacking in sexual . . ." He lit his cigarette.

"You," she interrupted. "A reptile in fine wool . . ."

"A reptile, and possibly a father, eh?" He gestured with his cigarette at Benjamin.

"Not so," she snarled. "A much finer man than you."

"Not mine, I agree. He's a crying baby and of little use."

He laughed and turned away. "Ernst, let me have a look at our treasure."

Rebecca shielded Benjamin from him. She watched Steinmetz take the manila envelope from the big blond. He pulled the first page of the concerto out for just a second. A few snowflakes fell on it. He hastily pushed it back inside and took a plastic bag from his overcoat pocket. While he wrapped the bag around the envelope, he commented on it to her. "Anna Magdalena, nein?"

"So."

"Why did you never play it? Once I recognized who you really were, I went to every concert, certain that this would be the time you would choose to reveal the concerto."

Rebecca saw a way to buffer Abraham from Steinmetz's anger after he killed her. "I was never absolutely sure what it was," she replied slowly, "There are many unexplained peculiarities in the manuscripts and I didn't want to claim them as Bach's, only to find that I was wrong."

Rebecca hoped her explanation would throw Steinmetz off the trail of the real manuscripts. If she had to die here, she wanted no one to suspect that Abraham had anything more real than the obvious forgeries Steinmetz now held.

"You should have played them. You would have lived longer, darling Rebecca." He tucked the envelope under his arm and stepped back from her. "Now my dear, you must take off those skis. You will have no more use for them."

"May I first have a few moments with Benjamin?"

"For all the good it will do you, go ahead." He turned away, crumpling his cigarette package and tossing it. He gestured at Ernst and the smaller man to give her a little privacy with her son.

She took off her coat and unbuttoned her wool sweater. This she put on Benjamin, saying out loud. "I want you to be warm, my little one." Then her whispers to him were low and calm as she buttoned the sweater and rolled up the sleeves to make him a coat. "I'm going to hit him with the ski. When I do, you run for the woods. Go uphill until there are very few trees. That's the timber line. Turn right and run until you come to the lodge. Get help from the lodge. Do you understand?"

"Yes, but Mama . . ."

"I'll knock out all of them. You keep running no matter what you hear. When I'm done, I will meet you at the lodge. But you have to go, or they'll try to grab you. If they have you, that would keep me from hitting them, yes?"

Benjamin looked at her with fear. He knew his mother couldn't hit all these men before one of them hit her. "Mama," he whispered urgently, "the big one, Ernst, has a gun. Hit him first. I will hit the little one."

"No. You have to be gone. Please, Benji . . ."

Ernst's voice interrupted them, complaining to Steinmetz. "Can't Willie take these two to the cliff now? What difference does it make if they have time to talk?"

The smaller man, Willie, started toward her.

Steinmetz grew angry at having his authority questioned. His hand shot out, grabbing Willie. "Stand still." He turned to Rebecca. "Take off your skis and say goodbye to your son."

She hugged Benjamin quickly and whispered as she released him, "Please run when I hit him. Please run."

"I will, Mama."

Rebecca put Benjamin between her and the forest. "Get back Benjamin," she whispered.

He stepped toward the forest a few feet and turned to face her. Then he took slow steps backward while the men watched his mother fold her coat and lay it on the snow. She set the poles far to her left away from Benjamin before she bent to release her skis. Stepping back and to the left, she lifted the first ski and plunged it upright into the snow. Backing still farther, she grasped the other ski near its heel, lifting it slowly.

*   *

As her ski tip drew an arch in the air, Lewis threw a rock at the snow-loaded Douglas Fir branch directly over Steinmetz. The side of the ski slammed into Ernst's head. At the same time the branch dropped several pounds of snow on Steinmetz. Lewis leapt out of the woods behind the stunned Steinmetz, yelling, "Get to the woods and get down, Benji!" Lewis hit Steinmetz in the jaw, sending him sprawling into the upright ski.

Lewis turned to see Willie fumbling for something in his coat pocket. Grabbing one of the ski poles, Lewis lunged and knocked the gun from Willie's hand. Willie's eyes locked Lewis's as they circled each other. Willie forgot everything except his anger, but Lewis knew exactly where Rebecca was. He circled to his left, menacing Willie with the makeshift ski-pole saber.

Willie smiled, circling to Lewis' right, closer to the other ski pole. When Rebecca's ski came down on the man's head, his look of utter amazement ended only when he collapsed.

"Behind you, Daddy!" Benjamin's shout made Lewis duck and turn in time to catch Steinmetz's bullet in his arm instead of his back. Steinmetz clambered up, waving Ernst's gun at them both.

His command hissed at Rebecca, "Sit on the ground next to him."

Slowly, she did as she was told, staring in horror at the blood next to Lewis in the snow. The pool darkened as she watched. Steinmetz moved carefully toward her skis, one hand holding the gun on them, the other fumbling with the binding, putting the skis on his feet. When he stood, he reached for the pole still stuck in the snow.

Then he pointed the gun, sighting down the barrel at Lewis' head. His smile was cold.

"The dogs are coming!" It was Rebecca speaking, surely, quietly. "Listen, Harald. Dogs! Ernst never turned off my GPS."

Steinmetz glanced up the path. Dogs bayed. Lewis saw him waver.

"Your gun will be heard."

"I can kill you anyway and be gone."

"My radio messages identified you," Lewis said. "You won't get past airport security."

Steinmetz wavered, hate in his eyes. The hounds were still far away. He pointed the gun at Lewis' head and began to squeeze the trigger. At that moment, the baying of a hound only yards away brought his attention again toward the woods. His shot whanged into the Douglas fir behind Lewis. The hound bayed louder.

Eyes wide, Steinmetz grabbed up the envelope, turned and fled downhill on the skis. Within thirty seconds he was out of sight in the snow and the wind.

*   *

Lewis lay back on the snow. The flakes that landed softly on his face were clean and fresh. The tightness at his head loosened and the sharp stab in his right arm seemed to withdraw. Peace descended on him suddenly and without warning. He began to let go, to slip into unconsciousness. Sharply, the memory of Benjamin's voice cut through the peace and made him blink.

"Where is Benji?" he mumbled. Then louder, "Becca, help me get to him. I have his clothes in my jacket pockets."

Rebecca helped Lewis to his feet. Together they stumbled across the wide opening to the trees. Behind the first Spruce, they found the little boy, burrowing into the melt-cave near the trunk. He was whimpering, "Mama, Daddy. Mama, Daddy."

Lewis collapsed next to him, trying to raise him up. "We're all right, Benji. We're here. Look at me, little buddy. . . Benji!"

The boy whimpered, "I cried like . . . like the dogs . . . coming." His shivering grew uncontrollable. Lewis sagged over him. Rebecca pushed Lewis against the tree and pulled Benji onto his lap.

"The dogs come . . . Burford comes," the child murmured deliriously, "Ah-ooh, ah-ooh." Benji's weakening voice was the voice of the hound which had sent Steinmetz flying.

Rebecca and Lewis stared at each other, open-mouthed. Then Lewis numbly tried to pull clothes from his jacket pocket.

Rebecca reached into Lewis' pockets. She pulled the winter clothes on Benji over what he already wore, a second hat, mittens, jacket. Lewis' eyes closed, his head lolling against the tree trunk. Rebecca touched his arm to awaken him. Her hand came away covered with blood.

Steinmetz's bullet. How can I stop the blood? Lewis' scarf – and this branch. Where? Up here? God let this be right.

She tied what she could remember as a tourniquet above the wound, tightening it until the bleeding stopped. It was difficult to tell how long it would be effective because of the jacket. Yet she was afraid to expose Lewis to the cold. She had to get help, but what if Ernst and Willie should regain consciousness?

"The gun," she said hoarsely, "Willie's gun." Rebecca ran to the path, picked up her coat and put it on while frantically searching for the gun.

She hadn't realized how cold she was until she put the coat on. With it off, she'd had the mobility she needed to fight. Now the fight was all gone from her and she desperately wanted to be able to quit, but they were a long way from done with this thing.

Lewis had lost a lot of blood and Benjamin needed more heat than two hats and two pairs of mittens could give him.

She found the gun near Willie's inert body. In his pockets, she found more bullets and a switchblade knife. She hurried back to Lewis whose eyes were barely open. His good arm held Benji in his lap. She covered both of them with her coat and put the gun in his hand.

He nodded and whispered. "I've got it. Can you find the lodge?"

"Yes. I'll be back soon."

"Get ski patrol. Get police."

"Fight, Lewis. Stay awake."

"Fight. . ." he chuckled, a little giddy with pain, "You kidding about dogs . . .?"

"Couldn't you hear them? Even before Benjamin bayed. I don't know why. I'll be back soon." She hurried uphill to Willie's body again, took his skis and began the ascent of the trail.

Within minutes, the sound of real dogs drew closer. Rebecca began to be afraid. These dogs were hunting. What if they smelled Lewis's blood?

She stood in the middle of the open space, ski poles raised to defend those behind her.

Around the curve came three hounds, noses to the ground, leading several county sheriff's men. The man in front of the police seemed as imposing as a bear. Rebecca lowered her poles, leaned heavily on them and sank to her knees. The dogs milled around her, howling and barking.

Uncle Tobias caught her in his arms. "Becca, where are they?"

Her arm gestured downhill. Her voice caught in a long sob.

"Steinmetz?" he asked.

"Gone down Highland Trail."

Tobias shouted. "On down the path, Joseph. Follow her ski tracks." Tobias turned to the other men. "Get her in that sled. She's exhausted. And Sheriff, get Officer Williams on the phone. City police need to get to the Heathman Hotel before Steinmetz clears it out."

CHAPTER THIRTY-NINE

Tuesday morning, Lewis awoke in the same hospital with the same sun, the same chrome bed frame and a new pain. Surprise turned out to be only part of his disorientation – he'd been strapped in the bed.

He remembered holding Benjamin so tightly that the men who came to steal him decided to take them both in the same sled. He remembered protecting Benjamin from the dogs, but the sight of Rebecca tied tightly in another of their sleds – that had made him go berserk – before they'd stabbed him with that needle. At least he'd fooled them with his strength – kept a good grip on Benjamin's hand. But Becca . . .

"Levy?"

He turned his head a little and refocused his wandering vision. Rebecca held his hand, her redbrown hair atumble about her pale face. A deep bruise on her cheek marred her white skin. An angry cut reddened her eyelid – Willie's mark. He tried to raise his hand to caress her cheek. His damned hand would not move.

She saw what he tried to do. "They had to sedate you and strap you in bed. You were fighting mad most of the night."

"Where's Benji?"

"Sleeping in the next bed. We couldn't separate the two of you unless you could see him." She grinned. A dimple he had never seen before appeared in the bruised area, and he tried again to touch her.

"Damn! Untie me. I want to hold you."

Her long eyelashes brushed her cheek as the peach color of embarrassment spread over her. She glanced at the door and began furtively to loosen the straps. After a few moments' frustration, she went to the door. "Abraham, could you help me in here?"

Abe's grin mixed tease and admiration. "Crazy man last night. We had to do this." He began with the feet straps. He looked up at Lewis every once in a while, as he loosed various levers and the straps fell away.

"You had the nurses convinced for a while there. We were all evil men who stole your wife and child. But you fought to keep us away from the child. You would see us all dead before any of us laid a finger on him."

Rebecca had colored thoroughly peach now, her gaze on the floor, her hands twisting the bed draperies. Lewis lifted his arms, dropped the one with the new pain and reached for her with the other. Abraham dropped back toward the door.

"Rebecca, hold my hand please."

She took a tentative step toward him, her hand reached for his. Abe grinned and left the room. Lewis drew her down onto the bed next to him. "You are a great one, Becca. You were going to just keep thwacking those guys until one of them killed you, giving Benjamin a chance to escape."

"I am so glad you followed us, Levy. But you made yourself very sick."

He put her fingers to his lips. "Sick is very temporary. I couldn't lose you or Benjamin." After a moment, Lewis chuckled, "I wish you could have seen Willie's face when you beaned him. He couldn't believe it had happened."

Rebecca smiled and then frowned. "I guess I hit Ernst too hard. He is still in a coma. Willie is in jail, and they haven't found Steinmetz yet."

"Ernst intended to kill you. He had his hand on the gun in his pocket the whole time. How did you know to hit him first?"

"Benjamin whispered to me about the gun. Benjamin planned to take out the little one, Willie, if I hit Ernst. I begged Benji to run for help instead."

"Oh, God! That would have been …" Lewis closed his eyes at the thought of how it all could have turned out.

She put her hand on his chest to make him relax. "It could have been bad, but it turned out better than I ever … Now you need to stop worrying. By the way, how did you know to go for Steinmetz first?"

"Steinmetz made the mistake of standing under a branch full of Oregon's heavy wet snow. Actually, you helped me make the choice. You telegraphed your own move by the way you got off the skis. It's just that none of them knew you well enough to think you would ever do such a thing."

Lewis became aware of her hand on his chest. It had come there because she didn't want him to worry. The touching had been the natural expression of her concern for him. That light weight rested there now because it comforted both of them. He put his hand over hers and decided to work back toward the topic that had embarrassed her.

"I guess my secret is out after last night."

"What secret?"

"That I think of you as my wife, just as Benjamin thinks of me as Daddy." He saw the beautiful color rising and hastened on, holding the hand to him. "Will you marry me, Rebecca?"

She tried to pull away, but he kept a firm grip. "Levy, I can't. You know it yourself. I can't be anyone's wife, not really."

Lewis stopped a moment, and then decided to be open with her. "I heard what Steinmetz asked you at the end. He meant for you to know who he was – the man in the fine wool, the kidnapper in the castle in Northern Hungary."

"Yes."

"He wants to control you still. Just by telling you who he is, he controls your fears."

"I . . . you have to know by now that I . . ."

"I don't know any such thing. When I first met you, you were virtually untouchable. Look how far we've come in such a little time. Back then, it was hard for you to sit in the same small space with me. Now, when I hold you, I can feel your wanting. Your body knows you will overcome it. Only your mind doesn't know it fully yet."

"But my dream. I will hurt you. "

"Yes, that will happen sometimes for a while. It is painful to go through, but it won't go on forever – not if you challenge it with the same kind of courage I saw on the mountain. You want it. I want it. And I'm patient and persistent. It will become all right."

"I can't marry you in the hope that it will be all right. That would be like promising something I can't . . ."

"You've got me in a sort of "Catch 22" here."

"A what?"

"You won't marry me unless you're sure you can have a physical relationship with me, but you're the kind of woman who wouldn't have that relationship outside of marriage. How are we going to solve that paradox?"

She put her head down on his chest. "Levy, please!"

He lifted his useless arm as far as he could, mussing her curly mane and trying to soothe her. "Be brave, my little lion. Concentrate on what you want, let your wanting be greater than your fears. What I want is not to lose you. I want you with me in my house, playing piano duets, doing laundry together, weeding the garden together, raising Benjamin. And I know that making love will come naturally when we are doing those other things, too – maybe not right away, but someday."

CHAPTER FORTY

On the opening night of the concerts, Officer June Williams talked to Lewis before the auditorium opened.

"That guy – his real name in Hungary is Steiermark, not Steinmetz – well known to the Hungarian, Russian and Ukrainian police. Anyway, that bastard is still out there somewhere, and he'll have revenge on his mind," she said.

Lewis nodded. "Sarge said he had the whole auditorium covered with plainclothes officers."

"Yes, and at the doors as people come in. They've got his photo and every one of them has studied the situation."

"I'd like to be able to picnic with Benjamin at the fountain, from six o'clock to seven-fifteen. Then we'll come in close to concert time." Lewis said. "Will that work?"

"Out there, that's my beat," she said. "Your friend, Rabbi Stamps and the immigration fellow are going to be nearby and watching."

"Rebecca and I want Benji safe, but we also want him to start recovering, be able to feel free while safe. Is there a better place than the fountain? Where should we be while Rebecca rehearses this evening?"

June thought a minute. "Frankly, I think down close to the fountain is best. You've got police coverage, and not just from me. Also, the grass near the fountain is lower, and there's a berm between you and the sidewalks near the auditorium. From the street it will be hard for him to see you. Easier for you to see him."

"Okay. When we're ready to go backstage …"

"Wave at me. We'll escort you to the stage door. Rabbi Stamps and Mr. …"

"Joseph Selig," Lewis supplied.

"Yes, they'll come to the stage door with me and the other officers at that time."

*   *

Close to seven in the evening, Benjamin sat with Lewis across the street from the Civic Auditorium, on the lawn near the tall cliffs and water fall of the Ira Keller Fountain. The water sheeted down over steep cliffs. They reminded him of the cliffs near Timberline. It seemed as if a part of the trail on the mountain had erupted in the center of Portland. But here, he was warm and with his beloved Lewis.

He glanced at Lewis. His friend kept watching the people around them. Benjamin knew he watched for that Steiermark, because Steiermark had escaped. Benjamin had overheard talk that police would be everywhere. The police searched for that Steiermark and thought he would be really angry, maybe try something bad.

Benjamin also kept watch. He knew Steiermark better than all of them.

That man had called him 'son', once, but Benjamin had stomped on his foot and yelled "Not your son. You stink."

The greasy hair man had started to laugh, until Steiermark glared at him.

And then Steiermark had smacked Benji and said to him, "You are the son of a whore."

Benji had stood up again. He knew 'whore' sounded bad. And he didn't believe it. He'd shouted, "I am the son of Rebecca Gregory and you shut up."

He remembered that night's hunger and pain. He watched for Steiermark with Lewis. Neither of them ate much of the picnic they had chosen from New Season's deli.

Benji noticed all the people coming to the concert. "Lewis, all those ladies are very dressed up."

"Yes, they are. This is a special night – a suit and dress concert for opening night."

Benji nodded. He had never been to one of his mother's late-night concerts. They usually began at his bedtime. He felt very grown up to be dressed in a suit, sharing a spring picnic on the lawn near the mountain-like waterfall.

Lewis looked handsome in his dark suit, even if his arm still hung in a sling. Benjamin secretly glanced with pride at that sling. Lewis had told him that if he hadn't yelled at just the right time, the bullet would have gone someplace worse. Lewis said that was a good fight the three of them had on the mountain. Everyone had done everything just right, and now they were all safe.

And tonight, Benjamin had been chosen to take a bouquet of Healall and Heart'sEase from Lewis' green house garden to his mother, right after she played her songs. He felt very proud.

But he knew they were not all safe. Not as long as that Steiermark was out there somewhere.

"Worried?" Lewis asked.

"No. Mama knows that music. She will be all right."

"Yes, she does," Lewis answered while checking out the crowd again.

So, Benji looked around again, too.

Lewis asked Benji. "Hey Little Buddy, where does all this water for the falls come from?"

Benji looked closely. "Is there a river on the top? I thought our river went north."

"You're right. The Willamette goes north, and there isn't a river up there running east over this cliff, so where else might it all come from?"

He watched the falls for a time and couldn't figure it out, except for some reason all that water didn't make the lake at the bottom get any fuller. He stood up to see if the water ran underground anywhere near their picnic.

But he became distracted by how the crowd outside his mama's auditorium changed.

The crowd grew, and the doors weren't open yet. In that bunch, it got hard to see people clearly. What I if the man came and he dressed in one of those suits, like all the orchestra guys, and the conductor and lots of the men lining up with their dressy ladies waiting to get into the concert?

Nearby, in the waterfalls park, he saw the rabbi and the Selig man. He saw Officer June and another policeman. He knew there were police who didn't wear uniforms. They tried to look like other people. So, Benji studied to decide who stood like police.

The times when Mama and Lewis went to the station to talk to Sarge and June, Benji had seen other police. A lot of them stood with their feet apart and their hands near their belt.

Ready for action, that's what June said, when he asked.

Covering up extra weight, Sarge said, and then he'd laughed so hard his own belly went up and down.

Benji saw two guys standing like policemen, so maybe they were Plainclothes. That's what June called them.

Benji felt real safe now, but he knew Lewis was watching all the time he talked to Benji, so he tried to eat and watch, to help.

He bent down and picked up another piece of Anna Banana's yummy bread. Next to him, Lewis jerked.

Benji stood up again. In the tuxedo crowd, he saw that man coming straight at them, pointing at them with his coat pocket.

Benji's breath stopped, but he raised a finger to show Lewis.

Before he could point at Steiermark, Lewis grabbed Benji up in his arms and ran across the wide flat stones toward the concrete cliffs at the back of the fountain. They ducked behind the sheet of water that cascaded from the top of the cliffs. Thick spray soaked Benjamin's suit almost immediately.

Lewis held him across the stomach with his one good arm and moved so fast that Benjamin's breath came in wheezes. They stopped in a cave behind the waterfall. At the back of the cave, Lewis tried a door, but couldn't open it. Behind the door, loud pumping sounds created a rhythm like the fall of water at the front of the cave.

Lewis set Benjamin down between him and the wall and took out his cell phone as it rang.

"June! Yes. He has a gun. I have Benjamin behind the waterfall. We're trapped back here. The door to the fountain motor-works is locked."

Lewis listened a moment, then said, "Hurry. I think he will have trouble seeing at first when he comes through the falls. Yes . . . Hurry. This kid's had enough scare."

Lewis knelt down next to Benjamin. "Sorry about your suit, little buddy."

"You saw him too? With a gun?"

"Steiermark."

The name jabbed Benjamin in the stomach. He grabbed at Lewis's jacket sleeve. "Will he come back here?"

"He might. But I am ready for him. Joseph is near. And so are Sergeant Hardy and Officer Williams."

All the time they talked, Benjamin saw Lewis watching the water sheet down over the concrete into the pool. Lewis took Benjamin's suit jacket off of him and began taking off his good shoes. "Benji, if he comes back here, I'm going to toss you into that pool. You're a good swimmer now. This water is coming down hard and it is cold, but you swim across the pool out of the falls and to the shore. Then run like the fox up into the trees on the other side of the lawn. Hide back there until Joseph says it is safe."

"But your arm . . ."

"If you're gone, I'll have the advantage. I've cleared my eyes from the water. He has not. You must swim away."

They both saw the shadow on the other side of the falls, a familiar height. As Steiermark stepped through the falls, Lewis pushed Benjamin into the pool. He came up sputtering, surprised by the coldness, but he remembered all that Lewis had said. In spite of the heavy water sheeting down on his head, he swam. In ten strokes he was across the pool. He pulled himself onto the concrete steps and saw Office Williams duck behind the falls. Two shots rang out. Joseph Selig pulled Benjamin into his arms.

Moments dragged by. Picnickers and passersby froze in place, staring at the constant motion of the water. Benjamin shook in Joseph's arms. "Is he dead? Is he dead?"

Joseph carried him up into the trees and hugged him tight. "Wait, Benji. We . . ."

And then, he said nothing and all Benji could hear was Joseph's heart pounding, and the water pounding, and his own rattling fear.

A tall figure stepped through the falls. Lewis James raked his fingers through his sandy hair. "Joseph, we need an ambulance. Officer Williams is shot in the leg. Steiermark is dead."

And then he turned back into the falls to take care of June.

*   *

A last-minute insert in the concert program explained the probable history of the Bach manuscripts. Briefly, it detailed the dangerous situation ownership had caused in the lives of all who had cared for them. The insert explained how the manuscripts would be taken care of after the concert – ownership by the Smithsonian Institute, with money from an endowment by Reed College working with several universities in the United States, in the East, and in Europe, including the Zeneakadémia, to make certain the manuscripts would be shared with scholars and seen in exhibit in many countries.

The evening's concert and the Bach Endowment was dedicated to Count Feodor Czigler, musician Anton Batislav, the artist, Casimir Annensky, and composer, Raphael Atemvoll for their part in keeping the manuscripts safe at the possible cost of their lives. The announcement was signed by Abraham and Miriam Friedenberg, as if they had discovered the music. No mention was made of Rebecca's ownership, because they still wanted to throw Steiermark and his revenge off of her trail.

The audience chatter died as more and more members read the insert. When Maestro Tovey and Rebecca Gregory strode onstage, the audience members stood as if at attention, and then silently took their seats.

Rebecca swished the pleats of her blue gown out of the way, raised her violin and began the known Allegro. She played as if dancing with joy.

The second movement, a lovely singing adagio held everyone in thrall, especially because of its soulful pianissimo. By the end of the first concerto, the audience could hardly contain its enthusiasm.

Rebecca and B.K. Price, the symphony's well-loved oboist, played the newly discovered double concerto together, and the crowd broke into cheers.

Rebecca played the third of the Bach concerti. As the last chord rang out, the hall erupted into stomping and clapping. Orchestra members stood, clapping and shouting. The words "Brava! And 'Encore!" rang from all sides. Rebecca pulled Price, the oboist, conductor Tovey, and Abraham and Miriam Friedenberg to the stage.

When the clapping and cheering didn't subside, Rebecca lifted her violin to her shoulder. Abraham and the others stood nearby. The audience quieted. She said, "I want to play for you a song of hope by Raphael Atemvoll."

Lewis stood backstage, his hand on Benjamin's shoulder. Benji had been newly re-clothed in something donated by a local merchant and rustled up by Uncle Tobias after Benji's swim. Benji had stayed awake, jazzed on adrenaline and crowd watching, but now, Lewis felt him start to sink toward sleep.

Rebecca played Raphael's song with such depth of feeling that Lewis saw one of the trombone players take a handkerchief swipe at his eyes. In the music, Lewis heard her longing, her grief, and her own hope.

In that moment, he knew she needed his help with that grief.

As she held the last note, Lewis sent Benjamin out with his bouquet of flowers. Benji stood nearby as she bowed and then she saw him.

The audience seemed to hold its breath. Tovey took her violin. She swung Benji up in her arms and the audience roared.

Afterward, in the stairwells and open spaces, backstage and at the stage door, praise for the newly found concerti filled the hall. The Oregon Symphony violinists compared them favorably with the brilliant and singing A major concerto of Mozart. The less musically inclined asked questions about the conspiracy to steal the concerti from Abraham and Miriam Friedenberg, about last weekend's kidnapping of Rebecca's son, and about tonight's sinister events by the waterfall fountain. All of this, Lewis didn't wanted Rebecca to be aware of yet.

So, Lewis took Rebecca by the arm, steering her and her burden of sleeping boy through the crowd of reporters. "Ladies and gentlemen,

Miss Gregory appreciates your interest, but she and her son also need to get some rest. If you have more questions, please ask the people who helped protect the concerti, Reed College professors, Abraham and Miriam Friedenberg. I'm sure they can help you fill in the details."

Abe and Miriam stepped into the fray like veterans. Their gentle presence and the ease with which they handled questions allowed Rebecca to retreat. Uncle Tobias lifted her proud, tired lion cub and his wilted flowers from Rebecca's arms, saying he would put Benjamin to bed at Abe's while she drove to Abe's with Lewis.

Minutes later, Rebecca settled back into the velvet upholstery of Lewis' sports car. She closed her eyes and seemed almost to sleep, a small smile on her quiet features. Lewis took full advantage of the opportunity to gaze at her for a moment. The soft delicacy of her beauty was an amazing contrast to the steely strength he now knew lay within her. Someday . . . someday she would find the strength to trust as well, to let go of her hard-won independence and allow love to protect her.

He started to reach for the ignition. The pain in his right arm shot through, reminding him of all he hadn't told her. He glanced at her. She watched him. "Better let me drive," she whispered. "You can't use that arm, can you?"

"No, I . . ."

"I know. You hurt it again at the fountain. Tobias told me. From all the commotion backstage, I knew something had happened. We delayed the concert until I knew how you were."

"You mean you knew about the shooting at the fountain? You went on stage and played like that even though you knew?"

"I played like that because I knew. When Benji, you and June Williams were safe I went into my dressing room and played such a fast Wieniawski that there was no room to breathe between phrases. After that, I was ready to play with control, so I went on stage. Don't treat me like a child, I'll play like one."

Lewis' relief was as instantaneous as his laughter. He leaned his head on the steering wheel, his weariness suddenly overwhelming him.

"Scoot over, Superman." Rebecca's voice brimmed with good humored teasing. "I'm coming around."

All his adrenaline drained away in the happy knowledge that she would take care of him.

CHAPTER FORTY-ONE

THREE WEEKS LATER

The white birch of her skis had been sanded and varnished to perfection – a beautiful gift from Abraham and Miriam. Rebecca looked up from the skis to the expanse of new snow beginning to melt in the afternoon sun. She listened to the joyous laughter of her son. He skied with Lewis, out of sight on the upper part of the trail.

She inhaled the pungent odor of the dark fir trees and the sweetness of budded vine maples surrounding the hill on which she stood. Her glance followed the trees from this hill to row upon row of hills into the distance. Light, distance, and intervening mist diluted the intensity of color in succeeding hills. A small bird flitted across her line of sight, swooping close to the ground after an unseen insect. Rebecca remembered such mountain snow birds in Hungary where she'd skied like this with her mother and father, racing Piotr, her brother.

The smell of fresh snow and pine pitch reminded her of her homeland. The longer she stood here looking at the birds and the trees, the more the yearning for lost things engulfed her. She had so much here. Having so much made her want to share with those she'd left behind. How Raphael Atemvoll would love Abraham and Miriam! Piotr, and her mother and father would value the love that Levy offered her.

And Zoltan . . . whom she knew as the source of strength in a time which had threatened to shatter her – what did she have to share with Zoltan?

She had freedom. Was he even alive? Her mind turned in on itself, the whiteness of the snow dimmed, her field of vision narrowed, darkness threatened.

At that moment, a joy of the present brought a brilliant sunlight to drive out the past. She listened to the bubbling laughter of her son and the deeper vibrancy of Lewis. They were schussing toward her, Lewis holding Benjamin's right hand on his left side and guiding his skis with his left ski. In the mile they'd traversed Benjamin had gained in confidence and was willing to tackle the smaller hills by himself. On the longer hills like this one, only the guiding hand of Lewis James was good enough.

During last week, while Lewis had gone on his mysterious research trip, Benjamin had missed him greatly. Rebecca had missed him as well, but it had surprised her that it was the physical contact she missed the most – his hand on her shoulder, fluffing her messy curls, caressing her wrist – the hundred safe ways he'd expressed his sensuality. She'd imagined that she allowed him these moments. Now she knew she needed them as much as he.

"Look Mama! We're going all the way down!"

Rebecca waved encouragement as they whizzed past her. Her little boy glowed with exhilaration. His red and white hat sat crookedly on his curls, testimony to hard work and near mishaps. His fat little red snowsuit was caked with snow from his last dramatic stop. His trust of Lewis was complete.

Lewis acknowledged her with the humorous raise of one eyebrow. On his back he carried the bright blue pack they'd retrieved from the Timberline Trail. Benjamin's ski poles encumbered Lewis' healing right arm, so he dropped them near her. He concentrated on the best route to keep Benji upright and successful.

Rebecca shrugged her own pack back into place, picked up Lewis's ski poles and retied his parka around her waist. He worked so hard to teach Benjamin that he'd become too warm even for his sweater. It too had been removed to his pack somewhere before this last hill. She found herself watching his long arms and straight firm shoulders under the blue cotton turtleneck. When he turned at the bottom of the hill to wave at her, she felt a warmth she couldn't name. He looked so like Benjamin in his enthusiasm and triumph.

Shivers ran through her body. She'd been looking forward to their weekend at his cabin, knowing he would control his obvious desire as much as she wanted. Now a frightening thought invaded her safety with him. She didn't know how much she wanted. His mysterious journey had made her aware of his physical absence. His touch and then his kiss at the airport last night had forced her to admit that he wasn't the only one with a desire for intimacy. Yet, if she encouraged his subtle expressions of awareness, how far could she go before her past took control? She loved him too much to allow her nightmare to shatter his ego over and over again.

*   *

Lewis admired Rebecca's fluid motions as she skied. He hugged Benjamin who hung on his leg while they both waited for Rebecca to come down the last steep incline to the cabin path. Her ridiculous snow suit was a blue version of Benjamin's. On a five-year-old, it was practical. On her, it was a way of hiding her body. That surprised him especially today. It was part of the mixed signals he was getting from her since his return.

Last night at the airport, he felt her need for his touch as if she had spoken of it out loud. Her response to his greeting had been so sensual that for a moment he'd forgotten how public the airport was.

This morning, her greeting was as excited as Benjamin's. He knew she looked forward to their long weekend together, but in the car, she'd sat far from him and kept all zippers closed on this over-padded snow suit.

Then, as she napped during the drive, she'd leaned against him as naturally as if she always slept with him. What was happening to her?

Rebecca could stop her crosscountry skis on a dime, with all the skill of a downhill racer. Obviously, she'd skied a great deal in the mountains of Hungary. Perhaps this trip reminded her of those times.

During the last week, he'd become aware of how beautiful a country she'd lost. He'd made a point of going to the site of the Sopron Festival where she last played for her countrymen. He followed her route up into the hills, stopped where she and Tobias must have stopped to send the car into the ravine with the unidentified woman's body afire inside.

He'd driven to the Neusiedler See and been overwhelmed with the enormity of that inland lake and the swampy atmosphere of it. How she had the strength to swim for several miles into that steel gray vastness was a wonder to him.

"What are you thinking about, Levy? You're so quiet since you came home." Rebecca's dark eyes caressed his rough face.

He hadn't been aware that she'd caught up to them. "I was thinking about how beautifully you ski in spite of the snow suit."

"Thank you, I think." She saw that he wasn't going to talk about what was really bothering him. "Are we nearly there? This trail seems very little used."

"I haven't driven up here once since I returned from Ireland in August. You're that much of a distraction, you two."

Benjamin was quick to hop on that opening. "We could come every weekend."

Lewis grinned at Rebecca over Benjamin's head. "You're welcome to come up here whenever you need to get away." His attention returned to Benji. "I thought of this as an escape route, last time we were in the mountains. However, your mother took care of those guys before the rest of us knew what was up."

It still amazed Rebecca how closely he'd read her mind when that fight started. "Lewis," she said, "we took care of them in concert."

"Mama, we took care of them before the concert."

Lewis laughter echoed in the surrounding hills. "You're right little man. I don't know what I'd have done if you hadn't been able to swim that night. Now let's get out of the cold, into the cabin."

He led the way down the winding path to what looked like the top of a gothic barn nestled in the snow among lodge-pole pine, Engelmann spruce and huckleberry bushes.

*   *

Having begun the game on his knees, Benjamin sank lower and lower with each play. His yawns came closer together. After Rebecca offered her lap for his head, he bought Reading Railroad and marched past Boardwalk one more time before he fell asleep.

Gratefully, Lewis had watched the progress from knees to elbows, to stomach and finally to thumb-in-the-mouth. Much as he loved Benjamin, he sensed that something was changing in his relationship to Rebecca and he wanted the peace to find out where they headed. After he could read her a little more clearly, he would know how to tell her about his journey last week.

After the concert, at Abraham's home, Uncle Tobias had taken him aside, shown him his correspondence with a man who owned a storage building in Budapest.

Tobias said, "About a year after Rebecca came with me to New York, my storage unit correspondent told me that a man named Andras

Sospiro came to see what had happened to the boxes belonging to Raphael Atemvoll."

"Sospiro?" Lewis said.

Tobias nodded, "I see she has told you about that name."

"Why haven't you told her about this Sospiro?"

"Because until Steiermark – Steinmetz died, it would have been dangerous for either of them to be connected to the other. She loves him. It would have been just like her to insist on going back to take care of him."

"Even with Steiermark dead," Lewis said, "the gang still exists. I don't think all of his men were on Mount Hood with him."

"Right," Tobias said, "We need to check out the situation there."

Lewis then looked over the letters. He saw right away that Andras Feodor Sospiro had been careful not to reveal anything certain that might bring danger to Rebecca, and did not reveal himself as Atemvoll even to Tobias. But it became apparent also that it wasn't only Tobias who had figured out the name of the Russian count that once owned the Bach manuscripts. Abraham and Steiermark had understood as well. It took Lewis only a moment to figure out what to do.

"I am at term's end," Lewis had said. "Can you stay with Rebecca while I go on a five-day trip to Austria to visit science colleagues? I know a guy who will help me test the waters for her."

Now that he'd returned from that trip, he longed for the chance to give Rebecca all the news he had discovered. He needed this time alone to help her through his revelations. And he wanted to test the next steps in their relationship.

He rose from the floor and reached for her son. "I'll carry this mighty mite to your bedroom while you get more apple crisp for both of us. That was a marvelous dessert for what you call a "novice" cook."

"Thank you, sir. Would you like some more tea to go with it?"

"Yes, thanks. I'll be right back." He ducked under the main beam at the bottom of the stairs as he started up, then turned back remembering something that would amuse her. "Benjamin said my cabin is like the inside of your lute and this beam is the sound bar."

They both chuckled. Benji had been listening to their preparations for next month's lectures on the physics of sound. Rebecca stood on tiptoe to hit the beam with one fist, making a dull thud. "I'm afraid the purpose of this beam is to inhibit vibration not transmit it.

Silently, Lewis thought, just as the purpose of that snow suit is to inhibit any erotic thoughts I might have. Well, it isn't working, young lady.

* *

Rebecca saw the way his eyes flickered over her snow suit in disgust.

Damn this thing! Why can't I get the zipper to work? I'd have changed to levis and sweater long ago. It's hot and uncomfortable.

She'd been tired when she took Benjamin shopping for his snow suit. It had seemed so easy to buy a larger boys' suit. Not beautiful, but it had saved her time and energy when she wanted to be practicing. She'd already tried vegetable oil on the zipper while she made dessert. Nothing seemed to make it budge. She sighed and went into the kitchen to wash dishes and start tea.

When she heard his footsteps coming down the stairs, she stiffened. She wanted to be alone with him, though not in this buffoon's suit. She wanted his closeness, but she was unsure how much closeness she wanted. His strength and his desire had both frightened and attracted her for months.

Now she only feared she wouldn't be able to finish what she started with him. And that finally would turn him away. She put her soapy wet hands to her head, trying for a last shred of control over the war between her wants and her ghosts.

* *

Lewis came around the corner and immediately backed into the dining area again. He spoke to warn her of his presence as he retraced his steps to the kitchen. "Rebecca, your sleeves will get wet if you wash dishes in that suit. Go on upstairs and change out of it while I wash. It can't be comfortable anymore – unless you got a chill . . ."

The pale face that turned toward him was distress. He opened his arms. She came into them, laughing and sniffing back tears. "I can't get this zipper to move. It is so . . . so obstinate a one!"

He held her close. "Is that what the tension has been about all day?"

"Yes. No. I don't know. Please what can you do?"

He stood back surveying not only the zipper, but the state of her mind. What he saw was an industrial strength zipper and a small, fragile sign. Her eyes plead for help – she wanted out of her emotional fortress. If he were very careful tonight, the walls could be trumpeted down.

"Let me see what's going on with this thing." He couldn't hide the sudden roughness in his voice. "Could you come into the living room by the fire? The light's better." He put an arm around her shoulder and walked her to the warmer room. When he got this snow suit open, he wanted no cold air to blow away her new warmth. His fingers shook slightly as he reached for the talon. He tried to remember what had helped him get through to her on the two or three other occasions when he knew for certain that she wanted him.

That morning long ago, on his living room floor, it had been release from the burden of bearing her secrets alone. During Gabriel's visit, as they retrieved the coats, it had been her need for strength to cope with the pianist's control. In the hospital, they'd needed each other in the face of losing Benjamin. And since he came home from Hungary – what was it that made her want his kiss last night – what was it today?

His fingers nudged her throat, forcing her chin to tilt up and back as he got a purchase on the top sections of the zipper. His index finger reached inside to protect her from the teeth. He felt the tightening of her muscles as his finger invaded. He caressed her throat with his thumb and began a running commentary.

"What is this? Why a boy's snow suit? Boys of sixteen are an entirely different species from a small woman. No wonder this zipper won't work, it's designed to zip straight down. Tilt back a little more and stop laughing, you're making it harder. Is this cooking oil on here? Boy, you tried everything, didn't you?"

He tried to banter on with a straight face, but he couldn't do it. His felt his smile deepen and his brows knit together with the effort to be serious. His hand tugged at the zipper. He looked intently at the crooked cross tie that stopped the talon.

"This is a job for a crowbar." He pulled the zipper to one side and then the other, growing more frustrated and more determined. Suddenly the talon moved six inches down, stopping with his hand between her breasts.

Her laughter and his banter stopped in a heavy silence. He looked at her face, a question in his green eyes and his slightly raised eyebrows. In her limpid wide gaze, he saw a clear "Please, yes." Both of his hands moved to the zipper, one hand pulling up on the fabric, the other down on the talon. Carefully, watching for any change in her, praying that the door to her past would not slam, he moved down.

The path of the mechanism swung from her torso to follow her inner right thigh and down to the ankle. As he knelt to unzip the turn to her leg, her eyes closed. She did not grow rigid. Instead, she swayed toward his hand. Her prison door was not closing. He reached a hand to her hip to steady her as he freed the zipper at her ankle. The suit fell open.

He stood, pushing his hand inside the collar to the dark green cotton of the thermal suit he'd given her as a present. He took her shoulders in his hands. "Rebecca, stop me if you need to. I want to love you, not scare you."

"Please, Levy, if something happens, it's not because of you." Her whisper was almost inaudible.

"Becca, just look at me. Remember this is me. I will always take care of you." Barely touching her, he slipped the nylon snow suit off of her shoulders and let it fall at her feet.

She pulled him closer. Her hands pressed against his back. She stroked his arms at first softly and then with an urgency he'd rarely glimpsed in her. One hand moved to his hips, drawing him to her. His breath stopped, his eyes closed, willing her to continue seducing him. Her hand moved lower until he knew that if he let her continue, he'd move too fast for her.

Reluctantly, he stepped back. His hands ran down her arms and took her hands in his. Her unfocused look bolstered his ego. He wanted her to live through this as if in a dream – completely separate from the ugly reality of her nightmare. That dream state was in her eyes now. When he knelt beside her, he kept his gaze on her face. Her eyes followed his and then briefly flickered as he put his arm around her hips. He leaned the side of his head against her abdomen remembering the reaction his kiss in the hospital had achieved.

With one hand, he pulled the second leg of her snow suit from her foot, encouraging her to lean into his arm as he drew it off.

Her hands caressed his hair. He smiled up at her and received a tender look just before she turned his head into her body. He took her gesture as a pleading, but he kissed her more gently than his desperation at the hospital had allowed. His hands moved upward inside the back of her cotton shirt.

The warmth of her invaded his arms, enticing him from his selfcontrol. In the back of his mind, the need to retain control nagged at him, forced him to stop his explorations for a moment and gauge her reactions. The color that suffused her throat and cheeks told him she was aware of where they were headed.

Lewis stood, holding her close, gentling her with his hands. "I want to carry you upstairs and love you well and slowly."

She wrapped her arms around his neck. "I want to be with you, Levy. I want to give you love."

He lifted her in his arms and ascended the stairs to the room across from Benjamin. He had set a small lamp to illuminate the white pine ceiling in the high-arched gothic frame of the cabin. Bookcases and two leather chairs surrounded a sheepskin rug in one half of the room. In the other half, another warm wool rug lay beside a wide futon on a low frame of rosewood.

Lewis watched Rebecca's eyes follow the curved wooden beams that were the frame of his small castle. When her head tilted back to see the high peak, he lowered his head to nuzzle her throat. In his arms, he could feel her react to his touch. There was no pulling away, only invitation to more.

The smile on her face was in full play when he set her feet in the comforter on the low bed. "Are you warm enough, darling?"

"Oh, yes!" Her hands still rested on his shoulders, her fingers caressing his neck and the hair that brushed his collar. She didn't seem to notice that the covers had been carefully turned open and the light set low before he brought her in here. She seemed aware only of the present – of him. His hope deepened.

"Rebecca, you are breathtaking!"

For a moment he thought he'd made a mistake. If the focus were turned on her beauty, she would remember how it had victimized her. She blinked as if awakening. His heart stopped. His hand touched her chin, breaking her thought.

"Rebecca, help me take off my shirt."

She looked surprised.

"Please," he said. "I want to feel your hands on me. I want you to wrap your arms around me and give me the love we've both waited for."

A slow smile dimpled her cheeks. Even where the bruise had disappeared, the new dimple remained. She reached tentative hands to the hem of his shirt. He raised his arms, watching her face as his body appeared. He knew by the flicker of her eyelid that she reacted to the sight of him. Raising his arms higher, he made her the aggressor and himself the lamb. As his face reappeared from the collar, he knew he was right.

He had found a way to vanquish the foe. From the love in her gaze, he knew that they had joined forces and would conquer fear together.

*   *

Even through the strong response of her body to the heat and electricity of his skin, Rebecca became aware that he'd given her the dominant role. She knew that she alone now determined the direction of their love making. Her hesitation was from long years of feeling dominated except when repulsing. She tried to imagine what Lewis would want, how he would feel as he stood in front of the woman he wanted to love. Her hands reached slowly toward his chest. The initial contact made both of them start. She heard his quick intake of breath.

Under her hands his chest expanded, begging for more. She moved over him, savoring the smoothness of skin and the roughness of sandy hair. Her hands and her eyes enjoyed the affirmation of her feminine powers that his reaction gave her. The nipples of his breasts rose at her touch. His skin grew warmer and his breath became uneven. Tense expectancy pervaded the room.

Rebecca brushed over his shoulders and down his arms where his muscles tightened. She pulled him to her. Her lips touched his hairline, moving aside the forelock that always defied his comb. She followed the hollows at the side of his temples and felt his pulse. The laugh lines around his eyes and the furrows between his unruly eyebrows fell victim to the tip of her tongue. Her lips swept down the aristocratic cliff of his nose and surprised his parted lips.

In self-defense he broke her hold on him and surrounded her with his long arms. He held back enough to allow her tongue its explorations. He dropped his injured arm to his side, giving her the upper hand once more.

Rebecca looked at his waiting, hopeful eyes and the encouraging smile latent in his quiet features. She took a deep breath and reached for his belt buckle. It stuck, and he helped her unhook it. He pulled at it as was his habit, removing it from its loops.

When it snaked out in his hand, she drew back suddenly. He saw the old trance threatening to control her. Immediately, he dropped the belt. "No, Rebecca. Look at me!"

The urgency in his voice brought her back to him. "I'm sorry, Becca. I didn't know. Please, stay with me."

She caught herself, touching his shoulders again to stay in the present.

A few breaths later she was able to reorient herself to his needs. She let her fingers arouse him. They grazed from his broad shoulders over his breasts, down his rib cage to his waist. One hand followed his belt line around to his back. Her other hand rested at the button of his levis, her fingers splayed across his taut stomach. She leaned forward to kiss him once, and then again. Something deep inside made her want to taste him – all of him – now. She heard herself moan as her lips returned to his.

Somehow, her body and not her mind took over loving him. Her mouth found his jaw, his throat, the hollow near his collar bone. She took new and deeper satisfaction from each part of him. When she stroked his nipples with her tongue, even he lost control. His arms surrounded her, cradling her head at his chest, prolonging the ecstasy. Moments later, she slid from his arms and knelt on the bed before him.

Her hand worked his top button undone. Lewis's hand, now impatient, covered hers and swiftly opened the rest. She watched as he bent to remove the levis. He stood up, magnificent in his unselfconsciousness.

He took her hands, lovingly kissing each fingertip. "Yes, I want to be with you completely – to know you fully. But it does not have to be – not until you want it as well. I love you enough to take this only as far as you are ready to take it."

"I want it now, Levy. I have wanted it for a long time. I have trust of you and love for you for so long. But I do not trust myself. I am afraid to encourage this between us and then to disappear from you into that other world."

"Just be here, now, with me." He bent again to kiss her upturned face.

"I am with you," she whispered. Her arms encircled his waist. She rose on her knees as he straightened. His hands tightened on her back pulling her full against him. They clung to each other, waiting for breath and time.

When the wave of wanting subsided, his strong hands pulled her to stand again on the low bed. His eyes probed hers, trying to gauge her will.

"Please, Levy. Help me with my shirt."

His pride in her courage was evident through his teasing. "I thought you would never ask." His fingers fumbled at first and then deftly opened the five buttons of the warm shirt he'd given her.

She saw his gaze widen as he saw the scars on her left shoulder. He leaned over and kissed each burn mark from the cigarette.

"My brave darling," he whispered.

She caressed his hair and let his lips bring healing.

After a few moments, he touched the front clasp of her bra but left it for the moment. Instead, he slipped his hands in the elastic of the thermal tights. "I want to take these, Becca."

She nodded. The unconscious movements she made to help him were like a slow seductive dance, driving him to the edge with anticipation. Breathing hard, he returned to her open shirt, then drew her arms from the sleeves. The light in his eyes was far from teasing.

His hands returned to warm her shoulders, massaging the tightness from her neck and back. He slid a finger under each bra strap and let them fall from her shoulders. The light fabric clung to the fullness of her breasts. The clasp opened easily to one hand while his other arm supported her back. His mouth began a tortuous exploration of every curve and shadow.

Rebecca pushed her breasts toward the tantalizing moistness of his mouth. His arms held her just a little away from him. His lips created a desire for his touch in every part of her body, but he seemed determined to keep her wanting. She strained toward him, crying softly in her final awareness of how much she wanted him. "Levy, please, now!"

He lifted her in his arms, kissed first one and then the other nipple before he lowered her into the bed and knelt beside her. His hand under her thighs moved up to remove her linen pants. She turned on her side toward him, her breast pushing into his thigh. He stroked the long curve of her side down to her naked hips. With his fingers spread over her hip and his thumb brushing toward her abdomen, he turned her onto her back.

Lewis gazed at her smile and the curls that framed her delicate face, her wide-set eyes and prominent cheekbones that had first hinted to him of her heritage. Her too soft lips where the corners still shadowed sadness, her small firm chin, so like the child's chin of Benjamin – these were the first that had drawn him to her. Even then, his male awareness had known the rest was there, waiting to be unsheathed.

He let himself take pleasure in her uncovered beauty. His hand covered the soft mound between her legs. And then his fingers stroked her lightly and they both came to life.

The shudder of passion that moved through her, jolted him. He lay next to her, caressing her ever more intimately until his touch told him she was more than ready. She pulled his body to her, opening her thighs to his hand. And when his hand was replaced by his body, she sighed and welcomed him through the last of her defenses.

*   *

As their passion crested, he buried his face in her curls on the pillow. It was then that he focused on the point of light that had flickered through his mind during their joining. A delicate white flower turned to face him, opening to the heat of the evening light. The scent of it was her scent and had driven him from the beginning – a fragile blossom waiting for his careful love.

An hour later, she snuggled next to him. They had made love a second time and now she let her breast rest against his chest as if she had always slept with him.

She whispered, "I've been so afraid of destroying our love with my nightmares."

His hand cupped her head as he kissed her hair. "Rebecca, the darkness of that other world is losing its grip on you. When you are with me and the other world threatens, let yourself think about it. But think about the theater at Sopron in the sunlight of summer, about the skiing in the mountains with your family, about the evenings playing duets with your teacher and your brother. Think about the beauty of that world."

She stared, wideeyed, surprised that he should have guessed in such detail what she had lost.

His strong voice became caressing whisper. "I know you have that other world inside you and that it pulls at you. But I know too that you will always come back to me. Because I am a part of you as well."

Rebecca's eyes grew round. "You've been to look for them, haven't you? This mysterious trip – it was to Hungary."

"Yes." He stroked her cheeks, breathing deeply of the jasmine. "Yes. I didn't want to get your hopes up before I left. I was able only to get a one-week visa to visit a physics colleague from Budapest. I met him in Germany last year. He fell in with my real needs and took me everywhere. I found them – at least some of them."

She was frightened. "Steiermark's gang . . ."

"The gang still exists, I was told, but they have a new leader named Russman. He controls the town and the region around it. Their goals now seem to be different. In fact, they recently sold much of Steiermark's music collection to the Zeneakadémia and his art to a museum in Vienna."

"Your friend, does he know who I really am?"

"No. He knows that my wife is of Hungarian grandparents, that she lived in Budapest, but had a cabin in the mountains near Sopron and used to swim in the Neusiedler See as a child. He was quite sorry to have to tell me that he'd researched the microfiche files of the newspapers in Budapest and found that my wife's' one distant cousin, Zoltan Nagy, was a convicted rapist, but released on parole. Zoltan was re-sentenced to do socially reconstructive work, acting as a nurse to an elderly invalid."

"Oh! Zoltan! You saw him?"

"I did. He opened up very much when I showed him my wife's picture. When I showed him the picture of the son she loves so much, the son I wish to adopt, he invited me into his small apartment. Inside, I met his patient – a wise and gentle man who is confined to a wheel chair, but is otherwise in very good health – good enough health to play his violin and continue to compose music."

"Raphael . . ." her voice trailed off.

"Yes – a man of great love. His legs were made useless by Steiermark's attack. But his becoming an invalid allowed him to work a poetic justice of sorts. Tobias' messages got through to him, though, for your safety, he knew he could not respond. Thus, Raphael convinced a judge that it would serve well to sentence Zoltan Nagy, the man who supposedly raped Darya Zolesku and caused her suicide, to spend the rest of his prison term caring for her old teacher. Thus,

Zoltan is free of the dark prison. He lives with his cello, with the music he loves and a man who is like a father to him. His parole has allowed him to marry and live next door to Raphael. His life is not ideal, but it is much improved."

"He is not bitter?"

"No. He is very quiet – a shy man, I think. But he does many small thoughtful things for Raphael. A bitter man would be too full of his hate to be aware of Raphael Atemvoll's needs. And his wife is a happy woman who is now about to give birth to a son. Zoltan has not continued the cycle of hatred any more than you have."

Rebecca looked down at her hands, twisting together in her lap. She felt enormous weights falling from her heart. What Lewis had done freed her from guilt. She had always known that she had no choice but to leave. To know at last that they were safe was a gift beyond compare.

Lewis watched her bowed head and slowly relaxing hands. He hoped to convince her to stop blaming herself. "I took some pictures. They are in my new camera. Raphael looks well, really. His color is healthy, his eyes bright and he smiles a good deal. If there is pain, I could not detect it. He said for me to tell you that he considers the wheel chair a mere nuisance."

Her head dropped to her hands, a small whimper of grief escaped her. Lewis knelt to comfort her. He smoothed her hair and wiped her cheek of its tears. "Zoltan looks quite well. His hair is beginning to gray early, but he has no physical problems. Emotionally, I know it has taken a great load from him, from both of them, to know that you have and love your son, and that you are safe."

Rebecca turned glistening eyes to him. "Levy, did you . . . were you able to . . ."

". . . to find your parents and brother? Not yet. Six years ago, Steiermark came after them as well as Atemvoll. But Atemvoll had a friend who took them away before Steiermark arrived. From their house, he stole the picture of you that eventually allowed his people to recognize you in New York. Your parents gave your teacher a way to get them in emergencies through the newspaper. Then they disappeared into the mountains. He promised to let us know when they answer his advertisements. Through my friends in science, I have worked out a way for you to correspond with all of them without the gang knowing who you really are."

"Would this Russman care who I am?"

"We can't tell, yet. Zoltan and Raphael feel he is probably glad to be his own boss at last, not interested in revenge for Steiermark, but they are not certain."

"Maybe we can test this. If Raphael finds my family…"

"He has thought of that. He'd love to arrange a concert, when it is safe to resurrect Darya Zolesku."

Her face radiated relief and happiness. Suddenly, it embarrassed him to have brought about such a transformation. He felt both godlike and humbled by her. He stood naked from the bed, pacing about the room. When he faced her again, he could see that she was both happy and amused by his nervousness.

But he'd gone out of control. He talked, blathering on about did she know who was the real son of that Russian count? About a little book Raphael has waiting for her when she can come visit him. About how much Lewis loved her, was she warm enough? Would she like some of that apple crisp?

"Levy, stop. I want you. I wanted you before you left, I want you now."

He closed his eyes, rejoicing. A smile he knew threatened to become a grin, spread through his face. His laugh lines warmed up for frequent future use. "Rebecca, if you love me, you'll make an honest man of me."

She looked up, confused.

"I told them all you were my wife."

A set of laugh lines, faint twins to his, framed her mouth. "To protect your honor, I accept."

His deep chuckle warmed her whole being. He strode to the bed and took her face in his trembling hands. "Then may we have many children as wonderful as Benjamin."

She lay back, arms out, inviting him to her again.

EPILOGUE

Inside the gold and green pillared Zeneakadémia in Budapest, Hungary, the lines of curious people had left. Only eight-year old Benjamin and his sister, known as Little Miriam, still stood next to the music display case. Their parents and their mama's family and friends still talked and laughed, and sometimes cried nearby.

Little Miriam said, "Someday, I'm going to learn to play the violin."

"Mama started when she was three, so you could start soon."

Miriam pointed at the yellowed and brittle music within the glass. "I want to play this song that Mama played tonight."

"These songs are why Mama met Daddy. They discovered them together."

"Tell me the story again, about the bad guys and the dogs." Miriam said.

Benjamin smiled. He stood up very straight and said, "I'll tell you about the day I saved Daddy's life by howling like Burford."

He took Miriam by the hand. As he spun his fantastic tale, they wandered around the tall pillars, past Mama and Daddy, where Mama knelt, holding the hand of an old man in a wheel chair, past Mama's special friend, Zoltan, who played the cello at this concert.

They wandered past Judge Otto, who played the viola, past their mama's brother who played the piano, past mama's own mother and father, who hugged Mama and Uncle Tobias over and over again, past Grandpa Abraham and Grandma, who was called Big Miriam.

At last, surrounded by those who loved them, Benjamin and Little Miriam sat on the marble steps and enjoyed a shivery memory, a moment of danger on a mountain in another part of their big, warm world.

JS BACH: VIOLIN CONCERTI

The three known concerti in A minor, E major and D minor, are listed first. Three missing concerti, listed after, are mentioned in letters and playbills.

Violin Concerto No. 1 in A minor, BWV1041

Violin Concerto No. 2 in E major, BWV1042

Concerto for Two Violins in D minor, BWV1043

Missing but reconstructed by well-known musicians from harpsichord versions.

Violin Concerto in G minor, BWV1056, Reconstructed after the Harpsichord Concerto BWV 1056 by Marco Serino

Solo Violin Concerto in D minor, BWV1052, Reconstructed after the Harpsichord Concerto BWV 1052 by Marco Serino

Concerto for 2 Harpsichords, Strings and Continuo in C Minor, BVW 1060, May originally have been arranged for violin, oboe and strings, or may have been a second concerto for two violins and orchestra

ABOUT THE AUTHOR

Rae Richen's stories and novels, articles and interviews bring focus to the themes that drive our human race.

Richen's characters face a confusing world of hypocrisy and greed with courageous honesty. Humor and friendship help them forge new solutions to age-old problems.

Rae has worked in many capacities that show up in her writing: historical researcher, musician, teacher and landscape designer. She teaches writing to adults, young adults, and the reluctant reader.

Rae Richen is the author of adventures for adults and young adults, of romantic suspense and of the recent Glyn Jones and Grandma Willie mystery series. Join Rae Richen as we explore fear and power, greed and human need in short stories and novels, articles, interviews and essays.

Learn more about this author at www.raerichen.com or contact her at rae@raerichen.com.

OTHER BOOKS BY RAE RICHEN

For a good read of all first chapters, and the history and back story of these novels, sign in as the author's friendly reader at https://www.raerichen.com/guest-area.

Uncharted Territory – a father-son adventure in the mountains and in learning to accept and love despite the fragility of life. Learn more: https://www.raerichen.com/books

Scapegoat: The Price of Freedom – a teen and his friends struggle with a culture of easy accusation during the McCarthy Anti-Communist era. Learn more: https://www.raerichen.com/books

Scapegoat: The Hounded – after September 11, 2001, a grandfather and grandson work to create safety and freedom for friends falsely accused of treason. Learn more: https://www.raerichen.com/books

In Concert – A novel of suspense and romance when a famous musician is stalked by a vicious man who wants to own her and her son. Visit https://www.raerichen.com/in-concert and read the first chapter for free.

Frozen Trust – a novel of espionage and romance within the United States during World War II. Visit https://www.raerichen.com/frozen-trust and read the first chapter for free.

Sentinels of Solitude – a novel of suspense and love during a murderous land grab in the lush Willamette Valley of Oregon. Visit www.raerichen.com/blog for the stories behind the story.

A Fool's Gold – a novel of treachery and romance in the Rocky Mountains of Colorado during the mining fever of the 1880s. Visitwww.raerichen.com/books for more information

Those Who Curse You --A Murder Mystery of Unlikely Bonds and Unrelenting Peril – Can inner-city architect, Sarah Rohann ,and her client, Abraham Hallowell save their families from the murderous drug gang that threatens all of their lives?

Without Trace: A Glyn Jones and Grandma Willie Mystery – When Trace Gowan, drummer in Glyn Jones' hip-hop band, goes missing, Glyn and his friends involve Grandma Willie and her connections to prison and police in the search. They find there is a lot more than a kidnapping going on and all of them are in danger. www.raerichen.com/books

Coming Soon: *Calling The Shots, An Anthology of Short Stories:* A confection especially for readers who asked "What happened to Elizabeth in The *Price of Freedom*? To Dick Street of *In Concert* and in *Those Who Curse You?*"

Learn what caused Gryf and his brother Sam to be the targets of a madman even before they came to the United States – the back story of *A Fool's Gold.*

And see what happened to Lewis James's missing brother, Dicken – a follow-up on Lewis's search for Dicken during *In Concert.*

In this and other anthologies soon to be published, Rae Richen has given us short stories to reveal where these characters lives intersected with the stories in the novels and where they went after we last saw them.

At the same time, in other tales, Rae Richen also has created whole new worlds and characters that you will want to follow and cheer for as they attempt to untangle their complicated lives.